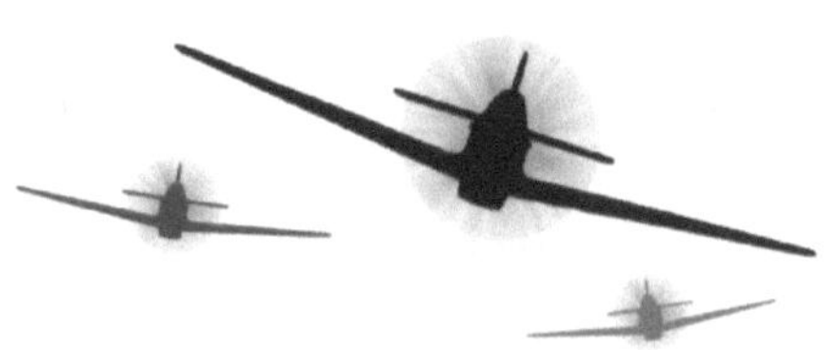

DL JUNG

SPARROW SQUADRON

THE WARBIRD BOOK 1

SPARROW SQUADRON. Copyright © 2018 Darius Jung
This edition published in 2022 by Xinlishi Press

Cover and book design by Kit Foster
Cover illustration by Daria Tikhomolova

Xinlishi Press
300 Coxwell Ave.
PO Box 22591
Toronto, Ontario, Canada
M4L 3B6

SECOND EDITION

ISBN 978-1-990554-02-5 (ebook)
ISBN 978-1-990554-01-8 (print)

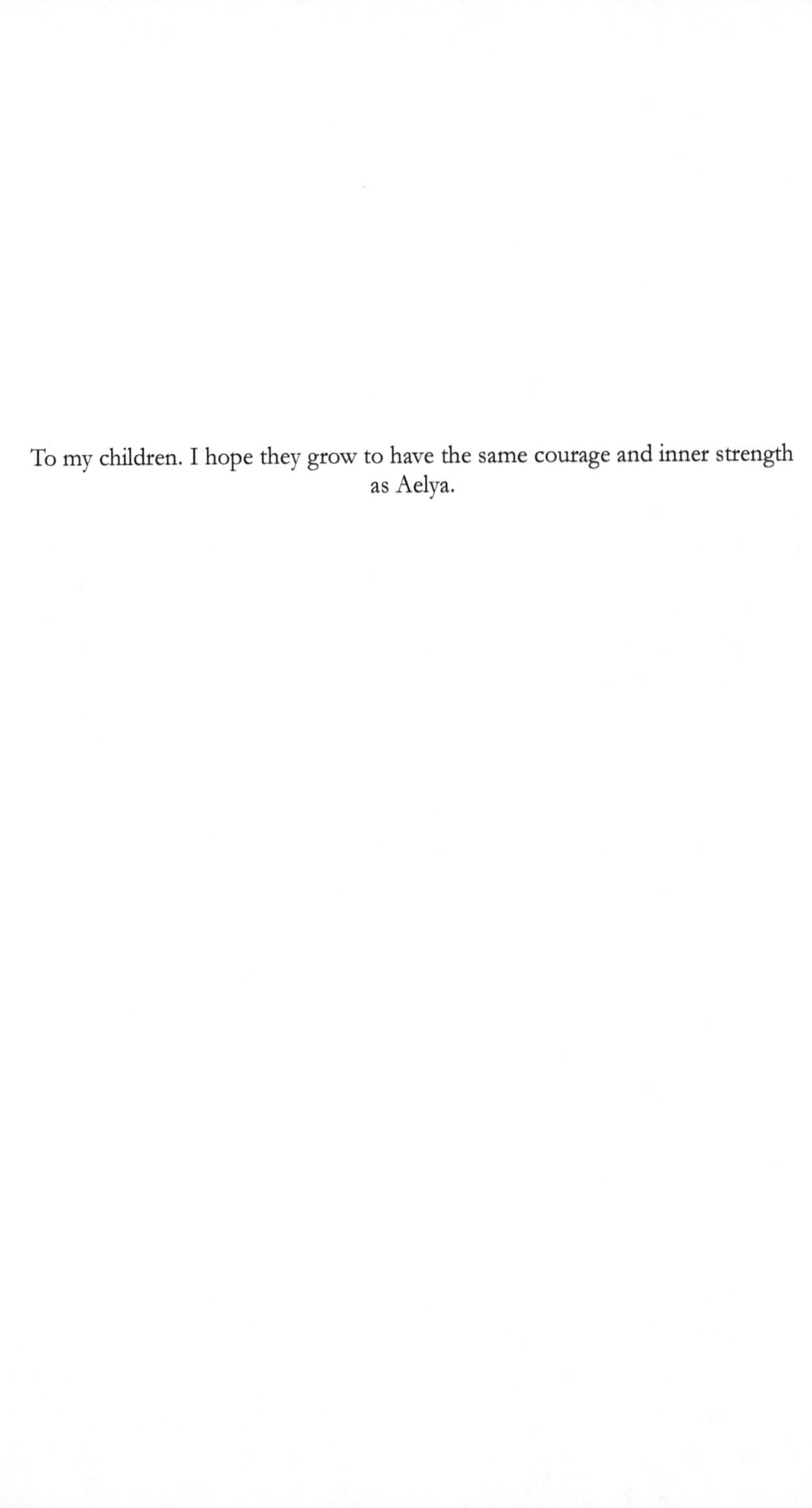

To my children. I hope they grow to have the same courage and inner strength as Aelya.

A NOTE ON RUSSIAN NAMES

Russian speakers use many different names to address the same person, depending on the situation. A Russian's full name consists of a first name, a patronymic, and a surname. The patronymic is derived from the first name of that person's father. Calling a person by their first name and patronymic usually denotes a level of respect or formality. In more casual situations, a diminutive form of the first name might be used. Very close friends, family or children might also be addressed by a "pet" form of the first name.

Take, for example, this novel's main character: Aelita Petrovna Makarova. Her father is Pyotr Makarov (note female surnames usually add an -a suffix.) Aelita's flight students generally call her Aelita Petrovna (derived from Pyotr.) Most friends just call her by the diminutive Aelya (I've chosen this particular spelling for ease of recognition.) Finally, her family refer to her as Aelitochka.

GLOSSARY OF SELECTED TERMS

There are many different systems for converting Russian Cyrillic spelling to Roman letters for those who read English. I've tried to use spellings of names most familiar or easy to pronounce for those readers, rather than any one system.

Aelita: science fiction novel by Alexey Tolstoy published in 1923; part of a trend for stories about Mars, its silent movie adaptation in 1924 became a box office hit in the Soviet Union; the story is about two intrepid Soviet explorers travelling to Mars, where they meet Aelita, daughter of the Martian ruler, and start a revolution

Babushka: Russian for "grandmother"

Bf 110: German fighter with two engines and a crew of two or three; was also used as a ground attack plane

bogatyr: term for a heroic knight in Russian legends

collimator: a special lens marked by fine lines, such as crosshairs, used to aim guns

Communist Party of the Soviet Union: In the single party system of the Soviet Union, the Communist Party controlled the government and all its operations. Among its policies were strict government control over the economy and property owned collectively by the people or the State.

deadstick: refers to flying and landing an aircraft without power

durak: meaning "fool," this card game remains popular in Russia and other nations of the former Soviet Union

ferry pilots: pilots specifically used to deliver aircraft, for instance, from the factory to a base at the front

flak: short for *Fliegerabwehrkanone* (German for "aircraft defence cannon;") the term became popular beyond Germany in the late 1930s and tended to be used as a term for both anti-aircraft cannons and the bursting explosives they fired *frontovik*: slang term for Soviet foot soldiers who fought at the front

Heinkel He 111: German medium bomber; frequently used against troop formations, installations or industrial targets; with two engines and a crew of five, it had a reputation for being able to sustain a lot of damage

Hero of the Soviet Union: a gold star medal; the Soviet Union's highest honour; during the war, fighter pilots were given this award after ten kills; they could be awarded the same medal additional times after scoring thirty kills and fifty kills

Ishak (I-16): primary Soviet fighter before the arrival of more modern planes like the Yak-1

Ilya Muromets: medieval Russian warrior (*bogatyr*) and folk hero

Junkers Ju 88: German medium bomber with a crew of four; two powerful engines gave it high speed that made it useful for many different roles

kolkhoz: short for *kollektivnoye khozyaystvo*; Soviet collective farm, where farmers collectively managed and worked land owned by the State, provided their agricultural output to the government and were paid for their labour

Komsomol: short for *Kommunisticheskiy soyuz molodyozhi* (Communist Youth League;) Soviet youth organization for both genders, aged 14-28; intended to promote Communist ideals and act as feeder for public service and the military; Komsomol groups frequently held activities for camping, sports, and other recreation; they also trained in paramilitary activities like shooting and flying in order to prepare young people for national defence

Kupala Night: summer solstice celebration for Kupala, an ancient fertility goddess of Eastern European origin

lend-lease: term referring to a program begun by the United States in 1941, intended to support the nations fighting against Germany and Japan; massive amounts of war supplies were given to the Soviet Union during the course of the war

Luftwaffe: the air force of Nazi Germany

makhra: Russian slang for a foot soldier, similar to "grunt" or "GI" in America

Messer (Messerschmitt Bf 109): the main German single-seat fighter throughout the war

NKVD: *Narodnyi Komissariat Vnutrennikh Del* (People's Commissariat for Internal Affairs); this Soviet organization was a combination spy agency and national police force; responsible for the political repression that maintained control over the country for the ruling Communist Party; it would eventually become the KGB; their uniforms were known for their blue-topped caps

Order of Lenin: Soviet award for outstanding service to the nation, both military and civilian; the medal depicted a portrait of Vladimir Lenin; it was considered second in honour only to Hero of the Soviet Union

Order of the Red Banner: Soviet military award, next in rank to the Order of Lenin; some servicemen and women valued it more highly because it was a purely military award; the medal depicted a red flag emblazoned with a Communist motto

Order of the Red Star: Soviet military award, next in rank to the Order of the Red Banner; the medal was a red star with a depiction of a soldier at its centre

Patriotic War (also Second Patriotic War, Great Patriotic War): name used for several wars Russia and the Soviet Union fought against invaders; Napoleon's invasion of Russia in 1812 was known as the "Patriotic War of 1812;" the First World War was known as the "Patriotic War" or "Second Patriotic War;" the conflict between Germany and the Soviet Union in World War II was known as the "Great Patriotic War."

Peshka (Pe-2): versatile Soviet light bomber, with two engines and a crew of three

Petrushka: traditional comedic character in Russian folk puppet shows; usually depicted as a court jester

pirozhki: traditional Russian stuffed buns; come in sweet or savoury varieties

pilotka: foldable military cap; it has a triangular appearance when viewed from the front; also known as a side cap

Pravda: Russian for "Truth", this was the name of the official newspaper of the Soviet Communist Party. It effectively provided the official news and opinions of the ruling class.

Rama (Fw 189): German reconnaissance plane; *rama* is Russian for "frame;" it had two engines mounted on parallel booms linked by the wings near the nose and a stabilizer near the tail, giving it the appearance of a window frame; a glass-enclosed crew compartment made it ideal for spotting and photographing enemy troops on the ground

Red Star (*Krasnaya Zvezda*): the official military newspaper of the Soviet Union; for the award, see Order of the Red Star

revetment: protective shelter for airplanes, often made with packed earth and sandbags

Sovnarkom: short for *Soviet narodnykh kommissarov* (Council of People's Commissars;) the highest government authority running the Soviet Union; effectively its Cabinet

starik: Russian for "old man"

Stuka: German dive bomber; with its gull-wing design (resembling a seagull's wings in flight) and fixed landing gear, it was one of the most recognizable planes in the war; to bomb targets, it dived directly at the enemy, dropping bombs with remarkable accuracy, only pulling out of the dive close to the ground

Sturmovik (IL-2): the main ground attack plane for the Soviet Air Force during the war; a combination of cannons, rockets, and bombs made it devastating to ground targets, such as tanks; despite heavy armour plating, the need to fly low and slow in attack runs made it vulnerable; most versions had a tail gunner in addition to the pilot

tracer: bullet or cannon shell designed to burn brightly when fired, assisting with aiming; typically, Soviet aircraft loaded one tracer in every four rounds of gun ammunition

U-2: incredibly versatile Soviet biplane used by both civilians and the military in many roles, from crop-duster to air ambulance; it was also the main aircraft used to train new pilots before and during the war

ushanka: fur-lined hat with ear flaps

usy: Russian for "moustache"

valenki: traditional Russian felt boots used in winter

VVS: *Voyenno-Vozdushnye Sily* (Military Air Forces;) the Soviet Air Force

Yak-1: the main Soviet single-seat fighter during the war

yellow-mouth (*zheltorotik*): literally yellow beak, referring to chicks, a derogatory term for novices

Young Pioneers: Soviet organization for children aged 10-15 that was equivalent to the Boy Scouts; open to both boys and girls, membership was heavily encouraged to help instill Communist ideals in children

CAST OF CHARACTERS

The Makarov Family
    Aelita Makarova - "Aelya" - flight instructor, Smolensk North Aeroclub
    Vasya Makarova - Aelya's older sister
    Galina Berezina - "Aelya's mother
    Petr Makarov - Aelya's father
    Nadezha Chernova - "Babushka" - Aelya's grandmother

Smolensk Communist Youth League
    Yuri Antonovich Khmelnikov - one of Aelya's flight students
    Andrei - a Komsomol member
    Fedor - Komsomol Leader
    Roman - a Komsomol member

Aviation Group 122
    Marina Raskova - Commander
    Militsa Krylova - Raskova's chief of staff
    Lara Rogacheva - an Air Force flight instructor
Prospective Pilots
    Dina Ivanova - a dedicated Communist
    Dunya Nestorenko - member, Red Banner Falcons aerobatics team
    Galya Borisova - an experienced pilot
    Klava Nikishina - leader of the Red Banner Falcons aerobatics team
    Masha Petrova - a Ukrainian peasant
    Olga Yunevich - "Everest" - twin sister to Yulia
    Roza Kulik - a late arrival
    Sveta Ryazanova - a sophisticated Muscovite
    Tonya Gorbataya - member, Red Banner Falcons aerobatics team
    Yulia Yunevich - "Elbrus" - twin sister to Olga
    Zina Borodina - Aelya's friend from the Smolensk North Aeroclub

586th Fighter Aviation Regiment

Tamara Volkova - Regimental Commander

Nadezhda Batyrskaya - Political Officer

Technicians

Sara Eisenach - Squadron Engineer

Oksana - Roza's crew chief

Liza - Roza's mechanic

Raya - Aelya's mechanic

Inga - Aelya's armourer

497th Fighter Aviation Regiment

Stanislav Rudenko - "Red" - Regimental Commander

Grigori Shepel - Chief of Staff

Yevgeny Dmitriev - Political Officer

Arkadiy Muromets - "The Legend" - Regimental Adjutant

Dr. Vera Krupenya - Regimental Doctor

Pilots

Yuri Zadorov - "Baby"

Igor Zhigulin - "Bison"

Hagop Demirdjian - "Dema"

Firuz Nabiyev - "Frost" - Flight Commander

Andrei Bykov - "Mouse"

Oleg Malinsky - "Petrushka" - Stitches's best friend and wingman

Stepan Badievich - "Sleepy"

Mark Akhmatov - "Stitches" - an ace

Taras Shaposhnik

Ruslan Fomachev - "Usy"

Yusupov - Squadron Commander

MAP

The
Soviet Union
Finland
Berlin
Germany
Poland
Hungary
Romania
Smolensk
★Moscow
Kuybyshev
Engels
Stalingrad
Volga R.
Don River
Germany and allied countries
Territory occupied by Germany
Soviet Union
Territory occupied by Soviet Union
Neutral countries
German offensives, 1941
German offensives, 1942

PART I:

Smolensk Communist Youth League

CHAPTER 1: A DAY OFF

Smolensk, June 22, 1941

Ceding control was the hardest part for Aelya.

"Yuri Antonovich!" she shouted over the wind. Formally addressing Yura always kept him on his toes. "Take over!"

"Yes, Comrade Instructor."

In the front seat of the biplane, Yura glanced furiously between the instruments and the ground, searching for the next waypoint. Aelya wished she could remove her goggles and helmet, let the wind flow through her hair, and allow the engine to calm her with its hypnotic juddering. But she hated taking her hands off the stick. It felt unnatural to her as a pilot.

Her mother would say that just being a pilot was supposed to feel unnatural. "Man was not meant to fly," the true red Socialist always said. "When you ascend in an airplane, you're proclaiming your triumph over nature."

Her father, when his wife was out of earshot, would counter, "When you're in the air, nothing feels more right. How can that be unnatural?"

Focus, Aelya thought. Let Yura learn the nuances for himself and observe. For Aelya, traversing the air came as easily as gliding through water did for an Olympic swimmer. It took hours and hours of practice for a complex machine to become an extension of oneself. She kept her patience, resisting the urge to correct her student.

The plane crossed the last of the waypoints, a marker flag in the vast open field behind Aviation Plant No. 35. Now for final approach. Time to take up the slack. If Yura made any mistakes trying to land, he could damage state property.

That would be on her, a blemish against her future Communist Party membership. She was already under enough scrutiny as the aeroclub's youngest instructor.

"Turn now. You're late!" she shouted.

The plane jerked violently as he overcorrected on the rudder. Aelya lined it up properly with her controls in the back seat. Now the descent.

"Flare up! Flare up!" He always nosed up late when touching down. The wheels hit the ground hard. The aeroclub had the privilege of using the paved runway at the plant's test facilities, so the plane remained level.

As the propeller made its last few revolutions, a technician met the slowing plane on the tarmac. They climbed out of the aircraft, Aelya declining Yura's hand despite her small frame. The technician guided the plane toward a hangar while they approached the aerodrome office to go through post-flight forms. Inside the low clapboard building, they removed their helmets and jackets in the stifling early-summer heat.

"I think you need more rudder pressure on takeoff," she said, looking at his neck. There was a gap of smooth, pale skin showing between his blue worker's jacket and white woollen scarf. She thought of another criticism and braced herself to look him in the eye, but his gaze fell somewhere over her shoulder. She turned and caught a glimpse of golden-blonde hair.

"Dear Spacegirl, you're not giving poor Yura a hard time, are you?" Vasya beamed. Though the nickname was meant to be derisive, Aelya had embraced it ages ago. Being named after a fictional Queen of Mars, she had to. Her elder sister only dredged up "Spacegirl" to belittle her in front of boys.

Vasya fidgeted with the strap of her fashionable red leather handbag and drew near to kiss Yura on both cheeks, her vibrant locks flicking from side to side. Aelya ran her fingers through her own matted hair. Why did she have to sweat so much in her flying helmet?

"Dear Vasya, were you waiting here for me?" asked Yura with a lopsided smile that other girls apparently found endearing.

"Oh Yura, I thought you were so wonderful. Surely Spacegirl will let you fly on your own soon?"

Yura turned the smile on Aelya. "What do you think, Aelya, er, Comrade Aelita Petrovna."

"Yuri Antonovich, you might need some more time yet." Aelya badly wanted to wipe his smile away. He was still too sloppy to solo. To let him do so would reflect badly on her teaching. But she just couldn't say it. She shoved the clipboard into Yura's chest. "Please complete these forms and I'll see you outside. I have to get changed. My sister and I have to be somewhere."

Yura frowned as Aelya hustled toward the ready room, dragging Vasya away from her shameless flirtation. She would have preferred keeping on her flying uniform to changing into a summer dress, but it made her father happy. Back outside, she completed the sign-offs with Yura, then said goodbye as quickly as she could and walked out of the aerodrome toward Frunze Street.

Vasya rushed to catch up. "That was very rude, Spacegirl."

"I thought I was being as polite as I could."

"Well, I didn't have a chance to say a proper goodbye," Vasya complained.

"Why don't you stay and talk some more? I don't need you to escort me to the tram."

"It's better this way. I can't seem too eager. Anyway, we're late enough for the picnic as it is." She turned to blow kisses at Yura as he crossed the street toward the workers' dormitories.

Aelya spotted a tram coming down the rails and started running.

"Wait, it hurts to run in these heels," said Vasya.

"You're the one worried about being late."

As they reached the stop just in time, Vasya caught her breath. "I just don't want to waste Mama and Papa's Sunday off. It's bad enough you had to use up the morning in your greasy contraption."

"Then you should be at Lopatinsky Garden already. No need to haul yourself up here to get me. Oh, I forgot—you're such a flying enthusiast." Aelya flicked her eyes back up the street toward Yura. Vasya burst out laughing.

They boarded and the tram squealed, pulling away from the stop, passing the massive cinder block edifice of the aviation plant where their parents worked. Two men offered their seats, doffing their hats toward Vasya.

"That greasy contraption," Aelya said, "lets us see the world from up high. Just think. A few decades ago, no one had ever done that. It's surely worth a smudge or two. I should take you in the trainer next time." She envisaged doing a roll and a couple of loops to make her sister sick, then terrifying her with a stall turn. She smiled.

"I wouldn't be caught dead in an airplane," Vasya said.

"But what if Yura wants to take you flying? He's going to be an Air Force pilot, after all."

"Oh come on, Aelitochka. Flirting with Yura's just a bit of a lark. I have university to think about."

Yura seemed to really be in love with Vasya. It was a bit cruel to lead him on, even if he was a blockhead. But Vasya would aim higher. Sometimes she thought Vasya had only joined the Komsomol to meet boys with good Party prospects.

Aelya sighed.

"Don't give me that," Vasya said. "You'll understand when you're old enough."

"I am—" The rattling tram wheels drowned her out as they crossed the Dnieper River bridge into Smolensk's old town. Some men at the front of the train chatted, sounding agitated.

Aelya looked out the window. Despite the Assumption Cathedral's czarist decadence, she admired the way its golden-capped towers reached up to the heavens. Its magnificence could only be fully appreciated from the air. Perhaps the builders had thought of that, intending only God to have the best view.

At the first stop across the bridge, the men at the front rushed off. There was a commotion on the street as the tram continued rolling alongside the river. More people than usual were lining up at the shops.

"Oh no," Aelya said. "Do you have the *pirozhki*?"

"Did you think they'd fit into my handbag? I thought you were bringing them."

The tram lurched to a halt to make way for a cluster of people heedlessly crossing the street as the driver cursed at them.

"It would have been just as easy for you to carry them as for me," Aelya muttered. "Except I had to fly an airplane. Molotov University will be humbled by your genius."

"Oh, don't get in huff. You could have stashed them in your ready room." Vasya strained to look past the passengers on the other side. "Let's get off at the next stop and head back across to the bazaar."

Aelya gathered her bearings. Two couples taking Sunday strolls alongside the river had stopped to talk. It didn't seem to be a happy conversation. Through the opposite window, she saw a group gathered around a radio set up in the doorway of an apartment block.

Vasya said, "Since it was supposed to be your job, we're getting the apple *pirozhki*."

"Ugh. Come on. Half apricot."

They got up and pushed their way toward the doors. Out on the street, more people were gathering in crowds. Other passengers craned their necks to see what was going on.

The tram came to the next stop. A man rushed up the vehicle's front stairs. He shouted two words that jolted everyone to attention.

"It's war!"

CHAPTER 2: THE CALL-UP

The locomotive blew its whistle. Vasya tilted her large summer hat as she hugged Yura. Aelya looked away. On the open platform, she shielded her eyes from the sun and scanned the mass of faces and the waving hands of those leaning out the windows of the carriages. She recognized a few people from the aeroclub and waved, but they were too preoccupied with their loved ones.

"Stay safe, please," Vasya told Yura.

"Don't worry," he said. "I had the best teacher."

Aelya's cheeks reddened and she cast her eyes downward. This was her last chance to say something. With his father already called up and his mother on factory shift, Yura had only her and Vasya to see him off.

"There's still so much for you to learn." What a terrible goodbye.

He smiled. "You sound like you want to go instead of me."

She grimaced. She was the better pilot. With the aeroclub shut down, he'd be flying and she'd be grounded. It wasn't fair.

"Maybe I should join up," she said, affecting a pout.

"A girl? In the Air Force?" Yura laughed.

"Marina Raskova teaches at the Air Force Academy."

"You're no Raskova. Or was that you who flew non-stop across Siberia? Was that last week?"

Actually, Raskova had crash-landed short of her goal, but Aelya would never disparage the great Raskova, even to put Yura in his place.

"Stop making this about you, Spacegirl," snapped Vasya. She was one to talk

"I'm not. It's just . . . why couldn't they wait to call you up?" Aelya said.

Yura shrugged. "If they had, the war might be over by the time I joined."

"I'll wait for you," said Vasya.

Aelya flashed her an angry look at her obviously empty promise.

"It might be a while." Yura smiled. "We'll probably be stuck for months teaching Communism to the Germans when we get to Berlin."

Vasya leaned in for a kiss. Yura seemed surprised for a moment, then reciprocated. Aelya didn't like standing there, watching it. If anything, Yura's attention should have been focused on her. Stupid Yura. Now that he was in the Air Force, suddenly he thought he was better than she was. The most important things he would be doing from now on were all based on the lessons she had taught him.

Catcalls from the train broke up the embrace. The carriages began to roll. Yura frantically picked up his bags and hauled himself on board. As he waved from the door, the train slowly pulling away, a compulsion struck Aelya and she ran alongside.

"Watch the nose, then the gauges," she shouted. "And pay attention to the checklists!"

What else, what else? Yura just nodded and waved. Seconds later, he had moved too far away to hear anything she might have to say.

At the last step, the bag of onions nearly fell out of Vasya's hands. Aelya scooped it up smoothly and took the handles from her sister.

"You really should find something new to wear," Vasya said. "That thing stinks."

Aelya looked down at her dark blue tunic and skirt. "I only have the two Komsomol outfits."

"You know what I mean."

No, Aelya didn't know what she meant. The problem was that Vasya had no healthy sense of shame. After seeing Yura off, they had spent the whole day with the rest of the youth leaguers accosting shoppers at the bazaar to donate goods for soldiers' care packages. Vasya ignored their area organizer Fedor's instructions and continued to wear a summer dress—a brilliant red number, more ostentatious than the white one she'd worn on Sunday, when the war had started. The dress that billowed in the wind as she'd kissed Yura. Why did the image of those two keep playing in Aelya's mind?

They trudged down the corridor of their dormitory. Their mother's voice barked through paper-thin walls, and they caught her in midsentence. "With that leg of yours? All a Nazi has to do is step to one side. Worse than useless is what it is!"

They strained to hear more as they neared their door, but their father, as always, kept his voice low.

Mama picked up her harangue once more, loud and clear as they stood by the door. "You'll do the most good here, at the plant. This is where you're needed."

Aelya leaned against the door. Her sister took the bag of onions from her and plopped them noisily on the floor. She then made a show of fumbling with the doorknob before opening it.

Mama stood at the kitchen counter facing them, her hands clasped in front of her. "About time."

Vasya kissed Papa, seated at their little round dining table, then took the onions over to Mama. Aelya sat opposite her father.

He looked from daughter to daughter, his lips trembling slightly. "My two princesses, back from their quest."

Mama said, "Aelitochka, dear, get some water from the washroom."

A door swung open and Babushka emerged from the bedroom she shared with her daughter and son-in-law. "I'll get it."

Aelya's grandmother knew to make herself scarce when Mama was on the warpath. It always surprised Aelya. From what her mother said, Babushka had been quite combative in her youth. She grabbed a bucket from the floor and headed out into the hall, escaping the tension.

"Why is there no mince?" Mama said, rifling through the bag.

"Meat? Are you joking?" said Vasya. "There's a run on everything at the bazaar. People are stockpiling."

"Watch your tone, Vasilisochka. You didn't think about simply substituting in mushrooms? I thought not. Too distracted by boys, weren't you?" Mama turned her gaze to Aelya. "Of course you weren't distracted, were you, Aelitochka? So what's your excuse?"

Aelya swallowed. She was never quite sure when Mama expected an answer. What could she say? She had no clue what ingredients went into *golubtsi*. That was Vasya's department.

Mama groaned and threw up her hands. "Just when there's a war on and everyone needs to pitch in, this is the help I get." Papa looked about to say something when Vasya flashed him a warning look. Mama continued, "You'd think, considering I have to plan a conversion of our whole factory line, that I might have a little help at home and not have everyone running off, thinking only of themselves."

"You're not alone in this," said Papa. "I'm not leaving."

Leave? What was he talking about? He was pushing forty, with a bad leg from an industrial accident. He thought he was going to join up?

A clatter at the window drew everyone's attention. Vasya stuck her head out.

"Roman!" she cried. "What are you doing here?"

Beside Vasya, Aelya squeezed through the narrow window. Three storeys below, their schoolmate Roman was leaning his bicycle against a lamppost.

"I just wanted to check you were home first," he shouted up, then bounded into the entrance.

Aelya and Vasya stepped into the hallway just as Babushka returned with a bucketful of water. Footfalls echoed from the stairwell at the end of the corridor. Roman emerged at the landing, out of breath. Like Aelya, he was sixteen, but the way his pale, skinny legs stuck out of his Komsomol shorts, he looked even younger.

"Big news," he said. "We're being called to duty. Building defences outside the city. Fedor says to pack overnight bags and extra uniforms. We're meeting down by the train station tonight."

He handed over a sheet with details to Vasya and Aelya, who looked at each other.

"What's this about defences? You digging trenches?" Papa called from inside.

"Why don't you come in, Roman?" said Aelya. "We're getting dinner ready."

She regretted the invitation immediately. Roman came from a family of leatherworkers, crammed into a low-rise with a dozen other families in the Iamskaya district. While he'd appreciate the luxury of a modern apartment with private bedrooms, what would Mama say to having an extra mouth to feed?

"Can't stay," the boy said. "I've got to finish my rounds." He nodded, then disappeared down the stairwell as quickly as he came.

Inside, Papa was standing next to Mama now, with Babushka seated, drinking something clear that was probably not water.

"Why are we digging trenches?" asked Mama. "We're hundreds and hundreds of kilometres from the border."

Vasya looked over the information on the sheet. "It doesn't say how long this will be for. There'd better be some way of washing our uniforms while we're there."

Mama dropped into a chair and slammed her palms on the table. "Why are they doing this to me? I'm going to lodge a protest with the workers' committee. They can't take you away like that, putting you in harm's way."

A protest built up within Aelya, but it caught in her throat. Mama was just blustering anyway. She would never publicly go against the Party. But Aelya didn't like her saying it. So what if Aelya wanted to dig trenches? It was better than sitting around not being able to fly.

"The enemy's still far away. It's just a precaution," Papa said, stroking his wife's arm. "It's a tactic. Trade space for time, then hit the enemy when they're overstretched, as we did Napoleon."

Babushka snorted. "Didn't Napoleon burn Smolensk?"

CHAPTER 3: ESSENTIAL TO THE WAR EFFORT

A *makhra* pointing a rifle was not to be disobeyed. Aelya and the other Komsomol members dutifully disembarked from their convoy of trucks. The Red Army soldier climbed onto the back and closed the tailgate, leaving himself plenty of room to stretch out his legs. Another *makhra* commandeered the driver's seat from Andrei, Roman's oversized puppy of a friend.

"You're just taking these empty?" Fedor complained to the driver.

Aelya couldn't muster any concern. One overcrowded, mud-caked village was the same as the next in the constant refrain of retreating to the next defensive line, just barely staying ahead of refugees and fleeing soldiers.

The driver shrugged. "My orders were to bring empty trucks to Mozhaisk, and that's just what I'm doing."

In the back, the soldier was standing now, warily brandishing his rifle and cursing at a swarm of refugees clawing to get on board.

"We're headed to Mozhaisk too," Fedor said. "Why don't you take us most of the way and drop us off just before you get there?"

A nasty squelch sounded as an old man tried to scramble aboard and got a rifle butt to the head for his trouble.

"If I take you," the driver said, "I'd have to let everyone on. Then we'd never get anywhere."

Empty or full, there was little chance of anyone getting anywhere. The line of vehicles had been swallowed up by the mass of people and animals bumping slowly into each other in this village, caked with so much dust and grime it was hard to tell one from the other. Just two months ago, this might have been a quaint farming settlement built around the intersection of two dirt roads. Now it was an artery for the defensive line in front of Moscow and clogged with twenty times its former population.

The truck's horn honked. But with no space for the other vehicles, horse wagons, soldiers, and overladen refugees to move out of the way, what was the point of honking? The driver put the truck into gear, honked once more, then lurched forward. Amazingly, the mass of creatures in front of it managed to scramble out of the way, but a horse wagon was overturned and two cars had their rear ends crumpled as the line of trucks forced its way through.

"So that's how you do it," said Andrei.

Fedor spent the rest of the day and half the night desperately negotiating with refugees and soldiers for alternate transport before making the inevitable decision to move out on foot the next morning.

Aelya had thought she'd be gone for a week. Near the forests west of Smolensk, her Komsomol group had made an outing of digging trenches and building defensive emplacements. The jovial atmosphere of a summer field trip continued even as the Germans crept closer and closer. Crept was the wrong word; the Germans *raced*. The news announcements Fedor received kept trumpeting heroic stands made by the Red Army. But anyone who'd taken a geography class noticed those stands moving eastward rapidly. By the time the air raids began, the unthinkable was reality: Smolensk was to be evacuated.

Not everyone had gone east, however—only workers and families essential to the war effort. Of course, Aviation Plant No. 35 was near the top of the list. The Komsomol group disintegrated, thinking only of themselves. Half of them scrabbled through their belongings, scooping up their bags, while others stepped aside, watching numbly. Roman and Andrei didn't even bother looking at the list of factories, knowing their families weren't important enough to evacuate. Fedor had no chance either and ruefully remarked, "No need for bakers in this war."

Anguish had clutched Aelya's chest while she watched Roman and Andrei struggle to collect the camping gear of departing Komsomol members, even as Vasya bullied her way into finding space for two on an evacuation truck. There weren't enough spaces on the trucks for everyone. Over Vasya's recriminations,

Aelya let a fourteen-year-old boy take her place. She would take the next convoy out—only there would be no other evacuation convoy, as Fedor told her after the truck had departed. When new trucks did arrive, they took the Komsomol members to the next line of defence east of Smolensk. In the two months since, Aelya's world had shrunk to one dirty patch of land after another.

Now dirt flew up with each step, crusting her fingernails and invading her nostrils. The ball of Aelya's foot chafed against the hole wearing in the sole of her right boot, socks long ago replaced by footwraps. A sore spot on her thigh flared every time she pulled up the ill-fitting trousers Roman had given her. Her Komsomol skirts had long ago shredded into rags used for wiping off mud.

The journey was hard, made worse by the congestion on the road to Mozhaisk, but at least it saved them from hearing Fedor's regular updates. The point of his litany of Nazi atrocities eluded Aelya. She was already torn up with worry over friends and family; she didn't need the horror stories. Her reserve of outrage was exhausted, and now she simply felt numb. For those who'd suffered loss, hearing Fedor's news picked away at their emotional sores.

She felt sorry for Fedor. Too young to be called up, he'd been burdened with responsibility for the youths in the group. Tall with cropped blond hair framing a square-jawed face that managed to be both boyish and rugged, he looked just like the young men in the posters TASS churned out extolling the virtues of the ideal Soviet worker. She suspected he'd been elected acting area organizer based on his looks.

Her pace slipped and she fell closer and closer to the back of their column. Roman and Andrei straggled behind, whispering conspiratorially. They were probably planning when to make a break and run away to the front. Roman had been obsessed with this since encountering a ragged group of retreating soldiers on the road outside the last village. They looked as though they'd been put through a wheat thresher. Not a single one had a clean spot anywhere on his body. Almost all of them wore bandages or splints. Bright red scabs and scars interrupted any exposed skin on these soldiers.

Roman had buzzed around them, peppering them with questions about the front. They weren't infantry, though. They were support troops—cooks, supply clerks, and mail carriers who'd been shattered by German bombers. One of them caught on to Roman's intentions. A bandage over his forehead covered only half the wound on the side of his head. What was left of his ear was lost amid a raw, lumpy mass that looked ready to bleed at any moment. Beneath the dirt on his face, his cheeks were smooth. He was barely older than Aelya was. This *frontovik* promised Roman a tip on how to join the front in exchange for the half-full packet of cigarettes Roman secreted in his boot. The advice was simply to head west and wander around, and eventually some frontline unit would pick him up and "volunteer" him for service. Roman was upset at spending all those cigarettes for such simple advice, but he'd been talking about going ever since.

Could she manage running away to the front? Not that she had an appetite for picking up a rifle. But pitching in for the Komsomol's war effort had lost its lustre after the third set of trenches. They were the future of the Socialist state, so surely they were destined for something more. But to disobey the Komsomol committee?

She noticed Roman and Andrei stop talking as she fell in step next to them. She said, "I know you're up to something. What is it?"

Roman looked around nervously. "Why, so you can tell your boyfriend?"

"What? Fedor's not—never mind that. You're planning to run away, aren't you?"

Roman shushed her so loudly, he drew a few glances. He dropped into a whisper. "Fine, that's what we're doing. And now that you know, you're part of this. You have to help us."

"No, I don't." She sighed. "Look, I understand what you must be thinking."

"How can you? You're a girl. No one expects you to fight."

"You're sixteen. No one expects you to either."

A distant rumbling caused the line of travellers to stop. Panic rose in their voices as they searched the skies in vain for the German bombers the deep sound signified. They were up there somewhere, hidden away by the streamer-like stratus and puffy cumulus clouds scattered across the blue.

Aelya heard Fedor's voice in her head: a story from the day before about a woman pushing her baby daughter in a pram and being strafed by a Fascist fighter looking for sport. The effect of a 20 mm cannon shell on a baby's body . . .

They cautiously took shelter in the long grasses next to the road, crouching down.

"Look!" A girl pointed behind Aelya, above a line of tall pines.

They saw them before they heard their high-pitched whines. A line of nine or ten Soviet I-16 fighters streaked over the horizon. Even from this distance, Aelya could recognize their distinct, snub-nosed shape. Pilots called the plane the Ishak because its ungainliness reminded them of a donkey, but in the hands of experts it was a nimble machine.

Aelya had always wanted to try her hand at an Ishak. It was said that if you could fly one, you could fly anything. She envied those pilots, the wind whipping their scarves like banners, the summer sun beaming down on them in their open cockpits. Aelya found herself joining in as the Komsomol members waved, even if the pilots couldn't possibly see them.

"Go get 'em, boys!" shouted Andrei, red-faced. He was twice the size of Roman, and when he patted the smaller boy on the back it almost knocked him over. Andrei had already lost a grandmother to bombing and his grandfather passed away from grief soon after. He made a point of loudly exhorting to battle any troops he encountered.

Aelya spotted the danger a second before anyone else on the ground did, and certainly before the Soviet pilots did. Little black dots, fly specks against the glare of the sun. They appeared quickly and transformed into sleek, angular silhouettes as they dived at the Ishaks from a high angle. There were four of them —Messerschmitt Bf-109s, probably. Another second later, one, two, three, then four of the Ishaks dropped out of formation, trailing smoke and airplane parts as the German fighters hit them.

The remaining Ishaks broke up their line, scattering in every direction like pigeons fluttering away when a dog barked at them in the park. Two of them flew flat out in the general direction of the Komsomol members. No, Aelya thought. You're a plane. Use the vertical space. The Messer pilot on their tail knew this. He arced smoothly into a climb until he was above the Ishaks and behind them. He must have been spotted by his prey, who banked hard to the left. The Messer streaked down at the trailing Ishak. It was close enough now that Aelya could make out the black cross on the Messer's grey fuselage and the swastika on its tail.

Cannon and machine-gun fire popped quietly in the distance, reminding Aelya of oil sizzling in a pan. The trailing Ishak broke apart, its pieces falling from the sky. One of them might have been a pilot, but no parachute opened. Someone gasped and another screamed. In the time between firing his cannon and the scream, the German pilot did something amazing. It looked as though he'd overtake the lead plane and fall within its gunsights, but the Messer pulled up from its dive, snaking and rolling upward until it crested an imaginary hill, slowing its momentum by just the right amount so that it finished its roll with its nose pointed just ahead of its target. Tracer rounds, mixed in with regular ammunition, burned bluish-white, streaking from its wings. The Ishak flew into the stream of shells and bullets and exploded.

Everyone on the ground fell silent as the Messers climbed back into the clouds. Aelya had no idea what happened to the remaining Soviet planes, but none could be seen. Fedor began hustling everyone back into the tall grass, in case the Messers lingered to strafe careless gawkers on the ground. Big Andrei supported himself on Roman, shaking his head. One girl was sobbing. A queasiness gripped Aelya. It had been disheartening to see the Air Force beaten so easily, and horrifying to witness the doom of those brave pilots. But her horror mixed with guilt, for she knew she had seen, in the enemy pilot's actions, something beautiful.

CHAPTER 4: THE LAST DITCH

Rain pelted the tent, droplets seeping along every seam and through every gap. The moisture spread from the ground, soaking in and turning the dirt beneath their sleeping rolls into a spongy brown carpet. In this weather, there was no use digging. The group was given a break to read their mail. Given their constant movement and the fractious state of the postal service, letters arrived in clumps, the delivery today the first since Vyazma, two retreats ago.

A heavy envelope awaited Aelya. A hardbound grey book with a familiar illustration of the red planet Mars on its cover fell out. A note written by her mother was tucked inside, simply saying, "For you." Nothing else was needed.

She clutched the novel close to her for a while. Her mother had read *Aelita* to her when she was child, only in her telling, Aelita was not just a Queen of Mars but also a fearless explorer, like the heroes she'd just heard brought to life. One day, she was destined to reach the stars. As time went on, Mama's drive manifested itself in pressing Aelya for academic achievements, and in working long hours herself researching new technologies at the aircraft plant. Aelya would fly to the stars in a craft her mother helped build. or that was what Aelya assumed; Mama had never found the time to articulate this. She would have welcomed a scolding from Mama right about now, just to hear her voice.

The envelope also contained a long letter. She recognized the flowery writing. The missive from Vasya was a change from the terse note she'd received weeks ago, written by her mother. It had simply told Aelya that everyone came out of the journey to Kuybyshev fine and they hoped she would stay safe.

Now Vasya's pen gave life to a long elaboration on everything they were up to. The whole community around the aviation plant was banding together to build anew in the Central Asian city, known in ancient times as Samara. But

Kuybyshev was far from being romantic or exotic; Vasya described vast open spaces that were rapidly being transformed into industrial complexes. Everyone was expected to pitch in, even her. There were terrible shortages of everything, as the front was given priority for supplies. As she read that part, Aelya could almost see the pout on Vasya's face. Mama and Papa were holding up fine, waiting for the day Aelya would come back to them. But they were all happy to do their part for the war effort, Vasya took pains to note.

I know you're only digging ditches, she read on the letter's last page, *but I hope you nonetheless stay safe.*

Aelya almost laughed at that.

> *I can barely bring myself to write this, but you should know we've started to have our fair share of sorrows. Do you remember Lyuba, who lived downstairs? Her husband has been killed. And Yuri Antonovich Khmelnikov's dead too. His mother told us. She passed on this letter he wrote to you. I've put it in with the envelope. I couldn't bear to open it.*

> *With love, Papa, Mama, Vasya, and Babushka*

Sitting on her bedroll, Aelya felt profoundly queasy. She stood and a little letter fell from within the envelope. Her hand paused above it. What kind of hurt would the words bring? Poor Yura. She never liked him that much. In truth, his overconfident demeanour and passive bemusement with Vasya's needling of her were infuriating. But they were part of her life, things she thought would still be around when the war was over. Now they had been taken away. That life was never coming back.

She tried to remember Yura's face. Tried to picture the way he ate sandwiches during a break at the aeroclub. What was his favourite movie? She had to try to remember these things, or else he would be gone forever, too. Although her heart pounded against her rib cage, she forced her shaking hand to retrieve the letter.

> *Aelya, forgive my familiarity, but I'm over the moon. I've made it. I'm now on active duty! I can't say much, but it looks like I'll be a flying messenger —using the same old crop-dusters you taught me to fly. I thought I'd get a chance with something newer, but I guess we all have to work our way up.*
> *I wish I could be out there hurting the fascists, but I'm happy to be con-*

tributing in my own way. For that, I am eternally grateful to you. I would never have had this chance without you guiding me. I'll make you proud of me.

Take care,
Yura

P.S. I still remember: checklist, checklist, checklist!

Aelya slogged her way through the mud to find Fedor in the mess tent conferring with the cooks. They were learning to be creative with what few ingredients were still getting through in the dwindling supply deliveries.

She caught his attention. "Some rain cloaks have arrived at the main depot, Comrade Organizer. Do I have your permission to grab them before some other group snatches them up?"

"Good thinking, Aelya."

"I'll take Roman and Andrei," she said, cutting him off before he could suggest anyone else. "They're a little down. No one's writing them letters. They could do with something to distract them."

She'd been too eager with the suggestion, she realized, because he didn't respond right away and his eyes narrowed at her. "How did you hear about the rain gear?"

"Oh, Vera told me." She'd had to think quickly. Vera had been sent off to pick up paperwork from the regional committee and wouldn't be back for a while.

"I just saw Vera before she left and she didn't say anything about it."

Stupid, Aelya thought, trying to keep her face straight. Don't say anything yet—think of something.

"Listen," Fedor said, looking serious. "Don't let those two boys rope you into some crazy scheme."

"I don't know what you're saying." He'd mistaken her guilty hesitation for uncertainty. That made her indignant. "If they are up to something, I wouldn't be getting roped into it." This was her idea, stupid as it was.

"I know they've been planning to run away to the front for a while, ever since we arrived here. You're not going with them, are you?" He laughed. "What will you do there? Pretend to be a boy? Hide in the trenches with the *makhras*? You'd just be a distraction. I'd give you three months before you get pregnant."

"What about the women driving trucks? The medics? The partisans fighting behind enemy lines? Are they distractions?" she said, seething. She might be implicating herself, but he'd sniffed out her intentions already. "You of all people should know the vital contribution men and women both make to our society. Isn't that what we're fighting for, comrade?"

"I'm sorry. I didn't really mean all I said. I'm just trying to point out how crazy you're being. I've seen this sort of thing already. Organizer Struganskaya just had three boys returned to her group. Lucky it was regular infantry that caught them, not the NKVD blue caps, or they might have been shot as deserters."

"How can it be deserting if they're heading to the front?"

"The Germans are moving so fast, every direction is the front. To the blue caps, every direction is also a retreat."

This punctured all the stiff-backed official bluster of his daily talks. Was he hearing the same rumours, or was his pessimism coming from some more official channels?

"Is it that bad?" she asked.

"Who knows?" He leaned over a mess table and ran a hand through his grimy hair. His face was lined with an extra decade's worth of worries. "Did you think there'd be more than this? I mean, when you gave up your spot on the truck back in Smolensk, is this what you'd thought you'd be doing?"

"I'm not sure I thought anything. I just . . . I needed to do something."

"You didn't hope this might be more of an adventure than digging trenches, retreating, then digging some more?" She didn't answer because whatever she might say would sound stupid. So he answered for himself. "That's how I feel. I should know better. My brother Sergei doesn't have much good to say about the army. He's stuck somewhere out east, watching the Japanese. It's sort of the same thing, but without the retreating. I'm still jealous of him. I feel embarrassed having to wait until next year to put on the Red Army uniform."

The idea of the war lasting another year was appalling but looked increasingly like the most optimistic outcome.

"Somehow this all feels lesser," Fedor continued. "I know what we're doing is important, but I guess I always wanted to be personally tested. I'm not getting that here. I want to know if I'd be like my father, during the Civil War.

Do you feel like you're destined for something greater?"

"Not really." Of course she did. "But I think I know what you mean. It doesn't really feel like I'm contributing. I mean, the State has given me skills. I can do more than just dig trenches."

Fedor grew animated. "That's right. You were a flight instructor before the war, weren't you?"

She nodded.

"If you're going to desert us, you might as well make the most of it."

She immediately wanted to deny deserting. Or not use that word anyway. But she flashed Fedor a quizzical look. What was that last part?

"You could teach flying. A lot of aeroclubs reopened after evacuation. We need more pilots than you could possibly imagine."

Would they really allow her to do it? Maybe she could make it back to Kuybyshev. She'd be back with her family, but it wouldn't be like it was before. She'd be an important contributor to the war effort. How much more valuable would training a new Air Force pilot be compared to all the digging she could do in a year? She felt a pang in her gut. She'd need to do a better job than she'd done with Yura. But they'd rushed him into battle. She owed it to the next man to be more thorough, to give him everything he needed to survive before the Air Force took him. If she could do that much, it would go some small way toward making up for her guilt—she hoped.

"You'd just let me leave?"

"The evacuation order still stands, so I could get the committee to approve it. You don't even need to get to Kuybyshev. We're close to Moscow now. There are tons of aeroclubs here. Maybe you can sign on with one?"

Elation took hold at the thought of leaving this muck behind, but she hesitated. "What about Roman and Andrei?"

"I'll keep them out of trouble. Don't feel like you're abandoning them. You're doing them a favour. I don't think they can pull off anything without you to help them. Now they won't get themselves killed trying something stupid."

She looked at this young boy, so condescending to her comrades. Who was he to say she was doing them a favour? It still felt as if she was letting Roman and Andrei down. That was hardly the way to embark on her destined course. But she also thought about watching the Messerschmitt as it gracefully manoeuvred, destroying two fighters in mere seconds. That was the way their own pilots needed to fly. And she would teach them.

CHAPTER 5: THE UNWANTED PASSENGER

Aelya banged on the door and tried the handle once more, knowing nothing would be different and it wouldn't open. Two drizzly days of hitchhiking had left her wet, grubby, and suffering from a cold. She tortured herself by gazing through the window in the door. The aeroclub's administrative building in Kostyakovo was a much larger affair than what Aelya had been used to back in Smolensk. Eyeing the wood panelling and carpet and thinking of the warmth within, she noticed her skin tingling.

They should have opened by now. The Kirov wristwatch she'd received two birthdays ago was still holding strong, and it said ten o'clock. She bit her lip and wrung her hands. Maybe their schedule had changed due to the war. Maybe Fedor's information was wrong.

On closer inspection, she saw outlines in dust on the walls where some of the pictures had been removed. Scuff marks on the carpet had been made by furniture recently removed. Behind the reception desk, file cabinets and desks sat with some drawers half opened. No one was coming.

She groaned and sat on the ground, gazing over the empty road in front of the aeroclub. Snowflakes gently dusted her shoulders. All energy deserted her and she sat in a stupor, oblivious to time passing.

A black car pulled up along the road. A young woman in a grey linen tunic and trousers, one of three such figures within, bolted out of the passenger seat and sprinted across the grass to the door beside Aelya, scarcely bothering to glance at her. She drew a key from her pocket, opened the door, and marched inside.

Brimming with new life, Aelya followed. Guilt nipped at her for tracking dirty, wet boots across the finely woven beige carpet. "Excuse me, are you still operating?" she asked.

The woman ignored her, looking over framed photographs on the wall flanking a poster for last year's Aviation Day flyover. She took several off their hangers and leaned them gently at the foot of the wall.

"Sorry, I'm in a hurry," she said, striding to a tall glass cabinet containing numerous trophies and souvenirs from pioneering flights. She jiggled the handle, but it was locked.

Aelya looked at the closest photo. Five women posed in front of a UT-1 aerobatic plane. The plaque beneath read, "Red Banner Falcons, 1940." As she glanced between the photo and the woman before her, recognition dawned on Aelya.

The car honked its horn. Cold air muffled shouts from another passenger.

The woman grunted and went to the reception desk, rifling through its drawers.

A year ago, when she was part of a group representing Smolensk North Aeroclub at Aviation Day, Aelya had watched the Falcons perform a synchronized loop in a star formation. It took her breath away. Afterward on the tarmac at Tushino airfield, as she watched them congratulate each other, their helmets and scarves off and hair flowing freely, she couldn't get over how beautiful they looked.

"You're one of them," she gushed.

The woman gave up her search, putting hands on her hips and pouting. "I'm sorry—what?"

Surely a distinguished pilot like her had been called to duty. "Are you still flying?" Aelya asked. "I'm looking for a job."

"Maybe you can ask the aeroclub's administrator."

"How do I find him?"

The woman shrugged. "Everyone got evacuated out east. Sverdlovsk, I hear."

"You're not going with the aeroclub?"

The woman laughed. "I'm joining the Air Force."

Aelya shivered with excitement.

A gust of wind blew the door open. A woman in the back seat leaned out the car's window and shouted, "Dunya! Hurry up or I'll leave you to hitch a ride with a panzer!"

Aelya shuddered at such blatantly defeatist talk, even if it was meant in jest.

Dunya smirked and went back to the display case. "As if you'd leave without these," she muttered. She turned to Aelya. "You didn't see this."

She slid her jacket sleeve over her hand and smashed the glass. Opening the door, she piled several medals around her neck and cradled three trophies. "Be a dear, uh . . ."

"Aelita Petrovna Makarova."

"Aelita. Get those photographs, please. Gently."

Aelya complied and followed Dunya in a careful procession outside. "Are they taking women instructors in the Air Force?" she asked.

"Maybe. But I'm going to fly a fighter."

Aelya nearly tripped. Dunya snarled at her, helping to brace the pile of photo frames with her shoulder.

"A fighter? Really?"

Dunya rolled her eyes as they continued. "Yes, we received word last night. Major Marina Raskova's forming three VVS regiments, entirely composed of women. The order came from Comrade Stalin himself."

Air Force regiments. Not just an instructor, but an Air Force pilot. Aelya's mind swirled with questions.

When they got to the car, she could tell it was American made from the winged figure on its hood ornament. A black-clad man sat in the driver's seat while two women were in the back, a suitcase between them.

The woman closest to them cocked an exquisitely shaped eyebrow at Aelya. She was young, in her late teens, with perfect makeup that gave her the look of a porcelain doll. "Who's this urchin?"

The woman on the far side emerged. "Don't be rude, Tonya." She was older, in her late twenties maybe, and not as glamorous as her fellow passenger. She opened the trunk, revealing more suitcases.

"I'm a pilot," said Aelya.

The older woman brightened, her smile captivating. "Are you joining Raskova's regiments?"

Dunya crammed the trophies and medals into the trunk and took the photos from Aelya.

Tonya sneered. "Don't waste your time, Klava. Under that layer of dirt, I see a Komsomol badge. If she were any good, she'd have gotten the notice."

Klava shrugged. "The order probably got lost in the mail, didn't it? Not exactly the best conditions for the postal system right now, is it?"

Yes, Fedor must never have seen the order, or why let her waste her time wandering around looking for the nearest aeroclub?

Aelya rubbed her nose. "Where is this happening? Where do I go?"

"Poor dear, you have the sniffles," Klava said. She handed her a handkerchief. "Why don't you join us? We're going to sign up today."

"Absolutely not!" said Tonya. "I'm suffocating as it is back here."

Klava twisted her lip, then said, "Take my place. We're not too far from the station, and I should be able to catch a train."

"No," said Tonya. "I can smell her from here. She is not sitting in here and stinking up my car."

"This is the State's car. You only get to use it because of your father."

Tonya's eyes widened. "The driver answers to me."

Dunya smiled weakly at Aelya as the driver opened the passenger door for her. Tonya cursed her colleague's slowness, then glared at Klava. The driver opened her door.

Klava looked at Aelya. "It's at Zhukovsky Air Force Academy," she said as she got in. "Do you know how to get there?"

The driver got behind the steering wheel and Tonya tapped his shoulder. "Move," she said, and he began to pull away.

Klava leaned out the window and shouted directions at Aelya, but most of it was obscured by the car revving. She could only make out "Belorussky Station."

She stuffed Klava's handkerchief into her pocket, wrapped her arms around herself, and started walking toward the train station.

PART II:

Aviation Group 122

CHAPTER 6: STORM CLOUDS

Moscow, October 9, 1941

The press of people and piles of supplies around Belorussky Station made it difficult for Aelya to breathe. Inside and out, throngs of refugees and soldiers commingled chaotically. Everyone was leaving the city. Half were fleeing to the east, the other half grimly determined to head toward the fighting.

Outside on the wide footpath of Leningrad Avenue, Aelya finally found space, though she tore her carpet bag on the corner of a crate in the process. The skies had brightened and the snow receded, but now the wind picked up, its full force chilling her damp overcoat and carrying an ominous rumbling from the west. The brisk air jolted her out of the lethargy that had dogged her since she managed to smuggle herself onto a military train stopping in Kostyakovo. It was supposedly reserved for wounded soldiers, but plenty of refugees were among the packed cars.

Despite the crowded conditions, she couldn't recall a time when she'd felt so alone. Aelya's body was exhausted, but her mind raced. She was alone with thoughts of her first flight instructor, old man Panarin. Would he be proud to have trained a girl for the Air Force? And were Roman and Andrei cursing her as they dug a new trench? She thought of Vasya, who if she'd known Aelya's plans, would probably be cursing her on the way to work at the new aircraft plant in Kuybyshev. She thought of Yura and his letter. She thought of beautiful things. She wouldn't be like Yura. She wouldn't be like that Ishak pilot. Only reading her novel had given her respite from those thoughts.

Moscow looked all wrong. There had been stopovers early in her childhood, on the way to see her father's family in Kalinin, but most vividly, she remembered Aviation Day. Last year, she had seen it from a thousand metres, majestic and expansive. The year before, from the ground, it had been even more impressive. She remembered the banners and the pageantry in Red Square, the venerable buildings around its edges standing as vibrant reminders of an imperial past.

Now the city was scarred. The bright green facade and tall windows of the station were hidden by sandbags and plywood. The same look of urgent worry was on every face Aelya saw. For so long, while things seemed bleak in the trenches, she'd thought of Moscow as this pillar of strength for the people to lean on. But now it was being hollowed out.

A line of trucks followed by soldiers on foot rumbled down the street, directed by an old man on a podium. Aelya blew her nose and tried smoothing out her coat, but there was little point. What a sight she was. Her coat was soggy and her oversized trousers were stained with mud.

Dodging two heavy trucks, Aelya scrambled to reach the traffic controller. "Excuse me, comrade, which way to Zhukovsky Air Force Academy?" she asked.

"Why do you want to go there, little girl?" he replied, only quickly glancing away from his duties.

"I'm going to be a fighter pilot."

The man laughed heartily. Deflated, Aelya began to turn away.

Annoyance gnawed at her. Flushed, she reversed herself and leaned in closer, on her tiptoes so he had to see her. "The Nazis are on our doorstep. Can you hear their guns in the distance? Is this the time to be joking?"

The man smiled. "That sound you hear is thunder, not artillery. I've seen a few more wars than you. Believe me, this is absolutely the time to joke." He pointed up the street. "Head that way, until you see the park on your right. You can cut across that to the academy. You can't miss it—it's a pink palace."

She thanked him and weaved her way back to the footpath. A woman in a dark blue uniform brushed by her, also heading toward the park. Aelya noticed the propeller insignia on her chest.

Hurrying to catch up, she said, "Excuse me, sorry, but are you with Marina Raskova's regiments?"

The woman was in her twenties, with dark hair tied in a bun and framing a face beneath a visored cap. "You're another one of the Komsomol members answering the call?"

"Yes," Aelya said. "I saw your flying badge. You're in the Air Force already?"

The woman nodded. "My poor dear, you're shivering. Why don't you take my coat?"

"Oh no, I couldn't." Aelya put her hand up to politely refuse the woman's offer. "Well, how far is Zhukovsky Academy?"

"It's at the far end of that park." The woman put an arm around her and conveyed her along the street. "I suppose you'd better know my name. Larissa Illyichna Rogacheva. You may call me Lara."

Aelya returned the courtesy, introducing herself. She had so many questions for the woman, a real pilot of the VVS, but she was wary of overwhelming her. Still, she had to ask. "Are you a combat pilot?"

"They only let me be an instructor, until now."

"That's better than me. I was digging trenches. Not that it wasn't rewarding to do something for my country."

Lara cast her a sidelong glance. "So, Aelya, what did you do before digging trenches?"

The rigidity of the words made Aelya straighten up. "I was a flying instructor at Smolensk North Aeroclub."

"Smolensk," Lara said. "That must have been awful."

"My family were evacuated with the aircraft plant."

"I'm happy to hear that." After a moment of silence, it occurred to Aelya to ask about Lara's family, but before she could speak, Lara continued, "What sort of plane do you want to be flying in the Air Force?"

"I hadn't really thought about that."

"Comrade Raskova's forming one regiment for fighters. Not sure if those will be MiGs, LaGGs or Yaks. One for dive-bombers, probably Su-2 or Pe-2. And the night bombers. Those lucky ones will get the crop-duster."

"I don't know. Which one of those will do the most damage to the Fascists?"

"The dive-bombers, I think."

"Oh."

"Don't try to hide it. I can tell from your face. You want to fly a fighter. Are you really interested in killing, or just showing off your flying skills?"

Aelya fumbled for an answer, so Lara continued. "You need to be ready for this. This isn't just about putting in your best for the war effort. This is about killing people."

Aelya wrapped her coat tighter against the cold.

"I'm sorry," Lara said. "Don't get too caught up in that. There's plenty of need for all sorts. My husband is a dive-bomber navigator." She looked at Aelya. "Zhenya. He has a gentle heart. And yet . . . here we are." She gestured with her hands in a way that made it seem as if she was giving up something.

A dark thought passed through Aelya's mind and she asked, "What if they do it? What if the Germans take Moscow?" She immediately wanted to bite back those words. They were the words of a defeatist.

Lara said, "Napoleon took Moscow and he lost anyway."

Napoleon again. What would Babushka say?

When they reached Petrovsky Park, they left the footpath, passing the trees and moving onto the expanse of grass beyond, which was dotted with defensive pits for anti-aircraft guns. Even the sky looked broken by the floating silver barrage balloons.

Aelya saw the former palace that housed the Zhukovsky Air Force Academy in the distance. A distinctive pair of curving walls enclosed its forecourt. The faded brick exterior, partly obscured by camouflage netting and sandbags, looked more a dull red than pink in the gloomy weather. She was amused that her little grubby self would enter a place nobles once used for decadent parties.

Once they passed through the guard post, Aelya was hit by a wall of noise that had been hidden by the outer walls. Masses of women crowded the edges of the courtyard, trying to find shelter from the rain. The whole thing was a mess, with different groups of women being herded around and officials shouting left and right with no clear order.

She clung closely to Lara. The VVS woman looked for where to go, standing authoritatively. Even among the press of people, a space seemed to open up around her.

A tall woman appeared and accosted her. "Lara!" It was the Red Banner Falcon, Klava. She hugged Lara, then stepped back to look at Aelya, seemingly searching her mind to make a connection.

"Aelita Makarova," Aelya responded. "We met at Kostyakovo yesterday."

"Oh yes! So glad you could join us."

Aelya fished through her coat pocket and found Klava's handkerchief. "I believe this is yours?"

Klava gritted her teeth in mild revulsion. "No thank you." She turned back to Lara. "Lariska, there's so much to catch you up on. But I'm afraid my turn will have to wait. Raskova wanted to know when you arrived."

"Perfect. Let's go meet her," said Lara. She turned to Aelya. "I'm sorry, dear, but I'm being called away. I hope we'll talk again soon. Good luck."

With that, she and Klava disappeared into the crowd, leaving Aelya smiling blankly. She had no idea what to do next. She hovered around each group of women in the courtyard, trying to make sense of what she should be doing. Finally, she asked one person, "Where do I sign up to fly fighters?"

"Everyone wants to be a fighter pilot. You have to be selected."

"Where do I go for that?"

The woman grimaced in annoyance, then pointed over to one line making its way indoors. Once she was inside the halls of the palace, the noise was unbearable. In front and behind her, women clustered together. Up ahead, one woman finishing her registration triggered a feeling of familiarity.

"Zina!" Aelya cried out. On any other day, she wouldn't have been nearly as excited. She remembered Zina from only a few encounters at the aeroclub, before the war.

"Aelya." The young woman kissed her on both cheeks, brushing her own long mousy brown hair out of the way. Zina was one of the few who didn't have a uniform, just a trench coat over her dress.

"What have they got you doing in this war?" Zina said.

"I went with the Komsomol to dig trenches. And you?"

"I went with the rest of the plant to Kuybyshev." Zina had been studying at the aviation plant's technical college to be an aircraft engineer like Aelya's parents. "I applied to be a trainer at the aeroclub once they set up there, but there weren't enough planes. Only Panarin and two others were allowed to fly. Not everyone can be a prodigy like you."

Aelya started. She opened her bag and retrieved her internal passport, Komsomol card, and record. She pored over the documents, realizing why Fedor hadn't mentioned the order. Why would he? Two years ago, when she'd first applied to the aeroclub, her father found a man who made a copy of her birth certificate, changing a five into a three. Would anything give it away?

Zina knew all about it. Aelya's real age had been an open secret at the aeroclub.

Aelya drew closer to the desk. Her heart pounded. She remembered now to stand taller, suck in her cheeks a little. Zina was saying something, but Aelya just nodded. It was ridiculous to be afraid. Surely if she hoped to be in combat, she'd need to be tougher than this.

Zina frowned slightly, her eyes distracted. Was that a good sign, meaning she would leave? Or would she say something about Aelya's age? Did she even remember?

Sweat made the documents in Aelya's hand slippery. She used her sleeves to wipe her forehead and hands. It was her turn now. Did the woman at the desk spot her anxiety? Zina began to walk away.

"Wait," Aelya said as she handed over her documents. Zina stood quietly as the woman took down the details quickly, then returned the documents. No questions, not even a second glance. Aelya's shoulders drooped and she shuffled away as quickly as she could, putting Zina between her and the desk.

"So . . . what next?" Aelya asked.

"There's a medical examination—"

An air-raid siren sounded. Zina rolled her eyes, then took Aelya's hand. "Come on. The key is to hide out under a doorway and wait for the line to the shelter to thin out."

Aelya didn't like the sound of that, but few people panicked, so she suppressed any reaction and followed Zina quietly.

CHAPTER 7: AN UNFAIR ADVANTAGE

Lightly brushing the black curtain aside, Aelya peered at the smoke enveloping Moscow's horizon, darkening the grey skies. She had lost count of the number of air raids over the past two days. It was different from the trenches, where German planes simply passed high overhead. This was where they dropped the bombs. Most of the fires were in the western part of the city, and no bombs had fallen near the academy. That hadn't stopped the anti-aircraft gunners outside from letting loose at imaginary targets.

After every all-clear, Aelya took the first opportunity to look outside. While most of the other recruits chatted away in the cramped halls of the academy, fussing over their new regulation uniforms, rearranging bunk assignments in the dormitories, or gossiping about test results, she yearned to be outside. She didn't like being walled away from the world by sandbags and blackout curtains like some princess in need of protection.

The door opened behind her. Zina stepped into the hall, smiling half-heartedly. She pushed past a gaggle of recruits and went over to Aelya by the window. "I'm going to be a mechanic," she blurted out.

Aelya's mouth opened, but she was unsure what to say.

"That's all right," Zina said. "You can say it. It's terrible." She leaned back against the whitewashed brick of the hallway and slid down to the floor.

Aelya crouched down next to her. "Is there any chance of appeal?"

"They won't know for sure until all the applicants have been screened, but there's no way I match even half the girls here in flying hours. I mean, how many do you have?"

Aelya felt guilty contemplating the answer. If it was just down to hours, surely that meant she was safe. But then what was the point of the interview?

"You're in the Air Force now. You'll be going to the front. Who knows what will happen?"

Zina looked anything but reassured. Aelya would have felt the same way hearing such empty platitudes. A few days ago, she'd contemplated a life in the trenches at the front. Now with the possibility of becoming a fighter pilot tantalizing her, she couldn't aspire to anything else.

The door opened again and the chattering in the hall fell silent. A stiff-collared adjutant stuck her head out. "Makarova, Aelita Petrovna," she called out.

Zina gave her a pat on the arm as she stood and took a deep breath. The adjutant guided her to a single seat in the middle of the classroom. Facing the chair were five uniformed women seated behind school desks pushed together in a row. Lara was at the far right. After a glimmer of recognition, Lara's face went blank once more. The adjutant sat at a writing desk in the back corner.

Aelya's attention was drawn to the woman at the centre. Although she'd known Major Marina Raskova would be conducting the interview, actually being in her presence caused Aelya's legs to judder. She tried to sit.

The woman on the left cleared her throat. She reminded Aelya of a forewoman at the aviation plant who, Mama remarked, always seemed on the verge of anger. Her dark hair was cropped in a man's style, parted to one side. "You're a civilian no longer, comrade."

Aelya stood again and saluted as Raskova raised her hand in a conciliatory gesture, nodding for her to sit down.

"Comrade Marina—er, Comrade Raskova," Aelya said. "This is an immense honour to finally meet you. I loved your book."

"Comrade Makarova," said the first woman, "you'll speak when spoken to."

"I'm sorry, comrade."

"You'll have plenty of time to adjust to military habits," Raskova said, smiling. "Please, put yourself at ease."

She introduced the panel. The one on the left was Krylova, her chief of staff. Then came the political officer. On the right was Raskova's adviser for technicians, and Lara, her adviser for pilots. "And you already seem to know who I am," Raskova continued. "We are not here to test you. That is what the examinations were for." She peered down at a stack of papers in front of her. "And it looks like you've done well enough at those."

"We're still awaiting your flying log and certifications from your aeroclub," Krylova said. "For now, we'll take the information you have given us at your word." She made a show of taking sheets from Raskova's pile and looking them over. "Over three hundred flying hours in just two years. Impressive."

Her voice sounded anything but impressed. A bead of sweat slid down from Aelya's temple.

The chief of staff continued, "You've written that you've flown the U-2, UT-1, R-5 and even the SB."

"I didn't solo in that last one," Aelya said.

"I'd be surprised if you did. Hmm, Smolensk North. For such a small aeroclub, you had access to an unusual assortment of planes."

"Well, some were sort of unofficial."

"Unofficial?"

"My parents are engineers at Aviation Plant No. 35. Different models of planes are always coming through for repairs."

For the first time, the political officer spoke. "So you've been exploiting your familial connections for unauthorized use of state property?"

"Those planes needed flight trials anyway. And I only wanted to maximize my flying time in order to serve the State to the best of my ability."

Aelya began wringing her hands. She'd thought her flying experience would be an advantage. Krylova leaned over to whisper to Raskova. Aelya stared at her idol, hoping to make eye contact with the great aviatrix so the woman could look into her heart. Surely she would see that Aelya's intentions were true.

The women proceeded to flip through more of her file.

"Your Komsomol records are rather thin," said the political officer.

Of course. Only two years. She had to explain why she'd only joined the Komsomol at sixteen, at least according to her record.

But Krylova spoke first. "Do you think you're ready to endure the hardships of the front line? I see very little participation in hiking activities in your history. No camping, no shooting. Just flying."

"I left my family to join the Komsomol digging trenches."

"So you can hold a shovel. What other skills do you have?"

"Umm . . ."

Raskova interceded. "What my comrade is getting at is that to be an Air Force pilot takes more than just flying experience, more even than skill. How do you work in a team? How do you react to adversity? What are you prepared to endure? What motivates you to do this?"

"I'm here because I want to defend my motherland." She thought that was the answer they were looking for, but everyone must have said that.

"As you know, there are many different contributors to an aviation regiment," Raskova said. "Many different roles to fill."

Aelya felt a chasm opening up beneath her feet.

"Even if you can't verify all of your flying experience, I can tell that your commitment to your country, as with all of our recruits, is beyond question. With your excellent theoretical knowledge in a wide variety of topics, I think you'd make a great navigator."

After coming so close to her goal, Aelya might as well have heard "sewer worker." She looked at Lara, who returned her gaze with intensity. Aelya felt as though she was being willed to do something.

The voice of that old salt, Instructor Panarin, echoed in her head. "Is that all you've got?" he'd said when she took the controls of a trainer for the first time and wanted to give them right back.

"No," Aelya said.

Raskova raised an eyebrow. "I beg your pardon, comrade?"

"I'm sorry, Comrade Raskova. What I meant was, I don't know how I'd fare in a war zone. I'm only good at one thing: flying. If it seems I've omitted other interests, well, what else is there to do when you already know what you're *meant* to do? Yes, I did exploit an unfair advantage because of my parents' occupations. But even before I was born, they knew I'd fly. It's in my name."

Krylova snorted. "They named you after some alien girl."

"They named me for a story. The story of a flight beyond the bounds of Earth."

"I thought it was all a dream," said the political officer.

That was the movie! Aelya screamed in her head. She composed herself. "My parents built experimental planes that have gone higher than ever thought possible. As an infant, I crawled the floors of the factory. My father used to joke that I'd fly before I learned to walk. Comrade Raskova, in your book, you talked about knowing flying was meant to be from the moment you took off. I knew it from the moment I was born. So I may not have these other skills, but that's because I've always known I was a pilot.

"You may not have my flying logs or certifications, but they're just pieces of paper. Put me in the air, and I'll prove myself."

The women flanking Raskova looked to her.

"Your body may be ready," Raskova said, "but we have to see whether you have the proper mentality." She made a show of sorting the papers and closing the file in front of her. "Thank you for your time, Comrade Makarova. We'll discuss this further and reserve a decision until after the interviews have been completed."

Aelya stood to attention. Lara was smiling, but the others remained inscrutable.

CHAPTER 8: CHANGEOVER

Dear Papa, Mama, Vasya, and Babushka,

I'm safe and well and no longer near the front lines. I've left Moscow, bound for flight school. I've joined the Air Force!

I hated digging trenches. I was happy to have been useful, but I'm happier now that I can do what I do best.

I know you worry about me, but I'm living out my dream, flying for my country. I'm in good hands with Marina Raskova. Yes, I finally met her and she's everything, more even, than I thought she'd be. I know this will be something special. But there's a lot of training yet to come.

I want to fly fighters, of course, but they have yet to make that decision. Comrade Raskova said I need to prove not only my flying ability but also that I think like a fighter pilot. How does a fighter pilot think? If you know the answer, please tell me!

In the meantime, you must tell me how things have settled in Kuybyshev. So sorry to hear about Lyuba's husband and about Yura. I hope you'll be able to help their families.

I should also mention that Zina Borodina is here. Seeing her reminds me of home. I wish you could be close by. I miss you so much, but it's such a small sacrifice I'm making compared to many others.

Please save up your letters. I'll send you the field post number as soon as that's been sorted out. In the meantime, I don't want your replies getting lost!

Hugs and kisses,
Your Aelitochka

Aelya was scrawling her signature as a bump jarred her hand. The prospective pilots were piled almost on top of each other in the converted freight car. More than half the passengers weren't even military; refugees continually straggled their way in. The nine days since the evacuation from Moscow had been all stoppages, switching trains, and struggling to obtain basic necessities like food and toilet facilities. It was a wonder none of the recruits had disappeared.

Aelya had carved out a corner of the car with Masha, daughter of Ukrainian peasants; Dina, a dedicated Communist from Moscow; and Sveta, who seemed too delicate to be a pilot—something that could be said about Aelya, when she thought about it.

When the academy was evacuated from the capital, the recruits had been divided strictly. Not only were prospective pilots separated from mechanics and navigators but among the pilots Komsomol aeroclub members were separated from the civilian and Air Force pilots. In this group, everyone seemed to be from Moscow or Leningrad. Aelya and the Ukrainian, Masha, were the bumpkins. They kept to the fringe while the others chatted away—mostly Sveta getting a rise out of the others with her controversial opinions about movies.

Aelya actually agreed with some of what she said. Aleksandrov was totally overrated, but she wasn't allowed a word in edgewise. It was as if no one believed they showed movies in Smolensk, so how could she have an opinion?

Over time, the conversation topics ran out. Dina helped to alleviate the boredom with her gifted singing, accompanied by Masha's accordion, but the novelty rapidly wore off. Having read her tattered copy of *Aelita* too many times to count, Aelya had lent it to Masha, who put Aelya's notions of peasant illiteracy to shame as she sped through the novel.

"Are there really lizards and cacti on Mars?" Masha asked.

"All I know," Aelya said, "is there can't be people there. It looks far too much like a waterless desert." If those lines seen in telescopes were canals, they had dried up long ago.

On the way, news had filtered in of the desperate fight at the gates of Moscow. The defensive lines of Mozhaisk had fallen. Aelya wondered about the fates of Andrei, Roman, Fedor, and the others. Had they fled in time? Were they now digging trenches on the other side of Moscow?

Someone banged on the side of the carriage. In spite of the cold, the door was wide open, granting relief from the sweaty, stale air.

Raskova appeared. "We're almost there, girls. This is Saratov. Just waiting for a change in locomotives that will take us across to Engels. That's our final destination. Be prepared to spend the night here, though."

A weak cheer went up among the pilots, and Raskova hustled to the next car.

With the sun going down, the light in the car was failing. Aelya navigated a path to the doorway, hoping to illuminate the address she was writing on her envelope. She finished and put away the letter in her coat pocket. Out there, an endless congestion of locomotives, carriages, and cargo, human or otherwise, littered the rail yard. Just one more night of this madness, she hoped.

Masha tapped her shoulder. "If it's going to be all night, we'll need more food." Tall, broad shouldered, and square jawed, she had no problem clearing a path to the doorway.

"There are always vendors at train stations," said Sveta. "Maybe you can find a farmer selling apples or something."

"Apples," Aelya said with a hint of disgust.

"You'll get whatever I can find," said Masha. "Unless you want to come and help."

Aelya nodded. "What about you, Sveta?"

The prim girl shook her head and simply reached over, holding out a few ruble notes.

"Dina?"

"I don't trust those peasant markets," she said, turning away.

Other pilots pooled their money and handed it over. Masha snatched it up and then she and Aelya were off. A sea of train carriages lay between them and the station platform. Some were moving, and the light continued to dim. Masha started by crawling under a flatbed.

"Shouldn't we find a crossing or something?" Aelya said as she struggled to follow.

"If you can't keep up, go back. I'm sure Sveta wants someone to agree that *The Deserter* was an overlooked gem."

They scrabbled, climbed, and rolled across one track after another. Aelya had to admit there was a certain thrill to dodging the moving carriages. It was the most exciting thing to happen since she'd witnessed that dogfight between the Messer and the Ishaks.

When they reached the platform, freight was moving in every direction. Soldiers and civilians clamoured. Masha picked her way to a fruit stall.

"We're all out," the vendor said. "Haven't had anything all day. There's a war on, you know."

"You've been sitting here all day with nothing to sell?" said Aelya.

The vendor shrugged.

"I appreciate your contribution to the war effort," said Masha scornfully. Then they moved on.

The story at each of the other three food vendors was the same. Aelya sighed. Those vendors sat listlessly reading their newspapers while the State paid them to sell nothing. "Now what?"

"There are more than just vendors, if you know what to look for." Masha scanned the crowd as Aelya fidgeted next to her.

A man in a pressed grey suit sidled up next to them. "Looking for some food? Don't bother with the stalls. They've had nothing for days."

Aelya opened her mouth, but the man turned away and melted into the crowd. A pair of blue-capped NKVD guards passed by on their rounds. Once they disappeared from view, the man returned.

"Outside the station, across the street, there's an AMO truck parked to one side. Meet me there in five minutes," he said and made himself scarce once more.

Masha checked her watch.

"You're not thinking of going, are you?" Aelya said.

Masha shrugged.

"The man's clearly a criminal. A speculator of some kind."

"Don't worry. I see this all the time. The guards are fine as long as it's not in front of them."

It was deplorable. Weren't profiteers like this the cause of all the food shortages?

"If you're so scared," Masha said with a sneer, "just stand on the street and look out for the blue caps."

Five minutes later Aelya was doing just that in front of the station. The truck was there, about a hundred metres from the entrance, still too close for Aelya's comfort. Dozens and dozens of people milled around. Masha approached the truck. With only glowing cigarettes to light the street, she quickly faded into the twilight.

For one minute, nothing happened. Then two. Then three. No blue caps appeared either.

"Comrade, can I help you?" The old man was a railway worker, not a blue cap, but his insinuation was clear. How could a lone loiterer be up to anything good?

Aelya went back into the station and bided her time on the platform. She heard a whistle and some shouting, though she couldn't tell from what direction. The whistle barely made an impression above the noise of the rail yard.

She kept scanning the faces in the crowd. Was anyone looking at her? The two blue caps came back around on their patrol, swinging their flashlights. Aelya scurried behind a stack of crates.

A face framed by peroxide-blonde hair and a head scarf poked out from one side. "VVS, I see," she said, pointing at the sky-blue collar facings on Aelya's crisp new khaki uniform. "Are you with Aviation Group 122?"

Aelya nodded.

"Perfect," said the newcomer. She was petite and looked even smaller as she dragged two heavy suitcases behind her. "You won't believe the trouble I've gone through to find you girls. I must have switched five trains between here and Ufa."

She introduced herself as Roza Vyacheslavichna Kulik. Aelya returned the courtesy.

"So which train is ours?" said Roza.

Aelya looked back out to the rail yard. "It's a bit of a hike."

Roza hefted the two suitcases. "Just show me the way."

"It's not that easy. Why are you asking anyway?"

"I'm a pilot. I'm reporting for duty."

"Why weren't you with us in Moscow?"

"I got a little delayed."

Aelya strained to see if Masha had come back. "Can you wait here one minute?"

She hurried back out to the street. The truck was gone. A blue cap was standing nearby. She quickly went back to Roza and said, "Let's go."

Aelya offered to take one of the suitcases. It was shockingly heavy. She had to drag rather than lift it as they made their way across. The sun had set so they had to carefully cross over couplings between cars, barely able to see farther than a metre in front. She wondered the whole time if Masha had been caught. What could she do if she had? But it seemed cowardly to leave her behind when they had been comrades in arms just moments before.

One more train to cross, if Aelya remembered correctly. They had just mounted a coupling between cars when it started to roll.

"Look out!" Roza pushed Aelya off and leaped after her. Aelya hit the gravel bed, the suitcase flying from her hands, its contents pouring out. Roza landed perfectly, still holding her luggage.

Aelya dusted herself off. "Just what's in this thing?"

She crouched down with Roza and started gathering lipstick tubes, perfume bottles, and powder kits that had clattered to the ground. She wanted to say something, but what was the point? She gave this lightweight a week at the most.

When they finally reached the carriage, Masha was there.

"Where did you run off to?" Aelya asked.

"I got chased off. Then when I came back, you were gone. Well, here you go." She handed Aelya an apple. As she groaned, Masha asked, "Who's this?"

Roza hefted both suitcases onto the train. "I'm your new best pilot."

CHAPTER 9: THE HAIRCUT

The new girl sidled up next to Aelya at the very back corner of the formation. Late. They all gave Roza a withering look as they shuffled over to make orderly ranks and files in time for Raskova's inspection on the parade ground.

The evening before, Raskova had delivered a rousing speech to the recruits. Too bad Aelya had barely heard it. The whitewashed clapboard one and two-storey buildings lining the parade ground offered little shelter from the merciless wind that blew in from the surrounding plains. Aelya had only just caught the mention of Nadezhda Durova. Babushka had assured her she was descended from the legendary cavalrywoman who fought Napoleon's armies disguised as a man.

This morning, Major Raskova paced back and forth through the four hundred women assembled on the parade ground of Engels Higher Aviation School, barking out criticisms of each mistake. With each scolding, the women tensed in unison, lips stiffening, cheeks drawing in.

"Hands at your sides . . . straight backs . . . button up . . . eyes front."

Aelya inspected her own presentation, surreptitiously adjusting her *pilotka* side cap. She glanced at Roza to her right. Something was off. The uniform sagged at the shoulders, her tunic too long and belt tightened high at the waist to compensate. Having missed out on processing in Moscow, she had probably received the only size available that came close to fitting her tiny figure.

Something else was wrong. The hair underneath the *pilotka* was too bulky, bulging out.

Raskova's boots clacked on the pavement as she came around. Her strict demeanour made Aelya want to shrink out of sight. Unfortunately, Roza was just about the only recruit shorter than she was.

"Eyes front, Makarova!"

Aelya complied. Then Raskova's gaze fell on Roza. With a flick of the wrist, she knocked the newest recruit's cap off. A cascade of white-blonde hair fell to Roza's waist.

"Just what is this?" asked Raskova.

"Comrade Commander?"

Raskova smirked. "Just because you were late doesn't mean I'm going to be easy on you. You had all the time in the world yesterday to get your regulation haircut. Five centimetres above the shoulder, like everyone else."

"Yes, I understand the concept, but I think I can fly just as effectively with my hair tied in a bun."

"That's not the point."

Roza clasped her hands, pleading, "Comrade Commander, I've been growing my hair out since childhood. It would be a terrible omen to cut it. My mother always said—"

"Aren't you from Moscow?" Raskova gestured at the mass of women staring at them. "If you want to play a superstitious farm girl, let me remind you that plenty of the peasants here overcame their anxiety for the motherland." She looked over her charges. "Did any of you think to remind Comrade Kulik of her duty to see the barber?"

There were a few snorts. Aelya rolled her eyes. She'd been preoccupied with grabbing a bunk in the barracks and arranging her own affairs. In any case, she wasn't the type to play mother hen. Let Roza learn to look after herself like everyone else did.

"Nothing?" said Raskova. "Very well. Comrade Kulik, report to the guardhouse immediately for punishment. Women of Aviation Group 122, I want ten laps around the parade ground, then report to the hangars. There are oil stains that need cleaning."

A groan rose from the throng.

Raskova put her hand up. "When one fails, you all fail. Now move!"

It took enormous willpower for Aelya to overcome the soreness in her muscles enough to remove her cap. Without seeing it, she could sense the disaster already: cutting her hair short had left it stiff and frizzy. The sweat and grime from the day's work had only made things worse.

Summoning all her strength, Aelya changed out of her uniform and into a nightdress. She folded everything according to how she'd been taught that first night at Zhukovsky Academy in Moscow.

All around her, row upon row of bunks stirred as, with newfound energy, the recruits began to chatter and pull out personal effects from their lockers by the light of bare incandescent bulbs. It felt like Young Pioneer camp all over again.

There wasn't much time until lights out. Aelya pulled her tattered, discoloured novel out of her carpet bag. She didn't want to read it, just hold it as she went to sleep.

A nearby clutch of girls dispersed as they prepared to sleep in their own bunks. Tonya plopped down and began checking herself in a hand mirror, rubbing off makeup with a wet cloth. How had it not run when she'd been scrubbing the floor of the hangar? Even bare, her face was unmistakeably beautiful, her almost feline eyes giving her an exotic quality. Perhaps she had some Asian blood in her.

As soon as Tonya finished with her mirror, Aelya asked to borrow it.

"Do I know you?" Tonya said.

"Yes, we actually met when you left Kostyakovo, and again at Zhu—" She saw Tonya chuckling and stopped. "So may I borrow it, please?"

"Sure. You need a hairbrush too? It's boar bristle, not steel, but it might still work on that mess." Tonya tossed it past Aelya's outstretched hand and onto her pillow. Her eyes narrowed at the sight of the book. "Are you some kind of narcissist? Or does your mother put your name on everything so you won't forget it?"

Aelya laughed uneasily. "I'm actually named for the book, or rather, the character."

"How's that working out? Have you become an all-knowing, exalted beauty? Do men travel the universe to fall at your feet, oh Queen of Mars?"

Not sure if Tonya was expecting a response, Aelya angled herself away, focusing on brushing the kinks out of her hair. Thankfully, a commotion arose as Roza finally returned to the barracks.

Guardhouse punishment consisted of standing at attention all day, no matter the weather, with submachine gun-toting men taking turns watching. They even watched during the few toilet breaks while the offender squatted on a patch of grass. Aelya didn't know if she could ever make it through such punishment.

The cold had made Roza's face as pale as her hair, which was now regulation length, albeit uneven, as if it had been cut by a knife. Her eyes still shone brightly with defiance as she dropped herself onto a bunk in the corner of the dormitory.

Her pert nose twisted in disgust. She stood up suddenly and leaned in close to her bunk. "Ugh! What's that?"

A few of the girls around Aelya laughed, none louder than Tonya.

Roza recovered quickly, lifting up the yellow-stained sheets. "You call yourself pilots, yet you can't even find the way to the toilets."

Some spare sheets sat on a shelf at one end of the barracks. Aelya rose to get them. Walking barefoot between the rows of bunks, she stubbed her toe on something and fell to the floor.

Tonya sat there, staring at her. As Aelya got up, she looked over to her neighbours. Masha was looking the other way. Dina gave a slight shake of her head.

She was reminded of fifth grade, when the teacher announced that Lev Geller's father was a "class enemy." Lev was placed at a desk in the corner, and no one shared work or ate lunch with him. No one spoke to him, except to call him "traitor's son" or "parasite." He would walk home, often just a dozen steps behind Aelya, as he lived in the next dormitory building over. She would scrupulously keep her eyes down, careful to turn her head so as to never face him. A month later, his mother lost her job at the plant and they were moved out.

She looked over at Roza, who was focused on replacing the sheets on the bunk herself. She couldn't meet her eyes, just as she hadn't been able to look at Lev Geller. Shame burned within her. But it was still better than being an outcast herself.

No. She was going to be a fighter pilot. She couldn't give in to such weakness.

The clamour of tin plates and spoons banging on the door to the barracks gave her a fright.

An officer screamed, "Alert drill, alert drill! Everybody up! You have five minutes to get your uniforms on and assemble on the parade ground!"

CHAPTER 10: TABLES

The late-night alert drill set the tone for the days to come. A fearsome toll was exacted on the recruits' minds and bodies. Military drills began in the mornings, as Aelya learned the basics of how to dress and even how to walk. Regulations seemed to be changing as rapidly as the situation at the front. Even those who were already in the Air Force, like Lara, had things to learn. She and the others with prior military experience had a separate dormitory down the hall, but they participated with the new recruits in many activities.

Afternoons continued with classroom learning, and physical training came in the evenings. They seemed to be getting every possible lesson that didn't involve the presence of actual planes, which were in short supply.

Before the final meal of each day, the political officers led classes. Aelya eagerly anticipated these—not for the blunt propaganda, which made the eyes of even dedicated Communists like Dina glaze over, but for the news of the outside world they offered. They learned to translate the commissars' language. If a humble village girl had suicidally stabbed a Nazi officer to death within sight of the venerable Volokolamsk Monastery, the real news was that the Germans had taken that town. If the Fascist beasts were being hurled back toward Germany, but no specifics were given, at least it meant things had come to a standstill. The recent torrential autumn downpours around Moscow had trapped both sides in the mud.

It took perhaps a day or two for groups to form along social lines at mealtimes. Older pilots, like Lara and Klava, formed one distinct group and sat at their own table. Tonya, now sporting a glamorous Hollywood-style do, held court with a number of mostly young but experienced pilots, including Sveta. Tonya herself was not more than nineteen but had well over five hundred flying hours under her belt.

The navigators and technicians were separated from the pilots for their own training. Aelya acutely felt the absence of Zina, whose initial assignment as a mechanic had been confirmed. As a result, Aelya milled around her own table with Dina and Masha, neither of whom seemed to fit in with another group. It was like Young Pioneer camp all over again.

Roza was on her own, when she wasn't missing meals due to punishment. Almost every day she gave an improper salute or backtalk to the instructors. Half the time, the punishment was visited upon all the pilots.

At the end of the first week, they got a whole afternoon of "structured" leisure time. The commissars' duties included fostering both Communist Party ideals and morale. They gleefully carried this out by forming recruits into a choir to sing Prokofiev's *Alexander Nevsky* chorale. A group also met in the school library, learning how to work a printing press to produce regimental newspapers. The only way to get out of these activities was to pursue aviation-related interests. Aelya volunteered to copy out tactical diagrams for the instructors. She enjoyed visualizing the movements of the little black silhouettes on the page, along with the actions of the pilots that would make such movements happen. Looking for any excuse to avoid the commissar, Roza tagged along.

There was another way to escape, though only one person knew how; Tonya simply disappeared during leisure time. All sorts of salacious rumours were whispered, though with schedules for male recruits at the school staggered with theirs, Aelya couldn't see how Tonya could arrange a liaison. It was amazing that she would so brazenly flout the rules when any recruit could have reported her. But that shamelessness worked in her favour. Roza pointed out that anyone unafraid of informers was doubtless well connected enough that informing on them would be hazardous.

The last sliver of time before bed was often dedicated to reading and writing letters. For many, it was a time of joy as they received greetings and care packages from dearly missed friends and family. Aelya was heartened to see the happy girls often sharing edible goodies and kind words with those who'd received nothing.

After a couple of weeks, Aelya began souring on letter time. She'd heard nothing from her family for about a month. It was fine, she reassured herself. She'd been moving around so much, it would take time for the mail to catch up. It could be worse. Masha anxiously scrunched up a letter from yet another relative who'd heard nothing from her family since their home village in Ukraine had been overrun. The fraternal twins, Olga and Yulia, known as Everest and Elbrus for their towering height, cried and hugged each other after learning their brother had been killed at the front, somewhere close to the Arctic Circle. It was easy to forget, with all the attention on Moscow, that the war was being fought across a whole continent.

Tonight, before the call for lights out, Aelya dashed off a quick note to Vasya about training and folded up some money into the envelope. She'd seen Lara sending money to her brother's widow when they received their first pay from the Air Force. Vasya had complained about conditions in Kuybyshev and terrible shortages there. If not for the war, she'd be in university right now, but instead she was working to re-establish the aircraft plant. Vasya would consider the money an insult but grudgingly take it.

A stocky, brown-haired girl stumbled back into the barracks in tears. Things had been moving so quickly that only now did Aelya remember the girl had been pulled aside earlier in the day. She sobbed as others moved closer to comfort her.

"The blue caps questioned me for ten hours," she moaned. "They shouted at me and roughed me up, calling me a traitor. They wouldn't let me go to the toilet, so I wet my pants. I kept telling them, you must mean another Polina Arshavina." She curled up into a ball.

Tonya, lying back on her bed, puffed on a cigarette, hands interlaced, arms behind her head. "I'll bet you she's a model Party type. It's always them."

"It sounds like a case of mistaken identity," said Aelya. "Otherwise, they wouldn't have released her."

Tonya shrugged.

For Aelya, training was at its dullest during theoretical classes. Never in the best physical shape, she found it difficult to maintain focus through her exhaustion. Worse still, the courses were designed for new pilots, ones with far less experience than all the women here.

She was itching to get flying, but the U-2 biplanes, the same ones she could have taken any day of the week from the aeroclub before the war, had been prioritized for the male students. So she was stuck in classrooms with half the instructors dry academics, hopeless at answering practical questions. Aelya had managed to befuddle one particularly imperious teacher with a bushy beard, older than her father, when she asked how environmental conditions might affect the performance of the Klimov engine.

Tonya tried to have some fun, batting her eyelashes at one slick-haired instructor. He kept his eyes straight down.

"What's the fun in that?" she whispered to her comrades.

Olga said, "I'm surprised none of them ever get fresh with us."

"They're afraid of Raskova," said Dina.

"It's not Raskova," said Tonya. "It's the letter she holds. The words 'by order of Josef Vissarionovich Stalin' have a strong effect on people."

The other instructors were frightening: dead-eyed veterans from the front. They all had stories about how bad things were: how the Luftwaffe destroyed thousands of planes on the ground in the first few days of the invasion, how the VVS was outmatched in every way except courage.

"When in doubt," said Instructor Loktionov, whose hair and beard were prematurely grey, "ram your plane into the enemy."

Two weeks into the routine, a new young tutor broke the monotony. It was an unusually clear day, so Instructor Savchenko took the pilots outside, to one of the endless stretches of grass that surrounded the school. As male pilots took off in U-2s on their training routes, he had the female recruits form into groups of nine. They stuck their arms out, pretending to be airplanes, complete with buzzing sound effects. He taught them to gauge their spacing and check their orientation.

Aelya couldn't help smiling. The scent of grass carried on the breeze was a relief from stuffy classrooms. It wasn't being in a real airplane, but she could almost imagine it.

No matter what directions Savchenko gave her, Tonya always seemed to brush up against him. When he corrected her, he did it with a laugh and she winked at him.

Then he taught them how to fly in a defensive circle. Roza stood still, her hands on her hips as the other eight in her group followed instructions.

"Comrade, don't fall behind or the Messers will gobble you up," he said brightly.

"I'm not in an airplane. I'm standing on the ground. And I want to know, if we're doing so badly against the Luftwaffe, why are we still studying tactics that obviously don't work? Fritz doesn't come from the side, politely asking to join your circle," said Roza.

Savchenko laughed. "The girl thinks she's an expert."

"Not me. Comrade Instructor Loktionov said they dive from above, pick you off, then climb away."

Savchenko flushed. "Kulik, is it? I've heard about you. What you say not only disrespects your superiors but sounds defeatist—even enamoured of the Fascist enemy."

Roza swallowed hard, shrugged, then joined her group. The rest of the lesson consisted of sober, repetitive drills, as Savchenko's mood had soured.

That night in the mess, Olga, the taller of the twins, "accidentally" bumped Roza as she got her porridge. Wordlessly, Roza knelt down to clean up the mess and scoop what was salvageable into her bowl.

"A bit clumsy to be a pilot, aren't you?" Tonya said, goading the girl.

As she did after every incident, Roza pretended nothing had happened. What on earth was Roza playing at, day in and day out? She had gone out of her way to catch up to the group when she could have stayed in Ufa, where apparently, she'd been an instructor at the aeroclub. When would Raskova end her misery and kick her out?

Aelya thought about Lev Geller again. At least those lunches had been boisterous for the rest of the fifth grade. She had almost forgotten he was there. Here, only the dull clang of cutlery could be heard as the tired recruits scooped up their meals.

Aelya sighed and left Masha and Dina to sit across from the brash and diminutive recruit. Roza kept her eyes on the porridge.

"Hi," Aelya said, only getting a grunt in response.

How was she going to broach this subject? Everything was always so clear and easy in an airplane. She tried to imagine herself in a cockpit, but that didn't help. Just get the job done, she told herself.

"You know," Aelya said in a low whisper, "what you said about tactics sounded quite reasonable to me. I've been wondering the same thing. But you know what's important? Working together as a team. Stop thinking you're some kind of lone wolf. You know what I think?"

"I don't care."

"If no one thinks they can count on you, they'll want you out before you hurt the rest of us. More than you've already done."

Roza looked up for the first time and stared at her, slowly slurping from her spoon. Aelya could sense the others slowing their movements and looking at them. Tonya and Sveta smiled like cats spying a mouse. Aelya sighed and went back to her own table.

The clanging of plates and spoons woke them at a mercifully normal time the next morning. Aelya had become so used to readying herself in fifteen minutes while half conscious, she'd initially thought the scream was part of a dream.

Only when Sveta, Olga, and Yulia gathered around Tonya's bunk did she register what was happening. Tonya's lustrous black hair, still in her Hollywood do, had been streaked with bleach while she slept.

In the corner of the barracks, Roza brushed her peroxide-blonde hair, cracking a smile.

CHAPTER 11: CUT OFF

All day, whenever Aelya glanced at her fellow recruits, they were watching Tonya and Roza, waiting for the inevitable explosion. Aelya kept her head down, trying to focus on the lessons and exercises flung at them at a blistering pace.

The big excitement that came in the evening wasn't a fight but the issuing of winter flight gear. As Aelya unfolded her fleece-lined suit against her body, it dropped down, a full half metre lying flat on the ground.

"I didn't know elephants could fly," remarked Tonya, her hair hidden tightly under her service cap. "We might lose Roza in one of these. What a shame."

Roza ignored her.

"They only have men's sizes," droned the logistics officer handing them out.

"These boots are huge too," said Olga. She did a little ballerina twirl, her foot fully rotating while the boot stayed in place on the ground.

Dinnertime was livelier than normal. It helped that the previous night hadn't been interrupted by an alert drill. Something about the enormous flying suits had also unlocked everyone's good humour.

One of the canteen servers delivered a wooden box to the prima donna table. Tonya lifted the lid and drew out a small silver rectangular block. "Chocolates. From America."

She looked at Aelya and nodded. "Queen of Mars?" She tossed the chocolate bar into Aelya's hands. As she comprehended the value, her fingers ran delicately over the English lettering on the foil wrapper. These were only supposed to be given out in hospitals.

A rush of women got up from their tables as Tonya dispensed the goods. Roza stayed rooted to her bench and exchanged a glare with Tonya.

When it came time to hit their bunks, Tonya still hadn't returned from the showers. She was risking the ire of NKVD women patrolling curfew. Aelya stepped lightly over to Roza as she was getting ready to sleep. She held out the remaining half of the chocolate bar to her.

"I don't want it," Roza said.

Aelya sighed.

"You know she's probably a denouncer," Roza said. "That's how she gets everything. She probably informed on Arshavina."

"No. How could any of us be an informer? Even Tonya?"

"It must be sweet to still think like that." Roza half smiled. She reached out softly, as though she wanted to stroke Aelya's cheek, but patted her on the shoulder.

Aelya brushed the hand away. She understood Roza's type—so privileged and well protected, used to saying and doing what she liked and getting away with it.

"I don't know why you have to be so difficult," said Aelya. "You can't be touched. We get it."

Roza laughed, then stopped, watching for reactions. But everyone's attention was turned toward Masha's bunk, where the rough and tumble tomboy was curled up, ripping at the sheets, tears streaming down her face. Masha let out a muted scream.

Aelya walked gingerly back toward her bunk.

Dina turned to her. "A letter from one of her brothers in the army. Her whole village has been wiped out. Her mother, baby brothers, and sister. All her grandparents. Uncles, aunts, cousins, neighbours. The Nazis machine-gunned them all. Only a friend of her brother's got out by playing dead."

An exclusion zone built up around Masha. Aelya took one step into this circle.

Masha lashed out at her. "I don't want your empty sympathy. Your pity. What do you know about it?"

But others did know; Aelya could see the looks on their faces. One girl mentioned her family had gone missing somewhere near Minsk. Galya, at twenty-three already one of the "old hands," obsessively checked off a list of friends and relatives trapped in besieged Leningrad. Olga and Yulia had experienced loss too—different, but no less profound.

"They slaughtered my uncle's family." Dina said. And the girl from the row behind nodded. More and more, they began share their stories of worry and loss.

Aelya backed away.

Tonya entered the room. Magically, she had somehow dyed her hair back to its normal black and she smilingly presented herself, until she noticed the mood in the room. She quietly went back to her bunk.

Aelya found herself sitting next to Roza once more. She placed her book gently on her pillow. "Your family's still in Moscow, aren't they?" she asked.

"My mother and a little brother. Zhora keeps talking about joining the army, but he doesn't even look twelve, let alone eighteen. There's a good air-raid shelter right underneath their building, so they're pretty safe."

"But what if . . . they take Moscow?"

"That's never going to happen. Old General Winter will take care of the Nazis, as it does everyone else who tries to beat us."

"I wish I could be as confident as you."

"Of course I'm not confident! But what choice do I have but to pretend? My mother's a clerk for the metro, and that's not moving anywhere, unlike some people."

Aelya pursed her lips. Her family had certainly been lucky, but Aelya was here by choice. She shifted uneasily on her bunk and only then noticed the parcel left underneath it during mail delivery. It was marked from Kuybyshev. Inside the care package were some plain biscuits, which looked pathetic next to Tonya's chocolate, and a white knitted scarf. The note from her father surprised her with its tone. He expressed no pride or encouragement over her enlistment. He was upset, imploring her to come back and be an instructor at the aeroclub, which had gotten a few new planes. There was another note from Vasya, who'd knitted the scarf as part of a voluntary aid committee. Aelya was amused by the image of Vasya in a knitting circle, making chit-chat with managers' wives. Her sister relayed that Babushka lacked the ingredients to bake any treats, which made Aelya more upset than she had any right to be. Vasya had earned the biscuits from donating blood and acknowledged their modesty, supposing that Aelya was being well fed by the Air Force already.

Aelya considered for a while what to write back. The sobs and anguished conversation around her died down as lights out approached. She decided to tell her family that training would take a long time and she would remain far from the front. She was indeed well cared for and wouldn't need anything special from them.

It took until the end of the next day before Tonya's payback manifested itself. Roza gingerly hobbled to her bunk without shedding her woollen greatcoat. She sat at its edge, her legs sticking out. When she didn't move for a minute, Aelya made her way over. Roza smirked and opened her coat.

Her flight suit had been cut off from the knees down, her legs bare and swollen red with frostbite.

"What were you thinking?"

"That's how I found them this morning. I didn't want a uniform violation, so I just hid them under the coat. It worked well enough, but the last two hours have been hell."

Roza gave Tonya a hard stare. Aelya lay her down on the bed, shaking her head. She had her own training to focus on. She didn't need to deal with this.

She went to the door and snooped outside. The hallway was empty. She scurried on bare feet to the senior pilots' dormitory down the hall.

"What are you doing here?" Lara asked.

"You have first aid supplies here, don't you?" Aelya filled her in on the feud between Roza and Tonya.

"They should be ashamed of themselves," said Lara.

"Maybe we should remind them we're in a war."

"Never underestimate the human capacity for pettiness, even in the face of unimaginable adversity. I'll go with you, see if I can sort this out."

Aelya couldn't see either party welcoming that sort of escalation. "I think it would be better for them to cool off."

Lara nodded. "That sort of judgment will serve you well. All right, but let's think practically. I have access to the fabrication shops. We can repair Roza's flight suit during our leisure time without anyone having to know. Then we'll make them accept that they're even now."

"I don't get the feeling Roza thinks things are even."

Lara frowned. "We'll have to force the issue somehow. Leave it with me—there's something I'd like to try. For the time being, just try to keep Roza from escalating the situation."

Sneaking back to her dormitory with a jar of ointment, Aelya found Roza still lying in bed, staring unwaveringly at Tonya, who was ignoring her with the same intensity. She treated Roza's legs, stewing about the absence of flying. Any moment now, Raskova might change her mind and assign her to navigation. She needed to stand out in some way, but now she had to be some bleached-blonde malcontent's minder.

"That's much better," said Roza with no indication she noticed hostility in Aelya's hand motions. "I should be back in action by first light."

"Great. Lara has access to the fabrication shop. She can use the sewing machines there to fix your suit."

"Does she now? Make sure she takes me there tomorrow."

"You're not going to do anything rash, are you?"

Roza smiled. "Don't worry. You'll like this idea. I guarantee it."

CHAPTER 12: AUNTIE

Aelya had to be grateful to her sister; the white scarf protected her face from the wind in the open back of the ZIS-5 truck. Next to her, Roza stretched out in her blue winter flight suit. Due to their warm fleece lining, most everyone was wearing them today, despite not performing any aviation duties. But Roza's was the only suit finely tailored to hug her petite form. The boots were still laughably big, but there were enough copies of *Pravda* and *Red Star* to stuff around the sides to make them snug.

The truck jostled when the convoy left the road. Even Roza had to break out of her pose to hang on. She showed no ill effects from the frostbite of a couple of days ago.

"Is this where they're building the secondary airfield?" Aelya asked.

"The airfield's done," said Lara. "The problem is the support buildings."

"I don't see any . . . oh."

"We have to dig reinforced bunkers for everything from the command post to ammunition storage."

"The commandant doesn't have labour he can set aside for this?"

"Don't complain. The deal Raskova cut with him is that if we dig out the bunkers, we get access to the U-2 trainers."

The line of trucks stopped at the edge of a featureless plain of snow, part of the massive void that surrounded Engels on three sides, with the Volga River on the fourth. Digging tools and building supplies were off-loaded. The eighty-odd pilot recruits disembarked and assembled in formation as Raskova announced their assignments. They were separated into work crews, with the officer candidates in charge.

Lara picked Aelya, Tonya, and Roza for her group. While she'd hinted that she would do this, it didn't make Aelya any less apprehensive when it happened.

Worse still, Tonya and Roza were smiling at each other like gluttons about to tear apart a roast pig.

"I know the days are getting short," Raskova said before departing, "but I expect you to be done your assignments by sundown."

She and the trucks pulled away toward somewhere much warmer.

Lara's group needed to dig four emplacements for anti-aircraft guns. Almost immediately after they started work, Roza and Tonya went at each other.

"I'm digging here."

"No, I'm digging here."

"Crack the ice with a shovel."

"No, it's thin enough to stomp with your feet. It'll be faster."

On and on they went, though at least they were working.

"Let's keep moving," said Lara. "You're doing well."

"Yes, Auntie," said Tonya with an insolent salute.

With the sun high in the sky, they had only completed one of the dugouts. Aelya noticed the other groups were all further along. Still, finishing by the end of the day seemed a stretch. What would Raskova think of this pathetic performance?

After a silent break eating tinned rations, Lara started off the afternoon by remarking, "There has to be a better way."

Roza ignored her, immediately picking up a shovel. Tonya puffed away on her cigarette.

Aelya piped up. "Well, maybe I have a suggestion."

"Yes?"

Aelya had no idea. She just didn't want Lara to be completely ignored. She furiously searched her brain. Didn't Mama always talk about improving productivity at the plant? Why hadn't she ever paid attention? She scanned the other work crews ending their breaks and tried to envision herself standing on the factory floor as a plane was being assembled.

"Pass me the sandbag, will you?" Roza asked Tonya.

"Busy." Tonya blew out a particularly thick plume of smoke. "Mars, you do it."

"Excuse me, they're right at your feet."

"So ungrateful. I thought you'd be full of energy after eating all that chocolate."

"Everything's a transaction for you," said Roza. "Now it makes sense. I wonder what you do for the officers to get their fancy Kazbek tobacco. Hmm?"

"There's nothing wrong with being charming," Tonya said. "Not that you'd have any idea. I wonder how you've managed to not get expelled."

"Maybe I'm so good at flying, they can't bear to lose me."

"Ha! Good at informing, more like. Those hours in the guardhouse . . . is that when you tell your stories to the blue caps?"

The war had gone on half a year, but this was the first time Aelya saw murder in someone's eyes. With a quick hop, Tonya dodged the shovel Roza hurled at her feet. Though Roza was a good fifteen centimetres shorter and ten kilos lighter than Tonya, her waist-high tackle knocked the girl to the snowy ground.

"I'm sick of rats who get fat off other people's misery. And now you call me an informer?" Roza screamed as she tried to wrap her hands around Tonya's neck.

Tonya crossed her arms and thrust them outward to break her attacker's grip, then hit her on the side of her head, knocking Roza down.

"A Party toady can't stand having her warts pointed out, eh?" Tonya said, struggling to her feet. "You think you're so superior, but you traffic in the same dirt as the rest of us."

"Enough!" Lara shouted, placing herself between them.

By now, work had stopped on every part of the field as the other crews were drawn in by the commotion.

Lara cleared her throat. "Excellent. Er, now that we have everyone's attention . . . Aelita Petrovna has . . . an idea. To improve our productivity."

Tonya and Roza temporarily forgot their animosity and gave Aelya perplexed looks. Everyone else seemed to look between the combatants and Aelya, as if she had somehow orchestrated the whole thing for nefarious purposes.

"Aircraft assembly," Aelya blurted, thinking aloud.

"Yes . . . we should be more like an aircraft plant, right, Aelya?" said Lara. "And that means . . ."

"That means . . . we would be more . . . productive."

A few groans emerged from the crowd.

Wait, Aelya thought. She remembered something her mother had said. "Each team should specialize in one duty and then pass the plane on to the others. Not the plane . . . I mean job."

A momentary silence followed. At least no one was asking questions. It gave Aelya enough time to recall what she had seen when her mother had walked her through the plant.

"One group can specialize in breaking the ice—the strongest among us. Then maybe the ones with the most stamina can dig out the pits. Another group finishes the edges. A fourth prepares the wooden planks and sandbags, while the fifth puts them in place. And maybe one last group for getting supplies out to each site."

Lara broke into a grin as she followed along. "We have a number of dugouts in different stages, so let's break up into groups and assign each to a different station."

With Lara taking the lead, the other officer candidates joined in the planning. The rest of the recruits fell in line quickly. Tonya and Roza walked as far away from each other as possible. With the sun arcing across the sky, they had little choice but to keep working. Soon, with assignments handed out and each group rotating between dugouts, they were operating with the efficiency of a factory. A military unit. They toiled wordlessly, though Aelya caught a nod of approval from "Auntie" Lara.

Neither Tonya nor Aelya had done much manual labour in their lives, so they were in the supply group.

Tonya shook her head as she watched Roza lining up and nailing boards together to form the base for a bunker. "Who would have thought a girl who spends so much effort on hair, makeup, and clothes would be so handy with a hammer?"

"Roza can't possibly be an informer," Aelya said. "An informer would be doing the opposite of driving everyone away."

"*I'm* not an informer," Tonya said as they hauled a stack of empty sandbags from the place where the trucks had dropped them off. "I'm guilty of many things, but I'm not an informer."

"Well, you can see—"

"What?"

"Uh . . . you seem to get your hands on a lot of stuff."

"Really, Mars, an informer would not be paid off in contraband. I happen to be very skilled at getting stuff."

Aelya tried not to let her imagination run wild speculating on what Tonya might be skilled at.

Tonya didn't notice Aelya blushing, for her eyes were on Roza. "I wish I could get a flight suit like that."

"She made it in the fabrication shop."

"I'm not very good at tailoring." She looked expectantly at Aelya.

"I suppose I could convince Roza to do one for you."

"I'm not apologizing, if that's what you're getting at."

"No, no, just a truce."

"A ceasefire. She does nothing to me, I do nothing to her."

For the first time that day, Aelya felt she'd truly accomplished something. Unfortunately, the sun went down with fewer than half of the dugouts completed. It was a deflated group of pilots who greeted the return of the trucks.

Raskova inspected their work by the illumination of the headlights. "Why so glum? This is brilliant. You've made more progress today that the commandant has managed in a month."

"But Comrade Major, we won't be getting the planes," said Lara.

"The commandant actually gave us three days. Don't look at me like that. If we didn't aim as high as we possibly could, what would be the point?"

CHAPTER 13: MINUET

The pilots filed back into their dormitory. Fatigue had reduced Aelya to a stupor. She hadn't noticed Krylova standing to one side until the chief of staff grabbed her arm. "Makarova. With me."

With the unbending Krylova marching behind her, Aelya couldn't help wondering if she was headed for the same treatment as Arshavina. But how could it be? She had done nothing wrong. Her whole family were upstanding Communists, her parents both Party members. She remembered the sound of heavy footsteps in the night, tramping down the halls of the workers' dormitory. Packs of black cars pulling away westward, out of the city. The next morning her mother telling her never to mention this or that neighbour ever again. Like Lev Geller's father.

She was about to turn toward the administrative block when Krylova surprised her, tugging her elbow and steering her along the path to the gymnasium. She made out a faint clinking noise.

The clinking coalesced in her ears with each step, forming into the tinkling of piano keys through the cold night air. The thought that she'd been recruited for a special part in a commissar's musical performance popped into her head. She clung to that absurd fear as she entered. Raskova sat, her delicate fingers tracing a melody across the keys of the piano situated in the corner, beneath the baleful eyes of Stalin's portrait. She seamlessly lifted a hand to wave Krylova away. Aelya stood to attention, the snow melting into a puddle at her feet.

When the piece finished, Raskova held her hands above the keys for a moment. She smiled slightly at Aelya and invited her to take one of the metal folding chairs arrayed around the piano.

"What do you think?" Raskova asked.

"I don't know much about music, but it sounded good, Comrade Major."

Raskova smiled. "Ah yes. You obsess only about flying. Have you begun widening your horizons?"

Aelya tensed. When did she have the time? Was she already failing at thinking like a fighter pilot? "It's been busy, Comrade Major. Morning, day, and night . . . the training's been relentless. But I'm enjoying it."

"Before the war, this training program took three years. We're trying to give you the same in six months. Don't look so nervous, Aelita Petrovna. I see you've taken well to your classes. Almost straight fives in your evaluations."

"I guess it comes naturally."

"You were born to it, you said."

Aelya felt embarrassed. It sounded arrogant coming from Raskova.

The door thudded open. This time, Krylova brought Lara in. They both saluted, then Krylova left. What was this about?

"Thank you for joining us," Raskova said.

Lara looked as though she wanted to say something but kept silent.

"I remember something else you said," the major continued to Aelya. "Actually, it was Lara who reminded me of this—about how you crawled on the floor of the aviation plant and your father thought you would fly before you walked."

Aelya's mind raced furiously. That was why she was called here? Because of a story she'd told that first review panel in Moscow? "Yes, that's right," she said.

"Tell me, were you a late walker?"

Aelya froze, trying to understand the question.

"Aviation Plant No. 35 was established in 1926. You would have been at least three years old then."

Aelya's heart went into free fall. What had Raskova seen? Her Komsomol record and internal passport said 1923 to match the birth certificate her father had acquired. Had Raskova talked to anyone from the aeroclub? Her real age had been an open secret, though old Panarin seemed completely oblivious.

She opened her mouth to speak. Would she lie to her commander? Raskova didn't seem angry. Lara appeared sad but didn't look away when their eyes met.

"It was Lara who brought this to my attention," Raskova said. "Don't look at her, look at me." Aelya obeyed immediately. "Ordinarily, I would keep Lara's confidence and not involve her. But she insisted that you have the right to face her."

Aelya resisted the urge to search Lara's face again for some sort of reaction. She was furious at Lara for cheating her out of her dream. It wasn't as if Lara had been in combat. How could she sit in judgment?

"I know, the Komsomol card, the passport—everything checks out," Raskova said. "I also know these things can be . . . arranged."

Lara spoke up. "Aelya, you must understand, I don't mean to disparage you —"

"That's not necessary, Lara." Raskova kept her eyes on Aelya. "As an officer candidate, she had a responsibility to report this to me, regardless of whatever evidence might or might not have been available. To omit any suspicions because she wasn't sure would be a dereliction of duty."

Aelya gripped the sides of her chair, her palms sweaty and tongue prickled with dryness. She squirmed under the gaze of Stalin's portrait. She wouldn't say anything unless forced to. That was the best thing.

The major said, "I haven't looked any further than that. But put yourself in my position. Could you allow a child to go to war under your command?"

Aelya had to word this carefully. "Would you hand a child over to the blue caps for lying?"

"What? No, what makes you think . . ." Raskova sighed. "In our system, there's only so much a commander has control of. But this is a different matter. It's entirely between the three of us."

The tension left Aelya's limbs, even though she knew she was still in trouble. At least the NKVD wasn't involved. Then she remembered that someone was talking about keeping her from flying, and her fear transformed into anger.

"I've put myself in your shoes," Aelya said. "You didn't stop trying to be a pilot when everyone said you couldn't. And what if your daughter has the same dream?"

"Don't bring Tanechka into this." Raskova sighed. "And set aside what *you* want for a moment. The duties of an officer are different from that of an ordinary pilot. We need to make hard decisions, knowing we may send people to their deaths. If Lara were your superior officer, what additional burden would you be putting on her?"

Aelya still hadn't really thought about the possibility of death. War or not, she felt invincible in an airplane, as all young pilots did. Aelya looked at Lara in a different light now, but something still seemed unfair to her. Had it been fair to throw Yura into a war zone with barely any solo time?

"Excuse me, Comrade Major, but I don't believe you're being fair. Yes, of course I gain some personal satisfaction from my service. But this isn't just some adventure cooked up by a daydreaming child. This is a matter of life and death. This is about . . . there was a pilot. A boy, you'd call him. He was eighteen. I trained him. He hadn't even soloed yet, but they threw him into a U-2, sent him to the front, and a few weeks later he was dead. He had written me that he wouldn't have had the chance without me. He thanked me for it."

"I'm sorry to hear that," Raskova said. "We've all suffered losses we wish to avenge, but—"

"This isn't about revenge!" Aelya said. Raskova was piqued by the interruption but visibly calmed. "If I'm good enough to send a boy to die, I must be good enough to put myself on the line."

Raskova sighed. "Thank you, Lara. You're dismissed. I'll handle this matter and discuss it with you later. Please keep this confidential."

Lara saluted, glanced briefly at Aelya, then left.

When they were alone, Raskova looked hard into Aelya's eyes, holding her gaze for a long time.

"Have a seat next to me," she finally said. She shuffled over on the piano bench. Aelya took her place to one side, sitting rigidly as Raskova began another piece. It ended after a minute or two.

"Comrade Major, what are you going to do?"

"I don't know!" Raskova snapped. "I'm sorry. I just need time to think. Let's just forget about it for now."

Aelya thought of the strain Raskova must be under, wrangling four hundred unruly charges through a merciless training regimen. With her connections in the Party, she must have been hearing troubling news from Moscow. Even Aelya had pieced together that the Germans had renewed their attack, their panzers now freely rumbling across frozen mud. Had Raskova's daughter been evacuated yet? She was only a few years younger than Aelya.

Finally, after the next piece, Raskova apologized for keeping her so late. She personally escorted her back to the barracks.

"Back so soon?" Tonya asked.

"It wasn't the blue caps."

"Pity. I was looking forward to some waterworks."

CHAPTER 14: TWO HUNDRED METRES

With a limited number of planes to go around, most of the pilot recruits had to endure a painful wait for their turns to be evaluated in the U-2. For Aelya, this became doubly frustrating, as the alternative training scheduled didn't involve aviation but ground survival. She should have been grateful she was still here, but she yearned for a chance to show what she could do. The longer the delay, the less time she had to impress Raskova and prove she belonged.

While there were lessons in finding food and shelter and ground orientation, the highlight was undoubtedly the introduction to their service pistols.

"This is the Tula-Tokarev Model 33," a young sergeant announced as he showed off the automatic pistol in front of an outdoor firing range. "It fires a 7.62 mm round from an eight-round detachable box."

As a bemused Instructor Loktionov looked on from the side, the sergeant demonstrated the different parts of the pistol, how to load it, and, with a chuckle, which end to point at the Nazis. He showed how to cock it halfway to engage the safety mechanism, which Aelya didn't think looked safe at all. Imagined injuries from the gun going off made her arm waver as she handled it.

"Get used to carrying this on you at all times while on duty, in the cockpit, or on the ground," the sergeant said. "You never know, there could be saboteurs."

"Or your air base could be overrun after the army bugs out," whispered Roza.

"And of course," continued the sergeant, "you'll need this handy if you bail out over enemy territory."

Aelya shuddered thinking about what would happen if she had to face the Germans on the ground. During several political sessions, a commissar harangued them with stories of disgraceful soldiers who'd joined the Nazis after capture. Comrade Stalin had declared that there were no prisoners of war, only traitors.

Once everyone familiarized themselves with the pistol, the fun began. Targets were set up at the far end of the range. Someone had attached pictures of Hitler, and a cheer went up as the sergeant announced they could take target practice after he showed them proper firing stances.

When Aelya took a turn, she squinted at the target. From this distance, she couldn't make out Hitler's moustache, so he just looked like any other man. She fired, flinching at the first percussive blast chopping the air. It got easier after that, and, once done, she and the other shooters went to collect their trophies. Only three of her shots managed to hit the poster.

"Just terrible," Tonya said, clucking from the next lane. "I hope you've got better aim in a plane."

Aelya shrugged off the insult, which was light compared to what Tonya regularly dished out to Roza, even after they'd called a truce. Roza, in turn, had been quick with her own insults. It was the state of their détente that they were content to leave it at verbal jousting.

Masha had put every bullet into Hitler's head. She threw the poster down and gave it a good stomp. Far from amusing anyone, she was given a wide berth. She'd been offered a furlough after the terrible news about her family, but there was no point. She had no home now and, with her father and two remaining brothers fighting at the front, no one to take comfort from. For her, the wait to get into a cockpit must have been excruciating. Just the previous week, she'd smashed her accordion in one of those sudden fits of rage she was now prone to.

After everyone had a go, Loktionov stepped forward. "You forgot the most important lesson, Sergeant. Show them how to load the ninth round."

"I was getting to that," said the younger instructor, annoyed. He loaded a pistol with eight rounds, chambered one, then pulled out the magazine to add another round.

"The reason I left this for the end," he said to the pilots, "is that you don't want to fool around with this. Make sure you unchamber this round when you're ready to put your pistol away. I remember one fellow came back to his barracks and tossed his holster on his bunk, and it went off. Shot his wingman in the, er, backside."

A few of the pilots laughed.

Loktionov said, "Before you go up, always load the ninth round. Use eight on Fritz. You know what to do with the last one."

"I c-c-can't do it, this is c-c-crazy," said Klava.

Aelya had never noticed the stutter before. Klava was shaking, even more than the twin-engined Li-2 transport they were riding in. The apprehension was understandable. Minimum altitude for safe bailout, the instructor had said, was two hundred metres. That would give just enough time for the parachute to open. They'd still hit the ground hard enough that they might break a leg, he'd said, but better that than going down in a flaming wreck. Today they would jump from three hundred metres. He seemed to derive joy from making his students squirm.

Klava grasped the frame of the plane tightly. This aggravated Aelya. How could such an accomplished pilot be afraid of this? She wanted to say something but hesitated. She thought about how much easier it was for her tell people what to do when she was flying.

"You're a great pilot," Aelya said. "Just imagine yourself in a cockpit."

"In a cockpit you have c-control. Here, nothing." How did Aelya expect her to react? That maxim never worked for her either.

"Come on, you must have done this lots of times." With the side door opened, Aelya had to shout to Klava.

Klava shook her head. Standing by the door, the instructor signalled for the women to ready themselves. Each recruit checked the parachute of the woman in front and the woman behind. Their packs all fit snugly against newly tailored flight suits. It had been a very busy leisure period for those students who were handy with a sewing machine.

"You haven't jumped before?" said Aelya as she checked Klava, her hands stinging with cold.

"Never had to. And I don't plan on it either."

The instructor gave the go-ahead, and the recruits at the front of the plane began filing out.

Aelya had to push Klava forward as the line moved. "How can you be a pilot and never learn to parachute?"

"It's safer to try to c-c-crash-land," said Klava.

Aelya shook her head. Now at the doorway, grey skies opening before her, Klava clutched the sides of the fuselage in terror.

"Get moving!" shouted the instructor.

Klava froze.

Aelya moved next to her. "It'll be all right. Just a few seconds and it will be over."

Now that she'd realized nothing was separating her from open air, Aelya's stomach lurched. From higher altitudes, the ground was an abstract concept. From here, it was solid matter ready to smash your body if the chute didn't open.

"Go!" the instructor ordered. "I can't go back with any students on board."

Aelya gave Klava a reassuring pat on the shoulder, but the older woman shook her head. Behind them, the remaining students shouted at Klava to move.

The intense attention made Aelya feel obligated to do something. She took a deep breath, then grabbed Klava. With one hand pulling the parachute's ring, she shoved her out the doorway, then toppled out after her.

The immediate sensation was the same exhilaration and terror of an uncontrolled dive. She yanked on her cord and felt her whole body pulled violently upward. Both her boots slipped away, their newspaper stuffing fluttering in the wind. She envisioned hitting the ground with a roll to absorb her momentum, but instead she thudded straight down into a knee-high snowdrift.

Uninjured, Aelya shrieked with joy and relief. She reoriented herself and spotted Klava struggling to her feet. Only when gathering up her chute did she feel the cold invading her stockinged feet. She made her way over to her comrade, looking in every direction for her lost footwear. Losing her boots wasn't how she wanted to stand out to Raskova.

Klava greeted her with angry abuse, then laughed, almost lifting her off the ground with a hug. "You lost your boots too?" Klava said.

Aelya looked across the snowy plain. Other pilots were also treading in circles, searching the ground.

A truck approached from the road, Raskova standing on the running board.

The pilots all stood to attention and saluted.

"My dear girls, I understand Comrade Instructor Blasov tried to frighten you." She looked them over from head to toe. "Why are you all barefoot?"

One of the pilots had found her boots and waved them.

Raskova looked them over again. "I can see how ridiculous they look with your finely tailored flight suits. How on earth did you acquire those suits?"

As the senior pilot in the area, Klava shifted nervously.

Then Raskova laughed. "Well, I must say I admire your enterprise. It will be worth calling in a favour from Moscow to get you properly fitted winter boots. You've earned them."

CHAPTER 15: SIX O'CLOCK

The long wait for a turn with the U-2s made it all the sweeter when Aelya finally found herself back in a cockpit. How long had it been? The first few days of the war, all the U-2s at the aeroclub had been commandeered for military use. She and Yura helped give them one last flight check before handing them over. Now the dials and gauges stared at her like a spider's multiple eyes. Were they the last things Yura had seen?

First came a simple twenty-minute tandem flight. She took to it like a fish being cast back into the water. Ailerons, elevators, and rudder moved completely in tune with her body.

Aerobatic drills came next. Easy. Then came flights in a designated zone along prescribed routes with multiple planes criss-crossing paths. Also easy. Unfortunately, the ease of the requirements meant almost everyone hit their marks. How on earth was Aelya going to stand out and prove that Raskova needed her?

The last exercise in the U-2 was to fly a more extensive route while in formation. She went out in a group of three, Dina in the lead, Aelya next, then Sveta on the tail.

Dina had struggled during the previous exercises. Sveta had done well but missed the last flying session due to guardhouse duty for some unspecified violation she wouldn't talk about. Uneasy, Aelya had a theory that Raskova had slotted her in with these two so she could be quietly downgraded and kicked out without getting into trouble for lying about her age.

Shortly before takeoff, they received a warning about a potential snowfall. The instructors had debated whether to continue, but Sveta and Dina were eager to go on regardless. Aelya thought her fate was already sealed but nodded meekly as the decision was made to go on.

Things weren't made any easier when the always grim Loktionov drew the lot to fly with her. Up they went, going through prescribed waypoints and changes in elevation. Loktionov occasionally broke things up by shouting over the wind, quizzing her on landmarks, distance, and timing estimates.

As he tested her, she determined to stop thinking the worst and focused on giving her best performance. Perhaps in a year's time, even after expulsion, they would let her join up again. Another year of war. General Winter had indeed given the invaders more than they could handle. Thousands of reinforcements from Siberia had stormed into the frozen, exhausted German ranks, hurling them back from the gates of Moscow. The tone of the political sessions was changing. Instead of sugar-coating military setbacks, they showed the recruits ghastly photos and films of corpses, young and old, strung up, frozen on newly recaptured ground, or burned to a crisp in their homes. If anything, being in a cockpit surrounded by comrades was the safest place she could be.

Push those thoughts away, she told herself. She kept her spacing with Dina constant, taking pride in this. Having rarely flown in formation before, she couldn't compete with the Red Banner Falcons like Tonya and Klava, but she hoped Loktionov would remember this was new to her.

Two-thirds of the way through the flight, a thick wall of snow clouds approached. A flare sparkled in the distance, above the airstrip, a prearranged signal in the absence of radio to come back to base. Not long after, snowflakes appeared.

Dina waggled her wings to signal a change in direction. Aelya banked and turned to follow, keeping a short distance above and to the right in perfect formation. A gust hit the plane. Aelya found herself pushed down and to the left, falling directly into Dina's slipstream. The plane juddered, in danger of rolling. By instinct, she fought to return it into formation.

"Check your six o'clock!" Loktionov shouted.

Too late, she glanced back. Sveta's nose had almost overtaken her. A loud crack ensued as its propeller struck the right wings of Aelya's plane. Time split into minuscule fragments as Aelya assessed what was happening.

Top right wing torn. Loss of lift. She compensated. In front, Dina had gone far ahead, already disappearing into the increasingly heavy snow. A glance back. No Sveta. Aelya looked over either side of her cockpit, growing frantic.

"We have to look for her," she shouted.

"Worry about yourself first," Loktionov answered. "Let's mark this position, then get back to base."

She made the plane descend, adapting to the damaged wing's behaviour. Getting away from the low clouds, she tried to orient herself. As she circled, she spotted Sveta's plane. It was wobbling as it glided down below.

Come on, Aelya thought. Fight for it.

Sveta looked as though she had taken the worst of the collision. The propeller must have broken. For once, Aelya was thankful for this miserable, desolate plain with just a few dips, trees, and hedges to avoid. Still, Sveta was taking too sharp an angle. The plane came down hard, its fixed landing gears bumping along the snow before it abruptly stopped and flipped over its nose.

Aelya continued her descent, circling around the crash site. She plotted the landing, finding the best stretch of open plain and angle to the wind.

"What are you doing?" said Loktionov.

"They say this thing can land on a postage stamp, right?"

"You're mad. Get out of here now—this is too dangerous."

He was right. She hesitated with the controls for a second, fear rushing through her in a sudden wave. This was a dumb mistake. But she felt compelled to keep going.

"Don't fight me for it," she said. "We're too low and slow."

Loktionov swore but let her take the controls. Sure, she could throttle up and pull away. But she kept on with the landing, knowing if she waited too long, she would be in danger of passing over rough terrain.

After a short, bumpy ride, the plane rolled to a stop and Aelya let out a breath. They were right—the U-2 really could land on anything.

Sveta's upside-down plane was within sight. Sveta crawled out. Aelya unharnessed and swung herself out, slogging through the snow toward her. Loktionov muttered curses and followed.

As she reached the crash, she quickly checked her comrade. Sveta was dazed but seemed physically all right. She pointed nervously at the man in the back: Savchenko. That sunny day on the grass pretending to be airplanes seemed years ago.

With Loktionov's help tilting the fuselage upward, Aelya managed to pull the barely conscious instructor out. She took off his leather flying helmet. A gash on his forehead bled profusely. Loktionov used his scarf to bandage it.

"We better get him back to the hospital on base," he said.

Together they dragged him toward their own plane and hauled him into the rear seat. As Aelya grabbed the side to climb in, Loktionov stopped her.

"I'll take it from here. Don't give me that look. I've landed a burning Ishak in fog. This is nothing."

Aelya didn't argue. She helped to turn the plane around, then watched as he took off. The storm was getting worse. She hoped the last bearings she'd given Loktionov were accurate.

Back at the crashed plane, she and Sveta sheltered beneath its wings.

"I'm in so much trouble," Sveta said. "Destruction of state property, and it's all my fault."

She pounded a fist against the side of the plane. "It's not fair! I try to be a good Communist. Why does trouble always find me?"

"Who says you're not a good Communist? What trouble?"

"And what if Savchenko . . ." Sveta sat down on the ground and buried her head in her arms.

"He'll be fine." What was the point in saying otherwise? Sveta was shaken. She wasn't thinking properly. If they were going to be stuck here for a while, she needed to get the girl's spirits up.

"You're a fantastic pilot," Aelya said. It was true. With her pretty auburn coif and her obsession with movies, Sveta had seemed a lightweight at first, but that was so long ago. "We're lucky to have you."

They huddled closely against the bitter wind, trying to cover every bit of skin.

"That was some doing getting your plane down," Aelya said.

"I nosed over. You landed perfectly."

"You were deadstick and lost altitude after the collision."

"The collision." Sveta smacked her forehead. "I wasn't thinking, just blindly trying to stay in formation."

As Aelya thought about it, she had a sinking feeling it was all her fault. She remembered Loktionov shouting to check behind her. Such a basic rule, and she'd forgotten.

"This will make a great story," Aelya said, as much to cheer up herself as Sveta. She got a slight smile for her efforts.

The cold seeped through every bit of clothing they had.

"We have to move to keep warm," Aelya said, "or we'll shut down."

She lost track of how long they stomped around, getting colder and colder. She tried not to worry. Would her Air Force career end with this? Wasn't flying her destiny? No, that was overconfidence—that's what caused the collision.

"They'll still let us fly, surely," she said, half questioning. "Or maybe we'll get busted to navigation and work our way back."

Sveta's eyes grew wide. "That's what you're worried about?"

Aelya was taken aback by her angry tone.

A horn honked faintly. The headlights of a truck appeared in the distance.

CHAPTER 16: FULL THROTTLE

"Ease up on the throttle! Too much rudder!"

This was the first time Aelya had flown with Instructor Golubev. She hated the way spittle flew as he barked complaints. At least Loktionov had the decency to glare his disapproval in silence. There was no way she could face him again, though, not after that collision.

What was she doing here anyway, at the controls of a UTI? The commandant was so impressed by the female recruits' work, he'd released these planes to them as well. The UTI was a two-seat trainer version of the newest Soviet fighter plane. By all rights, Aelya should have been removed from consideration. In fact, Sveta and Dina weren't getting this chance.

The list of prospects for the fighter regiment had been whittled down to thirty pilots, but only twenty would ultimately be selected. Once again, there was an apparent logic behind the order in which they got to take turns in the UTIs. The best pilots had already flown. Aelya had seen Lara's flight, so precise and correct. Tonya flew with a beautiful flair, each manoeuvre smoothly blending into the next.

"Stop that! Just hold it straight." Golubev snapped at every twitch she made, as if the slightest deviation would crash the plane. The closed canopy shut out the wind, making his tone unmistakable, even over of the roar of the engine. His barking was accusatory, as if to remind her the collision had been her fault.

Krylova had said as much. After Aelya had been taken to the hospital to recover from frostbite, she was confronted by the chief of staff. The woman was blunt, as always. Aelya relayed all she remembered of the incident. Krylova promptly said that, unused to formation flying, she'd erred in trying to force herself back into formation. A simple reading of the situation would have told her that a move to the left would have solved everything.

That painful truth hung in the air until Raskova came over to see how she was recovering. Aelya asked about the others, and Raskova confirmed that Savchenko had come out of surgery and was already joking about the crash. Sveta had a few bruises but was all right as well.

Raskova hugged her tightly, then left without giving Aelya a chance to ask how this might affect her situation. Fool, she thought. She'd almost killed four people, including herself.

Now Golubev's criticism of yet another wobble reminded her that even with her mistakes, they had let her get her hands on this thousand-horsepower beast, eight times more powerful than the U-2. No wonder some of the Air Force vets disparaged the old biplane as barely outmuscling a sewing machine.

The power of the UTI kept her on edge. She knew she would have less time to react to changes but more ability to recover from catastrophe. It was so much more streamlined than the U-2. All its characteristics differed from those of every plane she'd flown. When she'd done her first walk around, she remembered with some guilt what she felt that time she'd seen the dogfight. She admired the beauty of the Messerschmitts, even as they fired at and killed her compatriots. This was another beautiful plane.

She made another turn, but it was too abrupt.

"Hell, girl, you'll get us killed," Golubev muttered. "I must have really annoyed a blue cap to get this job. You girls flutter your eyelashes and wiggle your butts, and suddenly they give you a fighter plane! Guess it makes for good pictures, though."

Golubev's crassness reminded Aelya of Panarin. Her first instructor had been an old crust but at least he never once mentioned she was a girl. He'd said something like "Fly by the seat of your pants," only he put it more crudely. It wasn't meant to be an idiom.

She stifled a laugh, then took a deep breath. She stopped thinking through every possible action and reaction. She was going to feel the plane.

She took another turn, smoothly this time.

"What do you know? She knows how to turn," said Golubev. "One more turn and this agony will be done with."

These might be her last minutes flying for the Air Force. She had a notion to pull off a prank from her aeroclub days. It was against the rules, but what did she care now?

She throttled up.

"What are you doing?" Golubev said.

She banked sharply, the g-force whipping them both into the backs of their seats.

"Don't touch the controls," she said loudly.

She went down low and zoomed at top speed past the observers next to the airstrip. She waggled her wings in a gesture that felt obscene and screamed in exhilaration.

Aelya kept her eyes to the ground. All bravado had left her the moment she'd exited the cockpit. She sat in the pilots' ready room, Raskova pacing back and forth.

"What do you think I should do with you?" the major asked.

It took a couple of tries for Aelya to get words out. "If I'm going to be kicked out, it's better to do it now. You've already kept my hopes up for too long, Comrade Major."

Raskova sighed. "It was wrong to keep you in the dark all this time. But I needed to see what you did with this opportunity. The fact is, I also have a duty to make the regiments the best they can be. I believe you'll bring out the best in others, as well as yourself. It's better to have you as part of the VVS than to not have you."

Aelya covered her mouth to stop from squealing. She paused, fearful she'd heard wrongly.

"All your documents say you were born in 1923," Raskova said. "I'll leave it at that. Bear in mind, I wouldn't have allowed this if Lara hadn't spoken up for you."

"Auntie?"

"She heard all about what you did out there for Sveta and her instructor. If she didn't want to have you, I wouldn't have allowed you to continue. I wouldn't put responsibility for you on an unsuspecting officer."

Aelya didn't like the implication that she was some sort of burden on Lara's shoulders, but a lump hit her throat as she realized how selfish she was being. She knew she should be grateful.

"But the collision was my fault. Sveta and Dina deserve this chance, not me." She remembered how mortified Dina had been that she left her formation behind. But continuing to base had been the right thing to do. It was cruel to punish her for that. And Sveta, she'd done precisely what she was supposed to as the trailing plane.

The major placed a hand on her shoulder. "Dina's a good pilot. You all are. But there's another level of ability required to become a fighter pilot. The collision was a mistake anyone new to formations could have made. Formation flying can be learned. But your instinct to help your comrades, to land that plane under those conditions in a crisis . . . those can't be taught."

Aelya wanted to ask about Sveta, but Raskova's mood shifted suddenly and she laughed. "I heard Golubev threw up when they managed to pry him out of the UTI. He's insufferable. I can understand your urge to show him up."

The buzz of an engine that Aelya already recognized as a UTI drew their attention to the window. A plane on final approach executed the most daring manoeuvres Aelya had seen outside of an airshow: a low-altitude stall turn followed by multiple victory rolls.

"That's Roza Kulik, isn't it?" said Raskova. She rolled her eyes. "Well, get moving. I want you and Kulik to report to the canteen for kitchen duty. You're in the Air Force. No special treatment."

Hours of cleaning up couldn't wipe the smile from Aelya's face.

CHAPTER 17: THE ASSEMBLY LINE

The new year brought days of clear skies. Despite it being the coldest winter anyone could remember, the pilots assembled on the parade ground for morning exercises. It was a small group, just the fighter pilots, nineteen in all. It should have been twenty.

One night, Krylova had come for Sveta, just as she had for Aelya. But this time, blue caps followed and unceremoniously threw all of the girl's possessions into a cardboard box and left. Sveta didn't come back. In the days that followed, her name had disappeared from every roll call and group assignment. The instructors, even Raskova, acted as if she had never been there. It was understood among the recruits that her name couldn't be mentioned openly.

Whispered speculation was conducted during snatches of private time. During the muted New Year's celebrations in the canteen, the pilots milled around a pine tree wrapped in colourful garlands and sipped watered-down champagne-like liquid. Olga told Aelya that Sveta had an uncle who was a "class enemy." Sveta had exchanged letters with his son, who had to renounce his own father. The cousin himself had fallen afoul of the NKVD, and that's when Sveta was no longer welcome.

Olga was matter of fact as she passed this on—sad but resigned. Sveta had never been friendly to Aelya, but something had opened up when they were stranded. Now she was gone. That Aelya would turn seventeen the next day added to the bitterness. It wasn't fair that Sveta was expelled for merely writing letters while Aelya was allowed to fly fighters after lying about her age.

The winter flight suits allowed them some flexibility as a female instructor put them through calisthenics. Even with all the exertion, the cold seeped into every pore of Aelya's body. She relished it, though. Since she was ensconced so far behind the lines, the frigid weather gave her a feeling of kinship with the soldiers suffering through it at the front. The Soviet counterattack had petered out, and no amount of propagandizing could hide that fact. The excited optimism at the end of December had given way to the knowledge that it would still be a slog to push the Germans out. In the spring, one side or the other would be on the attack again, and Aelya knew that with training halfway done, her chance was coming. She would finally be joining something greater than herself, greater still than all of the pilots here, this school, and this corner of the motherland. Since birth, all her life had been leading to this.

She owed it all to Raskova and to "Auntie" Lara. By not acting on Aelya's lie, those two officers had taken a risk. She wanted to thank Lara, but when she'd tried to broach the subject, Lara put a finger to her lips. A look of determination, like the one they'd shared in that first panel interview, conveyed all that needed to be said.

Just as they finished their exercises, Raskova appeared, calling for them to line up at the airstrip. As they stood to attention, a single buzzing engine made itself known: the familiar drone of the UTI. But as the plane came in, Aelya spotted how different it was from others.

It was painted white. The gears that extended had skis instead of wheels. It skidded to a stop not far from where the recruits were standing. The canopy slid open and Raskova helped the pilot out of the single-seat cockpit. After saluting, they kissed each other on the cheeks in a perfunctory manner. The pilot took off her helmet and carefully fixed her slicked-back short dark hair. From the bars on her sky-blue collar patch, Aelya could tell she was a major. On her chest was a red-and-gold ribbon, hung with the wreathed portrait of Lenin. Except for the hair, she looked every bit the role Aelya had envisioned for herself: a real Air Force pilot.

The newcomer limped slightly, favouring her left side. A yellow strip sewn to her uniform confirmed she'd been wounded in battle.

"Girls, allow me to introduce your new commanding officer," said Raskova. "Comrade Major Tamara Volkova." Smiling slightly, Raskova nodded toward her.

Volkova limped to the nose of the plane. "And allow me to introduce the Yakovlev Model 1 fighter, or 'Yak' for short. It's quick and manoeuvrable. Simple to fly. But if you truly master this, it will be something . . . just beautiful. Like the *bogatyrs* of old, charging into battle. It's not much different from flying your UTIs. Except for this." She patted the nose and gestured for them to come closer, and they crowded around it. Its nose was very similar to the UTI's, but Aelya's attention was drawn to the hollow stub of a shaft protruding from the centre of the propeller spinner at the very tip of the plane.

"That's a 20 mm automatic cannon," said Volkova. "Two synchronous machine guns above the engine."

Masha whistled and the pilots began to chatter. Aelya had learned all the specifications in class, but seeing this up close in a live, working plane . . . there was something hypnotic in its power.

"Well, ladies," said Volkova, "would you like your own?"

The Yak-1s were manufactured right across the Volga River in Saratov. The plant was even larger than the one Aelya grew up around. Besides the main building, a huge brick structure with high windows, there were many outbuildings. Some looked like new additions since the war. It all covered a sprawling campus that dwarfed the base at Engels.

Trucks carrying the pilots pulled around the side of the main building and in front of a long section lined with tall barn doors. A man in a business suit stood before a row of technicians in neatly pressed and cleaned overalls. Without their uniforms, they would have been a motley crew—male and female, some wrinkled and grey haired, and several who looked to be of school age.

Raskova and Volkova stepped off and spoke with the man, who introduced himself as the plant manager. He mentioned how delighted he was to meet the protégés of the famous Marina Raskova, then led them all through one of the tall double doors.

Aelya nearly gasped. Twenty-five planes were parked perfectly, one in front of each door. They were painted white, with red stars on the fuselage and wings. Just behind the cockpit on either side were red numbers, going up in tens for each plane—10, 20, 30, and so on, up to 250. Unlike Volkova's, these had wheels for their landing gear.

They all looked expectantly at Raskova. The moment she nodded, the pilots scattered like schoolgirls on a field trip, inspecting the planes, gently poking and prodding them. Some grabbed stepladders so they could look in the cockpits and engine compartments.

"Do we get to pick which ones?" Tonya asked no one in particular.

Olga said, "I need one with a three or a seven.'"

Aelya was keen on choosing her own plane as well, but not out of superstition. Having grown up around an aircraft plant, she knew full well that there were massive variations depending on the parts batches used, the crews who built them, even the time of day they'd been assembled. The differences could mean rolling one right onto the runway versus needing a complete overhaul before even turning on the engine.

The manager cleared his throat. "Numbers 10, 100, and 200 are reserved for the regiment and squadron commanders. They're the ones with radio transmitters."

"No transmitters? I don't like the sound of that," said Roza.

Volkova shot her a glare.

Raskova put her hands up to stop further chatter. "Comrade Major Volkova will decide the squadron assignments and numbering. However, numbers can be repainted. So if you see one you like . . .'"

Volkova frowned.

A set of double doors leading from the factory floor opened, and a large group of women filed out. They wore blue military overalls.

"Zina!" Aelya shouted.

The technicians broke into a run, as more and more recognized familiar faces. The technicians had been housed close to the plant for the past two months as they learned their aircraft up close.

Aelya and Zina hugged tightly.

"Looks like we'll be in the same regiment," said Zina. "I've been assigned to fighter maintenance. They're making me a crew chief. Can you believe it? Me?"

Aelya was heartened to see that her friend's disappointment at not flying had dissipated. Zina paused, looking expectantly at her.

"I could request you for my crew," said Aelya. "Do you think they'd allow it?"

"Our instructors say it happens all the time. I'd be so grateful if you wanted me."

"Of course. I missed you."

Voices reverberated back and forth between the high walls and lofty roof.

It was all decidedly unmilitary, and Volkova looked on in disapproval. But Raskova happily chatted away with the manager, leaving them to their devices.

Aelya felt a tap on her shoulder.

"This boy says he can point out the good ones." Roza tilted her head to one shoulder, behind which a skinny youth with a crewcut stood in his overalls. Not even as tall as Roza, he definitely looked as though he should still be in school. "He says two in particular had good parts and good crews working on them."

Aelya shrugged. She and Zina walked over to the boy.

"Well?" said Roza.

"Payment first," he said.

"How much?" Aelya put her hands on her hips.

"Not money," said Roza. "He wants a kiss."

"What?"

"Just on the cheeks is fine. Unless you want to do it on the lips," he said with a smirk.

Aelya rolled her eyes. She pecked him lightly, eliciting a frown. Roza held him by the arms and kissed him on the cheek. He blushed slightly, then looked at Zina, who shook her head vehemently.

"Come on," said Roza with a withering look aimed at the boy, "that's two more than you've had in your life."

He sighed. Aelya nervously looked around, but everyone was so wrapped up in their conversations, they hadn't noticed. Finally, the boy shrugged and motioned for them to follow him down the length of the building.

Zina muttered, "He's, uh, a bit of a—"

"Creep?" said Aelya.

"I like him," said Roza. "Reminds me of my brother."

The boy brought them over to planes 180 and 190, making a grand, sweeping gesture as if he were introducing a stage act. "This one's a lucky one," he said, patting 180 on the nose.

"Why do you say that?" said Aelya.

"Because I worked on it. They usually only get me to do cleanup, but they let me attach the spinner on this one."

Zina examined the propeller cone, twisting it back and forth. "Seems solid."

Aelya looked at Roza. "Rock, paper, scissors?"

"You can have it. There's no such thing as luck."

Aelya ran her fingers over the wing fabric, the roughness of fresh paint rubbing against her fingertips. A heady mixture of engine oil and hydraulic fluid inundated her nostrils. Her plane. Her fighter plane. Six months ago, this was something she couldn't even dream of. It wasn't something she ever thought she wanted. Now it was the most important thing in the world. Everything she'd done before in life had no meaning compared to this.

By the end of the visit, the pilots had selected their planes through a combination of bribery, cajoling, and gambling. The recruits bubbled with joy. Yulia nearly knocked Aelya down with a spontaneous hug. Even Masha smiled. Before they boarded their trucks again, Raskova assembled them in a line.

"Ladies, as you're no doubt aware, our time here is coming to an end. I'll be restricting myself to commanding the dive-bomber regiment. Tomorrow, you'll assemble at the airfield and be presented with your regimental flag as the 586th Fighter Aviation Regiment. You'll be taking off for your first home base and your first assignment. Training will continue within your fighter regiment, under the supervision of Comrade Major Volkova." Raskova took a deep breath. "I'll save the platitudes for the commissars. I'll see you all again when we've won this war."

The plant technicians applauded, but all the recruits remained quiet. Wrapped up in their emotions, the pilots began filing into the trucks. Each one shared a few words with their soon-to-be-former commander. There were more than a few tears.

When it was Aelya's turn, she could almost see the pain in Raskova's face.

"Write to me on your next birthday," Raskova said. "Take care of yourself, Tanechka."

Aelya struggled for words, remembering Tanechka was her daughter.

Raskova covered her mouth, her tears welling up. She rapidly composed herself. "I'm sorry. Aelita. Like the book."

She hugged Aelya.

"I won't let you down," Aelya said.

PART III:

586th Fighter Aviation Regiment

CHAPTER 18: HONEYBEE

Kuybyshev, May 12, 1942

The air base at Kuybyshev was by far the largest Aelya had seen. After unharnessing her parachute, she straightened out her light service khakis, as if presenting herself for inspection to the hundreds of personnel scattered around the runway. In a way, she was. This was the regiment's first assignment off base since officially ending their training period. She followed Lara, Masha, Klava, and Roza into one of the low-lying support buildings that once sleepily serviced postal flights before becoming the airport of the nation's emergency capital.

The clerk in the office raised an eyebrow.

"Seagull Squadron reporting in," Lara said.

"You're Seagull Leader?" he said, letting out a low whistle. The other clerk behind him chuckled. They both continued to gawk as he issued passes for accommodation in on-site barracks. It was the sort of astonished look Aelya associated with the audience of puppet shows that travelled through peasant villages.

Tonya slipped into the office just as they were leaving. Lara cast her a sidelong glance.

"Just, uh, debriefing with the VIPs, Auntie," said Tonya.

"Is that what they call it?" said Roza. "Your lipstick's smudged."

Tonya frantically tried to find a good angle to check her face in the office's window.

"Made you look."

The sun was dipping low over the horizon, giving everything an orange hue. Lara led them out toward the barracks, each carrying the small regulation black suitcase they'd packed for this overnight.

"Sergeant Gorbataya," Lara said, still looking forward, "you're a professional in the VVS. I expect you to conduct yourself as such at all times while on duty."

"I was, Comrade Lieutenant," said Tonya. "Grisha—Colonel Davidenko—was reviewing our performance. He was delighted when he learned who we were. He called us his 'Flying Amazons.'"

They had escorted a passenger plane here for a meeting with government officials. Despite the German advances in the spring, there was little chance of being attacked this far east. Some might have called it a prestigious assignment; Aelya called it being sidelined.

"Colonel?" said Klava. "Very impressive."

"Yes, he's chief of something or other for Air Defence Command."

"It's always good to cozy up to the boss's boss," said Klava.

"Were his eyes blue or brown?" said Roza.

"Grey. Hard as steel, but I could see the little puppy dog within."

"Tonya, you're an incorrigible flirt." Even Lara was smiling as they found their barracks, a long, rectangular wooden building with two rows of bunks. It was reserved for women. Despite a number of mechanics and administrators on base, it was half empty.

"Too bad," said Tonya. "If this had been full, they'd have had to put us up in town."

They were in a mood to celebrate. Not only was this the first assignment off base, it would be their first night free of Major Volkova in three months.

"It's Kuybyshev," said Klava. "How much fun could you have here?"

"This is the capital now. There's bound to be something."

"A city of cowards," Masha said as she dropped her suitcase onto her chosen bunk.

"A city of dancing. Shows. Restaurants," said Tonya. "Though I suppose what we get in the canteen's already better than whatever peasant slop you get back home."

Had this come from anyone else, Aelya would have expected another explosion from Masha, but even she had grown immune to Tonya's constant stream of barbs.

"I'm fully expecting Grisha to invite me for a night on the town."

"I doubt even your colonel could authorize that," said Lara. "And now that you've told me, don't think you can sneak off in the middle of the night."

Tonya gave her a playful pout.

Roza sat by Aelya's bunk. "You could do it," she whispered. "Get permission to see your family. Auntie would allow it."

Could she? She thought about that last dinner when Roman had delivered the call-up order. Mama. Papa. Vasya. Babushka. She couldn't recall what they were wearing. How Vasya had done her hair. The expressions on their faces. She hadn't bothered looking carefully. She'd thought she'd be back in a week.

"I don't even know where the plant is. And how would I get there?"

"Aircraft plants have airfields. You could fly there. All right, maybe not, but there's bound to be some sort of military truck you could hitch a ride with."

Her father wrapping her up in his big bear arms. Showing off her uniform to her mother. Babushka grousing that things were harder still in her day. Vasya making fun of her hair. She wrung her hands over the possibility of seeing them again.

"No, I can't. What if I'm late? Can you imagine what Volkova would do if I didn't make it back to Anisovka tomorrow morning?"

Roza exhaled. If the situations were reversed, would she have dared?

They contented themselves with a visit to the pilot's club that evening. A few other women officers were there, so the sight of them didn't cause much stir, even with the pilot patches on their sleeves. Tonya did manage to hold out an unlit cigarette so seductively that half a dozen men lined up with matches and lighters.

The anguish of being so close to her family gripped Aelya's chest. She tried to push it out. Realizing that the postal service would be infinitely better here than in Anisovka, she returned to the barracks early to dash off a letter. She simply told her family that training had ended, although Lara would say that training never really ends. She was a full-fledged Air Force pilot. She used to imagine flying in a spaceship, landing on Mars. Now she was flying fighters. Circumstances had given substance to her dreams, and she was defending the motherland.

She wasn't sure why she felt like justifying herself. In the most recent letters, Vasya continued moaning about rationing, railing against unknown hoarders, but her parents had begun to fill her in on life in Kuybyshev. Updates from friends and relatives. How much they loved her. But they expressed no curiosity about what she was doing or experiencing. Perhaps they were too worried about what her answer might be.

She patted the breast pocket of her tunic, reassured by the constant presence of her copy of *Aelita*. Finishing the letter, she hurried to the base post office, hopeful to catch the last pickup.

After she dropped it off with the clerk, he noted her unit details. "The 586th? There's something for you."

It was a bouquet of flowers. These were not wildflowers picked from the fields, but a neatly cut and colourful arrangement purchased from a shop.

Aelya read the note.

To Sergeant A.S. Gorbataya,

My dear Amazon. My Greek goddess. My honeybee . . .

Aelya gagged from Colonel Davidenko's syrupy sentiments. A mischievous thought entered her head.

The others had come back by the time she returned to the barracks.

"Got something for you, Honeybee," said Aelya as she tossed the bouquet at Tonya.

CHAPTER 19: FOLLOW-THE-LEADER

"That's enough basic manoeuvres," Volkova's tinny voice announced through Aelya's headphones. "Time for follow-the-leader."

Aelya floated briefly against her harness as she straightened out her flight path and settled in, flying to the left of Roza.

"Kulik, you're to take the lead. Acknowledge."

In the absence of radio transmitters, waggling her wings within sight of the control tower was all Roza could do. She throttled up ahead of Aelya, flames spitting from her engine's exhaust stubs.

The object of this was not to simulate a dogfight, where each pilot tried to gain the upper hand in positioning. Instead, Roza would perform all sorts of manoeuvres as if she were in combat. Aelya, as wingman, would try to stay in a covering position, ready to shoot down any threats creeping up on her partner.

Since training had officially ended two months ago, they had been restricted to practice flights and uneventful patrols. Anisovka was less than ten kilometres away from their flight school in Engels. At first, they were to be assigned to defend the airspace over Moscow. But as the spring thaw came, the Germans began attacking in the south, rolling back the Red Army as they had the previous summer. Saratov and its critical industries fell within bomber range and needed protection. But the focus of the Germans lay elsewhere. So they spent day after day flying their patrol routes, almost hoping for Hitler to change his mind and order his armies toward Saratov. It was like a peasant leaving for Moscow to find a place in this new Socialist order, only to be assigned back to a collective in his home village.

"Go ahead," ordered Volkova.

Roza immediately jinked to the right and took off in a series of rapid turns and rolls, as if trying to gain a superior firing angle on a target. Aelya didn't try to directly copy her moves; that would have been pointless. She tried to anticipate, based on the way Roza entered each manoeuvre, and do whatever was necessary to stay in a good covering position.

After a few series of climb and dive combinations, Aelya started noticing the gap between them increasing. All of the angles and distances she was anticipating were a little off, as if Roza's plane had a little more jump than her own. Although they were flying identical model Yak-1 fighters, now painted camouflage green, mechanics could make adjustments and fine-tune to improve performance. They had been perfectly matched during the previous day's practice. How much could have changed?

Furious investigation of possible malfunctions churned through her mind as she followed Roza into an upward spiral. She powered up in an effort to close the gap, but Roza increased her own throttle, apparently trying to lose her own wingman. Soon they were at opposite sides of the arc that defined the spiral they were traversing. Aelya looked directly through the top of her canopy at Roza; her diminutive wingman was doing the same. Was that a wave? Cheeky.

Roza was showing her up in front of Volkova. In exercises like these, there was no benefit to the leader breaking free of her follower—it only made the follower look bad. If Roza had thought about this at all, it paled in comparison to her pathological need to show off her flying skills. Repeated groundings and other punishments for conducting unauthorized aerobatics during practices had done nothing to dull her enthusiasm. Aelya wasn't going to fall victim to that.

She pulled hard on the control stick, turning inward within the spiral and climbing fast. G-forces pulled her into her seat. Pressure built on her eyes and the sky began losing its blueness. She just needed to catch Roza, put a stop to this nonsense. She glanced to where Roza should have been, but the sky was empty.

Summoning the energy to turn her head to scan the horizon as she pulled back into level flight, she saw that Roza had stopped the spiral and was flying in the opposite direction.

"Sloppy, Makarova," said Volkova. "You tried to get too cute."

That was it for practice. After landing and the requisite criticism from the regiment commander, Aelya checked in with Zina for the post-flight inspection. The planes were parked in camouflaged revetments, surrounded on three sides by sandbag- and wood-reinforced earthen berms. A line of revetments capped one end of the packed dirt runway like the top of a *T*. Similarly constructed bunkers housed everything from fuel supplies to the command post along either side of the landing strip.

Aelya's head throbbed as she entered her revetment. Zina was on the stepladder, leaning into the open engine compartment while her assistant, Raya, examined the control surfaces on the tail assembly.

"Do you see anything, Zina?" Aelya asked.

"What do you mean?" Her crew chief straightened out, wiping a grease spot from her forehead, which merely spread the blackness.

"Something wasn't right out there."

"W-we inspected everything. Went through the checklist." Zina shifted nervously. "When did you notice something wrong?"

Aelya tried to remember a specific moment when the performance of her plane started falling off. But that didn't make any sense; it always felt fine. She could see Zina's earnest worry that she'd failed her pilot, and Aelya felt terrible. She only muttered an apology and left.

Roza and her crew were with her plane when Aelya visited their revetment. Roza stood up and put down her cup of tea as Oksana and Liza put down their tools. She stared at Aelya, waiting for her to say something.

Finally, Roza said, "I'm sorry for showing you up back there."

Aelya crossed her arms. When she frowned, Roza continued.

"It's just that . . ." Roza made a clicking noise with her mouth. "I needed to let loose some frustration. I didn't mean to shake you."

"You didn't shake me." said Aelya.

But she *had* been shaken off Roza's tail. Even though it hadn't been the objective, it bothered Aelya. They'd been so well matched in training till then. Volkova had conferred the senior pilot rank on Aelya months ago for her spotless if unspectacular showing during training. Although Roza couldn't care less about Air Force hierarchy, something clearly rankled about Aelya being her superior.

Aelya continued, "None of your moves were pushing the envelope. I could have caught you if you hadn't pulled that stunt at the end. But your plane did seem to have more jump for some reason."

She noticed Oksana's eyes widen, but the crew chief looked down when Aelya glanced her way. Oksana was almost a perfect physical counterpoint to Roza. She was of the same small stature, but dark haired where Roza was light.

She was also able to navigate her way through arcane forms and backroom trading, procuring just about any supply, including Roza's precious peroxide.

"Maybe the engine's been tuned better," said Roza. "Oksana could have a look at yours if you'd like."

"No, I trust Zina." Saying it made Aelya feel even worse for what she'd said to her crew chief minutes before. "So that's it? Your plane's just in better shape suddenly?"

Roza shrugged.

That evening, the barracks was overtaken by discussions on the upcoming midsummer's eve celebrations. While Volkova and the regimental commissar, Major Batyrskaya, frowned on the peasant religious aspects of Kupala Night, Lara had managed to sell it as a celebration of Communist youth. It was also a welcome morale boost after months without real action.

"Something needs to be done with our hair," said Sara Eisenach. "It's too short to braid. Do we have any experts at styling?" She was the lead technician for Auntie Lara's squadron and headed the delegation of ground crew.

Kupala Night would involve the whole regiment, as well as the support battalion and nearby male regiment. However, it was made clear that preparations would be the women's domain.

Tonya, lounging on her bunk, raised her hand. "I can get my hands on some hair products. But really, we're talking about Kupala here. It doesn't exactly scream modern." She flicked her own stylish do, making it clear she felt above this peasant ritual.

"Why don't we decorate our hair instead of braiding it?" said Roza. "Plenty of wildflowers grow around here."

She turned to Aelya, who was sitting in the next bunk, leaning intently. Roza started playing with her hair, demonstrating what could be done with garlands and smiling exuberantly at her. Aelya stared back, not listening to any of her words.

Roza had definitely done something to her plane. No sudden uptick in Roza's skill or change of flying habits had thrown Aelya off. It wasn't any manoeuvring—it was power. Pilots requested modifications all the time to see what they could get away with, to gain any sort of edge in combat, praying for the day they could show it off. Why not share her secret with Aelya? Wouldn't it make them all better pilots?

Roza finished her hair tutorial, and the planning session moved on to other mundane matters, like how to arrange a bonfire while they were in blackout conditions. Roza's eyes glazed over as she listened to these details.

"Anything you want to tell me?" Aelya whispered.

"Hmm?"

"About today."

"You're not still sore about that, are you?" Roza's lips twisted dismissively.

Aelya began grinding her teeth.

Lara said, "Mars, would you like to do the honours?"

"I'm sorry, what were we talking about?"

"We'd like you to read out the dedication to Communist youth. That should keep Volkova happy. You'll need to write it as well, of course, but you're good at that sort of thing."

Why her? She wasn't far removed from school, and in her last year she'd had to write out a similar assignment. Was Lara thinking that?

"Come on, Mars, you even look the part," said Roza. "You're the very model of a young Communist pioneer. Volkova will eat it up."

School homework was the last thing she wanted to be doing, but with everyone staring at her, Aelya meekly agreed.

CHAPTER 20: KUPALA NIGHT

When the midsummer day of Kupala came, Aelya spent most of it in readiness level two with the rest of Lara's squadron. That meant hovering around a sandbag-reinforced outdoor lounge, shaded by camouflage netting, waiting for any intercept alert over the radio loudspeaker fastened to a wooden post that supported the netting.

Aelya led one routine air patrol in the afternoon with Roza and Yulia. Since nothing unusual happened, there was no opportunity to notice differences in Roza's performance. Aelya decided to drop the subject for the time being. If Roza wasn't talking, neither would she.

In daytime, the ready area was the centre of social life for the regiment. It was a hive of activity now. Without once asking for payment, Tonya was painting a floral pattern on a banner made from sackcloth. Those who didn't have to fly did their own or each other's hair and makeup. Their appearance for the night's festivities was the overriding concern. As everyone was on active duty, summer dresses were forbidden; it was considered a grave tragedy.

Although they shared the same airfield, the men of the 383rd regiment had their own set of buildings with their own readiness and changing areas on the other side of the runway. Aelya wondered if they were as avid in their preparations as the women.

Next in importance to impressing the men was fortune-telling. Olga had put herself in charge of that and was pleading with Lara. "Now that Volkova can see how much effort we've put into this, can't you ask her for a curfew exemption?"

"I'm not dignifying that with an answer," said Lara. Volkova had already made concessions to the morale of the unit by scaling back practices and tactical lectures for the day.

"Well, the fortune-telling must take place by a bonfire at midnight." Olga scratched her head. "Masha, is there any custom that will let us do it earlier?"

"Why are you asking me?" Olga had a good five centimetres on Masha, but there was no question who was more imposing.

"I-I just thought—"

"That I'd be your token peasant bumpkin?"

Olga slunk away.

The sun went down and the readiness status ended. Everyone rushed to the technicians' canteen. Out front, a bonfire blazed under camouflage netting. The aroma of burnt charcoal brought Komsomol hiking trips to mind. Some men from both the support battalion and the 383rd had already arrived. Aelya patted her hair nervously. They'd given up trying to style it earlier in the day. She wished she could just hide it under a cap.

Zina quickly delivered a garland of camomile, lavender, and a few other flowers Aelya didn't recognize. She placed it on Aelya's head.

"Sorry, I forgot to bring a hand mirror," said Zina, whose own head was crested by a similar garland. In the sunset, her light brown hair took on an almost orange hue and the freckles on her face seemed illuminated. "It was such a rush job—I'm sorry. But it looks great on you, really."

"I'd expect nothing less." Aelya smiled.

Knowing Zina and her crew would need to work late into the night to make up for this break, she was all the more impressed with the handiwork. The technicians had made garlands for all the pilots. Katya, Masha's crew chief, had even prevailed upon her pilot to wear one. She'd also dabbed on a bit of makeup. Masha could be pretty if she tried, even with her hair cut shorter than everyone else's.

Postures straightened as Volkova and her counterpart from the 383rd made their appearance. Lara gave a signal and Aelya and Katya took their places next to the bonfire. They began to recite an ode to Communist youth they had written together under Commissar Batyrskaya's supervision. Aelya was so grateful that someone else was up there with her. Still, her body shook under the gaze of so many eyes. And so many men were looking at her. Were they now seeing her as a woman rather than a pilot? It was totally different from the teasing attentions of boys in school. She was terrified and curious in equal measure. At such a moment she would have welcomed Vasya's unsolicited advice. Ultimately, all anyone could hear was Katya's clear and unabashed delivery, while Aelya hid behind the piece of paper, speaking softly.

A flurry of activities was planned in the brief twilight period when they were allowed to have the open flame. Men and women paired up for the traditional leap over the bonfire while Olga and Yulia stood by, watching whether the flames flared or receded and the shapes the shadows made, interpreting the signs.

Aelya backed away and hid around the corner of the canteen building. She had no intention of joining up with some randomly chosen man and being trapped into dancing with him later in the evening. She thought dancing made people look like chickens, the way they flapped their arms. Her older sister used this as further evidence of her immaturity. Vasya always followed the latest jazz dances.

She peeked around the corner. The men seemed nervous as well, holding back, waiting for women to pick them off one by one. They'd coexisted well enough in the month since the 383rd had been stationed here. After their initial curiosity, the men had gotten over it and learned to treat the women like colleagues. Banter was normally easy between the two units, but something had gotten into the men, as if they were shocked by seeing femininity on display, even a version muted by uniforms and regulation haircuts.

After each couple leaped the bonfire, they were handed wreaths and they rushed off to the nearby pond to toss the wreaths into the water. A pair of technicians from the second squadron were in charge of interpreting the ripples in the pond water for omens.

Meals in the canteen were usually staggered, but tonight, members of both regiments and the support battalion crammed in for dinner after their outdoor activities. Pilots and technicians mingled freely. Despite many of the ground crews still coming in and out of their shifts, people passed around drinks much stronger than water or tea. Soon, several competing groups broke into spontaneous singing. It helped that Volkova had disappeared to do paperwork late into the night as she always did.

To open up space, they pushed tables and chairs to the outer edges. A group of male pilots pulled out guitars, balalaikas, accordions, and a tambourine to fill the hall with music. The pairs that had leaped the bonfire danced together before circulating and trading partners. Tonya "the honeybee" was in the thick of it, of course. But something about Roza seemed to catch the men's eyes.

With her short blonde hair tied in little braids going down to her neck and wreathed in red roses, she looked the picture of some virtuous peasant girl of legend.

Aelya drifted around the periphery, carefully avoiding eye contact with any man. She looked out onto the dance floor and there was Roza, switching again to another eager partner. As Aelya kept watching, she nearly bumped into Roza's mechanic, Liza, getting a refill of vodka. The puzzle that had tormented Aelya arose again.

"Liza, have you seen Oksana?" Aelya asked.

"She's busy, if you know what I mean." Liza gave a wink, then said, "She's down by the pond with a special friend. They're—"

"Yes, I know what you mean." Aelya blushed so much, she couldn't bring herself to say any more. Promptly, a man took Liza by the hand and pulled her onto the dance floor. So much for getting anything out of Roza's crew.

Aelya continued on her circuit, spotting Masha standing to one side. Masha's eyes flitted around intensely. A man approached her and she stared wide-eyed at him, as if frozen with fear. The man slowed down, then made a quick about-face. If only she hadn't destroyed her accordion. Aelya imagined that playing with the band was the only way Masha could be at ease among the men. Masha noticed Aelya looking at her and moved away to the other side of the room. In the corner behind her, Zina stood in the shadows cast by the dull oil lamps of the canteen.

Aelya approached. "I'm surprised you're not taking part. You contributed so much to this party."

"I don't dance."

"Why is that?"

"You're not dancing either," Zina said.

"I'm terrible. I don't want to be embarrassed."

"You never wanted to learn?"

"When would I find the time? What about you? You never answered my question."

Zina shrugged. "Same as you."

The song ended and one of the squadron leaders from the 383rd stood on a table to give a toast.

"I suppose we'll have to grab a glass," said Zina with little enthusiasm.

Aelya wrinkled her nose. She'd had a sip of vodka once as a child and hated it so much, she vowed never to drink.

Zina smiled. She tilted her head toward the back door of the canteen. They both sneaked out. After the overheated atmosphere, the cool air of a summer night was as refreshing as jumping into water.

"Are you done with the party?" said Aelya.

Zina twisted her lips. "But I'm having so much fun standing around, not dancing, not singing and not drinking vodka."

Aelya was fixated on her own concern. With the celebrations going on, it was a rare chance to move freely around the base. "Could I ask you a favour?"

Zina nodded. Aelya led them toward the revetments. It was pleasant, just walking in silence. If she closed her eyes, Aelya could imagine strolling with her family along the banks of the Dnieper.

Half-shuttered lamps swung gently from the tops of several of the shelters. Even now, mechanics were working on some of the planes. Those technicians still celebrating would have to work all through the night to catch up. Zina really should get a head start, even if Raya, her assistant, was still in the canteen. But Aelya liked having her by her side and she did need a favour from her.

A man was speaking low and a woman giggled from one of the darkened revetments. Aelya had the horrifying thought that she might walk in on a liaison, but when she arrived at the halfway point of the row of revetments, it was silent.

"Help me find a light," Aelya said as she went into the nearest revetment.

"This is Roza's. Ours is the next one over," said Zina.

"I know."

Aelya retrieved a half-shuttered electric lamp and switched it on, holding it up high. She beckoned for Zina to follow as she circled the plane, examining all the control surfaces.

"What are you expecting to find?" Zina said.

"Some sort of modification. It's probably the engine." She fetched a stepladder and together they climbed to view the engine compartment.

"Why don't you just ask Roza or Oksana?"

"I did."

When they opened the cowling, it was so obvious, Aelya was surprised no one had noticed until now. The two machine guns had been removed.

"Now I know why no one's talking," said Zina. "There's no way Volkova would approve of this. What could Roza be thinking?"

"Two guns with ammo—that's at least eighty kilos."

"Doesn't seem like a lot of weight savings."

"It's enough, trust me."

"But with just the cannon, she'd really have to make those shots count."

"Roza has no problem with that."

But how on earth did she think she was going to keep this from Volkova? There would eventually be an inspection or gunnery training. No question their commander would rain hell down on Roza for it.

"What should we do?" Aelya asked.

"I don't know. You're the senior pilot."

Aelya considered. "That's right, I am."

CHAPTER 21: TEST FIRE

"That should do it." Oksana slid from the wing onto the area of flattened grass around the Yak.

Sitting in the cockpit, Aelya held her hands up high, waiting for Liza to clear the target range. She felt wrong touching the controls to Roza's plane, telling Roza's crew chief and mechanic how to adjust the gun mountings.

No, it was more than that. Even with the guns uncharged, she felt as if the slightest movement might unleash the Yak's firepower. The image of Liza's short, muscular body torn apart played across her mind. Loktionov had said a 20 mm shell would split a man into thirds: a top part, a bottom part, and a splatter in the middle.

Roza's fighter was perched with its tailwheel propped up on bales of hay so that its guns pointed directly horizontal, aiming at a haystack three hundred metres away. In this farming region just south of Engels, haystacks were plentiful.

Liza waved to signal that the paper target was fastened securely to the haystack, then hurried away from the line of fire.

Aelya charged the pneumatic firing mechanisms, then gripped the rectangular "shovel handle" at the top of the control stick. She pressed the thumb levers. A short burst lasting just over a second was enough: two dozen cannon shells and machine-gun bullets shredded the target and set the hay bale alight.

"Just what is this?" shouted Roza from a hillock overlooking the firing range. She ran down the slope while Aelya got out to meet her.

"There was a problem with your guns," said Aelya from the top step of the ladder. "But we've got it sorted now. They're firing beautifully."

Roza looked at Oksana, then back to Aelya. "You don't give my crew orders."

"I tried to find you, but Oksana said you were out."

"I was collecting wildflowers."

"Kupala Night's over."

"They're for my cockpit. The air gets stale around here. If there's a problem with my plane, you come to me first."

"And if you want to make modifications, you tell me about them."

By now the test fire had caught the attention of other pilots.

"You're doing a test fire and you didn't tell us?" said Masha. She and Yulia came down the slope. Lara appeared behind them.

The outburst of excitement during Kupala Night had made the tedium of the every day worse. Now the only event to look forward to was the ride into Saratov every other week to make use of the bathhouse. In lieu of actual combat, any excuse to fire the guns was considered a big event.

"I need a turn," Masha said.

Aelya got off the stepladder and looked at Roza.

"Be my guest," Roza said. Giving Masha a chance to let off steam was generally accepted policy among the squadron.

Masha signalled to Liza to prepare the target again while she adjusted herself into the seat. Lara motioned to Roza and Aelya.

"We have a problem here, Roza," said Lara.

"If you're going to make modifications," said Aelya, "you need to tell me."

Roza snorted. "I knew this would happen."

"How long did you think you could get away with this?" said Lara.

"Did you think for one minute that maybe this was for your benefit? To show Volkova what could be done, without getting you in trouble?"

Aelya seethed, open-mouthed, searching for a response. Had it even occurred to Roza that the other pilots might be perfectly happy with their machineguns?

"There's a chain of command for these things," said Lara, looking at both of them in turn. Roza should have gone to Aelya, her senior pilot, first. But Aelya had been guilty of skipping over Klava, her flight commander, with her own concerns. Speaking with Klava about the matter felt awkward. She'd dreaded the idea, and when she came across Lara she'd just spilled everything to her squadron commander.

Roza addressed Lara. "So let's say I followed the chain of command. Mars, then Klava, then you. Would you all have approved the modification? Would

Volkova? No, of course not. But you know as well as anyone the machine guns are too weak to be of any use. Or don't you listen to your own lectures on frontline dispatches?"

"I know it makes sense," said Lara, "but we have to pick our battles. We're trying to squeeze enough changes out of Volkova as it is. Do you want a tiny bit of extra power, or do you want to get two-way radios? How about flying in pairs instead of bunching up in a circle?"

"How about getting a commander who understands these things? What kind of regiment commander doesn't even fly the planes?"

"It's not her fault she was wounded," said Aelya. She had no love for the commander, but holding the injury against the major offended her sense of fairness.

"If she's too feeble to fly in combat, she should have been signed off. I'll bet her own pilots shot her down."

"She has an Order of Lenin," Aelya said.

"I hear denouncers get those all the time."

Liza gave the all-clear and Masha let loose with a torrent of fire that lasted well over ten seconds, completely obliterating the hay bales set up at the opposite end. The whole time, she screamed with an intensity that made Aelya imagine a Cossack war cry. Masha's chest heaved from the exertion.

Aelya smiled weakly at Roza. "Why don't you have a go? It'll make you feel better."

"What's all this loitering?" Volkova called out from the top of the slope. "I hope you're not expending ammunition unnecessarily."

"We're just finishing up here," said Lara.

Masha quickly scrambled out of the cockpit. Aelya went toward the tail section of the plane to help move it off the hay bales.

Roza rushed over and slapped her hand away. "Don't touch my plane!" She turned her back on Aelya.

CHAPTER 22: THE WEATHER REPORT

A strangely inactive tension gripped the pilots of Lara's squadron. They had just completed their flights for the day. They crowded in the main room of the command bunker, leaning close to an alcove that acted as its radio room, straining to hear news of the twins. The radio operator periodically sent a direction-finding signal, but the planes didn't have onboard transmitters. The only responses coming in were from ground observer stations reporting the gloomy weather. There was little to be seen.

Olga and Yulia had been due back thirty minutes ago. Another ten minutes and they would likely run out of fuel.

Lara and Volkova conversed in hushed tones near the radio. Aelya, Roza, Tonya, Masha, and Klava lingered in the map area, trying to look as though they were conducting a tactical discussion. Sveta was there too, standing to one side. She'd made a reappearance shortly after Kupala Night. Apparently, she had been "rehabilitated." It wasn't something she would talk about, and no further details were coming from Volkova or Commissar Batyrskaya, if they even knew.

Ears perked up as the radio operator took a call. "It's from Meteorology," she reported. "They say to expect rain."

"Timely as always," said Roza bitterly as water seeped through gaps in the roof.

They heard Lara's raised voice: "Change the parameters, then."

"They send their bombers when the weather's bad," Volkova snapped back.

"I'm not saying don't defend against it, it's just a matter of prioritizing—"

Volkova put a hand up and looked at the other pilots. "Do you all really need to be here?"

They all looked to Lara, who stood slightly behind Volkova. She tilted her head toward the door.

Outside, the precipitation was forming a thick mist. It hadn't been raining when the patrol started, but they'd all known from the pervasive greyness what the day would be like. The heavy clouds and stinging raindrops made it clear what the twins were dealing with. Aelya wondered if they could even see each other. If she were flying with Roza and lost sight of her, would she use precious fuel to look for her, and risk disorienting herself further? All logic and operating procedures pointed to continuing to base, but could either twin have abandoned her sister?

They stayed in the lee formed by the command post's log wall. Roza pulled her tunic up over her head, her service cap offering little protection for her hair. "All those practice flights, and we never once trained for bad weather."

Was Roza criticizing her? Aelya was the senior pilot and helped to lead their practices as a pair.

"We need to make sure we get the basics of combat manoeuvres first. It's not like we're supposed to fly in bad weather anyway."

"You call the weave a basic manoeuvre?" Roza said.

"As I recall, it was your idea to try it."

"Practise this or practise that," Tonya said between puffs on her cigarette. "Does it matter? Even with good weather, we're too far from the action to be doing anything."

"The Germans did try to bomb the bridge a couple of weeks ago," said Aelya.

Tonya rolled her eyes. "We need to be down south."

As the summer had run on, it was clear that the German offensive in the south wasn't a diversion as early reports had guessed. They had truly abandoned Moscow as their goal. Not that there wasn't fighting all along the front—they just happened to be in one of the quietest sectors.

"We're still doing our part," said Aelya. "We keep the Luftwaffe from scoring cheap hits on Saratov. If we left, then they'd hit it for sure. Our time will come, and we'll be rewarded for this." How desperately she hoped that were true.

"Life has become better now," Roza said, mimicking one of Comrade Stalin's favourite slogans. "Our time will come. You're very good at repeating the Party line. No wonder you're such a favourite."

Sveta's eyes widened. Klava and Masha manoeuvred her a few steps to the side. They didn't want to be around for one of Roza's dangerously outspoken tangents.

"This isn't about the guns again, is it?" asked Aelya. "We have to accept and follow—"

"The chain of command. Yes, I've heard that. But I can only tolerate so much from a commander who doesn't even fly her own planes."

"Stop putting me in this position. I agree with you. But there's the matter of respect. We're all fighting for our country here."

"Life has become better now."

Aelya glared at her. Tonya just stood against the wall, grinning.

The crack of a flare gun interrupted them. Down at one end of the airstrip, technicians were lighting flares to mark out the runway. The pilots moved away from their shelter to get a better view.

They heard Olga's plane before seeing it. It came in a little too fast, as she had a tendency to do, dropping altitude abruptly, in little chunks. Another engine's racket confirmed that Yulia was nearby. Water sprayed as the first plane's wheels touched the ground. Aelya breathed a sigh of relief as it slowed at the end of the runway and began taxiing off.

After circling once, Yulia made her landing. Her wheels hit and she braked, the plane careening across the soggy dirt runway and spinning around. It dipped its right wing to the ground before coming back level with a jerk.

Aelya rushed out with the others, but thankfully, Yulia had climbed out on her own by the time they arrived.

"Is Everest all right?" Yulia said as Aelya helped her down.

"She landed fine. You guys had us worried there."

Volkova had emerged from the command post. She shouted something Aelya couldn't hear, then crossed her arms and went back inside. She did not look happy.

CHAPTER 23: THE NEW CLASSICS

Aelya took a deep breath. *You can do this,* she told herself.

She rapped her knuckles on the door. A singsong voice told her to enter.

The regiment's political officer rose from her desk, beaming. Major Nadezhda Batyrskaya was not much older than the pilots. She kept her blonde hair bundled under a dark blue beret. Her job was to ensure that all personnel productively adhered to the principles of the Communist Party. She seemed to measure success as the outward appearance of cheerful optimism at all times. In that the NKVD had seldom bothered anyone, aside from Sveta, it probably worked.

Batyrskaya skipped the required salute and embraced Aelya heartily with both hands, and they exchanged kisses on the cheeks.

"Welcome to my humble office. I'm always thrilled to speak with my charges, one on one."

According to regulations, the commissar held the same rank as the regiment's commander. In theory, she had the last say in every command decision, although disastrous results from the first year of the war led to an easing of this cumbersome command structure. Batyrskaya had a background in agricultural machinery, not aviation, and was happy to leave all decision making in Volkova's hands. She was satisfied with her domain over indoctrination and morale.

"Please, sit," said Batyrskaya. "Would you like some tea? I find it always helps with the free exchange of ideas."

Aelya accepted a cup, her mind turning. "I'm having difficulty coming up with ideas. That's why I sent you this note."

"You pilots are all so proud in the air yet so modest when you're out of your element. But believe me, our cultural activities would not be half as enriching without your input."

"Cultural activities? Comrade Major, I wanted to speak regarding the problem I wrote about."

Batyrskaya seemed not to notice Aelya's confusion. "These choir recitals just won't do. They're too backward, too folk oriented. We are at the cutting edge of modern technology. We need to reflect our role as the vanguard of society." The commissar drummed her fingers on her desk. "No, everyone resorts to music. It's a lazy choice. We need to mount a play. Have you seen any that have moved you?"

"No. Um, I'm not one for literature. I wouldn't know any." Aelya cleared her throat. "Excuse me, but I think our squadron's morale is an urgent situation."

Batyrskaya leaned forward, her hands together and elbows propped on the desk, her flowery perfume overpowering the earthiness of the bunker. Her smile swelled the rosiness of her cheeks. "Go ahead. You may speak freely."

"We're feeling a lot of frustration," Aelya said with some effort. It had been easier writing the note. After the twins had nearly been lost from flying in bad weather, Yulia had been further punished with guardhouse duty for missing her landing and damaging her plane. The squadron was ready to revolt.

"Yes, I know," said the commissar. "Perhaps it was a mistake to make such a big occasion of our youth celebration. It leaves everyone wanting more. That's why I want to keep us busy with a play." All the good cheer from Kupala Night seemed years ago.

"I . . . don't think cultural activities are what everyone's looking for. We need action."

"But action is precisely what Comrade Major Volkova is preparing you for. That's why she's so aggressive with her assignments."

"Patrol after patrol doesn't mean anything when we're so far away from the fighting."

"Well, I'm proud our regiment only wants to move forward. As Comrade Stalin says, 'Not one step back.'"

Aelya couldn't help chuckling at one of Tonya's jokes: "If we took one step back, we'd be in the Pacific Ocean."

Batyrskaya's eyes widened, the smile disappearing for once. "Do you find something amusing in the words of Comrade Stalin?"

"No, of course not. I'm sorry."

"Irreverence is a symptom of atrophied minds. You and your comrades have perhaps been stationed here too long. You've grown listless. I know . . . Svetlana Ryazanova's a new addition, isn't she? Let's get her opinion."

The mention of Sveta made Aelya freeze. Sveta was still catching up with her training so didn't participate in missions. Her dour presence and the vague terrors of what might have been done to her made her seem like a ghost haunting their home. Aelya scanned the commissar's face. She was smiling again, but was she hiding machinations for either poor Sveta or the squadron as a whole? Aelya had ruined everything with careless laughter.

"Opinion on what precisely, Comrade Major?" she asked.

"You all need to exercise your minds more. We need to have literary discussions. Come, Makarova, you're Russian—literature is in your blood. Don't be shy. What are your favourite books?'

"Books, Comrade Major? I suppose . . . *Aelita*?" She gave a half-hearted giggle. Ugh. She needed to stop doing that.

Batyrskaya frowned. "That is an immature piece. Too revolutionary. Aleksey Tolstoy's more recent work is better. Do you know them?"

Aelya shook her head.

"Who else have you read?" Batyrskaya sighed.

Aelya racked her brain. "Pushkin . . . Dostoevsky . . . Chekhov." Finally, literature class had come in handy, despite her abysmal marks.

"No, no, no, old, old, old. Let's talk about modern authors."

Modern authors? She needed to say something. "How about . . . Finne? Baidunov? Mikhailovich?"

Batyrskaya scratched her head. "I'm intrigued. I'm not familiar—" Her demeanour darkened. She placed her hands on the desk. "Don't insult my intelligence. I may not fly, but that doesn't mean I'm totally ignorant. Those are all aviation authors! Are you truly such a philistine?"

After staring for a moment, Batyrskaya snapped her fingers. "I know." She swivelled in her chair to the bookshelf behind her and ran her finger over the collection before pulling out a thin paperback and handing it to Aelya. *Tempo*, by Nikolai Pogodin. "Read this. It's the epitome of social realism. Modern," she said, emphasizing each syllable and pointing at Aelya. "It's a celebration of the Stalingrad tractor works. Topical, isn't it?"

Every day, the German advance in the south covered more and more space on the map, spreading like a stain. Its direction was unmistakable. Stalingrad. The city of Stalin.

Batyrskaya continued, "It also has a heroic American character. What better way to celebrate our new alliance?"

If such an alliance meant a continuing supply of American meat, biscuits, and chocolates, Aelya was all for it.

"Once you're done reading it," Batyrskaya said, "we can have a discussion on mounting the play. It will expand your horizons. And I think this will help your squadron to direct its energies properly. Sometimes we all need a reminder of what we're fighting for."

She ushered Aelya out and closed the door behind her.

Aelya hated being burdened with the extra homework. And redirecting the squadron's energies into a play was probably the worst thing to suggest. But she wasn't about to object and be tagged as a troublemaker. She decided never to do anything as foolish as volunteering time with a commissar again in the future. The only place she wanted to stand out was in the air.

CHAPTER 24: PARAMETERS

Patrol meant the constant drone of the engine, the tang of oil and burning fuel, and an intense chill rushing through the open canopy. Aelya sublimated every action and thought into the routine drilled into her by constant, repetitive training, her body bumping along with every disturbance in the air. Flying in a large figure eight. Scanning every segment of the sky, looking from one side to the other, beginning and ending with her six o'clock, checking up and down, squinting past the glare of her engine exhaust stubs. Checking her positioning against the other three members of the flight. Trying, hoping, for tiny telltale black dots to appear against the haze over the horizon. As the sun went lower, the long shadows cast by scattered clouds added their own dimension.

The greatest danger was a momentary lapse in concentration. If one pilot did it, Loktionov said, chances were all the pilots were doing it. As luck would have it, that was always the time when the enemy appeared.

The canopy was open, the better to see without distracting reflections in the warped glass. Her sister's scarf was wrapped tightly around her face, her goggles on to protect from the wind mercilessly whipping through the cockpit.

Klava called in to Zebra station to report moving on to the next waypoint. "Repeat, come in, Zebra, this is Seagull Two-Zero. Come in, Zebra."

After no response, Klava cursed into her transmitter. "We have to get Eisenach to improve the range on these."

"Be thankful we even have these," said Roza over the radio.

Aelya was indeed thankful. Their squadron engineer, Sara Eisenach, had somehow learned that the 383rd had been tuning their radio transmitters incorrectly and were about to junk them to save weight. She intercepted them before disposal and made the correct adjustments, and now every plane in the 586th could both receive and transmit communications.

"Making the turn at waypoint four, on my . . . mark," said Klava. "Come on, Roza, form up tighter. You too, Honeybee."

"Aye, aye," Tonya said sarcastically.

"Yes, Honeybee, tighten up," Aelya couldn't help adding. She imagined hearing steam coming out of Tonya's ears. It was still a strange experience listening to voices through the throat mic. It was as if they were speaking through a rolled-up piece of paper.

"Roza," she called out, "bring yourself closer. You're too high."

"I can see better this way, Mars."

"And you're too high to support the rest of us."

"Form up, Roza," ordered Klava. "And let's all try to remember a little something called radio discipline."

They kept on their course in two pairs, Aelya and Roza at a higher level on the "bookshelf" from Klava and Tonya. Lara had finally prevailed upon Volkova to switch to these tactics.

"Contact!" Roza said. "Ten o'clock low, height about twenty-five hundred."

Aelya was so used to the monotony, it took a second for the words to register. She was upset at not seeing them first: little silhouettes ahead and below them to the left. "Confirmed, bearing zero-seven-five. About a dozen—no, more. Maybe twenty. At this speed, I think we'll cut across their path."

"I see them too," Klava said. "Button up. Let's climb. Hope they haven't spotted us yet."

They closed their canopies and shed their goggles in readiness for battle. They gained altitude, following Klava as she turned to a more parallel course, so as not to close in too rapidly on the enemy formation.

"They're bombers all right," said Klava. "Anyone spot escorts?"

They all reported negative. At this distance from the front lines, it was unlikely German fighters had the range. Still, it always paid to be careful.

"I think they're Heinkels," said Aelya. She could make out the distinctive enclosed round glass nose of the medium German bomber. Veins in her neck throbbed from her pounding heart.

"Zebra," said Klava, "if you can hear this, this is Seagull Two-Zero. About twenty unescorted Heinkels. Moving to engage. Honeybee, come with me. You know the book on the Heinkel. We'll climb and turn, then dive head-on, take them from their twelve o'clock-high blind spot. Mars, Roza, you stay in a figure eight, watching for fighters."

Roza groaned but said nothing. This was it, Aelya thought. It was really happening. So fast. She put every extraneous thought out of her mind. Everything ingrained by her training kicked in.

Klava and Tonya made their attack run. It was textbook. The bombers didn't open up with their guns until the fighters were almost on top of them.

"I think I got one," shouted Tonya.

Diligently scanning every segment of sky, Aelya could only glance over briefly. Her two attacking comrades had already pulled away from the bombers.

"Looks like they're scattering," Aelya said. She spotted tiny dots dropping out of the bomb bays as the enemy jettisoned their loads, trying to shed weight to evade their attackers.

"Doesn't look like they have the fight in them today," said Roza. "I pity the poor cows in the fields down there."

"All right, enough joking," said Klava. "Your turn, Mars. We'll fly in coverage."

The bombers were turning in every direction, the worst mistake they could make, destroying any chance of forming a defensive wall with their gunfire.

"Let's pick off the one on the far right," said Aelya.

"Lead on," said Roza.

Aelya throttled up and chased after the bomber she'd chosen. She gained on it from the side, then turned in to dive steeply. Already, bright white tracers were streaming desperately back and forth in their general direction. She levelled out, just as she'd practised in training, hoping to rake the Heinkel across the wings just as she got into firing range.

By rote memory, she moved both hands to the control stick and pressed the levers. The *thunk thunk* of cannon and machine guns was muted over the noise of the engine and wind. Yellowish-orange tracers spat out from her machine and flew off into the sky behind the enemy.

How could she have missed so badly? The plane bucked from the recoil, and when she recovered her course, she was facing the enemy dorsal gunner, who let out a burst of machine-gun fire. She turned to the left and dived away from the fire. She glanced back and spotted Roza firing as she chased the Heinkel into a cloud.

She looked forward in time to see another bomber and a stream of white fire heading straight for her. She jinked away just as an explosion of sparks and glass burst in front of her.

"Mars, report," said Klava. The voice in Aelya's headphones barely registered above the roaring wind that shook everything in the cockpit.

"I'm all right."

Was she? Her face was freezing. Residual spots dotted her eyes as she looked herself over. She hadn't felt anything. A hole gaped in the windshield. Her evasion had already pulled her far away from the bombers, and they regrouped and took cover in a bank of clouds, hoping to hide as the light of day faded.

"I got one! I got one!" said Roza.

"Congratulations, we've done our job," said Klava. "Now climb to three thousand and form up."

"Mars, I'm not receiving Klava clearly. Permission to pursue the enemy?" said Roza.

Aelya tried to piece together what she was hearing from Roza.

Klava cut in over the radio. "Don't be ridiculous. You know the mission parameters. No pursuit. Stay over the patrol zone."

"Mars, I'm assuming by your silence you're affirmative," said Roza.

"Hold on," said Aelya.

"Sorry, I didn't copy. Beginning pursuit."

What was this nonsense? Where was Roza?

"The hell you're going without me," said Tonya.

"Honeybee, g-g-get back here!" said Klava.

As Aelya climbed, she spotted Tonya's plane diving into a cloud. She could only see a dot corresponding to Klava's plane now and moved to form up with her. Scanning the sky, she saw no sign of Roza. No Tonya. No bombers.

"Hell, I lost them," said Roza over the radio. "Ugh."

"What's wrong?" said Aelya.

"Just hitting some turbulence."

"Too rough for you?" said Tonya.

"C-climb and form up now!" said Klava.

"Yes, C-C-Comrade C-C-Commander," Tonya exclaimed.

Now flying close, Aelya and Klava circled, waiting for their wingmen. When they reappeared, it shocked Aelya how far apart they'd gotten; Tonya and Roza were on opposite sides of her.

"Come on," said Klava. "Let's find some open space, figure out where we are." Her voice returned to a neutral and dispassionate tone. If she was angry at their disobedience, there was no way of knowing.

Aelya opened her canopy and looked down. A puff of black smoke surprised her as it burst far below. Clusters of puffs appeared, creeping higher and higher. The rumble of explosions juddered the fuselage.

"We've got anti-aircraft fire!" she shouted.

"They're our own guns," said Klava. "Head for that cloud deck, bearing one hundred. Maintain altitude. Full throttle!"

Black bursts of shrapnel exploded above them. The anti-aircraft gunners below, mistaking them for much larger enemy bombers, must have been fooled into thinking they were much higher than they were. The explosions followed them but petered out as they hid in the clouds. Feeling the danger had passed, Klava ordered them to climb into clear flying space.

"Zebra, Zebra, come in," said Klava. She took a deep breath. "All right, switch to channel two, all of you."

Once off the main channel, Klava laid out the story. "We m-m-made one pass each. The Heinkels jettisoned and headed for home. We shot up two probables. We did not pursue. We never left the patrol zone. We were nowhere near anti-aircraft fire. Does everyone understand?"

All in agreement, they headed for home. Klava kept calling in to Zebra, finally picking up a response after a few minutes and gaining permission to thirty-three, or return to base. Only then did Aelya start to pay attention to the smashed windshield. A bullet had hit it. With creeping unease, she forced her mind to return to routines. Even heading back to base, there were procedures to follow. When the whole sky was a combat zone, they were never truly safe until they landed, and even then . . .

Only when she had taxied back to her revetment and hopped out, weak legged, did Aelya realize she'd barely been breathing. She took in huge gulps of air as her crew swarmed over the plane.

"You all right?" Zina asked, leading her down the stepladder. Aelya's hand shook as she held it.

"Your first combat!" Raya, the mechanic, said excitedly.

"We're just happy you're back, aren't we?" said Zina.

She sat Aelya down on a bench and ordered Inga, the armourer, to get her a tea. Then she climbed back onto the ladder to look in the cockpit. She gasped. Aelya climbed the ladder next to her.

Zina looked at her, lips quivering.

"What?" Aelya asked.

Zina pointed to the damaged windshield. She traced her finger to the gun-sight. From that shattered plate of glass, she continued on until her finger found a hole in the headrest of the seat.

"I'm surprised you don't have scorch marks on your helmet."

She reached into the hole and pulled out a flattened bullet. "That boy was right. This is a lucky plane."

CHAPTER 25: SANDBAGS

A year after the war began, Aelya was back in a world of dirt.

"Give me a hand here," she said.

First Roza, then Olga walked right past her.

She knew it was going to be bad today, just from the stares and whispers that floated around her. She braced the full sandbag between her legs, then tied it off. Knees bent, she heaved it upward and wobbled through slippery mud to the pile they were making. This was their punishment, to fill sandbags all day, in preparation for a new secure area to store hydraulic fluid, lubricants, and other chemicals closer to the revetments. Someone had finally figured out that the current location was too far from either the main depot or the planes to be of any use. The process of building an airfield, like training, was apparently a never-ending commitment.

As she placed her sandbag atop the waist-high pile, it began to lean to the right, threatening to pull several other bags with it. Lara put a hand in to stop it and helped Aelya get the sandbags in order.

"Thanks, Auntie," Aelya said. "You believe me, don't you?"

"It's what I do," Lara said, turning to continue her own work. Aelya had to wonder if Lara was talking about helping her or believing her.

Volkova had somehow found out that they left the patrol sector and wound up in the gunsights of their own anti-aircraft gunners. The day after the encounter, they were dragged into her office—not just Klava's offending four-some, but the whole squadron—and given a tongue-lashing. They were grounded indefinitely and assigned to sandbag duty.

Aelya's day had started with her socks being stolen. Then she was forced to do sandbagging on her own. Other petty mistreatments followed until, finally, Olga blurted out that she knew Aelya had ratted them out. She wouldn't say how she knew. Aelya wasn't sure who started the accusation or how it could be a mystery within such a small group. Until Volkova blew up at them, Aelya was sure only the four women in Klava's flight knew they had violated regulations.

She knelt down next to the dirt pile built up by a trench dug earlier in the week. She used her spade one-handed, holding a new sandbag open with the other hand.

"Even if I did say something, which I didn't, I'm not the one at fault. I didn't fly off against orders," Aelya said.

Klava walked past, deliberately looking the other way.

"You of all people should know that," Aelya said. She let out a short growl of frustration. No matter the disrespect that Roza and Tonya had shown their flight commander, they only violated regulations. Aelya was accused of committing a crime against her squadron mates. They'd been euphoric over the regiment's first engagement. Roza and Tonya were heroes for actually hitting something. Then all of that good feeling was killed off.

Yulia shuffled next to her. Although she too didn't look at Aelya, she quietly shovelled a couple of loads to help fill Aelya's sandbag when the others' attentions were elsewhere. Aelya gave her a quiet nod. Nicknamed Elbrus, the smaller, yet more ungainly of the twins always seemed so concerned about causing harm, going so far as to defend the occasional rat they found in their barracks. Aelya wondered if she'd ever be able to pull the trigger in combat. For that matter, Aelya still couldn't believe she herself had managed to fire at a bomber. It had never occurred to her that some living being might be affected.

The vivid memory of her gunsight exploding caused Aelya to flinch even as she stood there. Thankfully, everyone was still doing their best not to look at her. How close had she come to being the regiment's first casualty?

The roar of Klimov engines caused everyone to look up as Second Squadron prepared for takeoff. Lara's squadron could only look on wistfully as two pairs of Yaks took off for midday patrol.

"Actually, it's for the best that it comes out," said Tonya. "Now we can get credit for our kills if they find them outside the zone."

"If they haven't found them by now, they'll never find them," said Klava.

"That's not true. Just the other day, they found a wreck from the last war with Fritz. Rightfully credited it to Auntie after all these years."

The twins laughed half-heartedly while Roza groaned. Lara was not amused.

"Come on, then. You do better," Tonya said to no one in particular. "This silent treatment's a bore anyway. You can't blame poor Mars. She just doesn't have the guile to be an informer. She's a little slow."

"I think I'd rather be called an informer." Aelya surprised herself. Perhaps she was relieved someone was actually including her.

Tonya patted her on the back. "Congratulations on finding a sense of humour, little one."

The others continued ignoring her, except for Sveta, who gave her a terrible stare. Not angry—more full of sadness. Maybe even pity. She was worried about Sveta. Back in training, guardhouse duty had unnerved the girl, and Aelya knew why. Her demeanour now seemed different. Where was the worry? Perhaps she was relieved at no longer hiding a secret. Her shame was in the open now.

Lara rammed her spade into the dirt with particular force, a signal it was time to work. The thought of getting killed weighed on Aelya's mind. Death was still an abstract outcome—the memory of a gunsight exploding, then nothing more.

Was she really prepared to die? She had so much more life to live. She had never kissed a boy—had never wanted to, but it was something she should get a chance to do. Why had she gone out of her way to ignore the men at Kupala Night? More than a few gave her a look that night. The atmosphere was so charged. Until now, it had never occurred to her to think of boys' affections as anything but a distraction or annoyance. Boys had always been something abstract she would deal with the next summer, once she'd finished with high school and could spare time outside of flying hours. She missed Vasya, who would have caught her up with everything she needed to know, at least after considerable teasing. Her sister's fixation on the opposite sex had always seemed so frivolous, but now it was the most important thing in the world.

Stop it, she told herself. This isn't a Komsomol summer trip. You're fighting a war.

She placed her new sandbag on the pile and leaned on it to rest. A shove rebuked her; she was standing in someone's way. Her hands drew back, allowing Roza to place her sandbag. When it threatened to topple over, she rushed in to help Roza steady it. Roza smiled.

Aelya said, "I thought you didn't like informers."

"You're being punished, just like us."

That wasn't an exoneration.

"I didn't rat you out."

"I don't think you did."

There was something left hanging. "But?" Aelya said.

"You're so cozy with Batyrskaya, maybe you let something slip. By accident?"

"You practically brag about your violations, and yet somehow everyone blames me." Aelya was raising her voice now. "Really, this is your fault."

Tonya snorted.

"And yours too, Honeybee," Aelya said.

"Don't blame me. Roza needed someone to watch her back."

Roza growled something unintelligible.

"It seems to me," Olga interjected, "there's a fundamental problem affecting your whole flight."

Now it was Klava's turn to make a sound of frustration. "You think you'd be better? Try doing it with Volkova—"

"That's enough!" said Lara. "Put a sock in your mouths, all of you." She pointed at Aelya. "And no, I don't have any brilliant ideas how to get everything smoothed over. You all just need to grow up."

For a moment, they lingered, frozen in their positions. Lara twitched. She was often serious, but this was a rare show of anger. Chastened, her charges returned to their digging, holding silent recriminations as she walked away.

Roza and Aelya crossed paths once more at the dirt pile.

"Don't look at me," said Roza. "Volkova's the problem."

Klava shushed them from nearby. "You heard Auntie. Button up."

Masha moved closer with her sandbag to join the conversation. "The problem is, we're stuck here and not at the front," she said a little too loudly. "We're wasted here and Volkova's orders aren't helping."

"You know what happened to that leg of hers?" said Tonya. "She crash-landed in a meadow. A shepherd mistook her for a wolf and took a shot. You should have seen what happened to the shepherd."

"I'd believe it," said Olga. "She really enjoys giving orders with a snarl."

"That woman," said Tonya, "and I use the term broadly because there's no proof she isn't a wolf, would give orders to my ovaries to schedule my period if she could."

"Don't be so crude," said Klava.

"I'd wager there can't be one in ten regiment commanders as hard as her."

"What Honeybee means is, only nine in ten commanders will sleep with her," Roza said.

"Ha, ha. But admit it, we'd be better off with another commander."

"She was picked by Raskova. You can't just drive her out," said Aelya.

"Maybe we should leave," said Tonya.

"Shut it, you," said Klava. "You're dangerously skirting mutiny here."

By now, Lara had noticed the congregation. "What's going on here?"

"Honeybee's being a world-class complainer," said Klava.

"I'm merely a neutral observer of truth," said Tonya.

The squabbling reminded Aelya of Mama's nightly complaints after returning from the aircraft plant. Every colleague was a malcontent, sniping at everyone else. Papa would try to come up with solutions to her workplace problems, which inevitably led to Mama shouting back at him. Aelya would cover her ears, finding any corner of the apartment away from them. She'd never thought that pilots could suffer from the same inane griping. She lingered on one memory. "My father always said complaining could be a useful tool."

"What's that?" asked Tonya.

"Watch it in front of Mars," said Roza. "or it'll find its way to Volkova's ears."

Aelya glared at her and wasn't watching her step. She bumped into Masha, who had set down her sandbag for a moment. Their size difference meant she'd barely nudged Masha, but the girl immediately gave Aelya a shove anyway.

"Stop it!" said Lara. "This is not how we work. We're all in the same squadron."

"For now," said Roza.

"What's that supposed to mean?"

"If I can't trust someone down here, how can I trust them up there?"

"There you go again, presuming my guilt," said Aelya.

"It's not about guilt. It's about what works and what doesn't."

Something had fundamentally changed between her and Roza, and Aelya was disgusted. Roza, who had almost been driven out by her own comrades back in Engels, had turned on her. Roza twisted her lips, chewing over her own words. As Aelya tried to lock eyes with her, Roza turned her gaze downward.

"I'm sorry, I've taken it too far," Roza said. "Whatever happens, I do trust you up there."

She offered a hand to Aelya and she shook it, but there was no dismissing that an invisible wall had fallen between them. The next time a bullet came toward Aelya's head, would Roza be there to help?

CHAPTER 26: THE FOG

Zina's figure was hard to make out against the murky backdrop of the airfield. It wasn't yet night, but the fog made it seem that way. Aelya approached warily, softly patting Zina's arm. "You've done enough," she said. "There's plenty of punishment going around—do you need to do it to yourself? Someone from Second Squadron can relieve you."

Zina's eyes glistened. "It's not on them—it's on me. Something went wrong with Galya's plane. I just know it."

"And Dunya's plane? Somehow that was your fault too?"

Aelya could see how Zina could blame herself. Galya's mechanic had been caught trading vodka ration cards with the 383rd. Most of the women didn't drink, so rather than let the rations go to waste, an agreement had been worked out. Vodka in exchange for chocolates and biscuits, especially the American lend-lease packets. Another night and it might have been Zina's turn to run them over.

Short a mechanic, Second Squadron's Galya had gladly accepted Zina's offer to fill the void. How many missions had Galya flown without a hitch? And now, the first time with Zina on her crew, she failed to return. It was just bad luck.

"We all know it wasn't mechanical," said Aelya "Look at this weather. Well, you can't, because you can only see as far as your arm. It was mad to fly out in this."

It was also ridiculous to be waiting. It was already two hours past the point when Dunya and Galya would have run out of fuel. If they had safely crash-landed, it could be days before they managed to hitch a ride back to base. But perhaps Zina felt in her heart what Aelya did: no one was landing safely in this fog. She wasn't waiting for a return. This was a vigil for the dead.

If Aelya hadn't encountered Dunya pilfering her own trophies from the aeroclub, she wouldn't even be here. A lump caught in her throat, but she needed to be strong for Zina. Papa would've known the right thing to say.

Aelya yawned. As a pilot, she was used to turning in early. Meanwhile, the day was only half over for Zina. Working through the night was common for the technicians, who often slept in the revetments rather than in their quarters. When the planes were in the air, instead of resting they worried about their pilots, that some tiny oversight might cost a friend's life. They rarely ate dinner in the canteen and instead had food brought to them to eat under the wings, the better to get back to work quickly. Not that Aelya would have a chance to eat with Zina; technicians had a separate canteen, with food of a lesser grade. American rations were out of the question, so Aelya always shared what she got in trade from the 383rd. They were all supposed to be part of the same working class, Aelya thought, but in defending it, she'd never felt more privileged. One sleepless night was hardly a burden since she was still barred from flying.

"I was wondering if I could ask your advice," Aelya said, hoping to break the uncomfortable silence with small talk.

"Of course," Zina said in earnest.

"You've . . . kissed before, haven't you? I mean a man. On the lips."

Zina's expression darkened. "Why are you asking?"

"Oh, well, it's just . . . I haven't. But I want to. I guess I want to know what it's like, in case . . ."

"You don't even know how lucky you are. The men here treat us, well, maybe not as equals, but we're comrades. Why do you want to ruin that?" Zina crossed her arms and looked off into the blackening sky.

Aelya cursed herself for bringing up the subject. She needed something else to get Zina's mind off her worries. Something bland. "Had any letters from your family lately?"

"Yes. You know, it's the usual," said Zina. "Everyone's doing well. Telling me to keep safe."

"I know what you mean. Still nice to get them, though."

"Of course."

"My sister complains a lot. She makes knitting scarves for the *frontoviks* sound like the worst form of torture."

Now Zina chuckled, but in the silence that followed, her smile disappeared.

"Did I tell you about my cousin, Shurochka? She was the littler of two sisters. Four years old when the war started."

Back in her aeroclub days, Zina had mentioned a pair of young cousins she used to watch after school—another reason she'd never had the same opportunities to fly that Aelya did.

"She died in the evacuation," said Zina. "Got run over by a truck."

Aelya swallowed hard, not sure what to say.

Zina looked down at the ground. "I wonder how that truck driver feels." She kicked a bit of dirt. "Nothing's quite how I wanted things to turn out. With the war, I mean. I thought I'd be like you, flying—well, maybe not fighters, but at least a U-2. I should have kept coming to the aeroclub."

"It always sounded like you had so many things going on. You actually showed up for your Komsomol activities."

"Like knitting? Your sister's right. It's torture."

Aelya laughed. That brought a smile to Zina's face.

"Actually, I guess I liked learning to fish," Zina said. "I used to go down to the Dnieper with my uncle. I bagged a sturgeon once, down by Dubrovenka."

"There are bound to be lots of fish in the Volga. Maybe next time we're in Saratov, you can give it a try."

"Go fishing instead of a bath? No thanks."

Thinking of a bath reminded Aelya how much they all stank. What else? "You know what I miss about Smolensk? Going to the movies. You ever go to the October?"

"The one in the old synagogue?"

"Yes, that was the best. Better than the Palace. There's something about seeing the screen up there, where the altar should be. It felt like I should be praying to it. Like the movie was a message from heaven."

"Was that where you saw *Aelita*?"

"Don't talk to me about that movie."

"I'd have thought it would be your favourite."

"They turned her into a villain."

"But at least she does something. In the book, she just sort of waits around looking pretty."

Aelya had never thought about it that way. For her, the book hadn't really been about the Martian queen. It was a journey of discovery. Queen Aelita was a symbol of that. Maybe the movie deserved another chance. Perhaps she'd broach that with Sveta, try to get her to warm up.

They stood in silence for a while.

Finally, Zina said, "Thank you, Aelya."

"It's nothing. It's not like I'm flying tomorrow."

"No. It's more than that. Thanks for just being another Smolensk girl."

They were distracted by the rumble of an engine, but it was only an American-made jeep pulling up, its partially shuttered headlamps illuminating them before quickly being shut off. Lara got out from the passenger seat looking expectantly at them while Klava, Tonya, and the driver waited.

Aelya shook her head. Klava covered her mouth with a closed hand, biting on her fingers as Tonya patted her gingerly. They hadn't seemed all that close to Dunya, but she had been a Red Banner Falcon. Lara signalled to the driver, who continued on, taking Klava and Tonya back to their barracks.

"Can I speak with you for a second, Aelya?" Lara was already pulling her aside while Zina kept her watch. She leaned in to speak softly. "What did you mean, back when we were talking about our situation, about how complaining can be a good thing?"

Aelya could barely remember saying that. It was just something to relieve the tension. "My father used to talk about how it was easier to shuffle complainers around the factory than get rid of them. He said they were like the sparrows that built nests in the rafters. Every time they were chased from one area, another nest would pop up somewhere else."

"Why couldn't they get rid of the troublemakers?"

"Papa said it was always the shirkers who had important friends. There were always a few of them in every section. They rotated them around. That was the best they could do."

"I've been thinking about that." Lara pursed her lips. "It seems we need our own protector."

Aelya instinctively made sure they moved farther away from Zina. "You're not talking mutiny, are you?" she whispered.

"No, of course not. That path only leads to a bullet in the head. But the VVS isn't that different from factory bureaucracy in some ways. If we, say, were to show ourselves as unfit to fly, day after day, that would force the issue."

"You want to make enough trouble to get us transferred to the front?"

"Exactly."

It was a dangerous game Lara was proposing. What was to prevent Volkova from simply kicking them out of the Air Force? Or, if gutting half the regiment was unpalatable, what if Volkova just kicked Lara out as a threat to the others? As squadron commander, Lara would be exposing herself to far more danger than any of the eight women in her charge.

Aelya shuddered. "If this goes wrong . . ."

"We could wind up like Sveta, I know. That's why we'll need someone with more pull than Batyrskaya."

"She's not my friend. Have you tried Honeybee? What about her colonel?"

Lara smiled. "That sounds about right."

"Have you spoken to her about this?"

"No. I want to make sure every member of the squadron is part of this, voluntarily. I may be your commander, but I can't ask any of you to take this risk or be associated with it against your will."

"I don't think Sveta could go through with it. She's terrified of Volkova."

Lara put her hands on her hips. "We're her only friends. If we all back each other up, I think we can give her the courage. Roza would be in, for sure. So would Masha. Klava's trickier—she doesn't like going against orders. Being grounded has rattled her."

"And Honeybee?"

"I'm sure Honeybee will do the opposite of what Klava wants, just to spite her. And the twins will follow Honeybee's lead. For now, I think she'd be in. We just have to make sure she doesn't change her mind when Klava does."

A transfer to the front. Could it really happen? That was what Aelya wanted, wasn't it? She thought about the bullet missing her head by a whisker. There would be many more of those. A move to the front was a move closer to death.

"And Second Squadron?" she said. Was she looking for excuses to back out? "Have you asked them?"

Lara paused. "This is our best chance to get to the front. Is this something you want?"

"I'll do it if that's what you think is best for the squadron."

"No, I'm not asking you as your commander. You need to do this because you want to. I'm not telling you."

Aelya stared back at her.

Lara turned to Zina. "I'm getting another crew to relieve you. You both need some rest."

"No," Zina said.

"Zina—"

"No." Tears were streaming down her face.

Aelya approached her, and at first, Zina pulled away. But then by instinct, Aelya went in to hold her, and they embraced, Zina crying in her arms.

CHAPTER 27: A MISS

When the pilots weren't flying but still on alert, they were in one of two states of readiness. In readiness one, they sat in their planes, parked in their revetments, their engines warmed up and ready to go with the shot of a flare and a call on the radio. In readiness two, they waited in the ready area while their technicians kept the planes warm. Readiness two was the only time Aelya didn't feel as though she needed to be doing something.

She lay down on a slope of grass, shaded by the side of the ready bunker from the August sun, her scarf spread across her face. Nearby, Masha was reading *Tempo*. Batyrskaya had been determined that Lara's squadron use their time on the ground productively. Even after the pilots had been returned to active duty, preparations for the play continued. Masha had signed up to direct and stage-manage, if only to ensure she needn't act. Tonya was supposed to put her artistic talents to use on the backdrop. Perhaps she imagined set design was beneath her, because instead of catching up on that, she submitted to Klava's quizzing on tactical concepts. Aelya could hear the churlishness in her clipped answers.

Lara had broached the subject of forcing a transfer. With two pilots missing, the exiles had been recalled to duty, but Lara wanted them to deliberately refuse to fly anymore under Volkova. Klava was dead against the risk of being branded mutineers, so Tonya lashed out at her for being timid. "How bad does it have to be?" Tonya asked. Thankfully, Aelya wasn't asked to form her own opinion.

It wasn't clear what Roza or the twins were up to since they weren't around, pilots were allowed to wander as far as they could hear the radio speakers.

Galya and Dunya's disappearance had intensified Aelya's fear that she would never experience a kiss. She hated that she was obsessing over the trivial, but her mind kept running through possible candidates. Men in the support battalion she knew were so friendly, she almost thought of them as brothers. Perhaps it would be less awkward with some pilot from the 383rd, but after Kupala Night, they made her nervous. Certainly they would want more than she was willing to give. And how could she even arrange it? Any idea that came to mind seemed so tawdry. She wanted it to be pure and spontaneous, the way Vasya described it was with each new boyfriend. Who could she ask about it? Roza had turned cold. Tonya would only mock her. She wished Zina weren't so sensitive right now.

Overhead, Lara was taking Sveta through a training run. The periodic drone of their engines as they passed lulled Aelya to sleep.

She dreamed she was flying over a vast expanse of scrubland. As far as the eye could see, the landscape was the same. She spotted two figures waving at her from below and Aelya dived down toward them. Only she wasn't in her plane, so she just landed on her feet. Dunya and Galya stood there waving at her. She tried to speak, but an explosion cut her off. She flinched as more and more explosions went off, though she couldn't see where they were happening. The tall grasses around her swayed gently. The two missing pilots kept waving at her calmly.

Aelya felt grass prickling against her face.

"Get up, Mars! Get up!" Roza was tugging on her arm.

Aelya was awake now. She pushed herself up to her hands and knees with a start, gathering her senses. Her instinct kicked in and she looked in every direction as she would have in a cockpit.

Already, the other pilots were running to their revetments. Smoke rose from a camouflaged supply dump on the other side of the airfield. As she got to her feet, she felt a push on her back.

"Air raid. Let's go!" said Roza.

Aelya scanned the skies. Two dots, heading away. Where were Lara and Sveta? Was that them? She ran along the side of the runway, trying to keep close to any bunkers or trenches, in case the enemy made another attack run.

She sprinted the last open stretch to her revetment, not wasting energy or speed by looking around. She nearly toppled into Zina, who emerged from behind the wing of her fighter.

"What's going on?" the mechanic asked. "No one's said anything. Why hasn't the siren gone off?"

"Who . . . cares?" Aelya said between gasps. Zina quickly readied the ladder for her to climb. As she prepared to get into the cockpit, the radio speaker in the revetment crackled.

"This is Seagull Leader." Lara. "Misfire, misfire, repeat, we have a misfire."

The speaker hissed with static for a moment.

Then another voice. "This is command post. Confirming misfire. All-clear."

The anticlimax made Aelya's legs turn to jelly as she descended the stepladder.

From the next revetment, Tonya emerged, bent over and cackling. "That clown Sveta. I didn't think you could miss a ground target by that much! She must have fired high." Then she straightened her face in mock seriousness. "If she hit the vodka, I'll kill her."

Aelya and the other six pilots on the ground straggled alongside the runway toward the readiness area. They were in a state that mixed quiet amusement with embarrassed silence. At least Aelya knew she'd do well in a real air raid, because only now did she remember to be afraid. That unsheltered run toward her revetment was a moment of singular vulnerability. The idea of being fired on by planes and having no way to fight back made a knot in her gut.

Suddenly, Masha started running. Ahead of her, two men from the support battalion were climbing out of a trench.

"You cowards!" she shouted. "You pathetic weaklings." They covered their heads as she started hitting one, then the other. She drew her pistol.

"Masha! Easy!" said Klava.

"These idiots were supposed to be manning the anti-aircraft guns." She waved the pistol around, her eyes bulging. "I should kill you now, so we'll get some real gunners who don't hide like rats at the first sign of trouble."

Both Klava and Aelya took tentative steps toward Masha, who took a deep breath and began lowering her gun. The sound of a Yak fighter landing distracted everyone, and the two hapless gunners took the moment to slip away.

Sveta's plane taxied back toward her revetment while Lara landed next. As Sveta got out of her plane, the other pilots gathered near. Tonya led a round of applause, although Aelya didn't join in. She could see the worry in Sveta's face. Sveta ran through the line of pilots, heading toward the barracks. She stopped cold as Volkova approached from that direction, accompanied by two NKVD men armed with PPSh submachine guns.

By now, Lara had left her plane and moved into the space between them.

"I know," said Lara, her hands up in a conciliatory gesture. "There will have to be a full investigation. As the trainer in this incident, I take full responsibility."

This was a perilous statement. The VVS did not make mistakes. There was only sabotage.

"I'm already short two pilots," said Volkova. "I'm not ready to lose a squadron commander. Take that one in for questioning." She gestured at Sveta.

"No!"

The blue caps readied their submachine guns, and only then did Aelya realize that Sveta had drawn her pistol.

"Ryazanova, are you drawing your weapon on me?" Volkova was steely, her voice unchanged in tone.

"I'm not going back," said Sveta. She'd pivoted to face her commander. Aelya was behind her right shoulder. She should do something. Was she close enough to grab her?

Volkova barked, "This is ridiculous. You're only delaying the inevitable. Don't make it worse. Holster your weapon."

"I'm not going back."

The blue caps tightened the grips on their guns. Lara stepped carefully to shield Sveta from them. Sveta relaxed her own grip and raised her pistol. She turned it into the side of her own head and pulled the trigger.

CHAPTER 28: ROUSTING THE SPARROWS

"I appreciate your being here," said Volkova. It was the first time Aelya could recall her saying anything nice. "This is the best thing to do in these sorts of situations—get flying again."

The eight remaining pilots of Lara's squadron gathered in the musty command bunker. Bare lightbulbs cast sharp lines of shadow across the map table. They were now neatly sorted into two flights of four, each pilot paired up, just as in modern Luftwaffe tactics. That was the only way Sveta's absence was officially noted.

Volkova read out situational reports handed to her by her navigator and her adjutant. Batyrskaya was there too. Instead of being her usual ebullient self, the commissar wore a slight, close-mouthed smile.

"Air attacks in the Stalingrad sector are increasing in both volume and frequency," said Volkova. "So there's a good chance Fritz is shifting air assets to the south. But that's no reason to lose vigilance."

Aelya's thoughts turned to when she was twelve, and a neighbour down the hall had hanged himself. He was an engineer, though he worked in a different section from her father. She only heard about it because the NKVD men came around asking what he'd said and what his mood had been before committing suicide. Though she was ushered off to the room she shared with Vasya, she listened through the door. Her mother said the man had been a good Communist, always very vocal and demonstrative in their workers' committee meetings. No reason for him to kill himself. Later, her father came home. Told about the death, he gave a dismissive snort, as if the man deserved it. Mama told her not to think about it anymore. Only now did she truly understand: the man had been a denouncer. Thinking of all Sveta had gone through, she realized he might have killed himself over a guilty conscience.

Sveta's suicide marked the first time Aelya had seen someone die. In the back of her mind, she had been preparing herself for that moment. When she and Sveta had been stranded in the cold, waiting for rescue, she girded herself in case Savchenko died from his head injury. All that time since, she'd almost expected an accident or a comrade killed by enemy fire. Death in the abstract. Nothing like this.

Blood had spattered her uniform. That girl she'd huddled with in the snow near Engels had lain on the ground, missing pieces. She'd felt an urgent need to drop to her knees and put Sveta's head back together, but shock and revulsion paralyzed her.

As Volkova droned on about the orders for the day, anger rose within her. On some patch of land barely touched by humans, the bodies of Dunya Nestorenko and Galya Borisova were rotting away because of the regiment's commander. Now Aelya could draw a straight line between Volkova's harshness and Sveta's suicide. A commander was supposed to not only give orders but also look out for her charges. Perhaps since her arrest by the NKVD, Sveta's fate was inescapable, but Volkova had made no effort to help. Her inflexible rules and constant rounds of punishment had made things worse. Aelya couldn't imagine Raskova allowing things to get so desperate for Sveta.

"Any questions?" Volkova said.

Lara took a step in front of the squadron, standing opposite the map table from her commander. "Comrade Major, I need to self-report that every member of this squadron attempted to sell our vodka rations two days ago. Therefore, we should be removed from active duty."

"Is that so?" Volkova raised an eyebrow.

Lara's hand flexed nervously at her side. Roza stepped behind her, as if to hold her up. Volkova's eyes flitted around, looking at each of them. Aelya looked down when the gaze fell upon her. She took a deep breath. Sveta had been one of the squadron. One of them. Some safe zone had been violated. They all needed to do this.

Volkova looked as if she were sucking on a lemon. "I could have you all arrested. But I need at least one fully staffed squadron, so I'll defer your punishment."

"Then I have to report that we are planning to commit the same crime today," Lara said. "And the day after that. And the day after that."

"You're trying to get out of flying?"

Batyrskaya swiftly painted on a smile and stepped up to the map table. "I'm sure this is all a misunderstanding. Lara. You're no coward."

"Get out," said Volkova. Batyrskaya looked dumbstruck. "Everyone out except the squadron commander. Now!"

Batyrskaya and the other staff officers slunk away toward the door, but they stopped halfway when they realized the pilots were staying rooted to the floor.

"If you talk to me," said Lara, "you talk to all of us."

Volkova nodded tersely and the officers left, leaving the commander facing her eight insubordinate pilots.

"You all call her Auntie, don't you?" Volkova said. "You think she takes good care of you. Let me tell you this. Whatever your motives, your refusal to fly is treasonous. I'll have you all removed from the Air Force if I have to. Hand you over to the NKVD. You, Roza Kulik. You frilly, pretty girl . . . you want that? And you, Gorbataya." She sneered at Tonya. "You want to go down with Auntie?"

"We rise as one, we fall as one," said Roza.

Tonya stifled a giggle, somehow finding this all amusing.

"Makarova. You have such a promising career ahead of you. Do you really want to do this?"

Aelya looked up briefly but couldn't meet Volkova's stare. From some combination of fear and disgust, she couldn't bear looking at her. She knew she wanted out of this place. She felt like killing something. She felt like dying. Anything. Just some way to vent the formless rage building within her.

Lara said, "Are you sure you want to have this in your precious record, that you had an entire squadron arrested and removed? Do you think Air Defence Command will look fondly on you? Especially after Colonel Davidenko hears what we have to say?"

Tonya was smiling now. Her connection was well known, and more than a few gifts had been coming through regimental post.

"You want me out? Is that it?" said Volkova.

"*We* want out," said Lara. "Away from Air Defence."

"Batyrskaya may be dim, but she's right about you. You're no coward."

"If any other pilots had our experience, our training, they'd never be held back in Air Defence. Our country hangs in the balance—not here, two hundred kilometres from the nearest German—but in Stalingrad. We just want the chance to be treated like other pilots."

Volkova banged her fist on the table. "Everything I've tried to do has been for that reason. We can never leave one mission unfinished. We can never fail even the tiniest inspection. We have to be twice as good as any men's regiment just to be considered more than a joke, a novelty." She trembled as she spoke. Then the tension seeped away.

She limped around the table toward them. "You want to know how I got this?" She pointed at her left leg. "I flew a liaison plane, a U-2. Of course, I asked to fly a fighter. When they assigned me to liaison, I accepted it. It was just going to be a stepping stone. This was in that first summer, when we were being pushed back everywhere in Belarus, in Ukraine. Fritz had trapped thousands of our men in the Pripyat Marshes. Our men kept on fighting, though. Became partisans. My commander gave us a mission to fly an NKVD colonel in there to organize them. Can you imagine finding a landing place in those swamps? Behind enemy lines?

"We were all young and stupid, so immediately half of us volunteered. I was the only woman among them, so when they saw my hand go up, the rest of them volunteered as well. They couldn't bear to let their little 'Tamusya' fly into danger. Me. Their deputy commander. Regimental navigator. I had twice the hours of any man in that unit, and I had to beg and beg the commander to even let me draw lots with the men. I was lucky—I won.

"I flew the colonel in almost at dusk. I kept low, but even so, two Messers spotted me. They took turns shooting at my little crop-duster. I went so low, I was below the treetops, cutting through every open space in the swamp. The vultures finally got bored and left us alone. I delivered my passenger and stayed that night in the swamps. I already had my Order of Lenin then. The NKVD man said he'd recommend me for another.

"I was so proud of myself the next day. It was such a beautiful, sunny sky, I actually enjoyed myself. I spotted a dogfight between some Messers and Ishaks. I decided then I was sick of dodging through trees with my biplane, unable to fight back. I wanted to fly fighters. I determined to ask for a transfer as soon as I landed. I got sloppy thinking about that, and I didn't notice the Messer diving at me until it was almost too late. He set my plane on fire and when I crash-landed, I got a support strut lodged right here." She tapped her thigh.

"No Order of Lenin. I got reprimanded for losing a plane. Out of hospital, I wanted to return to my unit. They fawned over me when I visited, but no one wanted to fly with a cripple."

She walked over to stand next to Lara. Aelya cast her eyes down as she passed.

"You're all cogs in a machine. You're here to be ground down and tossed aside. Don't ever think you're special, that you're here to live out your dream. But I don't care if you do that here or at the front, so enjoy your little victory."

"We don't take any enjoyment from this," said Lara.

Volkova held up her hand. She pointed to the door. One by one, the women of the squadron filed past her. Aelya summoned the courage to look her in the eye. Volkova deserved that much. In her eyes, Aelya saw pure blackness. She had a gnawing feeling she was diving into an abyss.

PART IV:

497th Fighter Aviation Regiment

CHAPTER 29: INTO THE CAULDRON

Stalingrad, September 10, 1942

Zina's hand reached out from behind Aelya's seat. "Cheese sandwich?" she shouted as their Yak thundered across the sky.

Aelya looked away from the instruments. "How did you manage to pack that in?"

Her mechanic lay with their two standard-issue black suitcases in the empty fuselage space behind the pilot's seat and radio assembly.

The techs from the 383rd said that they travelled this way all the time during relocations: it was worth it to have a crew chief fly along instead of chancing the overloaded and erratic transportation network between bases. As Aelya grabbed the sandwich, she wondered if those men had been playing a trick.

The eight fighter planes of the squadron flew in two formations of four at just below four thousand metres. Although it was a beautiful late summer day, the clouds and gathering darkness provided some cover as they transferred to their new airfield. Considering they were running low on fuel and each had an extra passenger, an encounter with the Luftwaffe could prove disastrous.

Aelya leaned back. "Don't know why you bothered with the sandwich—it's not that long a trip."

"It's a very nice cheese we got in Anisovka," said Zina.

"The food's supposed to be even better at the front." Still she took a bite and thanked her crew chief.

"Are you nervous?" Zina asked. "I mean, how do you think the other pilots will be about getting a whole squadron of women?"

"Men and women mixed at the aeroclub, remember? It wasn't a big deal. I'd think it would be more of an issue for you. I don't remember any women technicians back at the club."

"I never really thought about that."

After a moment of quiet, the mechanic spoke up. "The men will all be different now. You'll be in danger. They'll want to protect you or maybe not want you there."

"The 383rd seemed all right with us."

"We were on the other side of the airfield. Now you'll be part of the same regiment. They'll be different—you'll see."

Aelya remembered Fedor deriding women at the front as distractions. She had as much right to be doing this as any man did. If they were distracted, that was their fault, wasn't it? Soon, her thoughts turned to her abortive quest for a first kiss. Wasn't that a distraction? Then again, wasn't Tonya's needling of her former air show colleague Klava also a distraction? So were Masha's vengeful thoughts and Roza's constant recklessness, driven by some burning need. This was war. They all just had to get on with it.

"The men might make a big fuss at first," Aelya said, "but they'll get used to it. This is the VVS. We're all professionals, aren't we?"

"Maybe. Remember when we got the radio sets from the 383rd? The boys there thought they were humouring us. It was a big joke to them. They never imagined we'd actually get them to work. After that, instead of asking us how we did it, they just got angry at us for tricking them. They might work with us, but I don't think they'll respect us."

Aelya searched her brain, recalling the men's stares during Kupala Night. It was the most she'd interacted with them the whole time in Anisovka. She remembered only keeping her head down and looking away. Nothing was ever as easy on the ground.

Aelya said, "When we show them what we can do in the air, they'll have to respect us."

"I hope so."

"You don't sound convinced."

"Well, maybe you or Masha. But I think about the way the men all looked at Tonya and Roza at Kupala Night. They were so glamorous, like movie stars. It's hard to take someone seriously after that."

Aelya wasn't sure which idea irked her more—that a woman could be too glamorous to be taken seriously or that she herself couldn't be glamorous. She thought about how Roza was willing to risk having only one gun on board to gain an edge.

"Roza will find a way," Aelya said. "She won't stop until she's some sort of hero. Or dead."

"She's running away from something," said Zina.

The receiver in Aelya's helmet buzzed to life.

"Sparrow Leader to Sparrow Squadron," said Lara. "Prepare to descend to three thousand and bank at waypoint."

"Copy that, Auntie," said Olga.

They each acknowledged in turn. The squadron descended through a thin layer of cloud.

Stalingrad first appeared as an orange glow over the southern horizon, like a second sunset. As they flew on, their angle toward it changed, and the full length and breadth of the city came into view. A wall of flames. Barely a square metre had been spared. From this distance, the sheer scale of it boggled Aelya's mind—not just the extent of the destruction but what it contained. It was a funeral pyre. It had been home to half a million people. How many of them were still within, caught by orders to join the defence when the German assault began a couple of weeks before? "Not one step back" applied to them as well as the military.

"Mars," Zina called. "Mars? What's wrong?"

Aelya paused. Too long. "Nothing."

"Your hands are shaking."

When Sveta died—was killed—Aelya had felt a hunger that urgently needed violence to sate it. Those thoughts seemed callow now. All she could think was, What had she gotten herself into?

"Next waypoint is in sight." Lara. Her voice betrayed nothing. "Prepare for heading two-five-five on my mark."

Aelya took a breath, ignoring her thumping chest, and oriented herself to the curve of the Volga, a dark band running along the ground to her left. She saw the bend in the river that Lara would use to key the next turn. Her eyes drank in the city once more as she hugged the right bank. The river looked oddly narrow there—until she realized the water was ablaze with oil from a destroyed refinery.

"Mark," called out Lara. The planes banked right and the nightmare landscape receded. Aelya had to force herself to look behind her, always wary of vultures.

It was worse not seeing the city. It invaded her imagination. She saw the flames transform into the sparks of an exploding gunsight. *What have I gotten myself into?* she thought. The river was on fire.

Lara broke radio silence once more to make contact with Maple Tree, the designation for their new base. Even with duelling sunsets, the real one to the west and the burning city to the east, the twilight conditions would make this almost a night landing, a feat none of the pilots had ever performed. The glare of the exhaust stubs in front made everything look black by comparison.

"This is Maple Tree," a voice barked on the radio. "Copy that, Sparrow Leader. Watch for the green flare."

A shimmering green dot soared into the sky, marking the location of their new airfield. Lara formed the squadron into a line with wide intervals and began final descent.

"I can just make out the landing *T*. This is against regs, but I'm going to flash my landing lights as I go in. Each plane following will do the same. Hopefully we'll just all follow each other down and not crash."

"As opposed to most days, when I do hope to crash," said Tonya.

"There's always next time, Honeybee."

The surprising levity in Lara's response had a calming effect on Aelya. She focused on Tonya's plane ahead of her and watched for the brief flicker of lights at the wingtips. Able to follow her path, she'd barely thought about the dark conditions by the time she touched down. Roza, the last plane, came in behind her, a little closer than Aelya thought necessary.

A ground technician flashed a half-shuttered lamp and guided her to park her plane with the rest of the squadron in a row. A stepladder was brought alongside her cockpit. She got out and, after awkwardly helping Zina disembark, a couple of technicians appeared. The man gawked at her as she removed her helmet, blinking a couple of times in surprise. The other was an Asian woman who watched her sullenly.

Zina quickly snapped them out of their moods as she went over the postflight checklist. With the engines off, Aelya noticed the sporadic rumble of artillery. It echoed back to her last day in Smolensk as the Germans drew near.

Lara gathered the pilots. They straightened out their summer khaki uniforms and lined up in a row as a bespectacled young officer bearing a clipboard came to greet them.

"You are . . . oh." He cleared his throat multiple times before continuing. "You're the replacements?"

Lara saluted. "Senior Lieutenant Rogacheva, commander of this squadron, formerly First Squadron of the 586th."

"The 586th," the officer muttered, looking at his clipboard. "Yes, oh, I see. Oh." He straightened himself up, then saluted. "Lieutenant Arkadiy Muromets. I'm the adjutant. Welcome to the 497th Fighter Aviation Regiment, part of the 212th Fighter Division, 16th Air Army. And welcome to Orlovka."

"We can see the commanding officer whenever he's ready."

"He's quite busy. He instructed me to sort you out, and he'll meet with you in the morning. Um, about that . . . we weren't expecting you. I mean, we were, but not that you're, uh . . ."

Lara raised an eyebrow.

"Uh, yes," said Muromets. Tonya giggled and he quickly looked at his clipboard. "We don't have any accommodations set up for you. Wait one moment. Armourer Ulanova," he called out. The Asian technician stalked toward them.

"I know the women's barracks is small, but would you perhaps have some space . . ."

She stared hard at Muromets. "You want me to do what?"

"Well, you see, we haven't arranged anything at the village. I mean, we had, but it's with the men, and, you know, regulations and all that."

Ulanova didn't blink.

"Comrade Lieutenant," said Lara, "we don't want to inconvenience any of you. We can only guess the hardships you've been facing. The weather is nice. We're happy to sleep under the wings."

When technicians worked through the night, they sometimes caught naps in the shelter of the Yak's wings.

Muromets's relief was palpable. "Yes, that would be good, I think. Thank you, Ulanova."

The armourer's expression didn't change as she left to help move the planes under camouflage tenting.

"Please excuse her—it's been a hard time. I probably shouldn't have mentioned the space. We had an air raid yesterday. Two of her female colleagues were killed manning the guns."

"Understood. We'll make ourselves comfortable and see you in the morning."

The long flight had been exhausting. Aelya had been so anxious about finally arriving at the front, she wasn't sure how to act. The mundane quality of the adjutant's search for accommodation had reminded her how tired she was. Many thoughts swirled in her head, but none formed coherently. Once the planes were secured, Aelya didn't bother with any niceties beyond laying a cloth sheet on the ground and lying down, falling asleep to the sounds of war.

CHAPTER 30: THE TALK

Orlovka was built near the ford of a shallow stream. Walking along the wooded banks for a few minutes east brought the pilots to a lightly wooded area where the water was waist high and large rocks dotted its sides. Yulia had seen a woman from the village adjacent to the airfield head down here to collect water in the morning. With the commanding officer still not ready to meet the squadron, and memories of the scummy pond in Anisovka, they eagerly took a plunge.

The fast-flowing water chilled Aelya, even as it refreshed a body made sore by lying on the lumpy ground all night. The dip in elevation masked the sounds of gunfire and artillery that intensified with the dawn. It was easy to paste over, in her mind, the image of the burning river.

"I wonder what the new commanding officer is like," said Klava.

"Can't be worse than Volkova," said Yulia.

Freed from the shadow of their former commander, they playfully splashed each other. Tonya even shared a bar of her special soap from the Central Universal Department Store in Moscow.

"They can *always* get worse," said Roza, though she smiled while saying it.

"I'll miss Batyrskaya, though," said Olga. She alone had any open regrets about leaving. It was the timing; she would never have a chance to star as Carter, the heroic engineer in *Tempo*. She'd been dying to try out an American accent.

Yulia passed the bar of red soap to Aelya. She sniffed at it enthusiastically. It had been ages since she'd had a proper bath. Volkova had outright banned the squadron's trips to Saratov after they'd been grounded. Nonetheless, Oksana, Roza's crew chief, had cleverly jury-rigged a shower from used fuel drums. Aelya had always left smelling of gasoline. Even that had been banned out of spite when Volkova got wind of it.

"I never realized how much we stank until now," Aelya said.

"Speak for yourself," said Tonya. That started a new round of splashing.

"Stop it—that's cold," said Klava, which only encouraged Tonya and the twins to redouble their efforts.

"All right," said Lara. "Settle down. We don't have all day here."

"Hello," came a male voice from the trees.

Instinctively, Aelya covered herself with her hands. Others went to shore for towels. Masha raced to her holster, which rested on a rock. She alone seemed to remember they were in a war zone.

"Hello?"

"Don't worry, it's just that adjutant," said Roza.

"Glasses guy," said Tonya.

"Lieutenant," Lara called out to Muromets as she wrapped a towel around herself.

"Are you decent?" he asked.

"Yes, we are," said Tonya.

Aelya rushed to grab a towel.

Tonya picked hers up casually, but as Muromets walked out from the trees holding on to his clipboard, she dropped it and stood naked, hands on her hips. "Oops."

"Tonya!" Lara said.

Muromets gasped and dropped his clipboard. He vacillated between retrieving it and covering his eyes. Finally, he turned around, his eyes on the ground, stepping back gingerly to pick up his papers. Aelya felt sorry for him and would have helped if she weren't standing so far away.

He cleared his throat. "Red will be out of the briefing soon. You'll have a few minutes to catch him."

"Red?" said Lara.

"Our commanding officer. I have a truck waiting by the road that will give you a ride to the command post." He made a hasty exit.

"Honestly, Tonya," Lara said. "How do you expect the men of this regiment to take you seriously when you act like that?"

"Oh, he's just the adjutant. Anyway, I don't see why I can't be an effective fighter pilot and have sex appeal at the same time."

Aelya had come to realize Tonya probably only played at being a good-time girl. These games were more about power for her. Tonya's behaviour was abrasive, but Aelya found something to respect in it.

Tonya shrugged. "We can't all be Mashas." And Aelya remembered why she couldn't stand Tonya.

Lara had them rush through drying and dressing so they wouldn't further delay Muromets. On the short truck ride to the airfield, Aelya sat with her near the front of the cargo compartment, listening to Muromets.

"First man you have to know is Red. Red is everything—the commanding officer, regimental navigator, and also commander of Second Squadron."

"That's a lot of hats," said Lara.

"We . . . gained a lot of vacancies over the summer."

"Why do you call him Red?" asked Aelya.

Muromets fiddled with the bridge of his glasses. "You'll see."

They disembarked in front of the command post, situated at about the halfway point along the landing strip. The distant outbursts of artillery grew in frequency. In daylight, Aelya could see the surrounding flat, grassy terrain. Yellow patches in the distance might have been crops of some sort, left unharvested after their farmers fled. Here and there, dirt-rimmed holes marked craters left over from the air raid. A half dozen civilians were busy filling in one of these. Were they villagers who'd stayed behind, perhaps unwillingly? Or refugees with nowhere to go?

Muromets pointed out a large bunker with a rounded, turf-covered roof among a cluster of smaller installations beside the dirt runway. "That's the operations bunker. And here they come."

Several officers emerged, chatting. In their midst was a tall man whose face was bright crimson. As they came closer, Aelya saw two gold-trimmed red bars on his sky-blue collar, marking him as a major. His face was blemished by smooth, red splotches, likely the product of burns. Behind him, one man lit up a cigarette, then looked over at the women, nudging his comrade. He ran back to shout through the open door of the bunker. Soon a dozen men emerged to have a look.

Lara led the squadron in a salute as Red arrived at the door of the command post.

"What is this, Muromets?" said the major. His smooth, youthful voice was incongruous with the ruined face, and Aelya realized he must have been thirty at most. "I wanted to meet the replacements, not the ferry pilots."

"Comrade Commander, these *are* the replacements."

"Senior Lieutenant Larissa Rogacheva reporting for duty, Comrade Major."

Red swore, which made Lara's eyes widen.

By now, the other male pilots had sauntered over, standing at a short distance, sizing up the new squadron. Aelya didn't enjoy feeling like a curiosity put on stage to be gawked at.

The pilot who had been smoking came over to clap Muromets on the back, hard enough to cause his glasses to tip forward. "Legend, you've been holding out on us. Where have you been hiding this harem?"

The man he'd been talking to earlier said, "You wish you were as cultured and courteous as The Legend, Petrushka. After all, when have you ever attracted such beauties?" An inflection to the word "beauties" made Aelya think he was being sarcastic.

"I demand a more respectful tone when you refer to us, Lieutenant," Lara warned him.

He maintained a slight smile but nodded.

"All right, enough fooling," said Red. "Flight and squadrons leaders, with me."

The sarcastic lieutenant saluted, then joined Red and two other men heading into the command post.

As Red turned away, Muromets spoke up. "But Comrade Commander, what should I do about the new pilots?"

"What do you mean?"

"There are induction procedures and orientation—"

"Can't you handle that? I'm busy enough with real pilots."

This last remark stunned Aelya. It reminded her of when Raskova had been considering assigning her as a navigator.

Red waved his hand dismissively. "I don't know—talk to Dmitriev. He always seems to have busywork."

Red entered the command post, slamming the door behind him. Lara and Muromets looked at each other for a moment. Finally, Muromets motioned for the squadron to follow him. He dismissed the truck and gave them a walking tour of the airfield. Most of the components were the same as at Anisovka, though the construction was hasty and several installations had multiple functions as a concession to frontline expediency. Aelya began to rapidly memorize the layout, hoping she wouldn't get confused if there was an alert.

Muromets arranged a ride into the village, where they had lunch in the officers' canteen, one of two camouflaged tents set up just outside the main cluster of buildings. By then, the sound of most explosions had become so consistent, they were easy to ignore, like the drone of an engine. Every now and then, a particularly loud blast would cause the women to start.

"Don't worry. Trick of the wind," said Muromets reassuringly. With his bookish manner, he would be right at home in a school library. But anyone could be hardened by war given the right circumstances.

Muromets met an elderly man, apparently the head of the village. Together they led the pilots to a grain storage shed, where space had been commandeered for them. Muromets left them to assess what needed to be done to make it their home—a gargantuan task. Then they got a pleasant surprise in the arrival of several trucks: Sara Eisenach and the remaining squadron ground crew were on board, along with bundles of supplies and other baggage they'd accumulated back with the 586th. An hour later, Zina and the other crew chiefs rejoined them from the airfield, completing the squadron.

The elderly man returned with other old people from the village. Few young people were still around. They proved helpful, bringing straw mattresses and blankets for the women, persisting past any attempts at refusal.

"How is your accommodation working out?" Aelya asked Zina.

"The women technicians let us stay with them, though there's a shortage of bunks. Newcomers will have to take turns sleeping on the floor. Oksana's on the case, so hopefully we'll all be sleeping properly soon."

"Have you met the commanding officer? I don't think he was happy to see us."

"Neither was the regimental engineer. It's one thing to work with women armourers and parachute packers, but having women mechanics feels like an invasion. That was his word—'invasion.'"

"It'll just take time. I'm sure they felt that way about their armourers."

"The women are even worse. Ulanova hates us. I haven't seen her smile once since we got here."

"Maybe she's always like that."

They spent much of the afternoon cleaning out the grain shed to make it more habitable. The technicians were happy to help. This was the first time they'd ever had better accommodations than the pilots.

Muromets returned to fetch them for a meeting with the political officer. Walking down the dirt track toward the canteen tents, Aelya accustomed herself again to the constant artillery fire. Then she noticed not a single airplane engine could be heard.

"Why isn't there more activity on the airfield?" she said.

"We're operating under strict limits right now. We've got shortages in everything. Planes, parts, fuel. Pilots."

The commissar was inside the officers' canteen. He was a blocky, middle-aged man whose crisp haircut shaved at the sides reminded Aelya of the eraser at the end of a pencil. All of the pilots and technicians transferring in from the 586th formed into groups according to their function and squeezed onto the benches.

From the back of the tent, Muromets made his introduction. "Comrades, this is Major Yevgeny Dmitriev, our political officer."

Dmitriev nodded approvingly. He watched as Muromets tapped his foot nervously and said, "Are you in a hurry to get somewhere, Muromets?"

"It's just, Shepel has got me—"

"All right, all right. You're dismissed. I don't need you here to protect me from these ladies."

There were a few quiet laughs. Muromets made himself scarce.

Dmitriev began, "I welcome you all to the 497th Fighter Aviation Regiment. I'm very pleased to see you here. No doubt some of my comrades have more backward views, but to me, you represent the very ideals we're fighting for. I know you've just arrived, so how are you settling in?"

The women looked uncertain whether to respond. Aelya glanced over at Lara and most did the same.

"Fine," Lara said flatly.

"Good, good. You may be in for more of a shock as you take on regular duties. This is the front line, comrades. You'll see we're much more strictly regimented than Air Defence."

What Aelya had seen so far pointed to the exact opposite. Muromets and other pilots were exceedingly familiar in front of Red. Their uniforms were shabby and disparate. A lot of the installations looked haphazard. None of that would have passed muster with Volkova.

"You are part of the best-prepared, most technologically advanced fighting force in the world. The VVS is the sharp point in the spear of our revolution."

Roza leaned in to whisper. "Shouldn't we be the shield? We always seem to be on defence."

"You're in the midst of the most colossal clash in the history of mankind, a battle for the very soul of the world. There's no room for laggards here. Retreat is cowardice. Surrender is treason. There are no leaves of absence. You're part of this fight until we destroy the Nazi scum utterly or you die."

"I still like him better than Batyrskaya," Roza said.

Aelya frowned. Much as she'd disliked working on the play, their old commissar's demeanour had never been as outright menacing as Dmitriev's. If she'd feared Batyrskaya, it was in the same manner as she'd fear a nosy neighbour her mother had cautioned her about. Dmitriev seemed of the same mould as the NKVD men in their black cars.

"I envy you your burden. Your duties shall be twofold: not only shall you be proud warriors of the motherland but exemplars of Soviet womanhood. A shining beacon of our ideals of equality and productivity." He grew animated now, pacing back and forth, his eyes gleaming. "Do your duty—no, go above and beyond your duty. Show everyone what you're capable of. Most importantly, show the enemy. Succeed here, in the same place our beloved leader forged his legend, and songs shall be sung of you until the end of time."

Aelya had been hearing the same message from the time she first dug trenches outside Smolensk. Everyone was going to be a hero, Fedor had declared. But now, so close to the centre of fighting, the Nazis a few minutes' flight away, she felt her destiny was almost tangible. She shivered, and not even Roza's eye roll could break her out of that spell.

Others must have felt the same. Hearty applause erupted when Dmitriev finished. With renewed vigour, the pilots returned to work on their lodgings while the technicians were sent to the airfield. At sundown, Tonya noted that the canteen had set up for dinner. They rushed in, eager to get first choice of food. It was a good thing, since Muromets came to fetch them shortly afterward.

They were driven out to the operations bunker, passing a truckload of exhausted-looking pilots on the way back.

"I don't know why they're so gutted," said Tonya. "Can't have flown more than two sorties each."

"They probably packed more action in those than we did in a whole month," said Roza.

The squadron squeezed into the ops bunker, where several staff officers were shuttling around with papers. Dmitriev sat in a corner with a cup of tea. Red was going over plans near a map pinned to the wall.

"What's this, Muromets? Can't it wait?" said Red.

"You asked to see the new pilots."

"Did I? Oh well, might as well get this done." He put down a sheaf of papers and stood with his arms crossed.

"Lieutenant," he said, addressing Lara, "I apologize for my earlier attitude. It was rude of me. I thank you for your service in bringing us the new planes. We'll arrange transport back to your unit."

"Excuse me, Comrade Major. This *is* our unit. We're not ferry pilots."

Red chuckled. "I'm sure VVS Command can classify you however they want, but the fact is, I don't think you'll be a good fit for my unit."

Muromets cleared his throat. "If you send them back, it will be a long time before they fly in more replacements."

"I don't care. We're fighting a war here. I need real pilots, not propaganda showpieces."

Dmitriev's ears perked up.

Lara barely hid her fury. "We have more experience than any of your so-called real pilots."

"Comrade Commander," said Dmitriev, striding over. "These women are graduates of the great Marina Raskova's aviation group. Comrade Stalin has taken a personal interest in their success. Whatever help you provide in facilitating this won't be forgotten."

Red looked from Dmitriev to Lara, sucking in his cheeks as he chewed on some imaginary morsel. "Fine. But you'll all need to be tested and reviewed, just like every new pilot. I need to know you won't get us all killed."

"I expect nothing less," said Dmitriev.

Lara smiled. "And we expect nothing more."

CHAPTER 31: THE PARTY

Tonya picked a careful path between the tall grass, then signalled for the rest of the squadron to follow. In the clear night, Aelya hunched over to hide from the moonlight, and she was relieved to enter the shadow of the next empty building.

"This is a really dumb idea," whispered Klava.

"You worry too much," said Tonya.

"There's a lot to worry about. We're under curfew. And what about the security patrols? And the blue caps? And just how late will this go?"

"Security is all about keeping intruders out, not stopping us from moving around. There are no female blue caps here, so that one knock on the door for lights out is all the checking they'll do. They're probably getting flat-on-the-floor drunk right now. And it's not like anyone's flying tomorrow, so what's a bit of lost sleep?"

"You've really thought a lot of about this," said Aelya.

"All in service to the squadron."

Lara shushed them. She exchanged a meaningful look with Klava, who shrugged. Klava wasn't one to take any risks if she could help it. Aelya had expected Lara to back her up, but once Tonya had mentioned being invited to a party with the other pilots, the women were buzzing about it. Tonya, Roza, and the twins were determined to go, thinking if a war was going on, they might as well have as much fun as possible. It threatened a rift between the pilots, so Lara relented but made everyone go. If they got into trouble, they would all go down together.

Tonya was right about one thing: there would be no flying tomorrow, at least no combat missions. They had spent their second full day in Orlovka reviewing situational reports and dealing with paperwork. Even the men made few combat sorties. The big excitement happened when a pilot who'd bailed out in the morning reappeared on the back of a passing infantry truck in the afternoon. Another pilot shot down in the same engagement hadn't been so lucky.

By the end of the day, the whole regiment was down to its last dregs of planes. The eight that the women had brought were fully operational, but the regimental engineer had been clear that they needed a full ground and air checkout before they were approved for use. Even then, the women weren't allowed near the planes. They could be trusted to fly them for dozens of Air Defence missions and transport them all the way from Anisovka but not to do routine checks.

Dinner in the canteen had been a quiet, strained affair, with the women sitting at a separate table from the male pilots. They traded glances but no one talked above low tones with their neighbours. The men seemed very reticent. Aelya wasn't sure if it had to do with the day's missions or the dawning realization they were stuck with the women. That bit of tension was a useful reminder she was fighting a war. Otherwise, battle seemed every bit as distant as it had been when she was a recruit at Engels. She hardly noticed the explosions anymore. Amid the malaise, it was hard to believe that nearby on the banks of the Volga, hundreds of thousands of soldiers were hurling themselves at each other.

Dmitriev had told them more shells and bombs were being lobbed into the corpse of the city than had been used in all of the Second Patriotic War, but she wasn't sure how accurate that was. He also told the story of a valiant defender in the city whose whole unit had been wiped out by an artillery blast that sheared off both his legs. He still manned a machine gun, mowing down wave after wave of Teutonic invaders. When they finally overwhelmed him, he set off a grenade, taking them with him. She wondered how that story got out if everyone had died.

They had been ready to turn the covers on a dreary day without flying when Tonya reported they'd been invited to a party thrown by the male pilots in honour of their arrival. How exactly she got this invitation, she didn't say.

The men were billeted in the centre of the village, which had mostly been abandoned by its inhabitants. Those who remained must have been moved somewhere else. It was hard to miss the party, with all the noise coming from the largest house. It had once housed the village headman and had a large adjoining hall. Light leaked out from the edges of blackout curtains.

Tonya opened the door to the hall. The dozen men within stopped their carousing, though one drunk, lying flat on a bench, continued mumbling loudly. A gramophone in the corner played scratchy Ukrainian *hutsulka* music.

The women crowded around just inside the threshold while the men stared. Aelya looked to Tonya for guidance, and she didn't disappoint. Someone had set up an array of liquor bottles on a low cabinet along one wall, and Tonya approached it with greedy eyes.

"Someone get me a drink," she said. "And not that watered-down crap we get for our hundred grams."

That broke the spell. Three different men rushed over to pour her glasses.

She sipped the first one offered, then signalled for Masha to come over, which she did, reluctantly. "I need stronger stuff. What do you think, Masha?"

Masha shook her head vehemently.

"Come on. Don't you lot start drinking before you can talk? I bet your babushka made this sort of stuff in her washtub."

She forced the glass to Masha's lips as the men cheered her on. Masha obliged, then turned bright red. She covered her mouth.

A chant went up among some of the men. "Puke! Puke! Puke!"

She held it in, then stood up straight, looking proud of herself.

A tall man with fine features and olive skin approached Lara and Aelya, still standing with the others by the door. He had silvery streaks of hair on either side of his head. "I apologize for the uncouth behaviour of my comrades. Let's civilize this a bit. Bison! Put on the Utyosov."

The record on the gramophone was changed, and the hall thumped to a big band, jazzy number. He held his hand out and Lara took it. They began to dance, though Aelya had no idea what style. It seemed very American. Tonya picked her own partner, and soon other men were approaching. Aelya dodged behind her comrades and made her way closer to the makeshift bar.

First Roza partnered off, then Olga, then Klava. A slight man with dark hair and a strong brow quickly pushed away Roza's first partner and took over. Tonya decided her first partner was hopeless and began doing a solo performance as three or four men looked on admiringly.

The pilot Aelya remembered as Petrushka roughly dragged a short man over to Masha. He only came up to her shoulders.

"Now this is a match made in heaven," said Petrushka.

The smaller man offered his hand gingerly.

"Try to dance with me and I'll break your arm," Masha said.

Petrushka laughed heartily as the other man slunk away to join others who were clapping and stomping along to the music.

"How about you?" Petrushka asked Yulia, who had quietly sidled up beside Masha. She blushed and shook her head. Before he could turn to Aelya, she looked away. Framed drawings of hunting scenes hung up high on the walls. The headman appeared to have lived well, for a peasant.

"Petrushka," she heard Masha remark, "you supposed to be a clown?"

"It's not a joke. Petrushka's a bona fide hero of the people, you know."

Masha snorted. Aelya had never seen a Petrushka show before. The garish puppets usually only played in the villages. A school friend had told of seeing one in the park. Apparently, Petrushka's whole act involved beating people over the head and breaking wind.

She turned back to see Petrushka smirking, then making a showy bow before returning to the fold. It was Kupala Night all over again. Why didn't she just dance? It wouldn't be hard. The man was supposed to lead, after all. Perhaps this was how her father had felt when the male engineers on their floor of the workers' apartments had frequent, noisy drinking blowouts. They would drunkenly hammer away at the door until Papa reluctantly agreed to join them.

"Poor Petrushka could die tomorrow, you know." It was Petrushka's sarcastic friend. Aelya noticed now in the light of the oil lamps that he had a tawny complexion to go with his dark wavy hair and didn't look altogether European.

"We could all die," said Aelya. He had been talking to Yulia, but she'd felt the need to interject. "We're not here to be your harem."

"You remember me? You should also recall that we thought you were The Legend's harem."

"Why do you call him The Legend?"

"After Ilya Muromets, of course. He's quite possibly a descendant. Also, I think Arkadiy would look very good in a suit of armour and a winged helmet."

"Does it make you feel good to mock him?" Aelya wasn't sure why her back was up.

"I'm not mocking him. Our dear adjutant is positively a hero for all the paperwork he saves us from doing."

Aelya looked at him with a sidelong glance.

"I'm serious," he said. "We all have our part to play. Just as you will make great propaganda for our cause."

Yulia leaned in. "We can fly, you know."

"Oh, I don't doubt that you can. I just doubt that's your primary mission."

This remark drew Masha's ire, and she and Yulia raised their voices in indignation as they laid into the man, who seemed amused by it all. Aelya needed to cool down, so she searched the bar for something to drink that wouldn't knock her out but found no options.

A new song came on the gramophone, and the partners on the floor switched. Tonya finally seemed to have found a worthy match in the silver-streaked man who'd called for the music. Roza started dancing with another man when Petrushka cut in.

Aelya observed the men in the room. It was one thing to meet with them during her leisure time, but soon she would be flying with them, trusting them with her life. She knew it was mostly propaganda, but she'd still been expecting strapping, classical statue-like men. Beyond the silver-haired one, they looked pretty similar to the men of the 383rd: some bookworms, some slouches, some oddballs. No real type among them.

"Pretty poor husband material, I know." The sarcastic man was back, now that Yulia had joined in a dance and Masha had busied herself staring into another drink.

"That's offensive. We're not here to chase men," said Aelya.

"I see you like Frost, our distinguished gentleman pilot. No chance. He's got a sweetheart back home he's madly in love with."

"Everyone has a nickname here. What's yours?"

"You can call me Mark." He hesitated a bit, and Aelya took satisfaction in tripping him up. She felt pleased enough to let him continue.

"Our unshaven friend clapping his hands and doing a little jig over there? That's Yusupov, but I wouldn't trust him. He always acts like he's serious, but half the time he's joking. His heart is unknowable, like a woman's."

He pointed to the stocky pilot who'd been operating the gramophone and was now spinning Olga around. "Bison. I can see your distaste already. Too rough at the edges. And Petrushka I know you hate already. What about our resident gypsy?" He pointed to the pilot who'd first cut in with Roza.

Aelya shook her head, surprising herself that she was playing along. But cutting these men down to size felt comforting.

"Too dark for you?"

She was mortified. Though until recently, she'd had little exposure to the panoply of races in the union, she was raised a proud internationalist. "No, no, it's not that. He was rude and butted in."

"Ah, but that's his right, you see. The other man was a new pilot, and Sleepy's been in combat already. What about Mouse over there? Baby? We're running out of choices. Wait too long and you'll wind up with Usy. He might seem harmless now that he's passed out, but . . ."

He furrowed his brow and seemed serious for once. Usy was so named for his ridiculous handlebar moustache, which extended far beyond the bounds of his face. He lay flat on a bench, arm to one side dangling above an empty vodka bottle on the floor. His face was pockmarked and even in slumber it looked alert.

"There are still a few more," Aelya said. "That tall one . . . what's his name?" He was the one Tonya had danced with before giving up. Despite his square jaw, there was a babyish quality to his face.

"I have no idea who that is."

"Are you serious?"

"He's too fresh. So are the rest. I don't bother knowing their names until they've flown at least a dozen missions. Then I know it's worth the effort."

The song ended and everyone applauded. Then a call went up for Frost to get his guitar.

"So, I suppose that just leaves you," said Aelya. "What's your clever nickname? I know you have one."

"Oh no, you haven't qualified to hear. You've not flown a dozen missions yet."

"We have nicknames too. You want to know mine?"

He shook his head. He was entirely too full of himself.

"They call him Stitches," said Tonya, barging in between them on her way to the cabinet of drinks. She was trailed by several admiring pilots. "Tore your pants that one time you bailed out, didn't you?" She reached up and pinched Mark's, or rather, Stitches's cheek.

They all used nicknames; Aelya thought she should get used to it in order to fit in.

"All right, my new friends," Tonya said, "find me something good to drink." She reached over and grabbed a clear bottle with a reddish liquor in it. She sniffed. "Smells sweet, might be just the thing."

"I wouldn't," said Stitches. "That's liquor chassis."

"Syrup and distilled brake fluid." It was Yusupov. Was he joking?

Tonya took a swig directly from the bottle. Her mouth wrinkled for a moment. Then she smiled.

"You're still standing," Stitches said with admiration. He and Tonya shared a laugh and talked with their backs turned to Aelya.

She found him irritating but nonetheless missed his attention. Frost began strumming a soft tune. It reminded her of the flamenco dancing she'd seen in newsreels when the war in Spain had been all the talk a few years ago. She sought out Masha, who was examining an intricately carved horn from an ox or some other large animal.

"That's our good luck charm," said Yusupov. "Took that from a Party boss's house when we hightailed it out of Vitebsk last summer."

"That's stealing from a Soviet citizen," said Masha.

"He can go to hell," he said. "I'll pay him back there."

Masha and Yusupov seemed intent on wallowing in the dead air between them, so Aelya turned to her other side where Yulia was chatting with the tall, baby-faced pilot. Yulia only gave up a couple of centimetres to him.

"Mars, this is Taras," said Yulia.

"Mars?"

"As in Aelita, Queen of Mars?"

"That's odd. I mean the name, not you. Not that it's bad to be odd." He fiddled with the buttons of his tunic. After Stitches's arrogance, there was something undeniably sweet about such a handsome man being so bashful, though Aelya realized he barely qualified as a man. Had he ever even shaved?

"So Taras," Aelya said, "everyone here seems to have some nickname. What's yours?" It felt good to be holding Taras's hand verbally. A charitable act.

"I don't know. Everyone in training just called me Taras. I suppose I'll go by Seventy. That's the bort number on my plane."

Aelya felt a little spark of excitement. "What a coincidence. My number is 70 as well." But this was no coincidence. She did a double take. "Wait a minute, white number 70?"

"Yes, that's it."

"That's my plane! They gave you my plane!"

The guitar stopped.

"What?" exclaimed Roza. "You took our planes?"

"Of course," said Stitches. "There's a war on. We have more pilots than planes, and you haven't been proven yet."

"Not proven?" said Aelya. "How many solo hours have you done in the Yak, Taras?"

"Fifteen," he said sheepishly.

"I've got two hundred."

"So what?" said Stitches. "You in a hurry to die?"

More arguments broke out. Whatever amity had concealed the previous tension disappeared, and open hostility replaced it. The voices only lowered when someone knocked loudly on the door.

"Quick, get the ladies out of here," said Frost.

The eight women bundled themselves through the rooms of the former headman's house, quietly lining up next to a side entrance as the men opened the main door of the hall.

"You knuckleheads!" It was Red's voice. "Shut this thing down before the NKVD remembers they have a job to do."

The women crept out quietly into the darkness. Masha was in full wobble and had to be supported by the twins. When they got back to their quarters, Aelya thought she'd never been so happy to see a dingy grain shed again. She burst out laughing. She had to admit, Tonya did have a good idea for once.

CHAPTER 32: THE CHECKOUT

A green flare soared over the runway.

"This is Maple Tree," came the call from the command post. "Vectoring station Gazelle reporting twenty-plus Stukas with escort. Bearing two-six-zero. Height twenty-five hundred. All units in readiness to intercept."

This was awkward. Aelya and Roza were already taxiing for takeoff. They would have to make way for the interceptors. To Aelya's right, Roza pushed her plane ahead toward the runway.

"Roza, what are you doing?"

"I'm clearing the runway. It's more efficient this way."

She had a point, but there was a hint of contempt in her tone.

"Stay behind your leader." Aelya throttled her plane ahead.

"Yes, Mars."

Aelya received clearance for takeoff, and the pair climbed to take their place with Klava and Tonya, who had taken off minutes earlier.

The men having commandeered the squadron's planes, Eisenach had set her team to work non-stop for the past day and a half to make four damaged planes operable. She, Zina, and the others were miracle workers. They still needed to be checked out, and, eager for any time in the air, Klava volunteered her flight. The male pilots didn't trust Eisenach, so there were no other takers.

"Sparrow Two flight, form up," Klava said. "We'll circle the eastern half of the flight zone until the boys get under way."

Aelya was bursting to throw her Yak into turns at top speed, to loop and roll, the g-forces slamming her into and out of her seat. Real flying. But for the next few minutes, Klava ran them carefully through manoeuvre drills, ensuring the planes were in top shape.

By now, six Yak fighters had lined up in pairs on the runway. With Yusupov in the lead, they took off.

"Only six? "Doesn't seem like a lot," said Roza.

"What are you getting at?" said Klava.

"Gazelle said over twenty dive-bombers plus escorts. And they called for all available units."

"All units in readiness."

"Splendid idea," Yusupov cut in.

There was a staticky silence for a moment. "Osprey Leader, what the hell are you playing at?" It was Red, from the command post.

"Observation purposes," said Yusupov. "Best way for rookies to learn is to watch the action."

"Yes, in ones and twos, not a whole flight."

"They can stay high in cover. Sparrow Two Leader, you can manage that, right?"

"Affirmative, Osprey Leader." Klava's reply was bubbling with joy.

Thank you, Yusupov, Aelya silently offered. It would be the perfect introduction to the front. This was it—she would finally see the war up close.

"Fine," said Red. "Observation only. No engagement by Sparrow flight."

"Copy that," said Klava.

Yusupov's six planes rapidly gained cruising altitude and formed up into three pairs at staggered heights. Yusupov and Bison formed the first pair. Then Stitches and Petrushka, then Frost and one of the younger pilots, whom they simply designated Forty. Klava took her four and formed up behind and above Frost. They quickly sorted out call signs and a general flight plan as they headed to intercept according to Gazelle Station's directions.

"We'll make this easy," said Yusupov. "You should be well versed in unit flying. You've had radios longer than we've had. Your techs are real wonders.

"I'll split your coverage. Mars, your pair will fly cover above me. Bison and I will be engaging any escorts we spot first. Klava, you'll be covering Stitches and Frost. Their one and only responsibility is the bombers. Based on Gazelle's vectoring, the vultures are probably headed for the northern flank of Stalingrad. There's a hell of a fight going on there right now. Whatever happens, we can't let their bombs fall on our boys. I know Red said observe, but if things get halry, I expect you ladies to throw yourselves into the fray."

"Yusupov," said Tonya, "I want to marry you and have your baby."

Yusupov momentarily switched off his transmitter. He was either laughing or swearing.

He switched back on. "All right, here are my last instructions before we go into strict radio discipline. If you're targeting the bombers, then enemy fighters are just a distraction. It doesn't matter if they're on your tail. Dive among the bombers, break them up, force their gunners to figure out friend from foe."

"We've done bomber intercepts before," said Klava.

"Perfect."

The distance to the front line was so short compared to rear-area defence, Aelya barely had time to absorb the instructions when first contact was made. A group of perhaps eight Messerschmitt Bf 109s. Remembering her tactical lectures, Aelya knew these were likely intended to clear the skies shortly before the bombers arrived.

While Stitches took his four planes, along with Klava and Tonya, to veer right, Yusupov took his group into a climb, trying to come right at the Messers from the direction of the sun. The enemy did the same, trying to gain an advantage. It was perfect. The German fighters were so eager for kills, they completely ignored Stitches's larger group. Aelya broke left with Roza following to observe at a higher altitude, as instructed.

Soon the space between Yusupov and the enemy closed and they tangled, their paths intertwining like a knot being tied. Tracers laced the air between the planes. Smoke trailed from one Messer. Her transmitter off, Aelya let out a cheer. Her heart raced so much, she thought it would be ripped out of her chest. In over a year of war, it was the very first strike against the invader she'd seen first-hand.

"I'm hit," Bison called out.

She glanced over in the midst of the dogfight to see one Yak dropping out perilously fast. A white bud separated itself, blooming into Bison's parachute. Yusupov was now badly outnumbered and dived hard toward a cloud formation, trailing five Messers on his tail. With one Messer out of action, the remaining two banked and flew toward Bison's helplessly descending figure. Streaks of white marked the trail of shells cutting through the air toward him. She couldn't see whether they hit him. The parachute continued gently floating down.

"Did you see that?" Roza swore and broke into a dive, veering toward the offending Messers. Aelya didn't bother calling her back. There was no point, and time enough to sort things out later. The most important thing was not to get isolated. In any case, her own blood was boiling.

The two Messers weren't interested in a dogfight and dived to disengage. Prudent, perhaps, but it felt unmistakably cowardly to Aelya.

Roza formed up again. "Apologies, Mars. I attacked before I heard you give permission." Overly formal, Roza's remorse was for the radio's benefit. Was it to excuse her insubordination or to save face for Aelya?

"Mars," said Yusupov. She felt relief he was still flying. "Regroup at height twenty-five hundred. I lost them in the clouds. Can you see me?"

Aelya searched the skies for his lone dot. "Negative."

Far away to the northwest was a cluster of dots moving in unison.

"The Stukas are here," Stitches called out. Soon more dots crashed together in the distant sky, swarming around each other. Aelya could make out Klava and Tonya staying high and away, as instructed. No idea where Yusupov could be.

"That's one Stuka down," Stitches said.

"That was mine, actually," said Petrushka.

"Knock it off," said Yusupov. "Radio discipline."

Where was he? Aelya asked for a heading. He tried to give her his bearing from the sun, but it was so high in the sky, that wasn't much help.

"Enemy fighters coming in, bearing one-nine-zero, height three thousand," said Roza.

Aelya had no idea if this group of six or so was the same one as before, but they had the height advantage.

"They're expecting us to dive and flee," said Roza. "Let's show them what they want, er, Comrade Senior Sergeant."

Flustered for want of any better ideas, Aelya entered into a dive, followed closely by Roza. The Messers turned toward them and dived at an angle to intercept.

"When the time is right, turn and climb toward them," said Roza.

"Then what?"

"Go head-on. Whatever you do, don't break first."

Aelya had heard about this tactic. Against the twin cannons and twin machine guns of the Messer, they would be seriously outgunned and had to rely on psychology more than anything else.

"All right, but I give the word." Would Roza listen? It didn't matter. There was no more time to think. "Now!" Aelya shouted.

Aelya and Roza turned as one, all those aerobatic practices paying off. They soon found themselves facing two Messers screaming directly at them. The other Messers couldn't get a firing angle on them without knocking into their comrades. A terror Aelya could barely comprehend gripped her, and she didn't move a muscle.

Closing speed was so rapid that within seconds the two Messers broke off. One of them trailed flames as Roza lit up its underside. Aelya realized she'd forgotten to fire.

She exhaled and looked behind. The other Messers disappeared.

Yusupov called once again for a regroup. He said it several times as the radio chatter became constant. Scanning the skies, Aelya deduced that another group of bombers and escorts had arrived. The Stukas had fled the scene.

"We'll take the fighters this time," said Stitches. "Sparrow Two Leader, want to take a run at the bombers?"

"Yes, Comrade Commander!" said Klava.

Aelya saw the new bombers. They were close. Junkers 88s. Big, twin-engined beasts with three gun turrets each. Much tougher nuts to crack than the little Stuka dive-bombers. Stitches certainly wasn't trying to coddle the women. Aelya was envious and it spurred her to action.

"This is Mars. We'll make a second pass when you're done."

"That's my girl," said Roza.

Well, she was senior pilot after all.

Klava and Tonya made their attack pass from above. A shiver gripped Aelya. Seeing two against twenty from afar made it seem like insanity. And her turn was next. She'd just volunteered. The flurry of tracers made it difficult to see who'd hit what. She exhaled when two Yak fighters emerged from the gauntlet. Her legs felt cold. Her stomach clenched. Time was up.

"Our turn," she said.

They made their attack run from below, at an oblique angle, so they could try to hit one after another of the bombers while forcing the gunners to avoid their fellow bombers.

She was firing too far behind again. Tracers ripped at her, too fast to dodge. Only luck would protect her. It took several bursts before she managed to strike one bomber, clipping it briefly across the tail. No smoke, no signs of damage. Her plane bucked, either from recoil or enemy hits. She and Roza climbed rapidly, looking back as angry lines of tracers chased them, then dissipated. Her heart leaped as she spotted one bomber spiralling down in flames—until Roza called out.

"Got one!"

The rest of the Junkers turned en masse, their bombs jettisoned into empty fields below.

Up high, Aelya finally spotted Yusupov and moved quickly to form up on his wing. His tail section was partially shredded, but otherwise his plane looked all right.

"I think I'm low on ammo," she reported. She had taken a few hits herself, but beyond a slight drop in oil pressure, everything seemed fine.

"Well, with Bison gone, you're covering me now," said Yusupov. "At least you can throw your plane in the way if we get attacked."

With the combat zone clear of the enemy, Stitches circled down low and spotted Bison waving on the ground. He called in Bison's location. Since they were over friendly territory, it wouldn't be long before some infantry picked him up. Yusupov called in to Gazelle for a thirty-three and they headed for home. Only then did Aelya notice Forty had gone down as well.

She wanted to talk so much but held on to her discipline. So that was combat. She could barely remember any of it. It was amazing to her that, knowing the danger even a single bullet posed, she'd so willingly hurled herself into the storm of gunfire from such a large group of bombers. She felt as though she was in a dream state and forced herself to continue checking the sky for trouble. Elation. Relief. Confusion. She didn't know what to feel.

She saw Klava's plane wobbling, struggling to keep a level flight path.

"Sparrow Two Leader, are you all right?"

"Fine," Klava said.

Aelya's legs itched. As she scratched, she realized she'd wet herself. The stench of urine made her nauseous. Forget that. Keep checking the sky.

They were soon back in the airspace above Orlovka. Klava started losing altitude. Yusupov asked her to report.

"N-no problem, Osprey Leader. Engine's a bit hot is all."

"Osprey Squadron, make a circuit," ordered Yusupov. "Sparrow Two Leader will land first."

"N-no. No need."

"She's not all right, Osprey Leader," Aelya said. "Klava, if you can't land it, bail out."

"N-n-no. I can land this."

"Don't worry about the plane. You can bail out. You've done it before."

Klava's plane made a sudden drop of several hundred metres. Then it nosed up slightly before falling into a spin. There was no chance to get out. Within seconds, the plane crashed into a field not far from the runway.

CHAPTER 33: BREAD AND VODKA

They dug a grave in the yard of Orlovka's little church. It was the first funeral of the war Aelya had witnessed. Sveta's body had been taken away and the death not spoken of officially. Galya and Dunya's bodies had never been found. Just one grave. Forty, whose name eluded most of the pilots, hadn't yet been found, though Petrushka assured them that no one could have survived the fireball that went down.

Klava, on the other hand, had been found badly mangled but mostly in one piece. Petrushka had reported on this so flippantly, he was scolded by several of his mates. Aelya wasn't sure if he'd crossed a line or if they were being especially sombre due to Klava's gender. If it was the latter, Aelya felt almost as angry at them as she did Petrushka.

Lara volunteered to speak so no one else had to. She uttered some standard platitudes, words that blended together indiscriminately to Aelya. In some ways, though the near miss she'd experienced back with the 586th reminded her of the closeness of death, it also made combat seem like no big deal. If she hadn't died then, what could possibly kill her? Sveta hadn't died in combat. Those who remained, they were invincible. And in their minds, Klava wasn't dead, just gone.

When the service was over, they stayed put for a moment. Frost approached the women and consoled Lara, putting his hand on her shoulder. "I'm so sorry we couldn't protect her." He was speaking to all of them.

"Klava didn't need protecting," Tonya said. "She died protecting you, trying to cover your landing instead of looking out for herself."

Frost nodded calmly despite the anger in her tone. Everyone filed slowly out of the yard to walk to the canteen for breakfast. A group of support personnel began filling the grave. Aelya was proud of Tonya for sticking up for the squadron. If the moment came, would she face her death as bravely as Klava had? She recalled the sheer terror that had kept her from breaking against the Messerschmitts, her only clear memory from the day before.

Pilots and staff officers breakfasted together. Sparrow Squadron, as the women had taken to calling themselves, found a table set for eight waiting for them. Aelya half expected Klava to join them at the table. In the corner place setting rested a single glass of vodka and a piece of bread laid atop it. Another similar setting sat on the table for Yusupov's squadron.

As the women stood looking at the bread and vodka quizzically, Petrushka said, "Don't you honour the dead in Air Defence?"

"Never had to do it before," said Lara. She gave an appreciative nod to the canteen servers, then took her seat.

Commissar Dmitriev, who'd also said a few generic words at the funeral, had made himself scarce, as had Muromets. Aelya felt that only those who'd been in combat were allowed to gather here in this moment.

Red, who'd seemed emotionally unaffected as he gave a brief boilerplate eulogy at the service, signalled for his chief of staff to speak. This was Captain Shepel, a squat, bull of a man with thin strands of grey hair swept across his bald scalp, making him look much older than his forty-odd years. His fingers were gnarled and beefy. He stood as they quietly ate spoonfuls of their porridge.

Shepel announced, "Senior Sergeant Zhigulin, who you may have forgotten is Bison, has been moved to a rear-area hospital. He has broken ribs and some internal bleeding but is expected to make a full recovery."

Yusupov's squadron patted the table in a quiet cheer.

Shepel continued, "For our newcomers, if you wish to send any gifts or notes to the families of either of our fallen comrades, please come and see me."

Frost stood up, placing a hand over his heart. "We honour Klavdiya Rodionovna," he said to the women. "We knew her only briefly, but she died as a member of this regiment. Her memory lives on through us who fight."

Petrushka stood up as well with hand over heart. "And we honour the other guy—"

"Petrushka," warned Stitches.

"His memory lives on in the boots I took."

Taras stood up abruptly. He'd looked pale and stricken all morning but now had some colour. "His name was Filip Semyonovich Harmash. None of you idiots knew him!" His lips trembled. "None of you knew him. I did." He hesitated, shaking his head. "I . . . I'm not a good talker but . . . I knew him."

Another pilot reached for him, but he swatted the hand away. "We came through flight school together. His family managed a grain collective. When Fascists overran the *kolkhoz*, they made them work day and night to feed the invaders. When they didn't collect enough, the Germans strangled them all with barbed wire, even his little brother." He cracked a bitter smile, looking off into empty space. "Filip always said his father was bad at farming."

Aelya regretted her anger with Taras at the party. Doubly so, since it hadn't been his idea to take her plane. The impression his friend had made on him was obvious. She only hoped her squadron mates would be as deeply affected if the worst befell her. What had she done for Klava? She hadn't said a word. Left it to Lara and Frost. And if she hadn't encouraged Klava to make her parachute jump, she might have been transferred to navigation and might still be alive.

Taras pounded the table. "He was here to kill Nazis. And I swear, I'll do it for him. I'll give him his revenge."

"No, you won't." Red waved his spoon with casual authority. "Forget all of Dmitriev's claptrap about honour and glory and vengeance. Your only mission, all of you, is to support the regiment's goals. You have no goals of your own. You're all just meat for the grinder."

"You're scaring the new pilots, Comrade Commander," said Stitches.

"We're not scared," said Roza.

"Oh, I believe that," said Stitches without a trace of sarcasm. Beside him, Petrushka nodded. They were looking at Roza differently. As an equal.

Red glared at Roza. "Well, you should be scared."

With a wry smile, Stitches shook his head.

"The point is," Shepel said loudly, "to remember that your living comrades take priority."

He had a very calm, conciliatory expression, and all who were standing knew to sit. He ceded the floor to Red.

"Now, if you're done breakfast," Red said, "here are the orders for the day. I want half of Second Squadron on readiness one, half on readiness two. Yusupov, you and Frost need to go to Division. General Platonov wants a conference on interception protocol. They need a navigator, so fish Chumak out of ops and take him with you. Stitches, take the rest of Yusupov's squadron on a review of yesterday's action. Bring your two new guys up to date. Did I miss anything, Shepel?"

The chief of staff leafed through some papers. "I'm sure you're all awaiting yesterday's confirmations with bated breath."

He went through the summary of yesterday's action. Stitches had one Stuka confirmed as a kill and one probable. Petrushka also got a kill, which he loudly celebrated. Several pilots, including Aelya, had damaged enemy planes. The big commotion was over Roza. She'd shot down both a Messer and a Ju 88. The men of Second Squadron, who hadn't seen the action, were positively buzzing as they reacted to the "new girl's" triumph. Roza only gave a slight smile, not forgetting the cost. Shepel broke it down for those who had: three planes lost; one dead; one missing, presumed dead; and one wounded.

On that sobering note, the pilots were dismissed from breakfast. Aelya nudged Lara; Red had yet to give them any orders.

Lara caught Red as he walked past their table. "Comrade Commander, a moment please?"

They spoke quietly away from the table.

Then he addressed the women. "You all still need to be tested before I give you any duties. As we do with all new pilots."

"I shot down two planes," said Roza. "What more testing do I need?" She added, "Comrade Commander."

"You, Comrade Sergeant, showed poor unit cohesion. You broke from cover without cause and lost track of your senior pilot. You got lucky."

Roza stewed over the criticism, but Lara put a hand on her shoulder.

Red's eyes flicked from side to side. "Go bother Shepel. He'll work out a plan to bring you along. But no more flying until you know you're part of a unit."

He left and everyone began to disperse. With no actual assignment, part of the squadron loitered out front while Lara sought out Shepel.

Roza pulled Aelya aside, back under the shade of the camouflage netting. "Listen, I'm sorry. A lot of things were going through my mind, but I shouldn't have brushed you aside and forced you to follow yesterday. After all, you're senior pilot."

"I . . ." After all that had happened, Aelya only remembered Roza's disobedience now. It should have angered her, but she just felt numb. She watched Roza carefully. Was she even sincere? No, because Aelya was a terrible leader. She'd failed in their first enemy encounter and failed at the first chance at redemption. Only Roza had saved them. "I guess I wouldn't have kept my head the way you did."

Roza nodded. They were uncomfortable standing there, so Roza wandered over to the other pilots. Aelya caught a glimpse of Tonya, still in the canteen. She had Klava's glass of vodka in her hand. As Aelya approached, she drank it in one gulp.

"What?" Tonya barked.

Aelya shook her head.

Tonya stared, but it took a moment for words to come out. "You know when I hit that Junkers, I caught it right in the top turret. It just went *spleh.*" She gestured with her hands, spreading them out. "All red. Who knew you could get so much blood out of one guy?"

Her eyes were wide, her breath shallow. Was this remorse? Fear? No, shock. Tonya, of all people, was shocked.

"How did you feel that first time you made a hit?" asked Aelya. "Last month?" That hadn't seemed to affect her, and perhaps getting her into that same frame of mind would help her.

Tonya said nothing. Her eyes wavered. Then she looked at her empty vodka glass.

Aelya sighed in frustration. "You lied about that?"

Tonya walked over to the glass left for Filip Semyonovich Harmash. Not looking at Aelya, she said, "One of the techs told me about that *thing* they pulled out—what was left of Klava. She—it lasted a whole hour on the ground." She heaved for breath. "I was the one who ratted to Volkova. That we left the patrol zone."

Aelya stared, open-mouthed.

"Yeah, I wanted to make Klava look bad. I spent a whole year in the Falcons with that cow yapping at me. Picking apart my every little move, even though I did them all better than she did. The centre of the star is the hardest part of the formation to fly. You know who flew it? Not her. I join the Air Force and I'm supposed to take orders from her again?"

She gulped down Harmash's vodka, then looked at Aelya.

What was Tonya telling her all this for? Did she want forgiveness? Aelya wanted to hate her. It only made sense. But she was numb. She had no idea what mattered, what to feel. She only knew numbness.

Tonya shrugged and walked past her out of the tent.

CHAPTER 34: THE FALLBACK

"Look down there," Stitches said, tapping the canopy on the left as he rolled to that side. "See that oxbow in the stream? That's the one at N-3 on your map."

In the rear of the two-seater Yak-7, Aelya flipped through laminated map sheets until she found the corresponding navigation landmark. Stitches was flying a wide circuit to orient her to the battlefield. She didn't spend all her time looking at the scenery. She also maintained her good habits of checking every sector of the sky, especially her six o'clock. It was much easier to do it with her shoulder harness unfastened. Stitches has suggested that change, as well as cutting off the shoulder strap to her holster.

Although their two-seater had a full load of guns and ammunition, they were on their own and sluggish with two passengers. Aelya didn't like their chances should they be bounced by Messers. Fortunately, the 466th, one of their sister regiments in the division, was responsible for protecting the skies today. This allowed them to focus on training flights. Yusupov was also up in the air, testing out Yulia, Taras and Masha, the four of them making tactical manoeuvres in regular Yak-1 fighters.

Stitches noted the next landmark, a village church with a tall onion dome. She familiarized herself with the whole map grid, laid out by vectoring station Gazelle. Gazelle acted as the director of this part of the front, moving different units in the air like game pieces. Up high, it was like floating over a map table. She recognized the zigzag entrenchments of the front lines and pictured the zones of responsibility of the different Red Army formations Shepel had gone through the day before.

The chief of staff was the most welcoming person Aelya had met so far in the 497th. While Muromets had been friendly enough, he always acted as though he was following orders. Shepel acted as if he didn't care about orders, so if he was friendly, he meant it. He'd worked in a lot of practical advice between all the situational reports and day-to-day operational details. When he sat the squadron down in ops, he showed them his hands, blocky and unnatural, like those of a giant ogre.

"Everyone asks me about these, so I'll get it out of the way," he said. "Back when we were supposed to be chummy with Fritz, I took part in an Air Force exchange program. Sometime in '36, someone high up decided we weren't supposed to be friends anymore. I was given a lengthy vacation in Luby-anka. Any of you seen the place? Beautiful building. The NKVD has good taste in architecture. They say it's the tallest building in Moscow, because you can see Siberia from the basement. After a while, they decided they needed experienced Air Force officers more than another enemy of the people. But as a souvenir, they took a hammer to my knuckles so I'd never fly again."

After that, Shepel simply moved on to the first topic, leaving Aelya taken aback. What was she supposed to make of that information? He was an enemy of the people, here in the midst of those charged with defending them. But hadn't Sveta been one as well?

"Stitches," she said, tapping his shoulder, "what do you think of Shepel? I mean, does he know what he's talking about?"

"He's a smart man. If the regiment is a plane, then Red's the pilot and Shepel's the crew chief. He knows how everything works under the cowling."

"He says I should hide my Komsomol badge in my boot."

"That's in case you get captured. The Nazis will kill you right away if they find that."

"I thought we weren't supposed to get captured. You know, shoot ourselves."

"What if you go unconscious or something? What if your gun jams?"

"Would you do it? If you had one bullet left?"

She knew she was being morbid, but everything she thought about lately involved death. When she climbed into the cockpit and looked at the gunsight, she remembered the bullet passing her head. She thought about Klava. Worst of all, she kept thinking about Tonya and a blood-filled turret. Could she do it when the time came? Was that why she kept missing?

"I like to think it's best to live to fight another day. Lots of downed pilots end up joining the partisans. Anyway, there's no telling what you'll do until it actually happens. If you girls aren't ready for that, maybe you shouldn't be here."

"We're ready," she snapped without thinking. The engine's pistons thumped in lockstep with the tension as she simmered over his attitude.

"You paying attention?" he said. "Memorize the landscape. Burn it into your mind. It won't always be this sunny, and that extra bit of knowledge might save your life."

She leaned back and focused on connecting the scenery below with what was on her maps. Flat, grassy terrain, cut with many rivers stretching to every horizon. She hated being a passenger, but that couldn't stop her from taking in all that she loved about flying: shadows cast by intermittent clouds distorting the landscape, the sway of the plane, the thrum of the engine.

He was right; it required the utmost concentration not to get lost under these calm conditions, let alone during combat. Far off, dark clouds of smoke marked the one unmistakable feature: the ruined city of Stalingrad.

"So what's your background?" Stitches asked. "When did you decide to fly?"

"I'm supposed to be watching the landscape."

"I'm testing you. A good pilot pays attention to multiple things at once." He laughed.

"Now you're interested in my story? I thought I didn't have enough missions."

He turned his face so she could see his strained smile. "Much as I hate to admit it, I saw enough during that interception. You're not without skill."

"Thanks, I guess." Was he telling her to be proud of herself? That was patronizing. The more she thought about it, the worse her performance had seemed.

"I don't doubt your ability," Stitches continued, "but combat's not just about being good. Only luck will determine when you go out. Whether you get shot down next week or make it through this war without a scratch, the odds are the same."

He seemed happy to hear himself talk. Stitches was a veteran. With four confirmed kills, he was almost an ace. She shifted to the edge of her seat, gripped with the urge to take advantage of this moment of openness.

"I probably could have done better." A lot better. "Any suggestions?"

"It's impossible to know what's going on with so many planes in the air. Half the time I have no clue what anyone else is doing. To be honest, I have no idea how well you did, but that you dived into a swarm of Junkers and came out all right speaks well of you."

"Wait . . . you saw enough to confirm I damaged one, right?"

"Caught me in a lie, I'm afraid."

She slapped him on the shoulder. "I don't need your pity."

"It's not pity." He lowered his voice, and she strained to hear him over the canopy rattling against the wind. "It's what we do for each other. Everyone plays up their numbers. Damaged planes don't count for anything anyway, just kills. If you added up all the planes we say we shoot up each month, it would be more than all the planes in Europe."

She had to calm down. Although it seemed patronizing, she realized that Stitches's little lie meant she was one of the group. In some small way, she belonged.

"To be honest," she said, "I barely hit anything before using up my ammo. Any ideas how to get better?"

"Practise?"

"Thanks, that's very helpful. Doesn't matter—I'm a crack shot in practice."

"Do you hit the towed targets every time?"

"Yes."

"When you fire in combat, do your tracers always fall behind the target?"

"How did you know?"

Stitches chuckled. "When you practise, you're tracking the plane towing the target and not the target itself, aren't you? That messes up your range. You fire too early and don't lead your target enough. Don't feel bad, it happens to a lot of yellow-mouths," he said, using the pejorative for new pilots. "Just wait until you're close enough to see the rivets in the enemy plane—then fire."

"But if I wait to get that close, won't they have a chance to hit me?"

"Not if you get your positioning right. That's the difference between an ace and a dead man. Positioning. And luck."

Suddenly it was all making sense, although it didn't explain why Roza or Tonya had no issues hitting their targets.

"So it's not some sort of mental block? I thought I was going mad," she said.

"It doesn't hurt to be mad in this line of work."

He banked the plane to the right and pointed out a thin line on the ground between two clouds. "That's the 466th's airfield. Let's pay them a visit."

He began to circle in a gradual descent.

"Shouldn't we call in, let them know we're friendly?"

"Nah, we shouldn't really be this far over anyway. Better to do this quick and get out."

Aelya gripped the sides of the cockpit tightly. Stitches seemed emboldened to prove his madness. She braced for a storm of flak bursts as they broke below cloud cover and descended, almost as if they were landing. He continued going low, down to a few metres off the ground, then throttled the engine, roaring down the runway. He waggled the wings in greeting as they passed the tower. They were close enough to the ground crews that she could make out surprised expressions and head scratches. Within seconds they were climbing at full power.

"See? Their anti-aircraft gunners are really going to get it for sleeping on the job. Chew on that, 466th! We hate them. Just kidding—not really."

After she collected herself, she understood the thrill they'd both gotten from that stunt. It was like being back in the aeroclub—just enough danger and illicit moves without being full-on terrifying.

"To answer your question," she said, "I never really decided to fly. I was born knowing I'd fly. I'm not trying to be arrogant. My parents are both aviation engineers, so there was never any question."

He remained silent.

"Your turn," she said.

"I started out in aeroclub. It was just something I wanted to join. I don't think there was any one thing that made me want to fly. It was just the thing every kid wanted to do back then. I got drafted in '40, and because I was an aeroclubber it made sense to put me in the Air Force."

"You don't sound overly enthusiastic."

"I really love it here, though maybe I don't show it. I get a bit . . . sad sometimes thinking about what else I could have been doing."

"What else do you want to be doing?"

"Nothing. That's the point. I had absolutely nothing better to do with my life back in Magnitogorsk. And after seeing the country, I realize how much of a hole of a town that place was."

"You still have family there?"

"I'm an orphan." He said this in a practised way. "What about your family? I hear you're from Smolensk."

"Yes. They got out all right. Being aviation engineers, my parents were evacuated along with my sister and babushka."

"Lucky you." She couldn't see his face, and over the din of the engine she couldn't guess at his tone, but something made her think he was full of bitterness.

The radio crackled to life. It was Gazelle Station. "Maple Tree has fallen within range of enemy artillery. Repeat, Maple Tree is hot. Fly immediately to backup airfield designated Maple Two."

"Copy that, Gazelle. We're combat ready. Any assistance required over Maple One's airspace?" said Stitches.

"Negative. This is a precautionary evacuation."

Stitches signed off, then made it a test for Aelya to navigate to the new airfield. Recalling Shepel's orientation information, she flipped through the map booklet to find the backup airfield marked with a circled red X and a number 2. She looked out the window to get her bearings. "That round hill down there, with that one tall tree growing out the top . . . that's Hill 206, isn't it?"

"Very good, Senior Sergeant."

"Then we need to head on bearing one-one-five for thirty-five kilometres. How much fuel do we have?" They had been flying for well over an hour.

"Uh-oh." Stitches called in for permission to refuel at their old airfield, only ten kilometres away, but it was denied since everything was already being packed up. "Typical," he said. "Not urgent enough to fight, too urgent to refuel. These gauges always have a bit extra, so I think we'll have enough."

He turned the plane in its new heading immediately and climbed very slightly, hoping for enough height if and when the fuel ran out.

"Your navigation skills are excellent," he said. "You should apply for advanced navigation training. Every squadron needs a good navigator."

"Not sure I want to be a pilot navigator. Would I have to be angry all the time like Red?"

Stitches laughed. "You're definitely a keeper."

Aelya estimated the engine would give out around ten kilometres short of their destination, but it lasted until they were eight kilometres away. They were high enough that he could circle the new airfield and come in for a proper landing. This was all routine. Aelya had flown deadstick landings as a precaution back in her aeroclub days. Nothing to it. Stitches made a point of quizzing her about everything he should handle differently, but aside from a few tweaks, it was almost like a regular landing.

Or it would have been if not for the nosed-over Yak-1 halfway down the runway.

Maple Two only gave out a warning as they were already coming in. Stitches had to pull up at the last moment, just enough not to lose control of their approach. The plane jolted as the tail caught something while clearing the wrecked fighter. It came down hard on its tail first, then the two main wheels, and skidded sideways. With no way to steer on the ground, Stitches and Aelya held on tightly as they spun. They were slow enough that the plane ground to a halt and listed toward the left. They threw themselves against the right wall of the cockpit and the plane settled down to level.

Ground crew were already rushing out to get them.

Stitches immediately unbuckled his straps and threw open the canopy. "Get out now! Fuel's not the only thing that might catch fire."

He threw his legs smoothly over the side of the cockpit and dismounted like a gymnast from a pommel horse. She was nowhere near as graceful, and as he tried to grab on to her legs, her belt caught on something and she fell into him, sending them sprawling in the dirt.

"Are you all right?" he said, quickly getting to his feet and helping her up.

Her heart was racing. It was such a surprise, she was full of adrenalin. Would she even know if she were hurt? She brushed the dirt off her uniform and looked at Stitches. They were standing close, and suddenly, with the ground crew blocked from view by the plane, she urgently needed to kiss him.

She had no idea what she was doing. She just put her arms around his neck and planted her lips on his. It lasted uncomfortably long. Then she pulled away suddenly, feeling regret.

"Sorry, that was embarrassing."

"No, no . . ."

"Let's never talk about that again."

"Right."

"It never happened."

"What happened?"

"Exactly."

CHAPTER 35: SHELTER

"Not this one," said Yulia.

Aelya looked over the contents of the truck. Its back was piled high with electric fans. Great. Just in time for the turn away from summer weather. She sighed, scanning the last two trucks parked at the crossroads of Urmanovsk village.

"Why are we doing this again?" asked Yulia.

"We need to find our personal gear."

"No, why are we stuck slogging through this mess while the others are twiddling their thumbs?"

Aelya tried to ignore the edge of snobbery in Yulia's tone. It brought her back to Engels, when being the only one from Smolensk among mostly Muscovite and Leningrader pilots had felt more acute.

Yulia added, "I'm sure it's because we've been tagged as juniors."

Aelya didn't like the sound of that, not least because she detected a bit of truth in it. She consoled herself that it must have felt worse for Yulia. Even her twin treated her like a child.

"Would you rather be cleaning up the gymnasium with everyone else?"

Neither of them wanted to be back in their new makeshift barracks. Yulia needed to keep busy so she could forget to blame herself for Yusupov's death. She had been supposed to land last, but Yusupov directed the pilots he had been training to land first. Then he glided in on low fuel, hit a rut on landing, and nosed over. Like a good fighter pilot, his shoulder harness was undone, so he smashed his head against the instrument panel. The leather helmet had been no better than a fashion accessory.

Aelya needed the fresh air, away from the caustic barbs accusing her of abandoning the old airfield with Stitches. She'd done nothing wrong, but she told herself it was only natural for the others to vent. Especially Roza.

The relocation had been a shambles, the regiment completely inoperative for two days. Supplies were so reduced that the number of planes available at any one time was never more than a handful. Worse still, personnel had gone missing. Even with the training and scouting craft, only so many could be transferred by air, and arrangements to move the rest by ground were inconsistent.

Sleepy turned up a day late, forced to hitchhike with five different trucks to get to the new base. Nemchinov, Stitches's crew chief, wound up at another air base, fifty kilometres away. He was stranded there with Ulanova, Stitches's armourer. Apparently, Nemchinov missed the truck he was supposed to take because he didn't want to be separated from Ulanova. That was when Aelya learned the two were in love. It was hard to imagine the fearsome Ulanova, who still hadn't warmed to the new arrivals, being in love with anyone.

Dangers abounded on the road. A convoy from the support battalion strayed too close to the fighting and came under fire. In the panic, one of the trucks crashed into a mud bog, killing two and wounding two. Shepel seemed less concerned over the casualties than the fact that the truck had taken a lot of critical electrical parts with it. Most distressing for Sparrow Squadron was that Oksana still wasn't accounted for.

Aelya and Yulia had no luck with the final two trucks at the centre of town, although they at least managed to redirect a shipment of wing fabric to their nearby airfield. They spoke with a driver, who suggested checking out the southern end of the village, which was acting as a sort of supply depot.

Urmanovsk was a farming collective renamed for some local hero of the Revolution. Its main road was situated on one of the arteries for the northern flank of the Stalingrad battle zone. It was packed with soldiers, mostly in a terrible state—dishevelled or injured, their eyes glazed. Although some residents had fled, contrary to Stalin's orders, the huge numbers of refugees from lands to the west overrun by the Germans more than made up for this.

Picking their way through the crowds, they reached the edge of the village. Piles of goods had been simply dumped at the side of the road. Aelya climbed a mountain of crates.

"I see some trunks over there," she said.

Sure enough, they soon accounted for seven trunks of personal effects. They quickly cajoled a peasant couple to transport their goods in an oxcart to the other end of the village.

Atop the trunks in the cart, Yulia whispered to Aelya, "They don't seem happy about it."

Glancing at the couple, Aelya wondered what misfortunes they had encountered before winding up here. "They're not used to all this," she said. As if she or Yulia had become used to death and destruction either.

The mood at Yusupov's funeral had reinforced Aelya's earlier suspicions that a woman's death was treated differently. Petrushka's cracks about Yusupov's valiant, fatal interception of two rocks and a drainage ditch went over much better than his previous attempts at funereal humour. Yusupov was also a veteran, an original from June 1941. He knew what this life at the front was all about. He'd have been disappointed if the regiment hadn't tried to laugh about it.

The humour was necessary. Inactivity bred tension. Given what was going on in Stalingrad itself—the Red Army hanging on to a tiny sliver of land on the banks of the Volga, rumours rife of the NKVD machine-gunning whole battalions of their own men when they tried to retreat—a sense of shame hung over the pilots and crew. This was officially called a strategic relocation, but it felt like defeat. Aelya worried tensions would boil over. Red tried to keep them busy. With not even a hint of combat, everyone concentrated their efforts on bringing the air base up to standard. Because it was a backup airfield, only the most basic facilities had been built.

The village had a number of collective buildings, such as a small school, which was where the women pilots were billeted. It was of modern brick construction, with toilet and shower facilities, but neither were currently working. It wasn't clear if they ever had been. Bunks were set up in the gymnasium. The situation was unimaginably luxurious compared to conditions in the rest of Urmanovsk.

"You girls are heroes." Olga gave her sister and Aelya a hug when they returned, then helped drag the heavy trunks of personal effects down from the wagon.

The other pilots were busy sprucing up their new quarters. Tonya was painting a geometric design on the walls, which she insisted was the latest trend in America. Everyone eagerly opened up the trunks. Aelya kept back and approached her own bed.

Next to the bunk she'd chosen, a small wire-haired tan-and-white mutt sat, eagerly chewing something. It had been found living on the school grounds, and Masha had unofficially adopted it. Tonya had named it Volkov, in a fit of spite over their former commander, and no one objected. Volkov was tearing apart some pages of a book. She looked at her jacket hung over the side of the bunk; the breast pocket where she always kept *Aelita* was empty.

"Get away!" she shouted at the dog. She stomped her feet near it, but rather than growling, Volkov seemed to shrug and clawed at the pages some more. The others were laughing and she picked up a stray page. On closer inspection, she realized it was from some children's novel about a horse.

"Very funny," she said. "Where is it?"

Roza flung the precious novel at her head, and she barely caught it, managing to avoid a black eye. Roza's look had a hint of malice. She was still sore about having to cram with Tonya and Olga into one little U-2 to escape the old airfield. What was Aelya supposed to have done about it? Nonetheless, it was a sore spot that she had effectively abandoned her comrades.

"If it's supposed to be not one step back, why weren't you shot?" Roza had asked, only half jokingly.

She ignored Roza. Her crew chief Oksana was still missing and she needed to let that anxiety boil over. Aelya sat down on her bunk and flipped open the cover of her book. Yura's letter was still folded up in there. She closed it and returned it to her breast pocket.

After hitching a ride on one of the vehicles that passed through Urmanovsk in a near-constant stream, Aelya disembarked at the airfield. She struggled to keep the pile of blankets upright in her arms. As it wobbled, she put a hand on top to keep a bottle of perfume from falling. The whole pile began to topple until a girl rushed up to brace it.

"Thanks," Aelya said.

The girl was about ten years old, part of a pack of a dozen kids, along with a few dogs, who were listlessly hanging around the margins of the airfield. The girl offered to help and she accepted. The technicians' quarters didn't have much, so Lara gathered up some extra bedding from the pilots' barracks to donate. Olga and Yulia pitched in with some perfume their family had sent, so the techs could freshen up their bunks. Tonya conspicuously refused to give up her mirror, even though the gymnasium already had tall mirrors of its own along one wall. Feeling the need to be doing something, Aelya had volunteered to take everything over.

As Aelya got a look at the girl, she remembered the first day the regiment arrived here, when an orphaned girl had spat on the ground. She didn't think much of pilots. When the Air Force had taken over her old hometown, the Luftwaffe bombed it, killing the rest of her family. Aelya worried this was the same girl but couldn't be sure.

An army of civilians was all over the airfield. Armed with spades, picks, and their bare hands, they were digging out bunkers, trenches, and gun pits. Large numbers of passing refugees clustered as well, hoping to contribute to the building efforts, if only to get their hands on military rations.

Passing through the work gangs, Aelya felt she as if was travelling through one of the propaganda posters hanging in Dmitriev's office. Soviet workers, young and old, all banding together. In this moment, that vision actually resonated with her. For all her suffering, a young girl was willing to lend a hand, along with so many others, contributing in their own ways. This was what she was defending: the people.

They arrived at the barracks for the women technicians, which was little more than a hole in the ground covered in camouflage netting. Still, some rudimentary wooden bunks had been set up, so Aelya left the blankets and perfume there and said goodbye to the girl.

None of the technicians were around, just old men putting up planking to brace the sides of the bunker. They stopped briefly when they saw her. They wore ragged clothes and looked decrepit. One of them glanced at another and shook his head, saying, "What have we come to?" The other man muttered something about women, and then they all continued working.

She walked out to escape the air of hostility. She couldn't be angry with them; for men of the older generations, it must have been enfeebling to have someone like Aelya defending them. It was the same sort of shame she herself felt watching battered infantry retreating while she fussed about living conditions, waiting for airplane parts to arrive. Thinking about the old men, she wondered if her father's opposition to her joining the VVS stemmed from a similar resentment.

"Hello, Mars."

Aelya straightened herself as she turned to face Stitches. She hesitated awkwardly, then exchanged a salute.

"Helping get our base up to scratch?" he said.

"Yes."

"Very good. Good job."

This was the way things had gone since that . . . she didn't want to think about it. He was very proper. Too proper, as though he was restraining his natural impishness. She could only think she had diminished herself in his eyes.

"Keep busy," he said.

As she turned to go on her way, not sure what she should be doing, Stitches caught her by the shoulder. "Don't go that way. Red will see you. He's giving out bad assignments like digging out latrines. Wants us to set an example for the people." He pointed her in the other direction. "I'm sure someone needs help over there."

She smiled and they parted. That was better.

Walking away, she nearly stumbled into a boy. He was standing still while everyone else was moving, so she'd expected him to get out of her way.

"I'm sorry," she said. "Are you looking for someone?"

The boy said nothing and didn't even look at her. He had cropped blond hair and skin so pale beneath dirty splotches, it looked ashen. Her nose wrinkled at his stench, noticeable even for a refugee. His eyes, creased all around, looked as if they belonged to an old man, though he must have been fourteen at the most. He focused on something behind her. She looked back. There was nothing of note.

Muromets tapped her on the arm and pulled her aside. "You won't get anywhere with him," he whispered. "He's gone."

"Gone?"

"Refugees found him wandering on the road heading away from the front lines, reeking of dung. Some brave soul who recognized him went back to check on his village. The Germans had been there. Gunned down all the adults. The boy must have hidden in a manure pile in a barn while all this happened."

"What about the rest of the children?"

Muromets shrugged.

She tried to block out all the horrific stories she'd been inundated with about what the Nazis did to ordinary people. Hearing one after the other had been draining, but now, with those boy's eyes piercing right through her, she struggled not to imagine vivid details of what could have happened. German logic was unfailing. If they wanted the children for slave labour, why not take the adults too? What else could they have done with the children? Stop it, she told herself.

"Air raid!" someone shouted. A bell began to ring.

Screams arose from all sides. Civilians scattered in every direction while uniformed soldiers tried to corral them into trenches. Others scrambled to get the camouflage netting up.

Aelya immediately looked to the skies, scanning for danger.

Muromets tugged on her sleeve. "Come on!"

She spotted a lone dot, high up and to the southwest, just breaking cloud cover. She ran with Muromets toward a trench, staying in a low crouch even as she reassured herself it was far off, probably headed elsewhere. They both dropped into a trench crowded with people piled on top of each other. Young children were screaming and sobbing.

She peered up again. More dots now, about ten or so. They were too high up to make out any sort of shape. Perhaps it wasn't even the enemy. In any case, she hoped the camouflage was set up well, or they might be getting more visits from the Luftwaffe.

The anti-aircraft guns opened up. Streams of tracers streaked upward while the bigger guns boomed and puffs of white flak bursts appeared near the intruders.

In the corner of her eye, Aelya saw the boy standing out where she had left him. She ran over as new, louder explosions shook the ground. Bombs, each one closer than the last.

"Let's go!" she shouted at the boy, grabbing his arms. He remained rooted on the spot. She wrapped him in a bear hug and pulled, only succeeding in bringing both of them to the ground. His eyes never wavered, staring outward. She looked to the trench, about to call for Muromets, but he was already running to them.

A bomb struck the other end of the airstrip, sending a fountain of dirt up into the sky. She wished dearly she could get into a fighter and hit back, but not a single plane was available. Where were those idiots from the 466th? It was their job to cover while they were inoperative.

Muromets got to her, and together they dragged the boy by his shoulders toward the trench.

Another bomb burst, thankfully on an empty field, but close enough that they stumbled from the shock wave. A thump followed behind them. They were almost at the trench when a supply dump exploded. Hands reached out from the trench and they awkwardly rolled in, landing on the people huddled there. The ground shook with another thump.

Aelya held her breath, as if any movement might bring a bomb screaming right at her from kilometres away. More explosions, but farther now. She dared to peek out.

The half-finished technicians' barracks had been struck near its side, collapsing one wall. The damage should have been much worse. An unexploded bomb, perhaps. Beyond that and the burning supply dump, the facility seemed largely unharmed.

Only then did she hear the distant whine of Yak fighters as the 466th finally arrived. The enemy bombers were already heading home as fast as possible.

"Oh, well done!" she shouted at the sister regiment. "Just a few minutes late, but who's counting?"

People began to clear out of the trench, just so they could breathe, before the bell rang the all-clear.

Muromets dusted himself off. "We were lucky," he said.

"Not lucky," said Aelya. "The enemy was lazy or scared. It was their luck they even managed to hit anything from that height."

They quickly moved among the civilians who'd been hiding in the trench. There were a few bumps and bruises and sprained ankles. Several children were crying. Aelya put her arm around a little girl who didn't seem to have anyone else. She was about six, with a white linen dress that made her look like a doll. She squealed loudly as Aelya hugged her. She had a deep red gash down one leg. Muromets had noticed as well.

He scooped her up in his arms. "I'll find Dr. Krupenya. Stay here and check on anyone else who's hurt."

She felt a twinge of resentment at taking orders from a pencil pusher, even though he outranked her, but she immediately chided herself for her pettiness.

She watched him carry the girl away, impressed at seeing this compassionate side of him.

She looked over everyone around her and ascertained that they were all right, then remembered the boy she'd left in the trench. He sat back against the wall of dirt, staring. He seemed unharmed, physically at least.

"Thank goodness," she said. "You really need to look after yourself."

He didn't respond to her offer of a hand, so she sat down in the trench next to him.

"Listen, I can't imagine what you're going through." What a mindless platitude, she thought. Breathing deeply, she struggled to think of some way to shake this boy out of his trance. She remembered how she'd felt after seeing Sveta kill herself.

"You know, there was a time when I was sort of like how you are. I . . . I didn't think I cared about myself." She put a hand on his shoulder.

He still didn't react.

"I was wrong. I'd forgotten about life. But after everything, I want to live. It's confusing in times like these, but we can't forget life is worth something. Once there was a time when flying didn't mean looking over my shoulder for death coming at me. I want to experience that again. Is there something you want to live for too?"

Nothing.

"Maybe that's my problem," she said. "I want to live too much."

She pounded a fist into the dirt. "I'm sorry. I'm supposed to defend you, but I haven't done a very good job so far. I'm a lousy shot. I couldn't even remember to fire. I wet myself. I'm a failure."

She looked at him. At least he wasn't judgmental.

"Maybe after the war, I'll take you flying. You need to experience that. Live for that."

A peasant woman called from the lip of the trench. "Stop wasting your time. Just get him up."

Together, they pulled the boy out of the trench. Other refugees soon embraced him and took him away. The whole time, his eyes never stopped staring at some invisible horror.

CHAPTER 36: LARCENY

The photographer motioned for Aelya to shift to her left, and she nudged Tonya, Masha, and Lara as if she were a freight train in a shunting yard.

"Perfect," he called out as he snapped a picture. The camera focused on the bomber regiment's officers and commissar, Dmitriev among them, framed by the reinforced structures of Koshkar air base. On the fringes of the group, Aelya wondered if she would even appear in this snap.

The photo session broke up, with the bomber regiment's commissar guiding the news crew on a tour of their airfield and its impressive hexagonal concrete grid runway.

"Has this visit from my Sparrow Squadron met all your expectations?" Dmitriev asked the bomber commander and his deputy. The commander pulled Dmitriev aside for a quiet chat.

Aelya rolled her eyes. They had been used as bait to lure the news crew from *Red Star*, the military newspaper. Now the bomber officers would get positive exposure that would help when the next round of promotions and awards were handed out. If that was the price for getting two of their own back, so be it. This was the base where Nemchinov and Ulanova had wound up, and the bomber regiment decided that, with a shortage of skilled technicians, they didn't want to give them back. When the deal had been struck, Dmitriev was so elated by showing off his clout with the media, he'd even driven the truck over himself.

One of the officers waved the women over to speak with them. He singled out Roza, Tonya, and Olga, and when Aelya stepped forward, he put a hand up. She shrugged. Standing around not doing much on a different airfield was an improvement over being stuck on their own airfield, standing around, not doing much. There had been no more air raids. The Luftwaffe was concentrating all its efforts over Stalingrad, where the beleaguered Red Army defenders were trading lives for time. The battle was close enough now that when the wind blew north, it brought the smoke and dust of the dead city with it. Making things worse, the showers weren't working and so couldn't wash the acridity away.

For the pilots of Sparrow Squadron, the frustration of inactivity was compounded by their still not having been given any normal duties, just ground-based training. Red told them that the active combat pilots took priority over them for maintaining their skills. Lara was a convenient target for her squadron's ire, which she took quietly, always reassuring them she was working on something.

The officers surrounded the three women they'd called over. Something in the way they stood put Aelya on edge.

"I don't like this," said Lara.

She approached Dmitriev and the bomber commander. An agitated discussion followed. The commander made a gesture to an enlisted man with a submachine gun, who jogged away into the warren of support buildings on the base.

In the meantime, Roza squeezed her way out of the press after pinching a cheek playfully. Still smiling at the men and waving, Roza said to Aelya, "There are some real wolves here. We'll have to make a break for it."

The enlisted man returned, Nemchinov and Ulanova trailing behind him.

"That's better," said Lara as she rejoined the group.

"What's going on?" Aelya wondered.

"I asked Dmitriev if he was a commissar or a procurer."

Stitches's crew chief gushed in relief and shook the hands of each of the pilots, as if they were liberators. Ulanova was sullen, as always, but exchanged a look with Aelya and nodded slightly. It was as close to a thanks as any of them would get and a sign they were all joined together in some way now. They'd all suffered losses. Oksana was still missing—dead, or worse, captured by the Germans.

The exchange done, Aelya didn't want to hang around one more minute. Tonya continued holding court, drawing laughs with her flirtatiousness.

A water tanker truck rumbled to a halt at the side of the motor pool area where they had been loitering.

"Perfect," said Masha. "Let's see if this guy will put the hose on so we can shower."

A driver emerged, looking at a clipboard and scratching his head. Roza narrowed her eyes at the truck.

"I know that look," Aelya said.

Roza glanced at her, arching an eyebrow. "Didn't Eisenach say we need a tanker truck to fill up the reservoir for our showers?"

"Yeah, I think that would do the trick," Masha said.

Roza caught Tonya's attention, then made some elaborate hand signals. Tonya nodded and returned her attention to the men.

"You two are getting chummy," Aelya said.

"She's proving useful," Roza shrugged. She approached the driver.

"Any idea where this is supposed to go?" he said. "I need someone to sign for this."

"Yes, it's a very busy time," said Roza. "Some big to-do with a news crew. We need this thing over in Urmanovsk. We're moving out there now. Isn't that right, Nemchinov?"

Nemchinov didn't miss a beat. "Yes, that's right."

"Roza, are you crazy?" Aelya whispered.

The driver eyed them suspiciously, then looked over their shoulders as Lara approached, straightening up as he saw the officer's insignia on her collar. Roza elbowed Aelya and moved over to stand in front of Lara.

"Right," Roza said loudly. "We better get a move on. They were expecting this in Urmanovsk already. Shall we move out, Comrade Major?" She looked over at Dmitriev and waved. He waved back. Tonya had a protective arm around Olga as they extracted themselves from the cordon of men. The officers waved and hurried their way around a supply shed.

Tonya beamed at Roza. "I told them to freshen up and that I'd round up the rest of the girls for a party in the repair shop."

"That's disgusting," said Aelya, catching Tonya's seductive tone.

"You're just upset they didn't pick you."

The driver nosed his way in front of Lara. "Comrade Lieutenant, can you sign for this?"

Lara looked at Aelya. Her eyes were wide, but with the driver close by, she said nothing. Lara picked up his pen, looking from Aelya to Roza. "Tell you what, let's get to Urmanovsk first. Then our chief of staff can do it."

The driver groaned.

Roza tapped him on the shoulder. "Come on, let's get a move on." She hustled among the pilots, motioning for them to go. "Get the truck, Mars."

"Roza . . ."

"No one's signed for it yet. Stuff goes missing all the time. Don't be a spoilsport. These perverts deserve to be had."

Aelya ran over to the truck with the other pilots. She glanced over at the bomber commander, who was already catching up with the news crew, oblivious to what was happening in the motor pool. Sweat dripped from her forehead as she got into the driver's seat. What was she doing here?

"Wait a minute—I can't drive," she said.

"What the hell," said Masha. She pushed Aelya out of the seat and started the engine.

Dmitriev and Tonya barely caught up as the truck pulled away from the motor pool, pausing briefly to let the tanker through first. Roza was sitting in the cab, with the liberated couple, Ulanova and Nemchinov, riding the running board. Roza leaned out the window and made an obscene gesture toward the air base.

"I really don't approve of that," said Dmitriev. "And why on earth are they riding in a tanker?"

"Comrade Commissar," Aelya said, "do you know what they'll print in *Red Star*?"

Dmitriev brightened immediately and gushed about what a success this trip was. Word of "his" Sparrow Squadron was spreading across the front. Aelya smiled and nodded along.

When they returned to Urmanovsk, they cajoled the driver into taking a victory lap around the airfield. The rousing cheers of the pilots and technicians made Aelya wonder if winning the war would be celebrated as much. She revelled in their welcome. These were their boys.

"I'm going to paint a dedication to Oksana on the side of the truck," said Tonya.

"Show some respect," said Lara.

Tonya shrugged. "The whole regiment will bow down to this every time it fills up the shower tanks. I'd take that over a tomb in Red Square."

They piled out and were mobbed by Ulanova's women comrades, eager to bring their unofficial leader back into the fold. New technicians and old now mingled as one. The clamour was only drowned out by a training flight coming in to land. Stitches emerged to give a hearty hug to his crew. He also congratulated the women on their acquisition before introducing his training partner, a new addition from Armenia named Demirdjian.

"You took this new guy up already?" said Roza.

Before Aelya or the others could turn to Lara, she was already on her way to see Red.

CHAPTER 37: THE CHALLENGE

Flying at low altitude limited the vertical space for manoeuvres and made the ground a factor in everything. It was a consideration that mucked up practised tactics. Just what combat was supposed to be like.

The two pairs of planes circled each other, trying to look for any weakness in their opponents. Aelya watched Roza, keeping one eye on her and one on the enemy. Even knowing her six o'clock was clear, she practised the instinct to check behind anyway.

Lara had been toying with the idea of switching their assignments and took this occasion to experiment. Roza was number one and Aelya was wingman. Perhaps it made sense. In their two previous combat encounters, Roza had pretty much taken the lead. More accurately, she had just done what she wanted and Aelya was forced to follow. And it seemed to work.

It was worth a shot. Win this challenge and they'd finally be accepted into the regiment. Lose to Stitches and Petrushka, and they'd be sent back to the 586th. That was the deal Lara had struck with Red.

"Let's mix in a barrel roll. Follow me," Roza ordered.

They moved in tandem, almost by instinct, as they chased the men in the air above Urmanovsk. They knew exactly the angle they wanted to get on their prey and, by climbing and rolling, they slowed and tightened their turn to get in behind their opponents. But Stitches and his wingman were too experienced to be caught out and broke in the opposite direction, looping back to threaten getting on their tail.

Roza climbed quickly with Aelya following.

"Don't you wish you'd dropped the two machine guns now?" Roza said.

Aelya said nothing. This demotion was aggravating, even if it made sense. She forced herself not to think about it and be aware of the now.

After opening a bit of space on their pursuers, Roza said, "Let them gain on us. Remember what we talked about?"

Before they'd taken off for this simulated dogfight, they discussed just what they would do in this situation. Aelya had accepted her role. She needed to be a good member of the team. Part of her could just barely admit that Roza was a better combat pilot. She certainly had an aggression few others had, something Aelya felt she could never match. That aggression might also get her in trouble. As wingman, Aelya would cover for that.

She lined up just behind and to the right of Roza, readying herself, both planes following an undulating path to keep the men from lining them up too easily as they closed the distance.

This was what the fight boiled down to: in the next minute or so, one pilot would lock another in a firing line for the requisite second and a half to register the "kill" and be halfway to winning the challenge.

"Let's do it," said Roza.

The two women broke into the weave they had practised so many times before, Roza going high, Aelya going low, crossing paths and forcing their pursuers to either split or drop one target from sight.

Both men pursued Aelya. She glanced behind, using a dive and turn to just keep Stitches at bay, jinking furiously and twisting her head from side to side to keep checking behind her. Somewhere farther back, Petrushka had peeled off to avoid being caught by Roza, but it hadn't worked.

Seconds later, Maple Tree's familiar voice said, "Petrushka is down, Petrushka is down. Exit the zone."

Curses followed over the radio.

Stitches picked up speed, closing fast on Aelya to try and get a quick kill. She was so low now that she had to either turn or climb, and he could catch her either way as she exposed her plane to his guns.

She climbed in the one direction with any escape, straight toward the sun, blinding her pursuer. She looked back. Stitches had broken off, now worried about Roza, whose plane screamed down toward him. He did what Roza had done that first time they'd faced Messers, turning to go at her head-on.

The simulation rules didn't allow head-on kills to avoid collisions in this sort of situation. But breaking early would make a fighter vulnerable. By now, Aelya knew both pilots were so competitive, they'd rather crash than back down.

Aelya dived back into an attack angle on Stitches. "Roza, break now, I have this." Trust me, I'm your wingman, she thought.

Roza pulled her plane out of her collision course. Stitches pulled in the opposite direction, not willing to risk a crash either.

He pulled a tight turn at lower speed to try to get Aelya to overshoot. She pulled hard on the stick, pitching her plane upward and arcing above him. She rolled her plane, her body lifting out of her seat. G-forces pulled on her eyeballs, tinging her sight with red.

There he was. She almost pushed the trigger levers by instinct, then remembered the guns weren't charged because this was a simulation. A second and a half with Stitches in her sight was enough.

"Good kill, Mars, good kill."

Levelling out, Roza pulled alongside her. "Time for a victory roll?"

They buzzed the airfield simultaneously, doubtless drawing the ire of Red.

Back on the ground, the women gathered around their two planes before they'd even rolled to a stop. Rising to stand astride the cockpit, Aelya let out a celebratory scream. The elation reminded her of the welcome after that first combat with Air Defence, only that time knowing the bullet had nearly hit her head muted her enjoyment.

"That was some slick flying, Mars," said Tonya. It was the first time she'd heard Tonya say anything genuinely nice to anyone. Masha wrapped her in a bear hug and hoisted her in the air as Volkov yapped his approval.

She met Roza halfway between their planes and they nodded at each other. Their actions in the air expressed more than words ever could.

They walked over to meet the men, who were mainly smiling and joking around. A group of pilots led by Frost linked arms and hoisted Roza up in the air and she bounced as if she was on a trampoline. After three bounces, they gave Aelya a turn. When she dismounted, she spotted Petrushka handing over a fold of rubles to Tonya. The fact that she had risked money on Aelya was an even greater compliment than anything Tonya said.

Stitches smiled awkwardly as Roza needled him. "Just so you know, you would have been dead earlier if they allowed head-on shots."

He shrugged.

"I'm coming for you. There's a new top dog in this regiment." Roza seemed almost angry.

Olga and Yulia came over to hoist Roza on their shoulders. She waved at an imaginary crowd, accepting invisible bouquets of flowers.

Stitches was visibly upset. Aelya wanted to speak with him. Don't think about the kiss, she reminded herself. They'd spoken a few times since, just routine things, but it always crossed her mind.

"Your friend has a real chip on her shoulder," he said to her.

"I guess you could say she's very motivated, in her way."

"Just watch that it doesn't get unhealthy." His shoulders were slumped.

"I'm sure you would have done better if Nemchinov had more time with your plane," she said in the most sympathetic voice she could manage. Roza made faces at him and he broke into a smirk. Aelya was being soft. She felt like a fool.

Red waded into the middle of the pilots, a sour look on his face as he met Lara.

"Comrade Commander," she said, "I think we've proven that we hit all the marks for ability, tactics, daring, and ruthlessness. Is there anything more you want out of 'real' fighter pilots?"

"Shepel."

"Yes, Comrade Commander?"

"Draw up new assignment rosters. We're putting the women into active combat duty."

CHAPTER 38: AUTUMN HARVEST

By the beginning of October, the regiment was close to fully operational, if not at full strength. Pilots flew several missions a day, though encounters were still sporadic. Orders held them back from the thick of combat. As clouds of burning oil enveloped the battlefield in a funereal shroud, they could do little to help the defenders of the city. What did it say about the VVS, the motherland's finest, most technologically advanced fighting force, that it still couldn't go head to head against the Luftwaffe?

Aelya pondered this as she sat in Dmitriev's office. She'd finally gotten her lucky number 70 plane back, only to have Zina declare that the engine had exceeded its maximum life. She was grounded until a replacement arrived. Of all the times for this to happen, it had to be just when she was going into frontline combat. It was as if some cosmic determination was made against her.

The plane hadn't proven lucky for Taras. He'd been helping to inspect the engine with his mechanic, foolishly gripping the side of the compartment, when the cowling slammed down accidentally, crushing the bones in his right hand. Dr. Krupenya had signed him off combat for good. Only after his tearful pleading had she been convinced to clear him to be a driver in a support battalion once the bones healed. He'd proven to be a lunkhead and a hopeless flyer, having never once taken a combat mission. Given how preternaturally clumsy he was and the way most truck drivers operated out here, Aelya wasn't sure Taras would be any safer when he returned. What else could he really do? He was unlikely to be able to help in his family's furniture workshop anymore.

"Makarova, pay attention," said Dmitriev, waving a pamphlet. "The duties of a Komsomol organizer are very important. I don't want to have to report your lack of diligence."

Aelya took the pamphlet, which outlined a series of activities to be regularly conducted among all the young aspiring Party members in the regiment. Dmitriev had been positively beaming with enthusiasm about this meeting. The regiment had been without a Komsomol organizer since the last one had been signed off for injury early in the summer, and the commissar had been doing double duty. Why had she been chosen for this assignment? Batyrskaya must have written something in her file about what a good little girl she was.

Her eyes glazed over and she nodded as the commissar droned through descriptions of each activity. She resented that everyone else was flying. While Aelya was stuck on the ground, Roza paired up with "Dema" Demirdjian. Masha had a new wingman as well, a beanpole of a boy from Siberia who everyone called Irkutsk. Both pairs, along with Aelya, were assigned to the new third squadron under Stitches. Lara had been passed over for squadron command and put into Red's own squadron, along with Tonya. Olga and Yulia flew for Frost, who'd taken over for Yusupov's squadron.

"Any questions?" asked Dmitriev. She shook her head. "All right, get to it. You're dismissed."

She saluted and left. What was it Dmitriev wanted her to do again? Who cared? She went straight to her revetment to check on the status of the new engine, but her crew was nowhere to be found. Wandering the aircraft shelters, she found Zina with Katya, Masha's crew chief, taking turns holding up a scrap of meat, getting Volkov to chase after it and jump over a hurdle improvised from a broom and two buckets. Back in Anisovka, both techs would have stood to attention when Aelya arrived, but here they continued laughing and cheering on the little mutt.

"What's going on with my engine, Zina?" Aelya surprised herself with the terse tone, but it felt good to be angry.

"It's on a train from Saratov."

"That's what they said yesterday."

Zina shrugged and grabbed another scrap of corned beef from an American tin.

"You can't give him that stuff," said Aelya.

"But he loves it," said Katya, as if that answered why they should be using precious lend-lease food on the dog. Volkov turned and barked at Aelya.

The growl of engines caught everyone's attention.

"It's Tonya and Usy," said Aelya.

"How can you tell from this distance?" asked Zina.

"Watch. See how smoothly Tonya lines up for landing? She always flies like it's part of an airshow. And now look at Usy. He'll drop like a rock on all three points. He only cares about shooting things up."

Sure enough, Tonya and Usy emerged from their cockpits after taxiing their planes to the revetments. Tonya threw off her helmet and immediately performed an energetic, jazzy dance. Sweat flicked away from her sopping wet black hair.

"What's that about?" asked Aelya.

"It's called the Lindy Hop, you peasant." Tonya pointed at Usy, who finished signing off the checklist with his crew chief. "How'd you like that? You make a mess of it and Honeybee cleans it up." She turned to Aelya and said loudly, "He couldn't even hit the guy coming down in his parachute."

So much for the shock from her previous battle.

"Think you'll keep dancing after I tell Dmitriev about your decadent Western celebration?" Usy replied.

Tonya laughed but stopped dancing.

A jeep rumbled to a halt near them.

Shepel was in the passenger seat. "I just got a call from an observation station. The enemy pilot bailed out not far from here. Shall we get him?"

Tonya and Usy piled in immediately. Aelya hesitated.

"Come on, Mars," said Tonya. "Ever met a German before?"

When it was put like that, Aelya had to satisfy her curiosity. She got into the rear compartment, next to the driver's submachine gun.

As the jeep started up the road from the runway, Dr. Krupenya waved them down from the side of the medical bunker. "I heard we might have a POW," she said.

"We will if we get there before the *makhras*," said Shepel.

"I better come with you, in case anyone does anything stupid."

Usy gave up his seat for the doctor and her medical kit, squeezing in the back across from Aelya. How on earth would they fit the prisoner in?

"Doc's a real bleeding heart," said Usy. "Hey doc, how much of him you think we can cut off before he bites it?"

"I don't know, but if you cut out half his brain he'd still have more than you do."

Shepel chortled loudly. Aelya froze, alarmed for a second that Usy might take out that knife that was always down his boot, but he just smiled. Had he been drinking before he flew? Muromets, who'd proven to be a fountain of information about personnel, had said a half-drunk Usy was the safest Usy.

They trundled along empty fields of grass and low scrub, Aelya hanging on to the sides of the jeep by her fingernails. It all looked so flat from up high. Tonya spotted a column of smoke, and they raced across the steppe.

The Messerschmitt Bf 109 had crashed at the edge of an unharvested wheat field, plowing a great furrow through golden-brown stalks. It lay in several pieces, fire smouldering from its nose while the main fuselage jutted up from the ground. A puddle of fuel leaked from the open end of the fuselage and soaked into the dry soil.

They ignored the possibility of an explosion so they could gawk at closer range.

Tonya whistled as she giddily pointed to several rows of swastikas painted on the side of the fuselage. "I got an ace! I got an ace!"

"There must be over forty of them," said Shepel. "I think you've avenged many comrades, Honeybee."

Usy grunted, rapping his knuckles against the aluminum skin of the cockpit. Aelya remembered seeing one of these for the first time last autumn. Now she envied how solid the German fighter looked even in death, compared to her fabric-and-wood Yak.

Shepel pulled out a pair of binoculars from the jeep. He stood on the hood, scanning the horizon.

"Who are these guys?" Tonya asked, pointing to an emblem on the nose depicting a black hand clutching a red plane.

Aelya remembered the symbol from her recognition lessons. "I Gruppe, JG 52," she said. "Must be new to the area."

"They're sending their big boys," said Usy.

Rumours buzzed all along the front about JG 52, the Luftwaffe's top fighter wing, with pilots regularly racking up kills in the dozens, possibly even into the hundreds.

"There he is," Shepel called out.

They got there in two minutes, easily spotting the crowd of infantry taking turns kicking a squirming figure in grey.

"Hold on, boys," Shepel said, hopping out before the jeep had even stopped. "This one's ours—we shot him down."

Dr. Krupenya ran over with her kit but was blocked by two soldiers. Two others pointed their submachine guns at Shepel.

A sergeant with a bent nose approached Shepel, completely heedless of being outranked. "You should have got here sooner. Now you have to wait your turn."

The driver retrieved his gun from the back of the jeep. Usy had his pistol out. Aelya felt her hand drifting to her holster even as her mind registered the insanity of shooting her own countrymen over a German.

"All right, you've had your fun," said Shepel, looking the sergeant in the eyes. "We have an interrogation to do. We need him to be able to talk. There will be a lot of disappointed people if we don't bring him back in talking condition. Understand, Sergeant?"

The sergeant spat on the ground. He eased his stance, seemingly ready to concede, but dragged out a silent pause anyway. "Fine," he finally said. "Give him some wine and take him to bed while you're at it, Fritz-lover." He signalled his men and they backed away, still brandishing their guns.

Krupenya looked over the pilot, who was conscious, wincing in pain. She said he was good enough to travel, so they hauled him into one of the back seats. Shepel took no chances and used his belt to tie the prisoner's hands. Short, with wiry muscles and brown, wispy hair, he wasn't the strapping blond Aryan Aelya had expected. The feeble shadow of a moustache covered his upper lip.

With the prisoner taking a seat, Tonya squeezed into the cargo compartment as they pulled away. The infantry jeered and made obscene gestures at them.

"They think we're soft," Tonya said.

"Probably true," said Shepel. "But the war needs all of us. Not every part of a machine needs to be forged of hardened steel."

"It's like the body," said Usy. "Some people are the hands, others are the —"

"Yes, thank you," said Shepel, knowing where this analogy was probably going.

When they returned, the prisoner was the talk of the regiment, but Krupenya kept everyone away while she bandaged and treated his injuries. The NKVD wanted their hands on him as well, but Shepel stalled them by emphasizing that they needed to glean intelligence about aerial operations first, and that required Air Force personnel. As night fell, Shepel managed to get into the guard post where the prisoner was held, bringing along Usy, Tonya, and Aelya. It seemed more like a reward for standing with him that afternoon than something that served any intelligence purpose. Krupenya insisted on coming.

Two guards stood at the back wall with submachine guns while the prisoner sat on the side of a bunk. His arm was in a sling and bandages were wrapped around his torso, his grey tunic draped across his shoulders. He looked so small and had such a soft face that Aelya thought of a teenaged classmate trying desperately to impress an older girl with his pathetic moustache. Shepel pulled up a chair and sat opposite. He began conversing in German.

After a brief exchange, Shepel said to the others, "Comrades, may I introduce you to Oberleutnant Dieter Kohlhaas. He won't tell us anything else. He's very clear about that."

"Maybe we should let Eisenach loose on him," said Usy. "She can make him an honorary Jew. I'll give her my knife."

Shepel continued his back and forth with Kohlhaas. It started out one-sided, with Shepel prodding him in fluent German, but after a while Kohlhaas started opening up.

Shepel chuckled, looking back over his shoulder. "Once I tell them it's either us or the blue caps, that always gets them talking. Hitler's propaganda is great. It's got them well and truly scared."

Shepel shoved a notepad at Aelya. "Sorry to put this on you, dear, but at least you look like you can write." His mangled hands couldn't hold a pen properly, so someone else had to record the interrogation.

Kohlhaas admitted he was with I/JG52, newly arrived to Pitomnik, just to the west of Stalingrad. He peppered this with bold pronouncements about how lucky these inferior Slavs should feel about shooting him down, how he was happy to be a martyr to his cause. Shepel gleefully translated these.

Kohlhaas stopped abruptly with a terse statement. Shepel said there'd be no further discussion until Kohlhaas met the pilot who'd shot him down.

"That was me." Tonya waved at the German.

Kohlhaas laughed, but his smile disappeared as Shepel told him she was serious.

"He thinks we're tricking him. Maybe you should give him a re-enactment."

Tonya obliged, using her hands to play out the battle as she narrated. Kohlhaas and his wingman had been heading southwestward, gaining altitude, probably done with their mission. Usy and Tonya crept up from below. Usy thought he could pick off the wingman quietly, but he got overeager, led the wingman too far with his tracer stream, and missed.

"I didn't miss," said Usy. "I was boxing him in for you." He sounded so earnest, Aelya almost believed him.

The German pair immediately swung hard right and went into a steep dive. Just then, Tonya, who had been lagging behind, saw Kohlhaas come across her view. Her guns hit his engine and right wing and caused it to catch fire as his wingman escaped. She talked almost admiringly about how Kohlhaas very calmly straightened his dive, popped the canopy, then pitched forward and bailed out.

Aelya watched as Shepel finished his translation. Kohlhaas's mouth was agape. He shook his head. *"Dieses Mädchen? Nein, nein, unmöglich. Unmöglich."*

Tonya laughed at him, hands on her hips. "You got careless, Kohlhaas. No, it's not impossible—you got shot down by a girl."

Usy tapped Shepel on the shoulder, eyeing the prisoner. "Wait, that wasn't what happened. I hit you with that first burst, didn't I? You were already bailing out by the time Honeybee fired. Tell him."

Shepel shrugged and told Kohlhaas.

He looked confused at first, before rapidly nodding. *"Ja, es war der Mann. Der Mann."*

Tonya swore loudly at Kohlhaas, who wouldn't look at her. Aelya declined to write any of it down. Then Tonya turned to Usy. She looked as if she was going to throw a punch. Aelya dropped the notebook and stepped in front of her. She worried for a moment she'd find Usy's knife in her back, but the door burst open.

"What the hell is this, a command performance?" Red yelled. "Shepel, get these gawkers out of here. Do this properly."

Shepel ushered the pilots and Dr. Krupenya out of the guard post.

"My kill. It's my kill." Usy did a twirl and strutted toward the airfield.

"We'll see about that," said Tonya. "Let's have a full inquiry."

The idea of Tonya and Usy fighting over credit felt sour to Aelya. Killing was an ugly necessity; they shouldn't be celebrating it.

Shepel put a hand on Tonya's shoulder. "Comrade Sergeant, a word of advice. Don't make a big deal of this. Think of who you're going up against."

"What, is he going to gut me with that fancy knife of his?"

With a wry smile, Shepel shrugged. "He's just as likely to stab you in the back by dropping a note to the commissar."

"I should have just shot Fritz back in that field. Made it easier for everyone."

"Don't joke about that," said Krupenya.

"Oh, you can be all high and mighty now," said Tonya. "Let's hear you tell that to the refugees."

Krupenya shook her head and walked away.

"You don't know her," said Shepel, losing his earlier levity.

"What's there to know? She's a doctor," said Tonya.

"Just lay off what you don't know."

"Unbelievable. I can't even talk about killing Fritz now?" Tonya let out a primal scream at the sky. A bit calmer, she said, "What kind of a war are you running here anyway?"

CHAPTER 39: THE WINDOW FRAME

The vibration of her fighter cutting through clouds made Aelya queasy. She regretted eating so much breakfast this morning. Dr. Krupenya had been threatening to strap her down and force-feed her before she flew. She'd been a very light eater before missions, ever since facing down those Messers with Roza. She'd been worried about losing control over her body again when the terror of combat struck. It was stupid. As the doctor said, she wasn't the only one to have lost control and not having enough nutrients was going to affect her performance.

It wasn't just the food and the vibrations that were making her queasy. With a rebuilt engine, she was back on Roza's wing. During the absence, Roza had scored another confirmed kill, flying with the rookie Dema, no less. She tweaked Red's nose with another low victory roll over the airfield, and her legend grew. The Roza who flew next to Aelya felt different—above her, somehow. Aelya felt hollowed out, yearning to belong the way Roza did.

The feeling of inferiority was only made worse by the rumour that Dmitriev had pressured Red into giving the women combat duties as fodder for propaganda. Forcing Stitches and Petrushka to lose the challenge provided a convenient cover for Red to save face.

Red showed no outward favour. As usual, he'd used his pre-flight briefing to alternately lecture and shout. Aelya caught heat for a failure to chase down vultures during a previous encounter. "The problem is, you think too much," he said.

How could that be true? Flying was the most natural thing for her. Scanning the sky, looking at the instruments, the movements of the plane reacting to her controls—it was all a fluid, continuous motion for her. Other pilots hung on to superstitions. Lara made whichever wingman she flew with tie on her scarf before going up. Olga and Yulia would exchange notes to tuck away in their cockpits. Masha made Volkov roll over three times. Aelya believed in rationality. Her flying instinct was physiological, not magical.

Today's flight of two was a token effort. Orders continued to forbid chasing the enemy into his territory. Tonya and Usy bagged a pair of Heinkels but couldn't claim them because they'd violated the order. It was part of the pattern of defensive behaviour established at the end of September. Sorties were being cut back, preserving the planes for some planned counterattack, which felt more mythical with each passing day. The slaughterhouse of Stalingrad, with its endless hunger for fresh meat, continued grinding thousands of men down each day.

During this time, the enemy seemed very happy to cooperate with keeping the sector quiet. The Germans knew the real fight was over the city. Kohlhaas said as much during his ongoing talks with Shepel, which were getting positively chummy.

When action did happen for the 497th, the odds were usually stacked against them. They'd been lucky. Masha and Petrushka had both made it back to base after being shot down. The only recent casualty occurred when a new pilot's landing gear failed during a training flight. He'd hesitated whether to manually lower them or land on the belly and wasn't paying attention as his plane went low and offline, shearing a wing on a radio aerial. In the crash, his legs were crushed. It was a horrific injury, but Aelya's overriding feeling was relief that such a lousy pilot wouldn't be endangering her during missions.

A speck in the distance caught her attention. "Vulture, ten o'clock, slightly low. Heading northwest." She congratulated herself a little for keeping her awareness even as all her worries simmered in her head. No time for those now.

"Any companions?" said Roza.

"No, I just see the one."

Roza waggled her wings, and Aelya knew immediately they were to climb and turn, trying to get up high in the enemy's blind spot. As they skirted a cloud layer, Aelya could make out more of its shape. Twin fuselages and a tail boom. Its overall square silhouette made it look like a window frame.

"It's a Rama," she said. An Fw 189 reconnaissance plane. Taking photos of Red Army positions. Gathering valuable intelligence. They needed to get this one.

They settled in about four hundred metres above the Rama, blocked from view by occasional clouds. Scanning everywhere, they still saw no enemy fighters.

"Ramas are slippery," said Roza. "Here's how we'll do it. I'll throttle ahead about two hundred metres. You dive straight at him and stay on his tail. You won't be able to out-turn him, but as he tries to escape, drive him to me."

"Copy that."

When they were in position, the Rama still showed no signs of noticing. Aelya went into a steep dive, aiming for such a sharp angle that the Rama's tail gunner wouldn't be able to hit her. Wait for the rivets. Wait for the rivets.

The Rama broke suddenly, pitching downward, giving his tail gun a straight shot at her. He fired from too far away, but she jinked anyway, struggling to keep the target in front of her. Suddenly, she was very close and fired before lining it up properly. The tracers fell into space behind its tail. She had to dodge a stream of machine-gun fire and felt a series of impacts on her right wing, like gravel striking the side of a truck on a country road.

And then the Rama disappeared from view. She took precious seconds to look for it before realizing she had overshot it. It dived even farther, and Roza chased it in a fruitless effort to line it up as it swerved madly.

Aelya squinted at the sun. New dots appeared. "Vultures, Roza. Four of them coming out of the sun. Messers, I think. They have the drop on us by about a thousand metres."

Roza broke off her attack and climbed. Aelya kept pace with her, constantly scanning for any move by the Messers, as well as any new threats. A pair of Messers dived down, but not to attack. They settled in above the Rama to escort it home, while the other pair circled menacingly.

"Should have taken those four when the chance was there," said Roza, her tone full of recrimination. "Regroup at two thousand. I'm calling this in and asking for thirty-three."

"We can still get them." They were outnumbered, but this was commonplace. Aelya wanted badly to make things up. Two to one was hardly terrible.

"No, the positioning is no good. Time to thirty-three."

Was this really Roza talking? "Are you sure?"

"Affirmative. Thirty-three."

Taking her hand off the throttle, Aelya clenched her fist, wanting to hit something, but thought better of it.

CHAPTER 40: FORTUNES ON THE TABLE

Even with most of the regiment present, there was still plenty of space in the readiness area. The lengthy rebuilding was a testament to the catastrophic losses they had suffered during the summer months, when they had been thrown at the German juggernaut advancing toward Stalingrad. It didn't help that Red had rejected two new pilots as inadequate and sent them back to flight school. They were even losing mechanics; a misfire loading a machine gun blew off one's hand.

Aelya waited in readiness two, along with the rest of Stitches's squadron. With crisp but fine weather, several squadron mates hung around outside eating biscuits or kicked around a soccer ball, led by Dema, who'd been a star player in school. Stitches was quizzing their newest member, Grishchuk, on the best ways to approach different types of enemy bombers. He was from Rostov, practically a local boy, and eager to kick the invaders out of the area.

Listening to Stitches's friendly, bantering way of teaching Grishchuk, Aelya couldn't help but contrast it with her own recent tactical review. It had been a tense session over the Rama incident, with a lot of arguments about what could have been done better. Red was furious about its escape. Even after the Messers arrived on the scene, she and Roza could have flown at the Rama and forced the escort into a dogfight where being outnumbered wouldn't be as adverse. Roza took full responsibility for the decision and admitted it was her fault. Knowing Roza, Aelya was convinced her senior pilot was covering for her. But did that also mean she didn't trust Aelya in battle?

She needed to distract herself. With the air base becoming more established, the postal system caught up. Aelya had received another letter from Vasya. Her sister seemed to finally accept, if not embrace, her role in the aircraft factory. Aelya took joy in the banality of Vasya's complaints that building the

IL-2 plane was back-breaking. Vasya's one consolation was that Aelya might one day fly a plane she'd built. Aelya wouldn't mention in her reply that the IL-2 was a Sturmovik, a ground attack plane, not a fighter.

The regiment received a long-delayed letter from Yusupov's sister. Unaware of his death, she wrote that her family had managed to get out of Kharkov before the Germans took the city, but they'd lost contact with her husband's family. Stitches took the initiative to throw the letter in a wood stove. Petrushka learned of a cousin who'd died in Leningrad. He was constitutionally incapable of taking anything seriously so immediately quipped, "I hope he made a good meal," referring to rumours of cannibalism in that besieged city.

"Want some new reading material?" Masha asked, waving a letter from Dina. Aelya snatched it up eagerly. Dina, along with the rest of the women night bombers, now the 588th regiment, were posted even farther south, down in the Caucasus. From Dina's account, they were in the thick of it, swooping in at night, their engines off, dropping bombs on the Fascists as they slept. Was it easier to kill when you couldn't see the victims?

Tonya bounded into the ready area, full of beans. Literally. At the table where half of Red's squadron was playing cards, she shoved a samovar to one corner and emptied a small burlap bag of little white beans.

"I thought Red would never finish his lecture," she said, holding a bean up to the sunlight like a jeweller examining a diamond.

Curious, Aelya put her letter down to peer over Tonya's shoulder. Beans seemed to be the most common, easiest thing to get a hold of, yet after weeks of hearing about them, this was the first one Aelya had seen.

"What's that for?" Petrushka asked.

"Fortune-telling," said Tonya. "Where's Yulia?"

"She's out on the field," said Aelya. "Some infantry found Olga after she bailed and they're sending her back. Should be due any moment. Yulia wanted to be the first to greet her."

"We better do this fast before Olga gets back," said Tonya. "I can't stand her butting in with her opinions."

"I didn't know you were an expert in fortune-telling," said Aelya. Olga certainly considered herself an expert.

"I'm a woman of many talents," said Tonya.

To Stitches's bemusement, she took a stick with one charred end from the stove and drew lines on the table.

Petrushka laughed. "I don't know about this beans business. Sleepy, you're a gypsy. Does Honeybee know what she's doing?"

"I'm the thieving kind of gypsy, not the fortune-telling kind," spat Sleepy, not looking up from his cards. Aelya could tell he didn't like the label of "regimental gypsy." He was like a chubby kid in school going out of his way to make fat jokes.

Frost sat in the corner strumming his guitar absently. Usy was next to him, whittling a sculpture with his knife that Aelya was sure was a naked figure of a woman. He was inordinately proud of his knife, supposedly taken from an Ottoman officer by his uncle during the Second Patriotic War. But there were whispers that Usy had murdered someone in a drunken brawl and took the knife from his victim. Aelya thought the truth was somewhere in between; Usy had probably murdered his uncle for the knife.

"Tell me how this works," said Stitches.

"You take half the beans and I take half the beans," explained Tonya. "Then we drop them on the table at the same time. I check how many fall within each section of lines, and I interpret the fortune."

"She's full of it," said Roza, hiding behind a copy of *Pravda*.

"Come on, Stitches," called Baby, a rotund pilot sitting at the card table. "That's for girls. We'll deal you in the next round."

"And what makes you think your games are just for boys?" said Tonya.

"Join us, Honeybee," said Sleepy. Other pilots joined in the calls.

Tonya enjoyed the attention like an opera singer accepting a standing ovation. "Sorry, but today's a fortune-telling day. I've already taken too much of your money, you degenerates."

Aelya watched the men laugh and return to their cards. For all of Tonya's talk, she never seemed to have liaisons with any of the men. Her constant supply of contraband stemmed from deal making and gambling, not unseemly favours.

"Shall we tell your fortune, Stitches?" said Tonya.

The squadron leader took the half of the beans offered by Tonya, and together they each dropped them on the table. Tonya began sorting where they fell with an intensity she normally reserved for combat.

"I see . . ." she said. "You will die a horrible death."

As Tonya cackled, Sleepy and Baby glanced over, looking pale. Petrushka found something interesting on the pages of Roza's newspaper. Stitches broke into an uncomfortable smirk. Tonya stopped laughing but kept smiling. She would never admit to crossing a line. Everyone loved to joke about dying, pretending they didn't care about each other, but they were also a superstitious lot, so Aelya suspected even pretending to predict misfortune felt wrong.

Usy broke into a laugh. "Now I like this. Do mine next."

"How about Roza?" said Aelya. She didn't want Usy coming over.

"I don't believe in fate," said Roza, still not looking up from her paper. Somehow that disappointed Aelya; it lacked a certain romance.

As Usy tromped over, she squirmed. Every pilot found joy and humour in some part of this war, but Usy and perhaps Tonya seemed to be downright revelling in it.

Thankfully, Muromets and Lara appeared, fresh from an operational briefing. Red didn't come. He believed in having some distance from the ordinary pilots and kept away when they were at leisure.

"Honeybee," Muromets said, adjusting his glasses, "I'm afraid your Messer had to be downgraded to a probable."

Tonya swore and tossed a handful of beans at his face. "That's a thousand rubles you cost me."

"Don't blame me. If the State is paying out bonuses, they're entitled to confirmation. Just because you see smoke doesn't mean it's a kill."

"Could be worse," Tonya said, shrugging. "Could have missed out on a Rama. That's fifteen hundred." She was looking at Roza. So was Aelya. Roza ignored the comment and went to get a cup of tea from the samovar. If she wasn't going to defend herself . . .

"I'd like to see how you deal with two pairs of Messers boxing you in," Aelya said.

"Please, talk to me when you've actually scored a kill," said Tonya.

"Now hold on, Honeybee," said Lara. "That's not fair. A lot of good pilots don't get kills."

"It's true," said Petrushka. "I took a full year before I bagged one."

"She said good pilots, Petrushka," Stitches said.

The two wingmen elbowed each other. Aelya felt they were having a joke at her expense.

Lara pulled her aside. "Don't worry about it. Don't overthink it. It's causing you to hesitate—"

"Don't you start with me," Aelya snapped. She didn't like being given remedial lessons like a classroom laggard—not in front of the others. The outburst only drew more attention to her. Roza sighed.

Aelya couldn't bear that her senior pilot appeared to be martyring herself, taking all the criticism, but making it clear she was protecting her wingman. Aelya pointed at her. "I don't need your protection. I'm your wingman—I'm supposed to protect you."

"I never said anything."

The radio crackled to life with an intercept order for Stitches's squadron. He looked over his charges. Aelya thought she caught Roza shrugging.

"Baby," Stitches called out. "Your flight's up."

Baby and Masha rose and headed out with their wingmen.

As soon as they left, Aelya grabbed Stitches and pulled him aside. "We need to talk."

"About?"

"A new senior pilot."

CHAPTER 41: RESTLESS

"Form up on my wing!" Lara called.

Aelya caught her breath, trying not to let adrenalin from the attack run affect her control. She throttled up gently, lining up slightly behind and to the right of Lara, stalking the smoke trail from the Ju 88. The crippled enemy bomber was falling farther behind its compatriots, the skies too clear to hide. She ignored Tonya and Usy as they swore at each other and the enemy over the radio, tangling with the German escort fighters, keeping them at bay. Her head swivelled around as she scanned, as always, for danger. She stole a quick glance at Sleepy and Mouse diving toward the edge of the main formation of Ju 88s for their own attack run, picking on a bomber to the left. The bombers had completed their run earlier, the VVS ground warning system having been late, so this was their last chance at revenge before they strayed into Luftwaffe-controlled airspace.

Lara took a high angle to the right tail of the ailing bomber. Aelya followed with practised precision, still scanning for any new threats. It was comfortable keeping up with Lara. Everything was so correct and procedural with her, and Aelya had little need to think. She didn't need explicit orders. Just follow along and watch her back.

Stitches had initially tried to shame her for her transfer request. He didn't like people running away from their problems. But Aelya explained that she'd lost trust with Roza and needed to rebuild that as someone else's wingman. Besides, switching to Red's squadron was hardly taking the easy route. When she put it that way, Stitches relented.

"Let's go, Mars."

Aelya hung back for a two-second interval after Lara plunged below the bomber to attack where its gun turret coverage was weakest. Then she followed the same path. Lara lined up her target and punched a tight pattern of cannon shells across its fuselage. Something exploded and a hole gaped in the side of the Ju 88, flames pouring out.

As Lara pulled away, Aelya drew close. The dual streams of machine gun tracers from the bomber's topside proved easy to dodge as she dipped below, and so much less frightening than the wall of bullets they'd dealt with when they first attacked the formation. She had to remind herself not to get lazy. One bullet could kill her just as easily as twenty.

The target crossed the red circles in her glass targeting collimator. She pushed the trigger levers. Streaks of yellowish light struck the burning bomber, and its fuselage broke into two pieces. A dark thing fell from the remains of the bomber's front section, the fiery bundle whipping close past her cockpit. It could only have been one thing.

"That's a kill. Time to break off and thirty-three," Lara ordered.

As Aelya sped up and climbed, the enemy bombers turned into small dots in her rear-view mirrors. The battle had so scattered the six Soviet fighters that it took some time for them to finally form up. They were low on fuel as they headed home.

"Shame to leave, Auntie. We had those Messers in a spot," Usy complained. "Did any of your bomber crew get out? I feel like shooting someone."

Although there was no doubt Usy would kill helpless crewmen, in this instance he was joking. Lara would never allow that to happen under her command. A lump caught in Aelya's throat. Had any parachutes come out of the destroyed Ju 88? The policy on shooting a bailed-out enemy depended entirely on who was in charge during an engagement. If they flew with Stitches, he wouldn't want them to go out of their way to gun airmen down, but he wouldn't reprimand them if they did. Under Red, they were expected to actively hunt down enemy pilots, provided the tactical situation allowed for it.

When Aelya blinked, she envisioned the burning thing again, enveloped in black smoke, tumbling past her down toward the earth.

Sleepy swore. "Where's Mouse? He was just here!"

"Mouse, come in," Lara called. "Mouse, do you read?"

His transmitter could be busted. Aelya's own transmitter had been shot up.

Aelya scanned every sector of the sky and ground, twice as fast as she normally would. Not a single telltale sign of a plane or a wreck. They all looked around. Nothing.

"Everyone stay in formation," said Lara. "We'll make a slow figure eight. Scan your segment and watch for vultures. Mouse might've gotten jumped when no one was looking."

They made their loping circuit. Lara continued to call for Mouse, with no success. Sleepy interjected with the occasional curse at losing his wingman.

Gazelle called in a report of enemy fighters sweeping inbound. The possibility that Mouse had been shot down made Aelya eager to stay and fight, but ammo and fuel were low.

"All right, we've got to move," said Lara. "Osprey flight's coming in. Let them handle this. I'll call in Mouse's last known location. Sleepy, when did you last spot him? Sleepy?"

Sleepy stumbled over his words.

"Sleepy," Lara said. "These things happen all the time. Did you see him when you broke off your last attack run?"

"Yes, I'm sure of it. We formed up with you. I don't know what happened after that."

Lara calculated the likely position and called it in. Then there was nothing left to do except head back to base.

Aelya clutched her book, staring at the wooden rafters of the gymnasium. Masha snored in the bunk next to hers. She shifted position again, as if that would somehow stop her from seeing and feeling everything again.

She was reliving what had happened. Not just that horrible moment, that image of the burning thing she couldn't quite wrap her head around. She was feeling the entirety of combat, her body experiencing each microsecond of every motion play out in full detail. Her stomach churned with the muscle memory of each lurch her plane made. Reliving her diving attack, she felt as if the bed was giving way beneath her. The jolt caused her to cry out and roll off.

Had she disturbed anyone? Masha's snoring continued unabated. Roza was in the next bunk over, on her side, her eyes closed and her face a perfect mask of calm innocence. She was tempted to wake them all and say, "How dare you sleep soundly like that?" Someone shuffled behind her.

"Mars," Lara whispered as she gently patted her shoulder. She reached down to take Aelya's hand and guide it to a steel flask she was holding. "Try this."

"What is it?" Aelya unscrewed the top and sniffed berries. She took a sip. The burning sensation almost made her cough.

"One of my concoctions," said Lara, "though I can't take credit for the recipe. Red learned it from the previous commander. Try some more—just little sips."

Aelya did as she was told, getting used to the off-putting mix of sweetness and foulness.

Lara said, "It's a vodka compote. We used some wild berries we found next to the airfield."

"They're not poisonous, are they?" In the dimness, Aelya made out Lara's smile.

"You can have the rest this time, but you'll need to start making your own."

Finally, the vodka ration made sense to Aelya. She took in a last, long sip. Her body warmed. Her senses dulled. Lara helped her down onto her bunk and pulled a blanket over her, tucking her in.

Even as her body collapsed into sleep, the image of the burning thing lingered.

CHAPTER 42: A SOFT FACE

"This is a good idea," said Shepel, sitting next to Aelya. Across the table, Kohlhaas, a slight smile on his face, drummed his fingers gently. "We should be squeezing as much as we can out of this guy. The blue caps are getting impatient." Shepel slid a cup of hot tea to the prisoner.

Kohlhaas had become quite talkative since his first interrogation, knowing that every cooperative act delayed the inevitable day the NKVD took him away. A steady stream of staff and intelligence officers, even individual pilots who had questions about tactics and the behaviour of their enemy counterparts, had spoken to him.

It was a pretty good deal for Kohlhaas, Aelya thought. He no longer had to suppress the terror of going into combat. He got to sleep in this backup guard post, which wouldn't be used until winter hit, and be fed every day. The interrogations were taking on an almost jovial air, with pilots often bringing snacks from the canteen and sharing cigarettes. It was wrong. This man was a killer. The biggest killer on the air base.

It was perfectly natural for Aelya to be asking questions. Red's pilots were always expected to try to find another edge.

Kohlhaas took a sip of tea.

"How many fighters do you usually send with Ramas?" Aelya asked.

Shepel translated, and she nodded but didn't even listen to the answer. She needed to know what it took to be a killer. Until then, she'd never measure up in the eyes of Roza, Tonya, Stitches, even Lara.

"You shot down forty four planes," Aelya said.

"Forty-six," Shepel said. "You forgot the two from the 466th the day we got him. Lucky for him we picked him up and not them."

"How many men do you think you've killed?" she asked the German.

Kohlhaas had an inquisitive look, but Shepel put a hand up to delay him. "I'm not assisting in your gawking, Makarova. Ask a serious question or we're done."

"This is a serious question. Did you ever strafe civilians?"

Shepel raised an eyebrow, then translated. "No, of course not," came the answer.

"What about anyone in your unit?" asked Aelya. "You never heard of anyone doing it?"

"What's this about?" translated Shepel. "Mistakes happen. It's war." Shepel leaned in and added, "He's right about that."

"This is a war you started," said Aelya.

"We were forced into it. We were the beating heart of Europe, but we were surrounded by leeches, until . . ." Shepel giggled while Kohlhaas's eyes grew large. Shepel composed himself. "Until Hitler showed us the way." Kohlhaas continued barking, Shepel translating flawlessly. "To seize the greatness we deserve. We, who gave the world Mozart, Goethe, Gauss." Shepel smiled and added, "Does he even know who those men are?" He turned to Kohlhaas. "Marx?"

"*Ein Juden.*"

"Your country's great. You love your country," said Aelya, "but does that make it all right to machine-gun villages, strangle families with barbed wire? I know people with these families. Do you want to talk to them?"

Kohlhaas's eyes flitted nervously as he talked. He probably thought this was the prelude to an NKVD execution. His voice was smaller now.

"Lies, propaganda," Shepel translated.

"There's this boy," said Aelya. "He used to . . . he hangs around here. He just sits there all day. Does nothing. Has to be spoon-fed. He must be thirteen or fourteen. Perfectly healthy body. But try to look into his eyes. You can only ever do it once. His mind's totally destroyed. You want to know why he's like that?"

She exchanged a look with Shepel. That boy had spooked everyone until thankfully he'd been moved away with some refugees. Would he ever talk again? His future was as cloudy as Kohlhaas's.

"We finally heard from someone who'd seen the village," she continued. "Every adult had been shot. At first they couldn't find any children. Then they looked in the well. The children had squirmed too much for their executioners. They gave up shooting and just grabbed them and threw them down there. They suffocated beneath each other. A few clawed their fingers to the bone on the stone until they starved. Let's bring the boy in here. Why don't you tell *him* it's all lies and propaganda?"

The story was just a rumour. No one knew if it was true, but it was perfectly believable after all the other horrors people had witnessed. And Kohlhaas knew it, too. His lips quivered. Tears glistened. His hands covered his eyes as he sobbed. He'd been perfectly happy to justify the Nazi war machine when the Soviets were just "leeches" in someone's speech. Up close it was always different, Aelya thought.

She stood up. "Tell me you're innocent. Tell me!"

Shepel stood and put a hand on her.

"Translate it," she said.

"Where are you going with this?"

She walked around the table. "Translate it!" she shouted at Shepel, but looked at Kohlhaas.

The German pilot stumbled back out of his chair, babbling something. He was on his hands and knees when he suddenly reached out and grabbed Aelya's legs. She reached for her holster. A call for the guards outside stuck in her throat. Kohlhaas was crying, banging his head on the floor by her boots. She pulled away in disgust. Shepel dragged her out.

"What was he saying?" she asked him when the door shut behind them.

"He said, 'I didn't want . . .' You know what? It doesn't matter." He sighed and put a meaty arm around her shoulder. "Are you disappointed he doesn't have horns?"

"I thought I could see something in him that I could use, but he's just an angry idiot."

"A few million idiots gave a true monster the power to destroy us all."

Knowing Shepel's history, was he even talking about Hitler? Aelya banished the treasonous thought.

"Look," he said. "Some of them are good, some bad. You just happened to find a guy who was somewhere in between. But maybe you're asking the wrong question."

"What question are you talking about?"

"You want to know if you're killing for revenge, or justice, or some other rot, as if there's time to feel anything but terror up there. The real question is, should you even ask?"

CHAPTER 43: LILY

"The angle's all wrong," Zina said. "He's come down way too sharp."

"Who's the expert here?" said Tonya.

"I'm not trying to be smart, but just look at what he's done."

Aelya followed the voices into Roza's revetment. She caught Zina's eye and her crew chief blushed slightly, though she was hardly shirking her duties. She had replaced virtually every part, some multiple times, but Aelya's ride had finally given out. There was nothing to work on.

Tonya groaned. "I taught him better than that." She went over to rattle the stepladder that Belenko, a new mechanic, was standing on, then climbed it, seizing the paintbrush from his hand.

"What's that supposed to be again?" Zina pointed to a white splotch on the side of Roza's cockpit.

"A hibiscus, I think," said Liza, now Roza's crew chief, as she walked down the length of the revetment, inspecting Belenko's handiwork.

"I thought it was an anemone," said Zina.

"Anemone Kulik," said Aelya. "Has a ring to it."

"Liza, shouldn't you be refitting the fabric on the wings?" said Roza, sitting at the controls.

"Already done."

Roza flashed a sharp look at Aelya and Zina. "What about you two?"

Aelya shrugged. "Still waiting on a replacement."

They locked eyes for a moment. Roza gave a slight nod. Just like that came the silent acknowledgement that Aelya was in a different squadron now and no more would be said about it.

Tonya screamed obscenities at Belenko as he once again failed to take in her instructions. She shoved him off the ladder.

"Off your butt, Belenko," said Liza with a tinge of malice, kicking some dirt at him. With Belenko slow on the uptake, she needed to double-check all of his work.

Aelya knew that somewhere within her she should empathize with Belenko, but she couldn't summon the effort. His work was shoddy. On a plane, that could be deadly. It was worthy of spite.

"Are you sure you want to advertise yourself in combat?" Aelya asked Roza. "What does Stitches think about your new decoration?"

"She's got Stitches wrapped around her finger," said Tonya.

Aelya didn't like the sound of that. It wasn't true anyway. Stitches was too independent minded.

"It's not much different from writing 'For Comrade Stalin' on the side," said Roza.

They'd seen someone in the 466th do that. Aelya disliked marring the beauty of the plane with writing. Roza's heart was in the right place. A rose would work.

"You can't do that anyway," said Zina. "You're not a Party member."

Not that it would have stopped Roza from trying. She was getting her way, as always. She'd recently been promoted to a flight leader, after Baby had been lost on an escort. Aelya wished she could be assigned to an escort mission. Only the best pilots were getting those, but it was a perverse reward. Escorting bombers was universally considered the worst type of work for fighter pilots. It was dangerous in the air, and it could be dangerous afterward. The 466th had lost a couple of Sturmoviks on a recent ground attack run and had to suffer through an inquiry. There were whispers that one pilot had been sent to fight with the infantry as punishment.

What was most notable about Roza's promotion was how little fuss the men made. Roza and Tonya had clearly been accepted by them. They loved Tonya's warped sense of humour, along with her access to luxuries and contraband. They admired Roza's ruthlessness in battle. Her star had risen considerably since she'd split from Aelya.

Tonya put down her brush and waved. Outside, Muromets's steps crunched across grass made white with frost, his greatcoat swaying with the wind. Aelya tensed, scanning the grey skies. Yesterday, a sneaky Messer had hit Grishchuk as he was taking off in the morning. It was supposed to have been his first combat mission. First mission. Last breath. Total flight time: fifteen seconds. They couldn't wait for the wreck to cool, so a truck had pushed it off the runway, roasting corpse and all, the burnt meat smell nauseating everyone. Now Aelya imagined Messers coming out of the clouds any time anyone walked across the open field.

"Senior Sergeant Kulik," Muromets said. "I'm happy to report confirmation of the Romanian IAR 80 from two days ago. I believe that makes . . ."

"Four," said Roza.

Belenko fetched paint from a workbench.

"Hold it," said Liza. "I don't want you butchering the plane. Tonya?"

"I don't paint kill stars. I'm an artist."

There was no way Tonya was going to paint stars marking someone else's kills, not when she was still bitter about Usy stealing credit for Kohlhaas. Aelya tried not to think about the German. The NKVD had come for him. Was he on a train to Siberia? Or in a ditch under a thin layer of dirt?

"Better make that five stars," said Muromets. "Keep this quiet, but Dmitriev wants a fifth for the photo shoot with *Red Star*. He wants the story to be about the world's first woman ace."

"Can we paint it white instead of red so we know it's fake?" said Tonya.

"It's not fake," said Roza. "Remember that Stuka Legend stole from me?"

"I don't steal kills," said Muromets. "There was no independent confirmation from the ground."

"That's because it blew into a million pieces."

Even Tonya laughed. Aelya's stomach knotted. They were so casual about killing now. She was envious. Every now and then, when she closed her eyes, she would see that flaming bundle that had once been a man, falling from the sky.

Muromets smiled and turned to leave.

"Wait," said Tonya. "We need you to fill us in on the latest."

During the flurry of activity in October, the rumours had been coming in as fast as the orders to fly. One moment the Germans were on the verge of taking Stalingrad. There was even talk that Comrade Stalin had ordered the unthinkable, abandoning the defenders in the city to prepare new defensive lines on the other side of the Volga. Just as suddenly, rumours swirled that masses of Red Army tanks were crossing the river to take the fight back to the invaders.

Ultimately, as the weather grew worse and the battle wore on, the missions and the rumours petered out.

"You'll have to be more specific," said Muromets.

"Is it on? Is there going to be a counterattack?" said Roza.

"Even if they told a lowly staffer like me, I couldn't tell you about it."

"That means there is," said Tonya. "When?"

"It would be terrible if it happens too soon," said Aelya. "Half of us don't have rides."

"About that," said Muromets. "I've definitely seen the paperwork. We should be getting a huge lot of equipment this week. And you'll be most interested to know, four new pilots have arrived, so that finally gets us to full strength."

"Know anything about them?" said Aelya.

"A couple are quite experienced. You might get your wish for a new wingman, Honeybee."

Tonya pumped her fist, then groaned, seeing the splatter she had made on the side of Roza's plane.

"What is that? A lily?" asked Muromets.

Roza rolled her eyes. "Oh for the love of—"

"I like that," said Tonya. "Lily of Stalingrad. Has a ring to it."

"It's supposed to be a rose," said Roza. "I thought it would be pretty obvious."

"Then why is it white?" said Muromets. "White symbolizes purity, innocence. Hardly fighter pilot material."

"I don't know, all right? It's just my favourite colour."

"Is Honeybee going to paint something for all the pilots?" asked Muromets.

"Not unless they can pay her with all their vodka rations," said Roza.

"I thought Roza was only paying you a week's worth," Aelya said to Tonya.

"Why, are you interested?"

"Maybe." Aelya smirked. What would look good on her plane?

"Well, it'll cost you a month's then."

"What?"

"Now I know there's demand."

"You're a dirty capitalist," said Liza.

Tonya hummed along as she continued correcting the rose on Roza's plane.

When they walked over to gawk at the new pilots, Aelya noticed Bison's familiar face first.

Tonya noticed the man next to him. "Holy hell, they sent us Nikolay Cherkasov!"

Aelya did a double take.

"That's not him," said Roza. He did bear a strong resemblance to the movie star, though, with his full, dark hair, strong jawline, and eyes that could only be described as smouldering.

Tonya whistled and started fanning herself.

"Why it's our very own Alexander Nevsky," said Roza. "I loved you in that one." She winked at him, and he responded with a sly smile.

Petrushka had a good laugh. This was the ritual for the new pilots: to stand with their suitcases and be poked and prodded in front of the operations bunker before they got their squadron assignments, the veterans circling like vultures to mock them.

Bison looked sheepish, and Aelya indulged a sudden urge to hug him. Roza and Tonya did the same. Lara gave him a pat on the back.

"Good to see you again," Aelya said.

"They couldn't keep me away." He said it without enthusiasm. His lips were curled in a smile, but his eyes didn't play along.

"All right," said Red. "Enough with the sightseeing." He waved for the pilots to give the newcomers space.

Aelya sidled next to Muromets. "You didn't say Bison would be back."

"I wanted it to be a surprise," he said. "Thought it would be fun."

"Doesn't look like he's having much fun."

Red waved his hands for silence. He introduced two yellow-mouths, Erdyniyev, a Mongolian with round cheeks and suntanned skin, and Tselner, a Siberian. Erdyniyev went to Frost's squadron while Tselner went to Stitches's.

"Ondarchuk," Red called out.

The matinee idol nodded, then stepped forward to shake hands with the commander. Aelya noticed the captain's bar on his collar.

"So tell me about him," Aelya whispered to Muromets. Getting Bison back was one thing, but a newcomer who was already a captain?

"He was in prison. Some sort of accident."

"Was it his fault?"

Muromets shrugged. "He's good, though. Ten kills."

A double ace. That put him at the top of the regiment's board, just ahead of Stitches.

"Comrades," said Red, "I'm putting Captain Ondarchuk into my squadron. We'll ease him into his responsibilities. Eventually, he'll take squadron command so I can focus on being the boss of all of you."

Aelya saw Lara's lips twist, but otherwise she didn't show any disappointment at being passed over for squadron command again.

Tonya leaned over to Lara. "At least he's nice to look at."

Red gestured for Bison to step forward. "Right, Zhigulin. Great to have you back in the fold."

"Yeah, who needs to be fawned over by pretty nurses and stuffed with delicacies from Britain and America anyway?" Was he joking?

"You'll be in my squadron as well. It wouldn't do for a rookie commander to have too many yellow-mouths in his squadron."

The pilots clustered around the newcomers, continuing the ribbing. Irkutsk joked that he and Tselner would fight it out over which one would be designated the squadron's official Siberian. Tselner looked frightened that it wasn't a joke. Ondarchuk was already being called "Nevsky." He looked thrilled to be back in action. Bison quietly accepted the slaps on the back from former comrades, looking anything but thrilled.

CHAPTER 44: GRUDGE MATCH

Rain turned the crossroads of Urmanovsk village into a morass of mud. The drops came down hard enough to splatter Aelya's trousers above her boots.

If only she hadn't let herself sleep in. First thing in the morning, she saw the men coming down to the school building to use the showers. She could tell from Petrushka's expression as he hauled himself down the main road of the *kolkhoz*, clad only in a greatcoat, towel, and boots, that the weather would be bad. It would be a non-flying day, the third in a row. She'd allowed herself an extra snooze. She made it just in time to catch the truck taking them to the command post for the official cancellation of flights. Unfortunately, by then the other pilots had volunteered her for her present duty.

A horse-drawn wagon gradually materialized through the driving rain. Sick of standing still, she waved at the elderly driver and climbed aboard while the horse still laboriously trotted through the mud.

"You're here for the tea?" she asked.

The man nodded, then said, "You want to take a look?"

Aelya hesitated. "It hasn't still got a head, has it?"

The man shook his head. She leaned over into the back of the wagon and pulled back a heavy cloth covering a lumpy form. The pig carcass was massive, probably weighing almost as much as Roza. Aelya was no judge of these things, but it looked freshly killed and cleaned.

One of the benefits of having an experienced arrival like Nevsky was learning how to get the most out of rations. Many local farmers hid their livestock but could be persuaded to part with it for tins of tea the military imported from China. Now the regiment could look forward to a roast pig for dinner

The thought of burning meat nearly made Aelya retch. She would skip this feast.

Huddled in her greatcoat next to the driver, she directed him as the horse pulled its way slowly through the village's muddy streets. She silently cursed the other pilots for sticking her with this, and she cursed Stitches for agreeing to it. With most of the senior pilots away at a navigation conference, he was in charge of the regiment. It could have all been a coincidence, but Aelya couldn't help but feel targeted. She was far from the most junior pilot and even had a shared kill now, yet they were picking on her. Stop thinking that way, she told herself. The idleness of downtime was making her paranoid.

They pulled up to the central hall of the *kolkhoz*, a concrete slab in the middle of the village. Out front, the kitchen personnel had set up a firepit beneath a tent. Two men came out to handle the pig carcass while a woman handed over several tins of VVS-issue tea leaves.

After waving farewell to the man and his wagon, Aelya took shelter in the relative warmth of the hall. A cacophony greeted her ears. It was so unexpected to hear such a noise indoors that she didn't immediately recognize it until she entered the main hall. Petrushka was making a circuit of the room on a motorcycle as the pilots around him cheered.

Finding Stitches standing close to the entrance, she raised her voice above the din. "Oh yeah, that definitely isn't a stupid idea."

"You know what the old men say: the difference between an Air Force pilot and a hooligan is the uniform."

They had to hop backward to prevent their toes from being run over.

Petrushka skidded to a stop. "Dema, you want a go?"

"No way," said Dema. "It would be just my luck to break my neck doing that."

A lively discussion ensued as several pilots vied to go next.

"I thought you were supposed to be lecturing us on cleanliness and grooming," she said to Stitches. The idea of missing out on that scintillating discussion had made waiting in the rain more bearable.

"Change of plan. Baby reappeared today and brought this toy with him. I think he stole it off some *makhras* on the other side of the river."

They had been expecting Baby back for a while. After he had been shot down close to Stalingrad, they gave up on him, only to get word a few days later that he made it across lines and was ferried back to the other side of the Volga by some helpful *frontoviks*. Then nothing until today. His reappearance was all the excuse anyone needed to celebrate on such a dreary day. Aelya noticed a few bottles of liquor chassis being passed around.

"The pig's here," she said, but Stitches was already occupied by something Roza was saying.

It was decided that Irkutsk would ride next, with Yulia on the back seat. It certainly didn't look as though he knew how to ride, as the bike wobbled around. After some jeers, interest waned. Dema found a soccer partner in Tselner, and they began bumping the ball from knee to knee, passing it back and forth. Others slumped to the floor for a rest.

Seeing Baby on his own for a moment, she welcomed him back. "Sure took you long enough," she said after a strong hug. "Is transport so bad you had to steal your own ride?"

"It wasn't transport that was the problem," said Baby, "although the bike definitely helped. I was stuck being checked."

"Checked?"

"NKVD. I never got picked up by Fritz, but I guess I took too long getting back to our lines. Soon as I made it out of the city and across the Volga, the blue caps hauled me into a camp."

Aelya stifled a gasp. "What did they do to you?"

"Not much. They just kept me there while they chased down the soldiers who found me. It took a while for that to get all sorted, but the wait wasn't bad. Had a bed. Nice food. Then they said I was done, and that was that."

He caught the disbelieving look on her face. "I didn't do anything wrong." He shrugged. "What did I have to worry about?"

The soccer ball got away from Dema and Tselner. Irkutsk swerved, then flipped the bike on its rear wheel. He and Yulia flopped to the ground while the bike motored on into an alcove, stopping with a crash. Far from hurt, the two riders laughed hysterically. Baby let out a horrified scream as he ran to check on his motorcycle.

Volkov barked and chased after the ball. Masha ran after him. The little mutt nuzzled the ball over to her feet, and she proceeded to play keep away. Aelya watched in fascination as she dribbled her way down one side of the hall, the dog nipping at her heels. Someone booted the ball away from her, to the other side of the room.

"Fetch," Petrushka said to Masha.

She glared at him, then went over to retrieve it.

"Who's a good girl?" he added.

Volkov trotted after her. She picked up the ball and ignored her dog's yapping. She let it drop, then gave a hard, swirling kick, sending it straight at Petrushka's head. He ducked just in time.

"I think we have a challenge," said Stitches.

"Let's make teams out of it," suggested Olga.

The motorcycle beyond any hope of recovery for the moment, they enthusiastically embraced the soccer match.

"How about men against women?" Tselner said. He had been mostly quiet since he joined, but the topic of soccer made him confident.

"We're long past that sort of thing," said Stitches. "Why don't we make the two duellists the captains?" He pointed to Masha and Petrushka. "You take turns choosing."

"Ladies first," said Petrushka.

Stitches lined up all prospective players. "You want in?" he asked Aelya.

"Of course." She was moderately athletic but had never really participated in team sports beyond what was required in Pioneers and Komsomol. The solitary nature of flying didn't really lend itself to teamwork.

Masha picked Dema and Petrushka countered with Tselner. The rest of the teams filled out, eight players each. Aelya was saved the ignominy of being picked last when Masha took her over Yulia; the towering Elbrus had never shown any of her sister's balletic grace. The benches were lined up on one side for a small but raucous cheering section. Roza and Tonya hollered loudly before the ball even dropped.

Two chairs at either end were set up as goalposts, with Aelya and Yulia tending their respective goals. When play started, the pilots in the "field" went at the ball with ferocity. Fighter pilots were an intense lot, and Aelya found herself swept up in emotion. She cheered as Masha stole the ball from Petrushka, then shoved her way past Bison to kick it through Yulia's legs.

Frost, who was supposed to be refereeing, looked up briefly from his book as he sat on the bench. "One-nil for Stone's team." That was what they called Masha. Heart of stone.

Masha jogged up to Petrushka, then pinched his cheeks. "Who's a good boy? Who's a good boy?"

Petrushka slapped her hand away. Play continued, more jostling and elbowing than passing and dribbling. Masha and Petrushka carried out a running fight, alternately shoving and pulling at each other's tunics. Irkutsk worked the ball loose, then hammered it at Aelya, slamming it right into her chest. She fell to the floor. It stung, but she was proud of herself for holding on. Then Usy came barrelling on top of her.

Aelya shoved him and rolled away. "Get off, you big oaf."

Usy was breathing hard, his eyes bulging. He reeked of liquor.

Aelya grasped at calming things to say when Stitches, also on Masha's team, shouted to Frost. "Come on, referee, that's a foul!"

"Hmm? All right, foul to Usy."

Usy grinned and walked away. Petrushka's team jeered.

"I'm a poet, not a referee," said Frost. "Leave me alone."

After that, the game got rougher. Masha pulled Petrushka down and Stitches was forced to do the honourable thing and call a foul on his own team. Then Tselner caught Aelya flat-footed. Luckily, his kick was blocked by Stitches, who cleared it from danger.

As Stitches settled into a defensive spot in front of Aelya, she needled him, remembering the last time they were in competition. "Feels good to be on the winning side of a challenge for once, huh?"

"I only lose when there's an unfair advantage."

"Excuse me?"

"Nothing."

"No, it's not. You meant that about our dogfight."

Stitches turned away from the play. "Sorry, bad joke." But he wouldn't look at her.

"It's true, then. Dmitriev made you lose."

"Dmitriev didn't make me do anything. He told me he wanted you two to win. What am I going to say to a commissar? But I swear to you, I was never going to let that happen. I don't lose. I was going to fly my best, then tell him I forgot in the heat of the moment."

She didn't know if she could believe him. Even if she could, would that make her feel any better? She was either an object of ridicule or some hopeless neophyte who needed to rely on Stitches's generosity.

Caught in that train of thought, she noticed too late as Olga tipped home the ball to score for the other side.

Masha went to retrieve the ball. Petrushka kicked it away. They chased after it as the play moved upfield. Aelya could see it coming, the way she could anticipate how a plane behaved in combat in split-second slices of time. Petrushka pulled on Masha's tunic and got there first, slamming his shoulder into the wall to stop himself. He worked the ball away and took one step as Masha came sliding in. They tangled awkwardly and the snap as Petrushka fell echoed around the cavernous hall. Hardened fighters winced at the sound.

After the briefest of delays, Petrushka screamed. He let out a few primal sounds and a stream of swear words. Masha froze, watching Stitches go over to help.

"You half-ton cow!" Petrushka screamed. "I'll kill you! I'll kill you!"

Volkov barked, sensing hostility toward his adoptive mother. Masha went to pick him up.

"He shouldn't have pulled my tunic," she said.

A crowd gathered around Petrushka. Frost seemed to have the most sensible ideas, ordering various pilots to apply pressure and makeshift bandages, get the doctor, clear space for Petrushka, and get a cloth soaked in cold water to stop the swelling.

As Aelya went over to see what she could do, Stitches stopped her. "You don't want to see him like this."

Dr. Krupenya arrived with a couple of orderlies. "What the hell happened here?" she asked.

Stitches seemed too distraught to answer. Aelya felt the need to give him a hug but held back.

"An accident," said Frost.

"Accident? How do you break a leg in an administrative meeting?"

To one side, Dema stepped in front of his soccer ball a little too obviously.

"You idiots," said Shepel, who'd appeared behind the doctor. "You know there'll be an investigation if you don't give a good explanation."

Dr. Krupenya knelt down and prepared to splint the leg.

Shepel leaned over Petrushka and spoke quietly. "Now, let's get things straight. What happened?"

Petrushka looked from Shepel to Masha, then to Stitches. Aelya wondered if Stitches was going to give some sort of signal, but his face remained frozen. She never knew how he wanted to be treated. At times he respected only those who were tough with him, while at others he seemed easily hurt.

"Tripped and fell in a trench," Petrushka said.

Masha exhaled and looked apologetic for the first time since they'd started playing.

Shepel nodded and stepped back to give the doctor some room. As space cleared around them, the wrecked motorcycle in the alcove caught his eye.

"What the hell is—never mind. Bury that thing before someone comes looking for it."

CHAPTER 45: RECOGNITION

Aelya watched as the cloud of vapour from her breath dissipated. She exhaled again, trying to make a bigger cloud. The new briefing room was a recent addition to the operations bunker. What it lacked in insulation, it made up for in decor. Dmitriev had issued everyone posters, which they were supposed to hang up in their barracks and all around the *kolkhoz*, but instead they'd used them as wallpaper for the briefing room. Bare electric bulbs illuminated the repeating patterns in different ways; a determined, youthful farmer at the centre of the room was transformed into a menacing agent of death in the corner.

Pay attention, Mars, Aelya told herself. She'd heard all of Red's information before. He was only filling in the escort pilots on the mission. But what if he mentioned one tiny little thing that might help?

"Roza, Dema, thanks for stepping in," Red said. "Hope you've got better aim than Usy. I'm slotting you in Nevsky's flight."

Roza yawned, causing Aelya to yawn in response. Even with sunrise arriving steadily later, the pre-dawn hours still felt too early.

"Nevsky, it's a lot to throw at you for your first mission with us, but you've seen worse, I'm sure."

Standing next to his new wingman, Yulia, Nevsky tipped his head with a smile. He said little but seemed to have charmed everyone on base, even Red. Tonya was watching him intently. Aelya was sure the two of them were sneaking around; Nevsky was trying a little too hard to ignore Tonya. Though playing up his matinee idol aura, he acted as if he were above the attentions of women. So used to men falling at her feet, Honeybee must have found this particularly enticing.

It was full squadron strength for this one—ten planes. Roza and Dema were on loan since Usy was in the guardhouse for firing his pistol at a rat in the canteen. Bison was taking over as Tonya's number one. She should have been happy to be free of Usy, but she wasted no time complaining about being passed over as a senior pilot.

Red was leading in person. His duties as commander prevented him from flying most missions, but this was important enough. He refused to fly with any inexperienced pilot, so Sleepy was on his wing.

"I'm not supposed to tell you anything specific," Red said. "Let's just say that if you happen to glance down when you're over the Lyska River, keep an eye out for vehicles and artillery. If we lose these two, I don't want to have to send out another recon."

He gestured at Lara and Aelya, the final pairing, sitting on a bench to one side. Aelya's cheeks burned from the attention.

Roza raised her hand. "I understand doing the escort, but why are they doing the recon? Shouldn't we be sending specialists? I mean no offence, Mars."

Aelya laughed uneasily.

"Air Army HQ sent a flight of Peshkas for a look a couple of days ago. They got blasted out of the sky by fighter cover. This isn't a photo job. We just need confirmation of what intel thinks is there. So better to send a pair who can fight their way out if need be."

Aelya's leg jackhammered uncontrollably. Another sortie, another chance to prove herself. To whom? Was anyone else fixated on this the way she was, convinced she was missing something vital in her makeup?

Red laid out a map on the table, going over the lay of the land where they'd be flying. She didn't bother with the map, closing her eyes and remembering the flight from yesterday, when Red had shown her the Lyska from afar. At that height, there was too much cloud cover in the way to make out details. It didn't matter. Today she would be going in low, where everything would look different.

She and Lara had been specially chosen for this mission—Lara for her navigation skills, Aelya because she consistently scored high in her recognition tests. She went over the images of different vehicles and weapons she was expecting to see. Panzer IIIs, Panzer IVs, StuGs, Marders, Sd.Kfz. 251 half-tracks, 88 mm Flak. 20 mm quads. She would have to capture it all in her mind in an instant. How much on either side of the Lyska River? Were they real or decoys?

"How much detail do they really need?" she had asked Shepel yesterday.

"As much as you can remember."

Aelya looked up as Red's briefing ended. Shepel was giving the weather report. Great. Just when she hoped for lots of clouds, he reported only three points at a thousand metres and up.

"Any questions?" asked Red. Hearing none, he led the pilots out.

"Ready for your starring role?" Roza whispered to Aelya.

She wanted to vomit, even though she hadn't eaten, but nothing came.

In front of the revetments, she and Lara tied each other's scarves, as they always did now.

Lara tilted her head toward Aelya's fighter. "You too?"

Tonya had painted a red disk, cut with lines representing the canals of Mars, just as it appeared on the cover of *Aelita*. That only served as backdrop to the streaking silver Goddard rocket soaring across the planet's equator.

"You're going to confuse everyone," said Lara. "They'll think you're a Japanese plane."

"Every little bit helps."

"All right, time to focus. No telling what we'll see. Just stay with me as much as you can. If you can't see me, just stay low. The anti-aircraft guns won't have time to find you, and the big guns won't be able to go that low." Lara patted her on the arm. "It'll be safer than you think."

Aelya's face was so tense, she couldn't even fake a smile. She breathed out.

"There you go," said Lara. "Let's do this."

The sun began to peek out over the horizon as Aelya's plane taxied. Silhouettes of cloud broke up the glow here and there. She wished there were more of them.

Red's squadron assembled quickly and headed westward, climbing to thirty-five hundred metres. The eight escorts went in a staircase formation of four pairs while Lara and Aelya trailed behind. They would be taking a roundabout route, hoping to cross the front lines southward at a spot where it followed a rough stretch of the Don River and enemy forces were thin.

Above the clouds, the sliver of sun washed everything in an orange glow. They maintained radio silence throughout. Aelya scanned the skies and spotted distant specks heading north, probably enemy bombers planning a rude wakeup call for the Red Army. She could neither say nor do anything about it; this mission took priority. If the enemy had spotted them, she would find out soon.

A few minutes into enemy territory, Bison's plane began to lag behind the formation. Tonya moved up next to Red. She must have signalled that Bison was experiencing some problem, because moments later she fell back next to Bison and they peeled away toward their own lines. It was standard procedure for pairs to return to base together if one experienced mechanical problems.

Aelya struggled to keep her breath from quickening. Two fewer fighters in her escort.

Soon they curled eastward and timed it so they would reach the target zone just as the full light of dawn hit. Red waggled his wings, and then he and Sleepy moved into high cover. Nevsky took the three remaining escorts in a loping figure-eight route, waiting for Lara to make her move. Aelya watched her as she signalled with her hands, then banked for a descent through the clouds. Aelya kept pace, with Nevsky's flight following at a distance.

Breaking through the thin white layer, Aelya oriented herself to the landscape. She saw the Lyska River as it split into its various sources, the small streams petering out through an elevated plateau covered in snow. She made out the bend in the river, several kilometres downstream of the largest settlement in the area. That would be their starting point.

Far away, from the corner of her eye, she spotted a half dozen dots sweeping the sky. Enemy fighter cover. More coming soon.

Lara broke radio silence. "This is Auntie. Go. Go. Go."

She veered into a steep dive, Aelya staying close to her tail. A few hundred metres from their start point, they began to level out, hitting the flaps and pitch controls to slow down. Lara banked and swerved, starting a zigzag path following the river upstream. Aelya locked her attention onto the snow-covered ground whipping by them, fighting the instinct to check the skies. That was Nevsky's job now.

Images flashed past at nearly two hundred kilometres an hour. Dark bands of roads cutting across the undulating snow fields. Trucks parked under white sheets. Splotches of foxholes and entrenchments clustered around clumps of trees. After a long, featureless stretch, they banked around a village. She warily skirted sandbagged anti-aircraft positions, their crews scrambling awake.

She heard Nevsky call an attack. Leaving the village behind, she and Lara moved through more wooded areas, the ground sloping slightly upward. She heard the booms of Flak guns opening up. She was too low to see any cloud-bursts. Someone swore on the radio.

Roza burst onto the comms. "This is Lily. I'm taking second flight. Follow me." That meant Nevsky was down.

More and more, the landscape was broken up by entrenchments, installations, and vehicles. A lot were painted white or covered by netting, but she was low enough to make out the distinct yellow ribbon insignia she was looking for. Were these decoys or the real thing?

As she flew between two thickets of conifers, she got her answer. Tracers whipped at her from all sides. She heard the whips and pings of bullets striking her fighter. She jinked, still eyeing Lara while scanning from side to side. Her muscle memory led her to make herself a difficult target, even as a stream of bullets threatened to slice her in half. Radio chatter was incessant and she vaguely understood that Red and Sleepy were entering the fray, that they had a lot of company.

She followed Lara to bank left, crossing the river's main tributary. For a moment, she thought they were getting away from the worst of it, but the Germans were more numerous on this side. Lara was sticking to the mission. This was what they were here for. More small arms fire opened up. Her plane felt achingly slow. A wetness washed over her legs. Her grip on the control stick was so tight, she thought she'd break it.

Finally, Lara called out, "All right, we got what we came for. Let's thirty-three."

They both cranked the throttle and began climbing northward.

"Lily?" called Lara.

Roza responded. "I'm just trying to catch sight of you, Auntie. There you are. Just trying to break away. Red?"

"We're tied up."

Their orders were to make for their own lines as fast as possible, regardless of what the escorts were doing. Lara and Aelya kept going, pushing their machines as hard as they could. Aelya's plane drifted rightward. She fought with the rudder to steer.

They were in the critical zone now. High enough for anti-aircraft guns to track them, not high enough to get away. No flak followed, though. Aelya suddenly remembered to check behind her.

"Vultures on your tail!" shouted Roza, just as Aelya spotted two Messers diving at them.

Lara broke left. In a split second, Aelya decided to go the way her plane wanted and broke right. Tracers streamed after her. She looked back.

The two Messers were climbing for another attack. A thin line of smoke billowed from Lara's engine, but she seemed able to climb as well. Aelya circled back, calling to Lara. No response. She moved in for a closer look. Lara's front windshield was completely blackened with oil.

"Lara, can you read me?"

Lara waved, then signalled that her transmitter was out. Her face was smeared with black.

Roza said, "Sorry we're late, Auntie. We'll take these vultures."

Aelya looked around. There were the two Messers, up high, curling around for another attack. Where was Roza? Was she chasing after another group of Messers?

"Auntie, you head back," Aelya said. "I'll try to draw the vultures away."

She didn't wait to see Lara's response. She climbed toward the enemy. She pushed the supercharger, forcing air at high pressure into the engine, which jolted the plane upward with more power. At this altitude, she was in danger of blowing out her engine, but it was her job to push her plane to the limits.

She flicked off the supercharger and turned to follow a path roughly parallel to the enemy. They stayed on course toward Lara, not wanting to give up an easy kill.

Aelya tried to will them to break: Come on. You don't want this. A moment later, worried about Aelya getting behind them, the two Messers turned to intercept her, exactly as she'd hoped. She broke once more into dive, glancing back as the Messers screamed after her. The lead fighter began firing. Part of her was pleased. If he was opening up at this distance, he was probably inexperienced. She couldn't tell if they were newer versions of the Bf 109. If they were, they'd probably catch up close enough to gun her down.

The ground approached rapidly. She pulled out very low, straining at the stick. Her vision faded to grey and then black, though she could still feel the plane responding to her. When she could see shapes and colours again, she saw that she had levelled out just a few metres off the snow. Gusts of white blew behind her. She couldn't see her pursuers, so she made a hard turn, staying low. Now she saw the two of them, still chasing, trying to line her up.

She kept circling, pulling hard, then began rolling her plane, turning, bleeding off speed, trying to fool them into overshooting. She jolted back and forth in her seat. The taste of bile filled her mouth. The enemy was struggling to keep up. Random shots chased after her, always late to the scene. She pushed her plane even harder now, climbing, then diving along with her rolls. Her body violently resisted the motions. Vomit spewed out of her mouth and splattered her face as she changed directions.

She heard a loud explosion. Behind her, a column of smoke rose from a black crater in the snow. One Messer climbed away. Two Yak fighters crossed into her vision. They left the fleeing Messer alone and caught up to Aelya.

"Sorry we're late, Mars," Roza said. "You're a popular girl."

"You with Dema?"

"Elbrus, actually," Yulia answered.

"Nevsky's gone," said Roza. "I had to send Dema home early. He was a bad boy and got hit. I just hope he makes it past the Don."

The Don River. If Dema could get north of it, he'd be safe to bail out. Aelya's heart leaped. Lara was in the same situation. "Auntie. Where's Auntie?"

"I see her," said Roza.

They caught up to her as she wobblily clawed for height, smoke still trailing. The line of the river came into view. They needed to get high enough so their own troops wouldn't think they were being strafed by the enemy. Now Aelya noticed the stench of vomit and tried to open her canopy, but it was jammed shut.

When they cleared the line of the river, Lara found a good clear spot close to a road, tipped her plane forward, then bailed out. Roza accompanied Aelya's own struggling fighter as Yulia stayed to confirm Lara's safe landing and call in the location.

Aelya felt weak by the time her airfield came into view. When her landing gear failed to deploy, she operated almost as if sleepwalking and belly landed straight down the runway. Zina had to use a hammer to slide the canopy open.

Aelya was stinking and wet when she came out. She was shaking uncontrollably. Red was there and held on to her. She could only think of how disgusting she must have seemed to him.

"What did you see?" he asked.

"The 14th Panzer. For sure. All over the west side of the river."

"Good job. Let's get you into ops for the full report."

She tried to stand up straight, then felt a wave of nausea. She threw up bilious green vomit all over Red's uniform.

CHAPTER 46: THE BIG SHOW

Outside the operations bunker, it was dark. Starlight diffused through fog gave a silvery glow to the surroundings, punctuated by a dozen orange pinpricks of cigarette light.

Aelya stood outside in snow that came up to the tops of her boots. It was too foggy to fly, but neither her body nor her mind would allow her to just flop back in her barracks and sleep. Before, she'd always been itching for another chance to prove herself, and now, after what she'd done, even earning praise from Red, she couldn't wait to get back out there. Her impatience was made worse knowing the Red Army had launched its long-awaited counterattack and she could do nothing to help. She breathed in the pre-dawn air, her mind racing over what to do.

Stitches emerged from the bunker, Erdyniyev trailing behind him. The squadron leader shot the yellow-mouth an angry look. "I don't know. What's the point? It'll be ages before you get to fly anyway."

Erdyniyev looked lost as Stitches stormed away.

"Don't worry about him," said Aelya. "He's not himself lately." She thought about her own ups and downs with Roza.

"Would you like one, Sergeant Makarova?" Erdyniyev pulled a packet of cigarettes from his coat pocket.

"I don't smoke. And you can call me Mars."

"Oh well, neither do I. Mars. I get them from rations anyway—thought it would be handy for sharing."

"You mean bribing?" The sweet plaintiveness in the way the new pilot spoke made Aelya feel confident in talking with him, as if he was a younger brother, though he must have been older than she. "Relax," she said. "You don't need to impress me."

"I thought that was my job. To impress all the veterans."

Veteran. She liked that.

"You need to impress with your flying. Though I guess bribery doesn't hurt." In his case, no amount of bribery would make any difference. From what Aelya heard, he was one of the worst new pilots the regiment had ever seen. Yet another raw foot soldier transferred to the VVS because he bowled over the medical commission with his superior eyesight and reflexes. But the regiment was stuck with him for a while. With the offensive in full swing, Red wouldn't be allowed to send Erdyniyev back as he had the two recruits earlier in the fall.

Aelya pulled a packet of dried apricots from her coat pocket. "Now here's something you should be bribing me with." She offered one to Erdyniyev. They stood there, chewing away like cows in a field.

Aelya savoured the taste, a pleasure she hadn't experienced since the war began. Her father must have begged, borrowed, or stolen to include them in the latest package from Kuybyshev. She really ought to think of that place as her home, even though she'd never seen it. Her real home was likely a smouldering ruin.

Her parents were fully absorbed in their work. Vasya seemed to derive some satisfaction, smug though it was, from playing the role of dutiful daughter. At home, she learned a dozen ways to make the meagre black bread rations tastier. At work, she was made an engineer's assistant and was now situated in the design shop, rather than the factory floor. Vasya had made it seem she was making the greater contribution to the war effort than Aelya, who after all, was supposed to be far away from the desperate fighting in Stalingrad. She still hadn't informed her family of the transfer. She couldn't bear to hear anguished pleas from her parents to stay safe. So she'd just given them a new field post number and never mentioned anything specific in her letters home.

Erdyniyev cleared his throat. He gave her a sheepish look. "I heard you took down a Bf 109 without firing a shot."

"Yeah, just flew him into the ground." Him. A dead man. Was he a good man? What was his family like? She'd thought these things would matter to her, but they didn't. She could only think of "him" as a machine, crashed on the Eurasian steppe. It was still exhilarating to remember.

"You must know a thing or two. You make any mods to your plane? I think I need every bit of help I can get."

She couldn't take credit for that, and she told him so. She just copied everything Lara had done. Back armour for the seat. Rear-view mirrors. Landing lights. Extra transmitter. Engine tweaks. Custom ammo loads. "Just talk to your crew chief. They'll know the latest."

Freely giving advice. She hadn't felt this authoritative since aeroclub. She remembered Panarin shaking her hand after she earned her flying certificate. The other students applauded as they gathered round and they shared sweet *pirozhki* Babushka had baked for the occasion.

By now, a bright yellow glow opened low across the gloom. As the sun rose, the pace and volume of explosions in the distance grew. Two mornings ago, a thunderous barrage lasting well over an hour had preceded the dawn. The ground shook, or at least she imagined it had.

"What do you think of the big show?" he asked.

She couldn't wait to get back. She could see his eagerness as well. But she remembered one of the first things Stitches had said to her. "You in a hurry to die?"

"What? Oh. I meant the movie. *Shining Path.*"

She laughed. She'd been so preoccupied, wanting to play the veteran, she'd forgotten about the movie that had been scheduled. Yet another reason everyone wished for bad weather.

She shrugged. "I'm glad we're getting a movie, but *Volga-Volga* was better."

As with just about everything else in the Air Force, the movie started behind schedule. It was mid-afternoon when the pilots were told to gather in the briefing room.

Aelya had occupied herself thawing berries in her revetment. Zina had dug out a little alcove in the snow to preserve wild berries they had harvested in the autumn to use in vodka compotes. Zina seemed to be in the same restless, joy-tinged mood as Aelya, flitting around in a daze. The thought that Zina might be in love with someone wandered into her head.

She was late to the movie. After being up for twelve hours, she'd lain down on a bench in her revetment for a short nap, kept warm by the engine heater. When she arrived, there weren't enough seats in the briefing room with the screen and projector set up. Muromets waved to her from the second row. He'd saved a seat by covering it with the notes and files he always seemed to have handy.

"Thanks. Are you sure this is all right?" she said as she scooted to a place between Muromets and Stitches.

"Ladies first," said Tonya from the row ahead. "And who am I to argue?"

"Who said you were a lady?" Aelya quipped.

She'd worried about Tonya's feelings after Nevsky's death, but her concern was quickly assuaged when Tonya said, "Better him than me," after she heard the news.

Crammed with people, the room was stifling hot. She folded her coat on the back of her seat, waving off Muromets's offer to take it. From next to Tonya, Roza smiled and greeted her. One seat over, Lara waved a bandaged hand. Officially, she was still in hospital, but she'd sneaked out for the occasion. In the low light of bare electric bulbs, her face almost looked normal, though Aelya knew it had been burned red, save for the area protected by goggles. Lara, always so correct in her procedures, wore them under most flying conditions. Any other pilot would have gone blind when the panel exploded in a gush of scalding oil.

Tonya leaned back. "Hey, Stitches, what's going on with Bison?"

Aelya looked around. Bison was standing at the back of the room.

"What do you mean?" Stitches asked.

Tonya let that hang in the air for a moment. "Last time out, he said his elevators were stuck. The tech couldn't find anything wrong. The time before, something was wrong with his engine, but it miraculously came back to life on the ground."

"Altitude effects."

"And the time before that—"

"What's your point?"

"I thought you said he was solid."

"Bison fought with us through the Rzhev meat grinder, when we were losing a pilot every day. Whatever it is you're trying to say, don't."

Tonya stared at him. "Right. Nothing's wrong with him. It just seems no matter which plane he takes up, there's always something wrong with it. Bad tech, I guess. Or maybe it's contagious." She turned around.

Aelya could see the intensity in Stitches's eyes. She put a hand on his arm and felt it shaking. "She just likes to get a rise," she whispered. "We put up with that for a whole year before we came here."

He smiled wryly. "If she weren't a woman . . . say, can you punch her for me?"

They both laughed. It was the most relaxed she'd seen him in a while. She liked that she felt at ease around him now.

"It wasn't my place to say it during the debriefings," he said, "but from Roza's report, that was some good flying you did on the recon."

She smiled but didn't say anything. She had done something impressive. Even Red had said so. This job was finally making sense to her.

"And taking out that Messer to boot," added Stitches.

"No-Shot Mars," Roza said without turning around.

"Well, it doesn't really count, does it?" Aelya said.

"No, it doesn't," said Tonya. "It's like getting your hand down someone's pants. Feels good, but you're still a virgin."

Aelya blushed and took her hand away from Stitches. She couldn't look at him.

Thankfully, Dmitriev clapped his hands for attention at the front of the room. "Comrades, the hour of our judgment is at hand. Though you all long to be forged into steel by the fires of battle, it's also necessary to temper—"

"Are we winning?" someone shouted from the back, to a few chuckles.

"How far have we advanced?"

"Is it true the Romanians have run off?"

It was unheard of for anyone to interrupt one of Dmitriev's speeches so boldly. Aelya noticed more than a few officers in various stages of drunkenness.

"Comrades, I can't possibly discuss the larger—"

The room erupted into jeers. The pilots threw crumpled balls of paper at the commissar.

"Start the movie!" A chant broke out. "Start the movie! Start the movie! Start the movie!"

Red ushered the commissar away from the line of fire and signalled for the projector to start up. There might be hell to pay later, but there was no arguing with a roomful of wired, half-drunk fighter pilots on a non-flying day.

"I think that's my cue," said Muromets. He shuffled over to the projector as the lights were turned off. Cheers and applause rocked the room.

The title cards came up. Muromets returned to his seat and smiled at her. Aelya found herself looking at Roza and Tonya's hair as they were bathed in the flickering glow cast by the projector. Red enforced few of the rigid grooming standards that had been Volkova's personal crusade. Roza and Tonya had washed and tied their shoulder-length hair into beautiful braids for the occasion.

As Lyubov Orlova appeared on screen to cheers, Aelya remembered how she'd imagined she'd look when her hair had been cut short: just like Orlova's character when she prepared to accept her award in Moscow. Instead, Aelya's hair remained a frizzy and matted nightmare even as it grew out. She'd tied it into a small ponytail and hid it under her service cap.

Most, if not all, had seen this movie before, so people wouldn't shut up. They either talked over the movie or sang along with the songs. Muromets quietly mouthed the lyrics. Stitches had a bemused smile.

"Too good to be caught singing?" she said to Stitches.

"That's what I tell everyone. The truth is, I'm tone-deaf."

"Come on, you can't be as bad as the rest of them."

He shook his head.

"Come on. Come on." She leaned in, poking and teasing him like a toddler. He giggled. She felt as if she was doing good, bringing the animated, lively Stitches back into the world.

"Quiet, you two," said Roza in a mocking tone. "Don't make me take my belt off."

"Will your pants fall down?" said Stitches. "I'd like to see that."

Roza pretended to be shocked. Aelya found this upsetting, but she smiled anyway.

With the scene in the women's shower, the room erupted into such loud hollering and clapping that the ground shook, making Aelya wonder if the noise was masking an artillery barrage.

"Show it again!" someone cried when it was over.

She looked over at Stitches, who was holding up a hand to his face, hiding his grin.

"Don't pretend you weren't drooling, you dirty sod." She playfully slapped his arm.

A few minutes later, the screen went white. Shepel cursed at the back of the room.

"Muromets. I need your help."

The adjutant went to look at the projector. The delay continued and the lights went on, followed by murmurs of discontent.

"Start it up at the shower again and you'll really be a Legend," said Sleepy from across the room.

Smoke wafted as Tonya took the opportunity to light a cigarette. A gust of cold air blew it away. Usy stumbled toward them. He seemed confused at the pile of papers on Muromets's seat and swept it to the floor.

"Muromets is sitting there," Aelya said as Usy leaned over her, about to sit down. Liquor emanated strongly from his every breath.

"I don't see him around."

"He's fixing the projector. Anyway, you're late. You should stand at the back." With anyone else, she would have felt bad about her hypocrisy. She remembered how *A Girl with Character* had been ruined when some drunken brute flopped down next to her at the October Cinema. She wasn't about to put up with that here.

"And pick those up," she added. She was in full flight.

Usy snorted, then picked up a notebook that had fallen out.

"What's this?" He showed her an open page. A poem was written on it, the title in large, flowery script. "Queen of Mars."

"Ha, I knew he was a pansy," Usy said.

The danger began registering in Aelya's head and she considered snatching the book away, but he held it up and began reading.

> *Fair maiden, do you come from Mars?*
> *Borne on wings to softly dance through the air*
> *You fly, crowned not with gold but stars,*
> *To conquer and tame the skies that few men dare,*
> *Practising a warrior's art,*
> *And thus, you vanquish my heart.*

Everyone around them had gone quiet. Stitches stood up. "That's enough, Usy. Now put it down and get over there." He pointed at the back of the room.

Muromets stared, motionless for a moment. He caught Aelya looking at him, then dropped the movie reel he was holding and ran out of the room.

"Hang on. Something's missing." Usy picked up a pencil that had rolled to the floor and began scribbling in the notebook. He turned the notebook toward Aelya. He'd drawn a stick figure woman with crudely correct anatomy.

Stitches tried to take a step forward, but Aelya stood in his way. She wasn't sure what she was going to do, but she certainly wasn't sitting down for it.

"Wait a minute," said Usy, taking the pencil to his drawing. He scribbled out the two circles on the figure's chest. "Should be flat. See?"

He dropped the pencil, then pressed his hand on Aelya's chest. Instinctively, she shoved him back on his chest. In his state, he fell down easily. Someone laughed. Usy shot back to his feet, his eyes wide. His hand drifted down toward his boot.

Stitches shoved Aelya aside and grabbed Usy's hand before he could reach his knife. None of Aelya's combat instincts kicked in. She just stood there. Men tackled Usy. She wasn't sure who they were.

A chant arose from the back. "Fight! Fight! Fight!"

Red stormed over. They let go of Usy. He held his hands up. Nothing was clear in Aelya's head as she lunged forward, her hand connecting with the side of his face. She winced at the pain in her hand, clutching it. Usy stared in shock for half a second. He barely moved forward before he was tackled once again.

"Get him out of here. Guardhouse. Now!" said Red. He was about to turn to Aelya, but she walked away before he could. She knew she shouldn't, but she sped up, heading out the door and up the steps, into the air laced with fog and snow. A gasp came from her right.

Muromets was shivering as he stared at her, wrapping his arms around himself. His glasses were fogging up.

"It's freezing," she said without thinking. "You should get inside."

He dropped to his knees in front of her. "I'm so sorry," he said. "I would never wish such embarrassment upon you. But now you know."

"What?"

"I love you, Aelita Petrovna."

She staggered backward. She remembered Valeri Popov in eighth grade, stealing looks at her during class. It was common knowledge how he felt. She'd always expected something like this to happen and rehearsed how she would break his heart as gently as possible. He never did work up the courage to talk to her and by the summer turned his attention to Zoya Kamenskaya.

She said nothing, only recoiled. She tried to regain her composure, but the excruciating look on Muromets's face meant it was too late. At that moment, he looked like an eighth grader himself. Muromets struggled back to his feet and ran away, disappearing around the corner of the bunker.

The door burst open. Frost and Lara.

"Where's The Legend?" said Frost.

Aelya pointed numbly.

"I'll look after him," he said and hurried off.

Lara put her arms around Aelya. "You'd best get inside before you catch a chill."

"No, I can't go back in there."

"They took Usy out through the operations room."

"It's not that. I can't go back and face everyone. Not after they heard . . . all that."

"That's on Muromets, not you."

Aelya shook her head until Lara grabbed her by the arms and said, "If you don't go back in right away, what do you think they'll say about you? You can face down Nazi aces but not this?" Lara smiled slightly.

She was right. This was stupid. Why was everything so much easier up in the air? She took a deep breath and headed back in.

CHAPTER 47: OVERSHOOT

At the end of the day, in his office, Red dropped the bomb on Aelya. "Grounded indefinitely?" Aelya said with indignation, forgetting her rank for a moment.

"You won't be out long," he said. "This weather won't hold forever. When the action heats up, we'll need every pilot. We're calling it a personal disagreement that got a little out of hand. Happens all the time, but we need to be seen taking action."

"What about Usy?"

Red nodded. "You want an apology? He'll apologize."

"I don't care about that, Comrade Commander," she said. "What's his punishment?"

"A day in the guardhouse."

"And then?"

He said nothing.

"He gets to fly while I don't?"

"We need men like him," said Red. "I think that's plenty of punishment for hurting your feelings."

"He did more than that."

"He put a hand on you," Red said, scoffing. "If you were a man, we wouldn't be talking about this. But you chose to strike a fellow pilot, while Dmitriev was in the room."

Was that what everyone was saying? Usy had humiliated her and now she was being punished as if she were the aggressor. But she'd hit him. That undisciplined flash of anger had lost her any moral superiority. She was angry at herself as well.

Red put up his hand for calm. "The important thing is that we all agree it wasn't an actual punch."

Instinctively, Aelya rubbed her swollen and red right hand. She realized it looked as if she was being cheeky. Red ignored that.

"As I said, let's keep this all at a low level. When the action heats up, there'll be no objections to putting you back on the roster. In the meantime, you'll be expected to help with administrative duties."

"Administrative duties? Does that mean . . ." It was bad enough to have to see Muromets to sign off on paperwork. But working side by side every day?

Red suppressed a smirk. "Now you're too good to work in the command post, are you?"

She hesitated, unsure how much he was joking.

Red pondered for a bit. "All right, fine. We'll figure something else out."

Taras took a step closer when the oil drum wobbled.

Aelya held up her hand. "No, thank you. You better get moving or you'll be late for your next assignment."

Taras nodded with a smile so earnest, she envied his satisfaction at so simple a job. Drive from point A to point B. How much could he ever really question himself? Remembering what a hopeless pilot he'd been, she thought his new assignment for the best.

The truck drove away. She strained with all her might to lower the drum gently on its side. It compacted the snow into a hard footpath as she rolled it into the first revetment. Masha's mechanic rushed over as soon as she spotted her and with an appreciative smile helped to roll it into a corner. One down, five to go.

The next drum was for Stitches's revetment. He was just leaving, his parachute and helmet in hand, when she got there.

"How was it?" she asked.

"We spent the whole day chasing. The front line's moving too fast, and the bombers on both sides keep getting revectored, looking for something to bomb. Every time we hit the zone, Fritz has disappeared."

"Still good to be back at it."

He dropped his gear to help her right the drum. His crew were hunched over the nose of his plane, their tools clanging against the engine.

Stitches followed Aelya as she headed back to the drop-off point. "How many more do you have?"

"Four."

"I'll help."

"I don't need your charity."

"Why are you doing this anyway?"

She gave him a sidelong look.

"Come on, how bad could it be?" he asked. "Just pretend nothing happened. I'm sure Muromets will do the same thing."

"That's standard operating procedure around here, isn't it? Don't talk about it, because eventually, one of you is going to die anyway."

She handled the next drum so roughly, it slipped and she had to jump backward as it slammed into the snow.

"You all right?" Stitches said.

She whistled. "Almost ended up like Petrushka there."

She began to roll the drum toward another revetment. She looked back. Stitches hadn't moved. As she came closer, she saw he was trembling. She moved to his side. He looked about to collapse.

"What's wrong?"

"Nothing. Sorry." He turned his face away. She moved around for a look. Tears streamed down his face. "I just . . . I . . ." He dropped to his knees and buried his face in his hands, sobbing loudly.

Aelya knelt next to him, her arm around his shoulder to soothe him because that was what she supposed she should do. Somewhere within was a version of herself who felt sympathy, but Aelya could only experience it at a remove. More immediately, she was disturbed; the sight of Stitches crying simply made no sense.

"I really wish he was here," he said, sniffling.

"We all miss Petrushka, even his terrible wisecracks."

"No, you don't understand. I'm being selfish. We always had this joke. A morbid competition, trying not to be the one to die first. How can I explain? It was as if, so long as he was there, it couldn't be so bad. Neither of us would die alone. Moscow. Rzhev. Kharkov. We made it through all of that. And now the dumb jerk's gone and broken his leg and left me to die here. I just know it. I'm going to die here."

He was screeching. He was the veteran. He was supposed to be strong.

Aelya couldn't hold back. "Stop it! Just stop it! What right do you have to crack up on me? You, Lieutenant I-Don't-Care-About-Them-Until-They've-Flown-a-Dozen-Missions. You're not supposed to do this. Pull yourself together!"

He didn't. He was bawling now, so she grabbed him by the arms and shook him, saying "Do I have to hit you like I did Usy?"

He took his hands from his face and stared for a second before giggling. He fell on his back to the snow, laughing uncontrollably. The swift motion pulled Aelya off balance and she fell next to him. He calmed down, gasping for breath. They looked at each other for a quiet moment.

Finally, she said, "I need to finish my rounds."

She got up and began rolling the oil drum.

"Mars—"

"I'll be fine. You better get some rest."

She didn't look back.

Roza was leaving her own revetment, coming to meet her. "What was that all about?"

"Just needed to knock some sense into Stitches."

"Stitches?" Roza cocked an eyebrow.

Aelya continued on her way, but Roza followed and said, "Don't get too full of yourself."

"What do you mean by that?"

"This strutting around."

"I am not strutting."

"You know why I called you No-Shot? It's not because that Messer crashed. It's because you had half a panzer division in front of you and you never touched the trigger."

Aelya stopped. She hadn't fired during the recon because she was saving ammo. No, that wasn't it; she simply never thought about it at the time. She'd been surprised during the debriefing to hear that Lara strafed the enemy at the end of the recon run. Aelya was so focused on not getting hit, she never noticed what Lara had been doing.

"I'm sorry I'm never good enough for you," she said, slamming a gloved hand on the side of the drum. Roza opened her mouth, but Aelya said, "Are we done?"

Roza screwed up her face, then shrugged and went away.

Aelya continued on her rounds. Great, she thought. Roza could go to hell. Who was she to tell Aelya she was getting too big for herself? Roza was soaking in all the adulation Dmitriev kept directing her way. News stories. Film crews. Word was she would be featured on a propaganda poster soon. The war was a big success story for Roza, though she was almost finished before it had even started. She should have been expelled by Raskova.

A memory gnawed at Aelya—the memory that she too should have been expelled, and would have been if not for Lara's good graces. But Roza was different. It wasn't fair. She was a good pilot, sure. But life must have always been easy for Roza. She was cagey about her past, because she wanted to pretend she wasn't one of those privileged Party types, always used to getting her way. Of course, it was easy for her to tell everyone else what they were doing wrong.

She found herself standing in the snow, clenching her fists. She'd been feeling as though she finally belonged, that she had figured out being a fighter pilot. Roza had ruined that feeling. And now she was wasting her time thinking about it.

"Bang, you're dead!" Aelya called out. "Overshoot."

She heard a familiar groan over the radio. How many times did they need to do this? Maybe she was being too difficult, her fighter instincts overwhelming her patience as an instructor. Erdyniyev wasn't a bad pilot really—he just exhibited poor decision making in combat. Not that she was any sort of expert in that regard, she thought ruefully.

"Let's try again," she said in a measured way.

Erdyniyev's plane climbed into cloud cover, which wasn't very far, given the weather.

Aelya took her own fighter into a low, loping circuit, mimicking a Stuka hunting for targets. She had to admit, she was enjoying being in the air again, even just for training. No one thought Erdyniyev was ready for combat and with the action heating up, the veterans had no patience to hold his hand. Red had even hinted it would be another day or so before she hit the active roster again.

She kept scanning all sectors of the sky. She spotted Erdyniyev's silhouette. He was trying to come from the direction of the sun, but the overcast muted any glare it might give.

"Spotted you. Try again. Use higher clouds," she said.

"Yes, comrade."

She loved the intense thrill of looking out for her stalker. Briefly, her heart thrummed with the rhythm of combat. How she wished her guns were primed and she could actually use them. She stewed over Roza calling her No-Shot. A vision passed through her mind: the burning man again. She hated thinking about it. She just wanted to get into action again. Everything would clear itself up then.

Erdyniyev was better this time, streaking out of the clouds ahead of her, trying to come from the high front, away from a Stuka's tail gunner. She broke hard, twisting to give her hypothetical gunner a shot. Erdyniyev was coming too fast again, probably pumped full of adrenalin. It was a simple matter to roll away from danger, then line him up as he overshot. A fat, juicy target. A Stuka only had two rifle-calibre frontal machine guns. Erdyniyev would have probably survived even point-blank hits. But a fighter pilot who felt safe was soon a dead fighter pilot. Best to drive the point home.

"Bang, you're dead!"

CHAPTER 48: NEW TENANTS

Though a parachute packer had already tugged on Lara's harness, Aelya did as well, making sure it was snug.

"It's nice to see you back in flight gear," Aelya said.

Lara held up her hands, red and raw with new skin. Her face still had the outline of goggles burned around the eyes, the scars covered in petroleum jelly. Those eyes now took in the sight of her plane in its revetment. She inhaled the intoxicating fumes of aviation fuel.

"I missed this. I can't believe Dr. Krupenya kept me away for so long."

"They needed help at the hospital."

Lara chuckled. "It wasn't about that. She was afraid I'd just pop into a fighter when she wasn't looking. It's hard for her, protecting us pilots from ourselves." Lara stopped herself from saying something more, and this wasn't the time to ask about it.

"Just don't push it, all right?" Aelya said.

"What's to push? It'll be easier than getting back on a bicycle." Lara smiled. "So how have you been doing?"

This was just a question to show interest. What could Aelya really say?

"Flying on Usy's wing . . . has been good."

"What was he like, when—"

"Oh, that's all sorted. He said sorry. Now we just act like nothing happened."

Lara raised an eyebrow. Perhaps she detected her bitterness, so Aelya added, "As long as I show him he doesn't scare me, he's quite manageable."

"Good for you. What's it like out there?"

"A lot of chasing."

It had been just as Stitches had described. In between bad weather and shorter daylight hours, it was a struggle to hunt down any action. There had been that one time with a Heinkel. She'd hit it hard, but it didn't go down. Baby claimed a kill shortly after. Was it the same one? There was a case for calling it a shared kill, but that would have involved lobbying Muromets, and she wasn't ready for that. It was awkward enough having to fly with Usy.

Aelya exhaled. "You ready, Comrade Commander?"

"Stop being so fussy. It's just a relocation."

"But your first mission as squadron commander."

Lara smiled. "I'll admit to feeling good. I hear you have reason to feel good too."

"The commendation? That might not lead to anything. From what I hear, even informants get medals."

"Don't be so cynical. That reconnaissance mission wasn't just busywork. You got crucial information that's helping us win this battle. Wars turn on that sort of thing. And don't forget, you saved my life too."

Accepting responsibility for someone else's life felt overwhelming for Aelya, and she couldn't meet Lara's eyes, not wishing to take the credit.

"Wish I could have saved your face too," she blurted out. "I'm sorry—that came out wrong."

Lara clapped her on the back. "Listen to you. Talking like a veteran."

Lara's new wingman approached. "Sergeant Erdyniyev," said Lara. "We haven't flown together, so let's spend a few minutes after takeoff going over how I operate."

"Absolutely, Comrade Commander."

"We call him Lucky now," said Aelya.

"I hope that's not meant to be ironic," said Lara.

"Definitely not," said Aelya. "He got his first kill on his first engagement."

Lucky looked bashful. "Believe me, I hardly knew what was going on. I'm amazed I made it back."

You got that right, thought Aelya. He'd sprayed the sky full of shells and somehow got in a freak hit that exploded a Ju 88. Meanwhile, he got separated from his wingman and his engine was hit multiple times yet kept working. He was alone and disoriented after the battle, and Caspian, the new radio beaconing station, found him and talked him back to base. When he landed, they found an unexploded cannon shell just under his seat and a nickname was born. But Lara didn't need to hear about that just yet.

"I just hope the luck rubs off on everyone," said Aelya.

Lara smiled and tied on Aelya's scarf, and Aelya did the same for her.

"Welcome to Maloye Zakharovo," said Red. "Beautiful place. I hear it's become quite desirable now that the old tenants have moved out."

That got a laugh out of the pilots. The Luftwaffe had abandoned this airfield, a cluster of camouflaged buildings over grassland with a few woods nearby and a dirt strip, now covered in compacted snow.

"Unfortunately, there's no way for our support battalion to make it here today, so you'll have to prepare some temporary accommodations in the woods." There were a few grumbles.

"Why not use the buildings on the base?" asked Dema.

"The crew that checks for booby traps is with the support battalion." The grumbling quieted. Red said, "The technicians will focus on sheltering the planes. You lot, split up into squadrons. Muromets will hand out supplies. And don't forget your new assignments."

He dismissed the pilots and they gathered into three squadrons by the edge of the woods. There had been a personnel shuffle. Stitches's squadron was now dedicated to "free hunting." With an entire German army of three hundred thousand caught in Stalingrad by the Red Army's pincers, the enemy was flying in supplies by air. The free hunters were charged with hitting those transports, along with any other targets of opportunity. They also got a couple of aces on loan from the 466th for this purpose, Wolf and KV.

Assignments had also been switched due to losses. Sleepy was killed while flying as Yulia's number one. Three of Yulia's wingmen had died, and there were whispers she was cursed. Now she flew with Olga, the only one willing to take her on. Tselner was gone too, and there had been a new pilot Aelya couldn't remember very well. He was badly burned and signed off. Tonya quipped it was a fair exchange for getting two aces, and no one disagreed.

A couple of technicians brought a crate over to Stitches's squadron. Inside were fur boots, donated by a sable-farming *kolkhoz* from Siberia.

Aelya eyed them. "Those will work much better than our *valenki*." She shook off snow from the felt boots she wore over her standard-issue winter footwear. It was still better than having nothing at all, which was apparently what the Germans trapped in Stalingrad had.

Tonya snorted. "Don't be so happy. Free hunters will be the only ones getting those. You'll see."

"Really?" she looked at Lara.

"They get priority," she said.

"Top choice in supplies, top choice in wingmen," Tonya said quietly. She was still moaning about Bison. There was some truth to her accusations that he'd bailed out early during their last engagement. No one could confirm, but Tonya insisted it was before they even tangled with the enemy.

While the supplies made Aelya envious of Stitches's squadron, she wanted to show him how she'd changed. She wasn't cowed by the enemy, nor by Roza. She must have been out of her mind to scold him when he'd been hurting. She just needed the chance to talk to him, one on one.

Muromets allotted them tents and sleeping rolls. Even in this cold, he held his ever-present clipboard with bare hands. Aelya refrained from eye contact.

"So what's it going to be?" asked Tonya. "Are the free hunters getting better tents as well?"

"Don't get too excited, Honeybee. The supplies are allotted by squadron, but accommodations will still be separated by sexes." Muromets seemed downright sunny. He caught Aelya's eye and smiled briefly. She was relieved. Frost must have given him another talking to. Now they could pretend nothing had happened. The usual.

They handed out hatchets and shovels, and the squadron began trekking through the woods to find a spot to set up. Usy sang the workers' march from *Shining Path* and Aelya found herself humming along. Within the shelter of the woods, the ubiquitous pounding of artillery lessened. Making new tracks through freshly fallen snow, Aelya could almost picture herself in some idyllic peasant landscape. She suddenly found herself short of breath, needing to rest next to a tree.

"Just slipped," she said when Lara came to help.

It was all hitting her: the idea that there could be life outside of this war for her. Just as she was starting to feel right about her place in it. The war itself seemed to be turning. Beyond Dmitriev's positive updates, the very fact that their base had moved westward, toward Germany, made victory almost tangible. And she was a part of it.

She stared at a silhouette of herself cast against the blank canvas of snow. Who was this person in the shadow? Could she be proud of herself? Was she whole? Would her family recognize her?

To one side of her, Stitches and Roza laughed as they debated whether or not the clearing they'd found would be a suitable spot to put up tents. This jovial banter grated on Aelya. Stitches felt like her responsibility. He had confided in her about his fears. She was the one who'd pulled the old Stitches away from the brink. She worried about him. Was his current humour just masking the fatalism he'd shown her? Was she just worried or something else? And that kiss they'd shared. An embarrassing loss of control in the moment, but it seemed to reflect some bond they shared as well.

She'd fallen behind and hustled through the snow to catch up to Lara.

"Feeling better?" Lara asked.

Aelya waved her hand dismissively and picked up the pace. After Roza's patronizing comments about getting too big for herself, the last thing Aelya wanted was someone else treating her like a child. With each hard breath as she stepped through the snow, however, her irritation dissipated. She knew she was being ungrateful to Lara. Lara had a husband to worry about, every day, not knowing if he was already dead, the notification tied up in the post somewhere. Yet Lara was still looking out for her, bearing the responsibility for her when she was still a month shy of the minimum age.

Aelya stopped to let her catch up. "How do you manage?" she asked. "How do you go on without worrying about Zhenya, without it driving you crazy?"

Lara halted next to her, planting her shovel in the snow. "Is there someone you're thinking about?"

"No." She hadn't meant it like that. But she thought about Stitches. "I mean, yes. Well, not like that . . ."

Lara held up her hand. "You don't need to tell me. With Zhenya, well, sometimes I'm angry at myself for falling in love with a pilot. Before the war, it was just a shared passion. Not even that—it was a hobby for him. We couldn't have known it would put us both in such danger. But I hear that all the time. 'If not for the war . . . if not for the war.' I can't live like that. If it's something that's meant to be, why fight fate? We can't let the war deny who we are."

Aelya's conception of destiny wasn't of something unavoidable. Like her mother said, there was a power in flying that was unnatural. Surely that meant fate was mutable too. It was her parents' rational determination that set her on her path to becoming a pilot.

Someone screamed. Lara and Aelya dropped their tools and ran toward the sound, Tokarevs already coming out of their holsters. They found Yulia at the edge of a clearing, buried in Olga's arms, Frost urging them to move away. Behind them, the snow was broken by lumpy ground. A second later, the truth registered. Bodies. Row upon row of frozen bodies in the rictus of death.

"Civilians," said Red, kneeling down for a closer look. "Bullets to the head."

Usy spat on the ground.

Baby cursed. "I don't want to wait for this base to get up and running. I want to shoot a Fritz now!"

"You'll be glad of the wait," said Red. "You'll kill more of them with a cooler head."

"Who's to say it was Fritz?" said Dema. "These might be collaborators. Maybe our side did them in."

"Nah, look at the noses on these ones," said Usy. "Gotta be Jews. This was a Nazi job."

Aelya ground her teeth. Usy would have made a great Nazi thug himself.

Stitches said, "Jews, collaborators, gypsies . . . maybe just wrong place at the wrong time. Does it matter? It's not like either side needs much reason to kill."

"Come on," ordered Red. "This is for the support boys to clean up. Let's go to the other end of the wood."

Everyone heartily agreed and moved away as quickly as possible. As Aelya retrieved her shovel, she was surprised at how calm she was. There was truth to what Stitches said. She couldn't summon the will to care about these people. At one time the very thought of defending the Socialist ideal had been enough for her to put her life on the line, even though her concept of sacrifice was abstract. Now she knew what sacrifice really involved. Some portion of herself had been taken away by the war. She had achieved her destiny, whatever that meant, but also gained the realization that all life, including hers, was worth less than she'd ever imagined.

They moved through the trees, which now obscured the bodies. It was as though they no longer existed.

CHAPTER 49: THE SHOPPING TRIP

Dmitriev's new office at Maloye Zakharovo was sumptuously appointed compared to anything else Aelya had seen since the school at Engels. The Luftwaffe certainly hadn't stinted on luxuries when they occupied this airfield. Dmitriev sat at a wooden desk inlaid with art deco enamel designs. Light was provided by a brass desk lamp. Behind him stood a cabinet filled with liquor, probably from every country the old Stuka unit had been based during their conquests. They'd left in an awful hurry. Only Stalin's portrait evinced a change in occupants.

"I feel we're lagging in progress," Dmitriev said.

"I feel it too," she said absently.

Despite the tardiness of the support battalion, the unit was up and running within a couple of days. But this relocation was more frustrating than the last one. The supply situation meant that only the free hunters were flying regularly. Aelya's flight time was limited to area orientation and the occasional airfield defence. On days like today, the poor visibility provided all the defence the base needed.

"Just look at this!" Dmitriev said, shaking a newspaper before tossing it on the desk. It was the official Air Force newspaper.

"'STURMOVIKS WIPE OUT PANZER BATTALION,'" Aelya read.

"No, not that, look down there."

"'FATHER'S FACTORY DONATES PLANE TO SON.'"

The article, tucked away in the corner, was about a pilot in the 466th. His father worked on the Yak assembly line in Saratov. The father and his fellow workers pooled money to "buy" one of their own fighters and deliver it to his son, complete with a dedication painted on its side. It was a fairly common occurrence, everyone pitching in for the war effort.

"It's that Berbatov—I know it," said Dmitriev. "He's got a friend in the Sovnarkom."

She tried to change her blank expression, to no avail.

"Ruslan Berbatov." Dmitriev wagged a finger at her. "He's the commissar for the 466th. You understand how wrong this is? We have the divisional free hunters. Us. We're the ones shooting down the transports. When the Luftwaffe's airlift fails and the Germans in Stalingrad surrender, it will be because of us. It'll be our victory."

Aelya twisted her lip, struggling not to smirk. Dmitriev liked to consider himself one of the pilots when times were good.

"So you want the news to acknowledge our role?" she asked.

"Our crucial role. Everybody seems to be getting a pat on the back except us. We can't be forgotten when the victory comes. You think the little Ivan *frontoviks* in the city could thrive without us? The tankists? Did you know they're making heroes out of lone snipers? One man with a measly rifle. Next they'll be giving gold stars to the barge captains on the river."

"Everyone contributes in some way," she said, repeating one of his past aphorisms.

"Yes, but some contribute more than others. The people need to know that."

And his higher-ups as well.

He took a deep breath. "All right, enough of that. What have you got for me?"

Aelya dreaded these quiet days. Dmitriev always chased her down for updates on her achievements as Komsomol organizer and conjured up new assignments for her.

"Well, I thought a piece about the perils of smoking would be a good place to start in promoting healthy living." She'd suggested it last time they'd met, mainly so she could irritate Tonya with a mandatory health lecture.

Dmitriev stared blankly at her. He rose violently from his chair and paced to a board covered in news clippings. The photos from that time they rescued Nemchinov and Ulanova from the bomber regiment had a prominent place.

"No, no, no, not that. What I need is this!" He waved his hands rapidly in front of the picture. "More of this! You're sitting on the greatest propaganda potential. Unleash it. Give me something!"

"Uh . . ." Her mouth hung open.

Dmitriev snapped his fingers repeatedly. "Come now, girl. You can do better than that. What about your comrades in the night bomber regiment?"

"The 588th?"

"Yes. They have a catchy nickname. What is it again?"

Dina hadn't mentioned their nickname in her letters, but word had been going around the front.

"The Night Witches," she said.

"Yes, that's right. The Germans are calling them that: *Nacht Hexen.* Because they bring terror in the night. That's perfect. Do you girls have a nickname?"

"Well, you like to call us your Sparrow Squadron."

Dmitriev paused briefly in his animated gesticulations. "That's no good. We need something—wait, you know what? We don't need to work the collective angle. We have a star. Roza Kulik!"

Aelya felt herself souring. Roza would hate this sort of attention. No, that was a total lie—Aelya was jealous.

"What do you call Roza? I hear you all have pet names for each other."

"Lily."

"Lily? Oh, a joke. But that's perfect. Lily of Stalingrad. A beauty who blossomed from the horrors of war. Yes, I can make that angle work."

"She'll love it," Aelya said with a sly smile.

Dmitriev wasn't the only beneficiary of the Luftwaffe's unintended largesse. The first bunker cleared of traps after the command post was the officer's club. It came complete with a bar and a mounted bear's head on the wall. Stains in the shape of beer kegs marked the wall behind the bar. Those amenities had been removed in case of booby-trapping and poisoning. Nonetheless, with a couple of wood stoves, comfortable chairs, and solid tables to play cards on, the place had become the pilots' ready area after the technicians wired radio speakers to the club's central pillar.

Aelya huddled in her winter flight suit with Lara, Olga, and Yulia over cups of hot chocolate. They surreptitiously checked how Tonya was faring at the next table. She seemed to have cornered half the pot in her game of *durak.*

The gramophone played a jazz recording by the American Paul Robeson, who rumour had it was performing for the Red Army—somewhere far from Stalingrad, unfortunately. The recording began to skip. Frost, who'd decided it was too cold to play the guitar, went over to hit it and it stopped playing altogether.

A jeep pulled up outside. The door opened, bringing in a gust of snow and biting air.

"Look who I found on the way here," Red said.

Bison ambled in with an infantryman's greatcoat and *ushanka* hat. He was greeted by a half-hearted cheer. Aelya caught Tonya rolling her eyes. He'd bailed out the day before and she'd taken to calling him "Breakdown."

"Now," said Red, closing the door behind him, "do I have any volunteers for a special assignment?"

No hands went up. If it were combat related, Red would've simply chosen the pilot. This was his idea of a joke.

"Shepel's had a successful shopping trip over at Kotluban. I need someone to take the two-seater there to pick up the new guy."

"Why doesn't Stitches just bring him back on his lap? He's over there anyway," said Baby.

The mention of Stitches caught Aelya's attention and her hand shot up.

Kotluban was distinctly disappointing after sampling a former Luftwaffe establishment. The Air Army headquarters consisted of many buildings, all lined with sandbags and partially covered with earth. Most had been newly built up, and so looked like grubby protuberances poking out from the snow.

After handing the two-seater over to technicians to stow, Aelya was told that the navigators' conference was being held in Building Three. Away from the airfield, all the installations were carefully spaced out. Wide alleys in between allowed a good look at the burned-out remnants of the air base's namesake village, the scene of savage fighting in the autumn.

Personnel of all ranks rushed around, looking very busy. She noticed one sergeant smoking a cigarette beside the door to a building with a large number 3 painted above it. He constantly stamped his boots, unprotected by *valenki*.

"You headed to the 497th?" she asked him.

He straightened up, surprised. "Yes, how did you know?"

She used her foot to tap a black suitcase at his feet. "You have 'new pilot' written all over you."

He stared at her aviator's badge. "You're one of them, aren't you? I heard the unit had women pilots, but it's another thing to see them. Er, apologies, Senior Sergeant."

Aelya smiled. She had gotten so used to being within the fighter regiment, she hadn't felt like a novelty in a while, despite Dmitriev's propagandizing.

They introduced themselves. He was Bohdan Borisovich Bronfman.

"You can call me Triple B, for short."

"Is that what they called you in flight school?"

His cheeks flushed. "They . . . just called me Bronfman."

"A piece of advice. Don't advertise your nickname. Everyone will call you the opposite."

"What's the opposite of Triple B?"

"I don't know, but I'm sure it will be something terrible."

He laughed nervously, only relaxing when she smiled. "You're not what I expected," he said.

She made a show of pouting. "You were expecting a moustache?"

"No, not at all. The opposite, really. I'd read so much about Roza Kulik. I'd just thought, uh, well, what I mean is . . ."

Now her expression soured. "You were expecting a glamorous movie star."

"No . . . shorter. I thought you'd be shorter, or something like that."

She rolled her eyes. Just keep it up, yellow-mouth.

"Mars!" Stitches jogged over, his new wingman, Starik, in tow. Under one arm he carried a small cardboard box. "We'd heard you were coming and were looking for you out on the airfield. You were too quick for us."

"Sorry, I was just dying to meet our newest member."

"Don't look so uptight." Stitches slapped Bronfman on the back. "Our women don't bite, although this one might puke on you." He tilted his head at his wingman. "Starik, get over to the controller's and get our planes readied. I want to fly out of here before it gets too snowy and they make us sleep in the hangars. Take the new fellow with you and start showing him how we do things. Sorry, we'll do proper introductions later. Mars and I will stay here and see how long Shepel and Chumak are going to be."

Starik nodded and signalled for Bronfman to follow him back toward the airfield. Aelya turned to Stitches. She needed to build up to talking with him about personal things. About how he was feeling.

"Starik's a bit new to be giving lessons, isn't he?" Great. Couldn't she have tried something other than small talk?

"I just wanted to get them out of the way." Stitches walked her over to the side of the building, where they were sheltered somewhat from the wind.

He knelt down to open the box and took out a small metal canister with a screw top. "This is fruit syrup. Peach, I think. Petrushka sent it from the hospital." Stitches paused, holding in his emotions. Then he unscrewed the lid and sniffed the contents before passing it to Aelya to examine.

"I'm not sure what peaches are supposed to smell like, but it's nice," she said.

He took the container back. "I'll show you a trick." He poured a generous helping of the red-orange syrup over a clean pile of snow. Putting the canister away, he took off his gloves and scooped the flavoured snow off the ground. He took two bites, then offered it to her. "Petrushka meant for this to be used with liquor chassis, but I thought you'd enjoy this more."

She certainly did, chomping off a mouthful of the snow. The syrup was so sweet it was overpowering, the ice crystals giving it a crunchy texture. They took turns, the sticky syrup rimming their lips.

Stitches said, "That's one good thing to come out of this war. I don't think I would have ever experienced this otherwise." He looked into the distance. "My family . . . when I lost my family, I could have given up. I had to make a choice. I had to do some things that made me question if it was all worth it, even if I got a chance to join the Air Force. When the war started, I thought I could do some good. But," he said, laughing, "I really wasn't sure until now. It was worth it."

"It must be hard being an orphan. Having to make tough choices on your own." She wanted to slap herself to stop the idiotic words coming out of her mouth.

Stitches looked confused for a moment, then just grunted as he returned his attention to the treat in front of him. Pretty soon, only a slick of melted, syrupy snow remained on his hands. He stuck one hand in his mouth to lick it off. Reflexively, she reached for his other hand, sticking out her tongue before she realized what she was doing. She let go and stepped back quickly. He cleared his throat, then plunged his hands into snow to clean them off. Rising, he shivered and stuck his hands in his armpits to warm them.

"Here," she said, stripping off her gloves and taking his hands. She rubbed them together. Her breath shortened and her pulse quickened. It was the same feeling as flying. She liked that he was so cheerful and open with her. But there was something else; she dared not think it.

He said, "Thanks. You're such a good person."

"Don't say that." Warmth rushed to her cheeks.

"It's true. I'm glad you're here. I really wanted to speak with you."

"You did?"

He took a look around, afraid of being overheard. "I just—I just needed to say something. I don't know how I should feel. There's someone I . . . I care about. I worry when she's in danger. More than with the others. Is that wrong?"

She found herself speechless. What could she say? She realized now how he made her feel. Out of all this madness, she mattered to someone. And he mattered to her. Was she in love?

Feet stamped in crescendo from the building behind her, momentarily distracting them. She felt her pulse rising almost in response to the pace of the noise around them.

"When you see someone every day," he continued, "and you can't be truthful, it's agony. What should I do?"

She inhaled sharply. He was asking her? Her brain focused as if she were in combat, homing in on the closest thing to wisdom she could grasp. She remembered what Lara had told her. "If it's something that's meant to be, why fight it? We can't let the war deny who we are."

Stitches brought her hands to his lips and kissed them. She couldn't bear to look him in the face. She'd never really been in love with someone. What if she did something wrong? She turned toward the thoroughfare between buildings, watching officers rush to and fro.

"You're right. Thank you," he said. "I know what to do now. You're such a good friend."

He hugged her. She was dazed with confusion. What he said didn't quite make sense. Unless . . . he wasn't talking about her. They pulled apart and she struggled to find words, but his attention was already drawn to the mass of people running past them. They stepped back out in front of the building. They quickly recognized Chumak exiting the conference building.

Stitches waved a hand to catch the attention of their regiment's deputy navigator. "What's going on?" he asked Chumak.

"We have to get back to base. The Germans have launched their counterattack."

CHAPTER 50: AFTER ACTION

Aelya stamped her feet on the floor of the operations bunker's annex. She was about to take off her fur-trimmed greatcoat when Muromets stopped her.

"You probably want to keep that on. It's almost as cold in here as it is out there." He had all his winter gear on as well. He pushed up the earflaps of his *ushanka* to adjust his glasses.

"Coffee?" he asked.

"No thank you. I'm jittery enough as it is. Do you know what this is about?" She nodded toward the briefing room, where presumably she was to report, though Muromets showed no signs of being in a hurry to usher her in.

"They usually tell me only after the fact, when I need to file the paperwork." He wrung his hands for a moment, then seemed to reset himself. "Been a hard day? Four sorties?"

"Three. Gear failed after the second one and I hit a rut belly landing. Tore off part of the tail assembly." It was a minor miracle, one she had gotten used to, that Zina's crew had her plane ready for the final mission of the day.

"Well, I'm glad you came back safely."

Aelya smiled. "It's good to talk to you. You know, maybe—"

The door to the briefing room opened and one of Shepel's deputies stuck his head out.

"Makarova, you're up."

Muromets squeezed her shoulder. She went into the briefing room. By virtue of the wood stove and the presence of Red, Shepel, and several staff officers, it was warmer than she'd expected, and she had no problem taking her fur cap off and standing to attention. Shepel gestured for her to take a seat. The way they had formed a semicircle around her put her on guard and she almost turned to check behind her, the way she did at any sign of trouble in the air. Her neck was sore from doing that relentlessly for the past several days.

Red sat directly opposite her, not moving a muscle. Next to him, Shepel sat on a chair turned backward, his arms resting on its back. Shepel began. "I know you must be exhausted. We'll try to get through this as quickly as we can so you can get some rest."

Exhausted didn't begin to describe it. Every day for nearly a week, she had flown multiple sorties per day and encountered the enemy about every other time. Bad weather only restricted mission parameters or reduced flying time but was no excuse to avoid combat. The Germans certainly weren't using it. And that they'd rarely closed within gun range didn't make it any less tiring.

Shepel continued, "We need you to go over the sweep you conducted over sector Zoya-6 yesterday."

She wracked her brain. "The airfield strike?" How could they be asking about that? Sure, they'd lost a couple of Sturmoviks to ground fire, but once they went on an attack run, fighter escorts could do little about that.

"No, that was two days ago. I'm talking about the sweep for the Peshka attack east of Molakonvsky."

The days were bleeding together, but she shouldn't have forgotten that. It had been a catastrophe. Perhaps her brain was blocking it out. But why should it stand out? They'd had other losses recently. A new pilot named Voronovsky. Another whose name she'd forgotten. She knew why this was different, though.

She swallowed. "Yes, Comrade Captain. What do you want to know?"

"Let's just go through the salient details," said Shepel. "What was the first deviation from the mission plan?"

What was the point of this? Memory was flawed and never more so than when flying hundreds of kilometres an hour with adrenalin pumping, ignoring radio traffic, tracking twenty or thirty fast-moving objects in the sky, trying to kill and not be killed, not to mention keeping an eye on the ground so as not to hit it. It was hard enough keeping control of her body. She was getting better at it now. She'd only wet herself three times and vomited twice in the past week.

"Makarova?" said Shepel.

"I'm sorry."

"It's all right. We know the strain you're under."

She looked over at Red, still stone-faced, and felt slightly ashamed. He slept in the command post, dealing with administration until the late hours, then woke up in the middle of the night as orders for the day came through. Even with all that, he'd insisted on flying at least one sortie a day. Shepel continued, "Take your time and retrace your own experience during the mission."

She closed her eyes and began imagining herself in the cockpit. She began to recall details of distances, headings, and waypoints. Just as quickly, she realized she was jumbling all her memories. That was a dead end. What was the first unusual moment?

"Baby had to turn back," she finally said. "He had an aileron problem. And Vino had to go with him, as standard procedure."

"Vino?" said one of the staff officers taking notes.

"Sergeant Bronfman."

He'd made out like a drunk his first night on base. Aelya thought it was all an act. The whole time flying him back from Kotluban, he'd fretted about what the other pilots would call him. He was worried he'd become Bignose, or Yid. He hit the liquor pretty soon after landing, and Frost happened to be there to declare, *"In vino veritas,"* and the name stuck. He probably preferred to be thought of as the unit drunk than the unit Jew.

"Let's move on to your arrival at the patrol sector, Zoya-6," Shepel said.

"Now I remember. Nothing was there." They'd already talked about this. "Our mission was to clear the skies for a close air support run over enemy ground formations, except there were no enemy formations in the air or on the ground, no battle to support."

"How long did you stay in the sector?"

"It couldn't have been more than a couple of minutes. We flew a figure eight to orient ourselves, then Auntie figured out the front line had moved on us."

"She gave the order to change sectors? Did she report this deviation to Antelope?"

"Yes, of course." This line of questioning was new.

"You heard their acknowledgement?"

She hesitated. This felt like a trap. "I couldn't make out much of anything. The reception was bad and there was so much traffic on the frequency. We had around two hundred planes in the air at the time."

"Don't get defensive, girl," said Red. "We're just trying to sort things out. You know this happens whenever we lose bombers."

"We didn't lose any bombers. Our job was to clear the skies over the target area and we did, and that was even after we were given the wrong directions. It was the 466th's job to escort the Peshkas, and they botched it." She took a deep breath. "Sorry, Comrade Commander, but here's what I can remember. We arrived at Zoya-6. Didn't find anything there. Then Auntie gave the order to move north, assuming our troops got pushed back. And she was right. We found a battle going on down there. Auntie talked more to Antelope. Next thing I know, someone called out 110s."

"The Bf 110s," Shepel said. "Who spotted them?"

"I'm not sure. It was either Auntie or Lucky. But everyone saw them maybe a second later."

"But they weren't 110s."

"We didn't know that, did we? I mean, someone called out 110s and we were all so excited. We'd heard a group of them had arrived in the area, painted wasps on their noses. We all wanted a crack at one."

"And you were told to expect German ground attackers in the area, so that's what you saw," said Shepel.

"Don't put words in her mouth, Comrade Captain," said Red.

"But it's true," said Aelya. "And we were also told not to expect our own bombers for another twenty minutes. Anyway, we got within four hundred metres, then Auntie called friendlies. I remember thinking they didn't quite look right for 110s. The shape of the canopies looked funny. As soon as she'd said it, it clicked. They weren't Bf 110s—they were the Peshkas."

"And no one fired?"

"I . . . honestly, it's hard to know." Together with the Peshkas, there must have been over twenty planes clumped together. And so much noise, outside and over the radio. "As far as I know, we aborted the attack in time. Then Honeybee spotted Messers. She and Bison had been flying high in coverage."

"Did the escorts from the 466th make contact yet?"

"No idea. I just remember we had a couple of seconds of warning. Then we were hit hard. Our formation was such a mess already. And Tonya and Bison dealt with the first sweep by the Messers. Then came the second wave of Messers. Then the third. It was all a mess."

Red and Shepel whispered to each other for a moment. They reviewed papers that might have been her initial report. She hoped she was being consistent. Shepel said, "So after the third strike, what happened?"

"Typical Fritz attack. They hit, then climbed away as fast as they could. We'd lost so much height initially, we had no chance to chase them. And in any case, Auntie gave the order to cover the bombers until they were done their attack run. The 466th lost a lot of guys, so we figured we should help out, but we were running low on fuel and couldn't stay long."

"What about your own losses?"

Aelya swallowed. "I didn't hear what happened to Bison. My radio was hit pretty early on. All I know is what Honeybee told me afterward."

"What did she say to you?"

She wasn't sure what she should say. Now she started remembering other things. Before he'd returned to base, Baby had made a crack that his plane must have caught Bison's disease. And before that, at least according to a rumour Lucky had passed on, Red had threatened to shoot Bison if he turned back early on one more mission.

"You should ask Honeybee."

"We're asking you."

"She said Bison was slow to attack. She dived at the Messers first. And then later someone else told Bison to get moving. That was when he rammed the enemy, apparently."

The words she'd heard had been more colourful. Tonya had told her the whole story. Usy swore at Bison, threatening all sorts of misery if he didn't do something. Ramming was survivable; earlier in the autumn, Masha had used her propeller to wreck the tail of a Heinkel after her cannon jammed, then bailed out. Bison didn't take much care; he simply throttled into the nearest Messer. "You want me to do something? How's this?" were his last words.

"So Honeybee positively identified Messerschmitt 109s in that first wave and attacked them? And that was after you'd positively identified your previous targets as Peshkas?"

"Yes."

They didn't care about Bison. This wasn't about his death.

"And you have no idea whether this was before or after the 466th made contact."

"No, I don't remember them acknowledging anything. We never saw them until after the Messers left. Not sure how they lost so many . . ."

The picture suddenly became clearer. A sickening roil built in her stomach.

The rest of the women were waiting for her in the club. All except Roza and Masha, who had already gone back to barracks, sleeping off another hard day of free hunting.

"Finally," said Tonya, taking her feet off the table. "Can we go now?"

"Not so fast," said Yulia, the shorter twin, sitting next to her. "Let me see that." She snatched a piece of paper Tonya was holding.

Lara, who'd been pacing the floor of the club, approached Aelya. Instead of any greeting, she said, "What did they ask you?"

Aelya tried to focus on an answer, but everything she'd said to Red and Shepel now seemed to have happened to someone else, a second-hand memory getting hazier by the minute. "I don't know. The usual stuff."

"What do you mean, 'I don't know?'" Lara snapped.

"They were redoing a debriefing. They talked to you too, right, Honeybee?"

"Yeah, it was just the usual. I hoped you remembered the part where I saved your life."

"We're not supposed to discuss details." Aelya looked from Tonya to Lara. Why was Lara trying to put her in an awkward position?

"Good," said Olga from next to her sister. "Now we can talk about New Year's. Maybe Fritz will surrender by then and we can do a proper celebration. We have to be prepared."

Lara twisted her lip. "You'd better go with them, Mars."

"What about you?"

"They're talking to everyone. I'll wait here until The Legend comes to get me," said Lara.

Olga and Yulia giggled.

"What's so funny?" Aelya asked.

"Nothing." The two sisters straightened up.

Tonya took the paper back from Yulia. "It's private." She stared at Aelya with a dark look, as if begging Aelya to snatch the sheet from her, so that was exactly what Aelya did.

The note was written in familiar handwriting. She began mouthing the words as she read it. "Sup from your sweetest nectar . . ."

"Ew, disgusting!" said Yulia, laughing.

Tonya snatched the sheet back with a wicked smile. "As I said. Private."

No wonder Muromets seemed so content. "Good," Aelya said. Why did she feel so angry about this? "Just treat him well."

"Oh, come on, Mars. Don't be prickly. You had your chance."

A chance. That's all she wanted. A chance to make things right with Stitches, one way or the other. Redness crept into her cheeks recalling the episode outside the navigation conference. It was Roza that he'd been talking about. As leader of the free hunters, he hardly saw Aelya, but he was with Roza all the time. She grimaced, trying to push everything from her mind.

"Oh dear," Tonya needled. "A bit of a sore spot? Tell you what. You can have The Legend back as a treat. I did you a favour. He's got a bit of flight time under his belt now."

She wanted to smack Tonya, but her arms felt numb. She said, "Next time he talks to you, he'll be taking a Messer off your count. Because guess what? It was a Yak from the 466th."

Tonya, Olga, and Yulia all froze. Aelya felt a hand on her shoulder.

"What are you saying?" Lara asked.

"It's true. That's what the debriefings are about. We spotted the Peshkas in time, but that first wave of Messers? Those were Yaks."

"You had a probable," said Tonya. "So you probably killed one of our guys too."

"Enough," said Lara. "You're comrades. Don't talk like that."

"She did it first," said Tonya.

"No," said Aelya, "I didn't hit a friendly. I hit one when the real Messers came."

"I said enough," Lara ordered. "Now get out of here and back to the barracks. Don't discuss this any more. This is my responsibility."

But Aelya needed to talk about this. What if she had hit a friendly? It wasn't just Lara's responsibility. That was on her too. How could Lara be so dismissive just when she needed her the most? Right away, Aelya knew how unfair she was being to her squadron commander. Lara had worry piled upon worry. Fighting and dying. The pilots in her squadron. This investigation. Her husband. Her brother's family.

Just as quickly, Lara softened. She put her hand on Aelya's shoulder, about to say something reassuring, as she always did. But no sound came out. Lara's eyes rolled into her eyelids and she collapsed to the floor.

CHAPTER 51: THE WAY HOME

"Anything?" asked Lara, back in the cockpit. That was best for her. "There's no one here," said Aelya. Below, black smoke, burn marks, and churned earth marred the white snow where the Red Army was coming to grips with the enemy. But everywhere above was a haze of grey and white.

"Even if there are vultures here, there's no way to see them," Usy remarked.

"Should we go down and strafe?" said Lucky.

"If you can figure out which side is which and get them to line up nicely, you're welcome to it," said Lara. "In the meantime . . ."

She shouted into the ether several times and finally caught the attention of Gazelle vectoring station. "This is Sparrow Leader. We've arrived at Ivan One-Three. No vultures. Almost at joker fuel."

Gazelle responded with a permission to thirty-three.

"Thank you for taking my call, Gazelle," Lara said.

"Ladies first," the operator responded.

"I'm happy to hear your sense of gallantry has survived this war."

Her levity continued with Aelya. "Hope you enjoyed the leisurely tour, Mars. Consider it an early birthday present."

There was something unsettling about Lara being so cheerful. She was an optimist but always treated flying seriously. Aelya knew she'd been given medication by Dr. Krupenya, but that was just the one time. She'd also been prescribed a day of rest. It had seemed to do wonders, but something wasn't sitting right. No, this wasn't the time to be questioning Lara's fitness. In any case, her navigation, even in this weather, was still spot on.

Lara gave the order to take a level course home.

"Shouldn't we climb to gain cloud cover?" Aelya asked.

"I'd rather take ground fire than fly through that." Up ahead, a towering wall of ominous clouds rolled across their path. "Throttle up. Let's see if we can outrun the storm."

Aelya watched Lucky struggling against turbulence and low visibility to keep formation on Lara's wing. He kept catching up, then falling behind, never settling on a speed. She wished she could be on Lara's wing right now, but if Lucky had to fly, best that it be with Lara. Usy would have left him for dead long ago.

Lara's voice broke through the background chatter on the radio. "Looks like the snow's going to hit us before we make it home. Stay on your bearings and descend at about twenty degrees. If you lose sight of the others, don't panic. We'll reform at four hundred. Let's go."

Sure enough, the moment Aelya hit the clouds, she was surrounded by grey plumes. She imagined flying through a smoke stack's fumes. The plane reacted violently to the air conditions, jolting her ride, pulling against the controls. The vibrations built to a crescendo, thrumming her body against the seat. It was hard enough to keep her head straight, let alone turn to constantly check for other planes, friend or foe.

The receiver crackled to life. "I can't see anything!" Lucky. "I think my wings are icing."

Why wasn't Lara responding? Aelya waited a half second for Usy to say something instead but realized quickly that was pointless.

"Lucky, stay calm," she called out. "Increase your descent, get out of the cloud."

"What if I hit something?"

"Have you forgotten where you are? There's not a single hill." Unless you got blown way off course, she was thinking.

She waited tense seconds for a response, all the while just hanging on to control of her own plane. Finally, at a touch below five hundred metres, she broke through into the grey-and-white expanse of an overcast day. The rims of her windshield were frosted over. Drifting snowflakes hindered her visibility. It was utterly insane to fly in this weather. So close to home, so close to home, she repeated to herself.

"I'm out!" called out Lucky. "I'm good." She couldn't make it out over the radio, but she imagined a deep sigh of relief.

She scanned the skies. Another dot on the horizon. "Lucky, is that you? I'm at four-fifty. I'm at bearing two-three-zero from you."

"I think that's me," called Usy.

"Forming up with you," said Aelya.

She looked all around. "Auntie, this is Mars. Where are you?"

Silence.

"Lucky, can you see anyone?"

"Uh, no. I don't know where I am."

When Aelya closed with Usy, she still couldn't see the other two planes.

Usy pointed out a familiar stream feeding the Don River and set a course for Maloye Zakharovo.

"What about Auntie and Lucky?" Aelya said. "We should circle, help them get their bearings."

"I'm not wasting any more fuel. What if the enemy hit the runway? We need to save up for contingencies."

"This *is* a contingency."

"Mars, this is an order."

"Should we at least check the runway condition?"

"Fine."

She waited a moment, then realized Usy was making her do it. "Maple Tree, this is Sparrow Two-Three. Come in, please."

She tried several times. All the way, she wondered if they were getting farther and farther away from Lara and Lucky.

When she finally got through to Chumak at Maple Tree, he reported the runway conditions were fine, if a bit slick. More importantly, he hadn't heard from Lara. She spent more precious time checking with Gazelle but got the same answer.

"Guys, help!" Lucky pleaded. "I have no idea where you are. Or where I am."

"Lucky, use the beaconing system," Aelya answered, holding back a groan. "Put in a call to Caspian."

She heard Lucky trying repeatedly to get through. There was so much noise over the radio, and his signal was getting faint.

Aelya fought off her own rising sense of panic. Lara had yet to respond to any calls. What if she was in distress? They needed to keep the frequency as clear as possible.

A stern but very feminine voice broke through the chatter. "Sparrow Two-One, this is Caspian." What she said next was garbled, lost amid the half-heard chatter of dozens of other planes in the air.

"Everyone shut up!" Caspian shouted, and the line went quiet. "Sparrow Two-One, switch your receiver to three-nine-zero-zero. I'll guide you on that."

"Thank you, Caspian," said Lucky. "Am I happy to hear your beautiful voice! You get me through this and I'll marry you after the war."

"That sounds like a punishment, not a reward, Sparrow Two-One," Caspian said in such a flat tone, it was almost soothing.

With the line cleared again, Aelya called for Lara to respond.

"Sparrow Leader, Sparrow Leader, do you read me? Auntie, please answer." More silence. "Usy, I'm going to circle back. If she's bailed out, we'll need to find her quickly in this weather."

"Negative, Mars. I'm your wing leader and I'm responsible for bringing you back. You're almost out of fuel. Land first, fuel up, and then you can search properly."

If Lara was out there, every minute was crucial. She remembered how badly frostbitten she and Sveta had been waiting for their own rescue. But she was Usy's wingman. He was right; she had a responsibility to him and to the regiment to bring her plane back safely.

"Auntie, if you can hear this, I'll be coming back for you."

She called in to Gazelle and reported Lara's last known location, to be passed on to ground units in the area. It was a faint hope. Even with an aerial search in this weather, they'd be hard pressed to find her. They had never found Mouse.

Aelya pushed these thoughts out of her mind. She still had a duty to watch Usy's wing. Fifteen minutes later, she was heading down the taxiway, her canopy open, as Zina came to meet her.

"Zina, I need this ship refuelled and ready to go immediately."

"We'll have to de-ice this thing first. And check for damage. Looks like it took a beating from Mother Nature."

"Can't wait that long. Auntie's still out there."

They locked eyes for a moment, remembering a lonely night on the airfield at Anisovka.

Zina nodded. Aelya hopped out to help guide the plane back to the revetment. Her mechanic fired up the heaters while her assistant quickly went to work checking all the control surfaces. Aelya and Zina rushed to connect a fuel drum.

The sound of a distant engine cut through the wind, and Aelya's heart leaped with excitement. She saw the Yak coming in high and too fast, its propeller cutting out abruptly. The flying was all wrong. She knew who it was before it was close enough to make out the bort number: Lucky. She should have been happy he'd made it, but she was furious he wasn't Lara.

The plane's wheels touched down hard and skidded on the icy runway. It began sliding sideways and continued past the end of the runway, hitting a rough patch close to the revetments before nosing over at the side of the taxiway.

She ran to the plane. It had to be moved. The canopy slid open. Lucky smiled at her as she climbed the inclined wing next to the cockpit. As he undid his harness, she grabbed him, intending to throw him to the ground, but they tangled up and fell together.

"You! This is all your fault!" She knelt over him.

All the joy in his face from a moment ago disappeared.

"Auntie's missing!" she shouted at him. "You're going to help me find her."

"What?"

"You left her out there. You're her wingman. You're supposed to look out for her."

"I'm sorry. It was impossible. How could I track her through that? You saw what it was like."

The memory of losing sight of Usy in the clouds didn't lessen her rage. She grabbed him by the collar, her fists balled.

A voice called out behind her. "Time for debriefing." It was Red. He glowered from the side of the plane, a scarf wrapped around his head underneath his peaked officer's cap. He had no use for bulky *ushankas*.

"No time," said Aelya. "We have to conduct a search for Auntie."

"Did you request permission to fly?" Red asked with a stern look.

"I'm asking for it now, Comrade Commander."

"Good of you to remember you're part of my regiment. Permission denied. I can't risk a plane in this weather for a non-combat sortie. With fuel stocks low, there are none to spare for a search anyway."

"Would you be saying that if Auntie were a free hunter?"

"Yes. It happens. Fighter pilots disappear. It's how we lost Tselner. How we lost Mouse. Maybe she'll be all right, but chances are she's not. In this weather? You'd better accept that she's already gone."

She thought about the struggle against Volkova—a whole lifetime ago, it seemed. She'd been certain Volkova was dead wrong about Galya and Dunya back then, but now she could only weakly say, "And you sent us out anyway."

"Because we have a job to do. Now I'll tell you what you're going to do next. You and Lucky will hop in a jeep with us, drive over to ops, get warmed up over a cup of tea, file your report, then hit your barracks for sleep. Understood?"

It was all a lie; Usy had known there was never a chance of going back out there once they landed. She had known as well and lied to herself. She chose to return safely and leave Lara behind.

Her hand dropped to her holster. She wanted to shoot something, someone. Anyone. Maybe even herself. Her thoughts had no coherence. She felt only overwhelming rage. A hand gently pressed her back, as if holding her up. Zina had quietly come over from the revetment.

Aelya found the strength to stand at attention.

"Yes, Comrade Commander."

CHAPTER 52: THE SPECIAL DEPARTMENT

Readiness one was the worst place to be. Alone in the cockpit. Alone with her thoughts. It made her miserable and yet, even though she had the choice, this was how Aelya wanted to be. She had skipped the brief, muted New Year's Eve celebrations, hiding in the barracks, a pillow pulled over her head. To shut out the feigned happiness while they were all in hell. She'd refused the entreaties of the other women and they left her alone to go off and celebrate, as if Lara weren't dead.

Zina started up the heater again, ensuring the engine wouldn't freeze up as they waited for a call to scramble that might never come. Her crew worked through every night to patch up her plane and every day, Aelya would fly it. In the air, she could forget about all the problems vexing her and focus on the immediate life-and-death tasks at hand. Every night she needed her vodka ration to sleep, but it wasn't enough.

She sat in the cockpit, too tired to be fully aware, too wired to sleep. Thoughts of Lara and Bison and Sveta and a burning man falling from the sky and every other loss haunted her so much, she couldn't be at peace. The weather, no matter how bad, provided no break in the action. The German breakout attempt had failed. Their army in Stalingrad was trapped, and the Luftwaffe futilely tried every day to feed them by air, stalked across the sky by the VVS. Pilots dying every day for men who were already dead. Yet still the Germans in Stalingrad wouldn't surrender.

Just die already, Aelya thought.

She patted the book in her breast pocket. The only thing she could rely on, that still gave her comfort. The last letter she'd received from Kuybyshev had been jarring. Both Papa and Mama excoriated her. They'd figured out with a neighbour's help that the new field post number she gave them was for a frontline unit. How dare she so recklessly gamble with her life? Everything they had done to nurture her, provide for her . . . all thrown away on a whim. They demanded that she ask for a transfer. As if she could, even if she wanted to. She didn't want anything.

She was startled when Red appeared next to her cockpit. He reached behind her and switched off her transmitter. He handed her a sheet of paper, then signalled for Zina and the rest of her crew to stand outside the revetment. "Read this. Memorize it. Then sign it."

Aelya's eyes pored over the sheet. A knot hardened in her stomach. "This is a lie," she said. "You're blaming Auntie for everything that happened with the Peshkas."

"War is ugly, in ways you can't even imagine."

"It's not right. Those Peshkas are on the 466th. It was their job and their mistake."

Shaming her comrades, even in another regiment, made her recoil in disgust. But Red was right. War was ugly.

"Absolutely true. But their commissar's too well connected. They'll never get blamed for this, and believe me, someone needs to be blamed. Losing five Peshkas in one go is a big hit. Mistakes were made all over the place."

"And so you're picking Auntie."

"Just read it properly. You'll see. A normally commendable pilot and squadron commander was suffering from health issues but soldiered on, unfortunately to the detriment of her own judgment."

She remembered the strain on Lara before she had fainted. Had it really affected her judgment? "You make her sound like a flake. Doctor Krupenya checked her out."

"Anyone can crack, even the best of us."

There wasn't much use in countering Red's arguments. But it angered her that he was doing this just before she might fly. She shook her head.

Red groaned. "Everyone who was on that mission has signed off. I left you for last because I knew you'd be a pain about it. I spent all night making these reports line up with each of your debriefings. Saved you the job of doing it. You should be thanking me."

"I want to talk to Shepel."

"He's gone."

She couldn't summon any words.

Red said, "We're pretty sure Gazelle messed up the vectoring that day. But they sit right at Air Army headquarters. You think they're going to get the heat for this? They were going to pin this on Chumak as a navigation error. Shepel decided to throw himself in the line of fire. He said he'd left his soul behind in Lubyanka and had nothing to lose."

"You let them do that to him," she said. "And now you want to stick a knife into Lara's reputation?"

"Time to grow up! This is for the good of the regiment. Auntie's a corpse. Shepel's on borrowed time. Better they be remembered as incompetents than as traitors."

"You're one to talk about betrayal."

"Did you notice the new man with the blue caps? Thought not. That's the way he likes it. He's with something called the Special Department. He's supposed to look for traitors, because of course it's only traitors that must be stopping us from winning this war.

"You want to talk about her reputation? You know what Dmitriev found out when we went through Auntie's things? That brother of hers isn't dead. He's up north somewhere, doing hard labour. He's an enemy of the people. I don't know how she got past the mandatory commission into a fighter regiment."

Raskova, Aelya thought. No wonder Lara was so studious about sending her relatives money. Even if her brother wasn't dead, his family still needed help. Perhaps now more than ever. Because he was a non-person, the job prospects, education opportunities, and access to goods for his wife and children would be severely limited.

Red tapped the note. "We sign off on this, we can close the book on Lara before the Special Department man does any digging. If Dmitriev could turn this up, you better believe that man will too. And then it's not just Auntie's memory that'll be destroyed—it'll be all of us. Can you imagine? A traitor in this regiment? A squadron commander?

"The Special Department would rip this unit apart like a buzzsaw. Maybe you can stand on your convictions, since I don't think they send women to infantry. But some of us don't want to be spilling our guts on some filthy alley in Stalingrad."

There was a fury in his gaze. I won't back down, Aelya told herself. She wanted to punch him in the face. She just wanted to fight. But to what end? What difference would it make?

Aelya breathed deeply. She picked up the pen. "I'll do this, but only so her brother's family can keep getting her pension."

Red held her hand before she could sign. "There'll be no pension. Auntie is missing in action. Missing means a potential POW, and that means potential traitor. They don't pay out pensions for those. You do this, you do it for the regiment."

He let go. Fighting back the bitter taste in her mouth, she signed.

It was dark by the time Aelya was discharged from her duties for the day. She declined a ride back and trudged through the snow to her barracks. She needed to think things over. By the time she arrived at her door, she'd decided on a course of action to make things right, or at least to assuage her guilt.

"I want to start up a collection," she told Tonya, Olga, and Yulia. The free hunters, Roza and Masha, were still completing their reports at ops.

"What did you have in mind?" said Olga. She and her sister were warming up melted snow over the wood stove to wash their faces. The former Luftwaffe barracks they'd moved into may have been spacious and well appointed, but it offered completely inadequate protection from the winter cold. This was exacerbated by the loose boards, which now covered the windows that had been blown out in an air raid a couple of weeks ago.

"You know how Auntie needed to support her brother's family? I thought it would be good to send them something. Take just a bit out of our pay for the next few months."

"I thought they had a pension for that sort of thing," said Olga.

"Yes, but she wouldn't qualify. Missing in action."

Olga looked at Yulia and they both slowly nodded.

"So how much?" Olga asked.

"Maybe a hundred a month. Just for a few months. Then I'd write them, see how they were getting on. Hopefully some other relatives could step in by then."

Olga shrugged. "Seems all right. With all of us chipping in, that would be six hundred a month."

"Five hundred," said Tonya, not looking up as she applied her nightly concoction of creams to her face.

Aelya walked over to her bunk, glaring at her, though Tonya resolutely refused to look away from her mirror.

"It's bad enough I have to hand over half my bonuses to the voluntary mandatory defence fund," Tonya said. "I don't see why Auntie's family should be getting any of my hard-earned money. They aren't putting their lives on the line."

"I don't know—maybe basic human decency?"

Tonya laughed. Aelya grabbed for the mirror, but Tonya coolly pulled it away from harm.

Aelya snapped at her. "Why are you such a—"

Tonya interrupted her with a word she'd only heard once before, when Vasya had fallen out with a school friend.

Aelya pretended not to be flustered. "No, I, uh, was going to say . . ." But she'd forgotten what exactly she'd been about to call Tonya.

"All right, my precious little flower, maybe you were going to say 'rat'? Was that it?" Tonya put down the mirror and stood up, the cream now smoothly absorbed into her face. "Listen, Mars. It's war."

"Oh, of course. It's the war that made you like this. I'm sure that's what the Nazis all say."

"No, I was always like this. People spat on me as a child. They preferred that I stayed hidden. Worse than that. My father was someone who made things happen. Criminals, they called us. Profiteers. We weren't model workers, our family. The revolution wasn't for our kind. But what we could do was survive. And when those revolutionaries and model workers got into trouble, do you know who they turned to? They started kissing up to my father. Because when everything goes to hell, it's we who thrive. The rats."

"I'm happy to know the future of the motherland is safe with the likes of you."

"Sure, keep hanging your hat on Socialist ideals while the world goes down in flames. Just what do you think has been going on? Blue caps gunning down our own soldiers. Children thrown down wells. Girls sent out to fight. There's no decency to be found. It's the time of the rats."

Tonya stared at her, shaking visibly. She was greedy, but this wasn't about her pay or her treasured kill bonuses. The world was full of swindlers and victims and she had only contempt for victims.

The door burst open, and Tonya quickly covered herself with her bedsheets. Roza and Masha stood in the doorway, looking stricken.

"Have you heard?" Roza said. "Raskova's dead."

Yulia gasped. "What? How?"

"Crashed in a snowstorm."

Aelya had completely forgotten until now. She had been planning on writing Raskova a letter on her eighteenth birthday, as she'd promised to do in what felt like another lifetime.

No one spoke. Masha turned to secure the door from rattling in the wind. Aelya looked down at Roza's hands. She was holding a package wrapped in parcel paper.

"Oh," Roza said, handing it to Aelya. "Sorry, this was a bit late. We had to wait for a delivery from central logistics. Happy birthday. From all of us."

Aelya placed it on her bunk and unwrapped it methodically. It was a leather jacket, the kind she'd seen worn by American lend-lease pilots in the newspapers. It was beautiful. She held it close, happy to experience beauty once more. Only Tonya could have managed to get a hold of something like this.

"Thank you," she said weakly.

Tonya stood and put a hand on the jacket. "Guess I'll be taking this back."

Aelya held on. The jacket's warmth at high altitude overrode her sense of dignity.

"Well," said Tonya, "looks like I'm not the only rat." She lay down on her bunk and turned away.

The rage welled up within Aelya, just as when she'd wanted to punch Red. She wanted to destroy something. She clutched her jacket so tightly, she was in danger of tearing it. Her hands relaxed their grip and her energy subsided. With no cause behind it, her will to fight collapsed and she was relieved. There was enough pointless violence around her.

CHAPTER 53: FROZEN

Roza screamed when she woke in the morning. With a bunk next to the wall, she found her hair had frozen to the side of the barracks. This was normally more of a problem for the technicians in their rudimentary dugouts, but with the shock over Raskova's death, no one had remembered to put extra logs in the stove for the night.

The duty officer gleefully banged on a helmet outside, walking toward the men's barracks to continue his wake-up call. Someone lit an oil lamp with a match.

"I'll get the fire going again," said Yulia, rubbing her eyes, then putting a greatcoat and boots on over her nightgown. When she opened the door, the dim light from the interior illuminated cascades of falling snowflakes in the still-dark morning.

"Snow bath!" Masha shouted and stripped off her nightclothes. Tonya and Olga followed suit and they ran out after Yulia, diving into the fresh piles of new snow.

Aelya sat next to Roza's bed and tried to warm the hair with her hands.

"And here I thought how great it was that Red let us grow out our hair," said Roza.

Aelya rubbed strands of hair in her hands, ignoring the biting cold. Roza lay flat on her back, trying not to move.

"She never threatened to kick me out, you know," Roza said. "Raskova didn't make me cut my hair. She didn't have to. She asked me where I wanted to be. She told me that the only thing holding me back was sacrifice."

"That's been your great sacrifice? A few centimetres of hair?" That came out harsher than Aelya had meant it but she felt unapologetic.

"It hardly seems like much now."

"It was all worth it," Aelya remarked. "Now you're famous. A great hero of the people. Your dreams have come true."

Roza's eyes narrowed. "What is your problem?"

"You're just—oh, it's not your fault." Aelya sighed. "You're just caught up in it all."

"Caught up in what?"

"The big lie. This great utopian system of ours that's just grinding us down. There are no heroes. Only potential traitors."

Roza laughed, then winced, her hair still stuck to the wall. "Oh, little girl, you've finally figured it out, have you?"

"Easy for you to be smug. You're getting everything you want."

Roza grabbed her by the arm. "Don't talk about me that way. What do you know? The system is using me as much as I'm using it."

"I know, you've had such a hard life." Aelya rubbed the hair vigorously, causing Roza obvious pain, though she was fighting to hide it.

"Get over yourself!" Roza exhaled a cloud of vapour. "What do you know about me?

You think I'm doing this for myself?"

"Calling yourself a patriot now?"

"I'm not talking about my country. I love it, but I hate the people running it."

Instinctively, Aelya scanned the room for anyone who might have heard. At first she thought Roza was throwing around her defiant personality again, but her eyes seemed to shrink; she knew she'd said too much. She looked vulnerable for once.

"I'm doing it for my name," Roza whispered. "My name is Roza Gromadina. Not Kulik."

Imagine being denied a name. Lara had always used her husband's name, not by choice but because she couldn't be associated with her brother. Roza nodded as the realization dawned on Aelya.

"That's right," Roza said. "One of my family was an 'unperson.' I wanted to win honour so I wouldn't have to hide who I was anymore."

"If you're supposed to be hiding, why do you keep breaking the rules?"

"Because that's how people who can't be touched always act. At least, until it's their turn." Roza smiled wryly. "I thought I was winning and flying my way, not letting the Air Force turn me into another part of the machine."

Roza grabbed her hand. "But I was wrong. Just watch. Raskova's a hero of the people. They'll give her a state funeral. And when she's put in the ground, they'll keep on using her. I realized all this a while ago, when Dmitriev told me I was his ticket out of this dump. I thought what I wanted to fight for—my name, my country, justice against the invaders—I thought they meant something. But I realized they don't mean anything to me anymore."

The others came back in, Yulia carrying logs for the stove. As she stoked the fire, Aelya put a steel helmet full of water on top to heat it and returned to Roza's side as the others started getting dressed.

"If you know all of this, and it means nothing, how can you keep going on?" Aelya asked.

Roza reached up and pulled Aelya closer. "You know what I remember feeling most from last night? Not Raskova's death. I remember being happy last night. I was happy we finally got that stupid jacket for you. It's because I know we're all that matters now. You, me, Tonya, Masha, and the twins."

"We're all this great Socialist collective."

"No, forget about that. It's the one thing that gets me through. I'm so anxious when I land because I want to see you guys again, hoping you'll all be there, even Tonya."

Aelya couldn't help smirking. "Tonya."

"That goes for the boys too. Dema, Stitches, Irkutsk. All of them."

Aelya contemplated for a moment. "I—I figured you all wrong."

"No you didn't. I'm still the best pilot in this unit."

Aelya laughed, grateful for the brief moment of levity. She stepped back to get the warmed-up water and used it to melt the remaining ice holding Roza's hair to the side of the barracks.

"But this stays between us, all right?" Roza said.

"Of course. Why did you tell me so much?"

Roza smiled, putting a hand on Aelya's cheek. "I don't know. I guess . . . you're my best friend."

Aelya thought about it. She didn't really have a best friend before the war. Maybe Zoya Kamenskaya had been, until eighth grade. Then who? Roman probably came closest. Pathetic. "I don't know what to say."

Roza sighed. "Don't let the machine chew you up completely. You can let them take pieces of you, but stay who you are."

A truck horn honked outside. It was time to get moving.

When Aelya arrived at ops, the large photos hung on the wall staggered her. One look at the bands of grey on the landscape depicted in the aerial reconnaissance photographs and she knew what was in the works: an attack on an enemy airfield.

Pilots from every squadron were there, along with most of the staff officers and two pilot officers Aelya didn't recognize. They were probably in their early twenties but already looked too lined and worn to be newcomers.

Red addressed the assembly. "First off, the good news. Too much snow, so no flying today. Don't lie, I know you're all thrilled."

Some half-hearted laughter followed.

"It also means we have more time to plan and get this right. Dmitriev wanted to give you guys homework assignments for the Lenin Day commemorations. I told him where to shove that. Anyway, if we pull this off, who knows, we might finally be done with Stalingrad in time for the big day. I'm sure that would please Comrade Stalin.

"Some of you, I'm sure, are too thick to have noticed that we've been focusing all training in the past few days on coordinating protection for Sturmovik attacks." Red pointed out the photographs. "Those among you who are bit brighter will no doubt recognize what these mean. We're attacking Gumrak airfield. These two gentlemen are from the IL-2 regiment that's going to be doing the bombing. We'll use this extra day to hammer out any questions and communication issues between our two regiments, so it's important—" He looked around at the back of the room. "Hang on—is everyone here?"

"Lily's still on her way," said Aelya. Roza had insisted on repairing the damage to her hair before going out and skipped the ride to ops.

"Lucky's missing as well," said Stitches.

"Oh yeah, I'm missing a wingman," said Tonya. Aelya gave her a reproachful look.

"Makarova, grab the jeep and get them now," said Red. "I don't want anyone using this as an excuse to mess things up."

Aelya couldn't be bothered to point out that she'd only just learned to drive, thanks to lessons from Zina. It would stupid to die crashing the jeep but at least her body would be found. She wrapped herself up in her greatcoat and *ushanka* and stepped back outside.

There was a motor pool tent on the other side of the bunker. As she rounded the corner, she spotted a lone figure wrapped up in winter gear.

"Lucky, you better get in there. Red's noticed you're missing."

"I can't go in."

"What's the problem?"

Lucky shook his head. "I know they don't trust me."

Great, Aelya thought. Just when she thought she'd pulled back from the verge of cracking, Lucky was losing his nerve. In truth, she was surprised he hadn't gone this way earlier. Or that he hadn't been shot down yet.

"No one thinks that, Lucky," she said. "Everyone here just likes giving people a hard time, especially when it gets a reaction."

"So you were just joking when you said Auntie's loss was my fault?"

Aelya felt as if she'd been punched in the gut.

He locked eyes with Aelya. "Did they make you sign the statement? Did you turn your back on her as well?"

"Yes." She was ashamed, but he had no right to judge her.

"Good. At least with that, you're no better than me."

He drew his pistol and pointed it at his head.

"Wait, stop!" Aelya stood ready to launch herself at him. She couldn't live with witnessing another suicide.

Lucky smiled slightly. "You know, I'm always terrified these things will go off when you put the extra round in. I always think I'm doing it wrong. I asked Auntie to load it for me before every flight, just to make sure. Anyone else would've said I was an idiot, but not her. That little bit of kindness might mean nothing to you. I had one last chance to repay it, and look what I've done."

He redoubled his grip on the pistol. "I'm just a liability here. This is the most useful thing I can do. And no one would really care."

"I would. I care."

"You're just saying that."

"I . . . look, I have no simple answers. Lara meant more to me that you could ever dream of. Whatever you might feel, I feel ten times worse. You think it's so easy for me? I can barely go on if I think too much about . . . I don't know, everything. But I do care about you. Not because I like you. Because I need you. We're all we have left for each other. It's the only reason to keep going. Us."

"Who do you mean?"

"All of us, right here. Forget about family, forget about the motherland or justice. We're only fighting for each other. Don't you dare take part of that away from me by killing yourself."

"Not everyone thinks like that," he said, but his grip on the gun was loosening. "Honeybee says I'm the worst in a line of terrible wingmen."

Aelya stifled a laugh. "Don't worry about her. In fact, stay close to her. She's a survivor. She's built for this war."

He began to nod slowly. She took a tentative step forward and he lowered the gun. She grasped his hand, then pulled him in for a hug. He returned the embrace tightly.

"Better give me the pistol," she said. "Don't want it going off."

He smiled as he handed it over. Snow crunched to Aelya's left. Roza approached them.

"Come on, they'll be waiting for us," Aelya urged. She patted Lucky and he led the way to ops.

"Did you see any of that?" Aelya whispered to Roza.

"I was ready to shoot him in the leg, but I knew you could handle it."

"Really?"

Roza shrugged. "Sure, why not?"

CHAPTER 54: BLACK DEATH

Aelya approached her plane as the rest of her squadron walked to theirs. Five others were left. Baby and Vino. Honeybee and Lucky. And Usy, her own wingman. Before Lucky headed to his revetment, he stopped by Aelya's. He held out his Tokarev pistol. She took it and he passed her a single bullet. She chambered a round, unloaded the magazine, then placed the extra bullet in the clip. She slapped the clip in, put the safety on, and handed the pistol back to him. He nodded and walked toward his plane.

On the other side of the runway, Stitches's squadron was already in their cockpits, being rolled out of their revetments. Stitches glanced over at Roza in the slot next to his. She kept on looking straight ahead. Had he told her anything? If he had, did she feel anything for him? Aelya watched him closely. She caught his eyes for a moment. She wasn't sure if his expression meant anything. Maybe it was all in her imagination and nothing was there. It didn't matter— they could both die today.

Aelya went over the pre-flight checklist with Zina. She kept glancing up at the other pilots. Baby signed a form for Muromets. With Lara gone, it was his squadron now. Bundled in his fur-trimmed winter flight suit, the portly new squadron commander reminded Aelya of a stuffed bear. Pilots said he looked as if he carried a baby in his belly and that's how he got his name.

As Muromets made his way back toward the command post, he passed Tonya's revetment. She winked at him. From his smile, Aelya knew she'd made his day.

"You ready?" Zina asked.

Aelya nodded.

Zina patted her on the back. "I hear this is big. Go get 'em."

As always, she gave Aelya's parachute harness a tug, then helped her climb into the cockpit. Inga, the armourer, cleared the weapons. Raya started the engine. Exhaust stubs flared brightly against the darkening grey skies. Aelya plugged her helmet headphones and throat microphone into the radio.

The entire regiment was involved with this mission. Red, with a yellow-mouthed pilot begrudgingly on his wing, was coming back in as part of Frost's squadron.

"Maple Tree, this is Osprey Leader," Red reported in. "Quiet day. No enemy transports spotted and the Messers weren't biting."

Aelya exhaled, calming herself. There was always an outside chance that the enemy fighter cover would take the bait. Red's sortie was meant to give the Luftwaffe the impression that the regiment was done their free hunt for the day. So much for that. Now Aelya would be facing full-strength enemy fighter squadrons, and a higher probability she would die today.

The thought of dying always triggered an initial anxiety in her, but it was going away faster and faster now. She'd figured it out. Even the basic desire to live wasn't enough to keep going, so she fought hard for her comrades, but not because she cared for them—although she did to varying degrees. Caring was a luxury that left her vulnerable, an opening that could be torn to shreds. She fought for her comrades so they'd stick around to keep her sane. So she could fight some more. And the machine kept grinding.

The setting sun reflected orange and gold against the undulations of drifting clouds. There were worse ways to bid farewell, if this was her final day.

The scope of her thoughts began to shrink as the turn came for the remaining two squadrons to take off. She waited patiently for her clearance and then rolled forward.

Once aloft, Stitches's squadron of free hunters assembled at a higher altitude. Together, they and Baby's squadron flew directly to the rendezvous point several kilometres from the front lines. They circled for a few minutes as the humpbacked silhouettes against the gathering dusk marked the arrival of the Sturmovik regiment: twenty-seven "flying tanks."

Every pilot in the regiment dreaded these missions. The IL-2s were deadly to enemy ground troops, but deadly to their crews too. They flew low, vulnerable to ground fire as well as enemy fighters. Escorts were exposed to the same dangers, flying far slower than was ideal.

Aelya watched as the free hunters went, taking a direct route toward their target airfield. Baby signalled with a wing waggle for the rest of the fighters to follow as they accompanied the Sturmoviks along a more circuitous route, hoping to avoid enemy formations. They stuck close to the ground. With visibility low and contours difficult to discern in the snow, Aelya felt her mouth go dry and her grip on the control column lock tight.

They approached Gumrak airfield as twilight set in. Against the cloud-blotted sky, she couldn't make out the free hunters. She could only hear Stitches give Wolf, one of the pilots on loan from the 466th, the order to patrol the air transport lanes with his flight while Stitches engaged an enemy fighter patrol.

The target came within sight, an expanse of dark forms, mostly uncamouflaged as they lay on the snow. One of the only two remaining lifelines to the outside world for the German 6th Army, Gumrak airfield was crowded with a mess of planes, supplies, and troops hoping for escape. Belts of anti-aircraft guns ringed the base.

Baby gave another signal and the fighters broke and climbed into a large figure-eight circuit around the airfield, hoping to avoid the worst of the anti-aircraft fire. The Sturmoviks went straight in. A series of bright white starbursts flared against the ground as the lead attacker dropped illumination rounds. Streaks of white and bluish tracers swept across the skies, like a hard rainfall in reverse. Aelya dodged and weaved with her plane, keeping Usy in sight, relying on pure gut instinct to determine where the enemy gunners might be aiming. Bursts of flak erupted around her. She jolted against the right side of the plane as she took hits, absorbing a sting in her arm but managed to get clear of the worst of it.

She kept watch on the ground between tensely scanning the sky. Orange flames spat from the Sturmoviks as they fired their cannons and rockets. Columns of fire spouted into the sky as their bombs struck anything flammable on the ground. Every outburst that rocked the ground sent a visceral thrill through Aelya.

There was movement down there. Little dots like ants, a pathetic mass barely seeking any cover. She could imagine the terror inflicted on those soldiers. The Germans called the IL-2 *schwarzer Tod*. Black Death. Perhaps for some, death was welcome, a relief from the misery of their freezing entrapment.

The radio filled with noisy chatter as Wolf spotted incoming enemy transports with escorts. The whole free hunter squadron was committed now. Reports of hits taken and given out were interspersed with fits of swearing, both at the enemy and each other.

"More vultures, about four of them," Aelya called out as soon as she spotted the silhouettes illuminated by the flames of the burning airfield. "Bearing two-five-zero. Height eleven hundred."

"This is Sparrow Leader," called Baby. "Usy, you're with me. Honeybee, stay in coverage."

Aelya fell in behind and to the right of Usy. As they moved to intercept the path of the enemy fighters, the Messers turned tail. Immediately, Aelya checked the skies above. Sure enough, another four enemy fighters were screaming down at them, hoping to catch them while they were too busy chasing the first group.

Baby and Vino already broke off their attack and flew up to engage a pair of the newcomers. Usy hadn't seemed to notice.

"Usy, Messers on your tail. Break off," Aelya said. There was no telling if the noise over the radio was too much, or if he was just ignoring the warning.

She rolled her plane to get in between Usy and his pursuers. Soon enough, she saw tracers fly by her windows and heard the ping of bullets striking her fuselage as she rolled away, drawing their fire. She pulled another roll, found a Messer moving in front of her, lined it up, and fired. Flames and specks of material spewed out from behind it, and she had to break to dodge the debris.

"Got one," Usy called out.

"Me too."

"I'm taking hits from the ground," said Usy.

She formed up with him as he climbed away from the danger.

"This is Gazelle. Ground observers reporting enemy taking off from Pitomnik. Expect company soon, Sparrow Leader."

"They'll have to queue up," said Baby.

"Sparrow Leader, this is Buzzard Leader," called the Sturmovik commander. "Disengaging and assembling to thirty-three. We're done our job here." The last statement was unnecessary; the orange glow bathing the ground was a testament to their deadly efficiency.

"Copy that," said Baby. "This is Sparrow Leader. I'm still engaged. Stitches?"

"No luck—we're still engaged too."

"All right," said Baby. "Usy, form up with Honeybee and take those hump-backs home."

Aelya moved into a climb to meet Tonya and Lucky. She saw Usy wobbling as he followed the same path ahead of her.

"Usy, you all right?"

"Just . . . tying off my leg. Plane's still good. Honeybee, take the high book-shelf."

Tonya led Lucky to a spot about two hundred metres above Usy and Aelya and a little ahead of them. Together, they linked up with the Sturmoviks a few kilometres to the northeast of Gumrak. They immediately set off in a straight line for home. From the cluster of humpbacked silhouettes, Aelya guessed that most, if not all, of the Sturmoviks made it out from the attack. As far as she could tell, the enemy fighters never even got close to them. She didn't relax, continuing to scan every part of the sky, especially behind her.

As if on cue, she spotted a pack of enemy fighters gaining on them rapidly, out to avenge the damage to the airfield. They were at about the same altitude as them, bearing down toward the Sturmoviks.

"Our friends from Pitomnik are here. Buzzard Leader, you better form into a circle," Usy called out. "We'll try to draw the Messers as bait. Honeybee, stay with the Sturmoviks."

Usy began to bank but immediately he struggled with the rudder, probably the result of his wounded leg.

"You're in no shape to fight," said Aelya. "Usy, you better stay with the Sturmoviks. I'll try to draw the vultures off. Honeybee, take anyone who's left."

"All right, sounds good," said Usy, his voice weaker than normal.

The Sturmoviks formed a defensive circle, covering each plane in front with guns in their wings, while tail gunners began forming an umbrella with their tracer fire to discourage the enemy. Tonya, and Lucky stayed high and away, ready to catch any Messer that tried their luck.

Aelya banked into her own circle, drifting into the space between the Stur-moviks and Messers, making herself a more tempting target. Four enemy planes dived toward her. She broke hard, watching a pair of Messers streak past her while the other two gave chase, trying to gain a good firing angle as she turned. She heard Tonya and Lucky talking over the radio but couldn't register what they were saying, as all her attention was focused on gaining every bit of edge on her pursuers. She pulled into a tight climb, then rolled, throwing her flaps open to bleed off more speed. The hard deceleration gave her vision a reddish tinge, and she felt satisfied she'd pushed herself to her limits. A Messer dropped close to her sights, just the right spacing from the red aiming circle. She fired and saw sparks as shots struck the metal body of the enemy fighter.

Aelya saw it dive away and didn't bother chasing it, already throttling to catch up to the other Messer. He'd spotted the danger and dived as well, and Aelya circled to watch for the other pair she'd lost. Their quick strike hadn't worked and they wanted no part in a low-visibility dogfight. They knew they weren't dealing with yellow-mouths.

"Vultures are disengaging, Mars," said Tonya. "I saw you. Nice shooting. I think Lucky and I got some hits in. Guess they're not that keen on revenge anymore."

Aelya was keen. It felt good to hit something, and she wanted to keep going. Everything was the enemy's fault and killing them would make it right, she thought. A moment later, she began to calm down and rational thought penetrated her brain.

They circled for a minute to ensure the skies were clear of the enemy before heading toward home again. It was now too dark to make out most navigation markers, but Aelya estimated they and the Sturmoviks were just crossing the front lines when Usy reported that his engine was giving out.

"We should be in a safe spot to bail out," she said to him.

He laughed. "My leg's stuck pretty bad. I think I'm nailed to the cockpit."

A belly landing in these conditions would be hazardous at best.

"All right," said Aelya. "Honeybee, continue the escort. I'll guide Usy down."

Abandoning her escort to help a fellow pilot, even her wingman, went against mission protocols, but at this point in the sortie, she felt it was the right decision. Tonya acknowledged and took her place with Lucky above the Sturmoviks. Aelya's right hand felt numb when she tried to take it off the control column, so she pulled a flashlight out of her cockpit's side pocket and put it in her mouth.

Spreading a map of the area out on her lap, she located a spot of flat, open space far enough away from the front lines to be safe from both Germans and trigger-happy infantry. She called over instructions to Usy on how to orient his plane and lose altitude at the right speed.

"Are you sure it's close enough? Usy said. "My engine's given out and I'm at nine hundred."

"I think it's going to be tight. You'll need to clear some uneven ground. Do you have the strength to keep pulling the nose up?"

"It's my leg that's been hit, not my arm."

She had been worried about blood loss, but his being testy was a good sign.

The ground was a nearly featureless sheet of white. They would have to rely on Aelya's blind navigation to find the right landing spot.

"I'll signal you when you're okay to make the final turn," she said. "Remember, you're going in deadstick on rough terrain, so throw the flaps early to bleed off speed when you're going in."

"I know how to land deadstick."

The beam from her flashlight caught a glimpse of something on her right arm. Dreading what she would see, she shone the light over it. Her sleeve was torn in several places and the leather glistened slick with blood. Pools of sticky matter had congealed in spots. She put the flashlight in her lap and used her left hand to untie her scarf. Holding one end in her teeth, she tied a tourniquet over her upper arm.

It was almost time. She went back to looking at the map. "All right, you should be at four hundred now."

"Closer to three."

"Good enough. Let's make this count. Bank now, heading zero-three-five."

She waited. Usy wasn't answering, hopefully focusing on the getting his plane down. She kept watch against the landscape, seeing the dark shadow of his fighter gently losing altitude. She could have let him die. It was his fault for getting hit by ground fire. That would teach him to do what he'd done to her and think he could get away with it. It felt better to think she had that power, but there had never been a question of doing anything but save him. She detested Usy. But he was her wingman.

"Usy, you've only got one wheel down."

"Which one?"

"Left. I think."

Seconds later, Usy's plane hit the sheet of white below. He kept it level for a moment, then touched the right wing down. It slowed rapidly and spun for the last few seconds before coming to a halt.

"I'm down."

Aelya exhaled. "I'm calling this in to Gazelle. And remember, when the *makhras* come, swear really loudly so they know you're Russian."

Usy's response came in loud and clear.

"Yeah, just like that," Aelya replied.

"Oh, and Mars? Thanks."

CHAPTER 55: RED STAR

February 5, 1942

e're all so proud of you. Everyone's saying victory is at hand at Stalingrad. Can it be true? We know you can't say, but for you to be contributing to such a moment in history is truly special. Now that you've done your duty, we hope to see you very soon.

Vasya promises she'll never, ever, ever, ever call you Spacegirl again if you'd just come home safe and sound.

With warmest love and affection,
Your Babushka and Mama and Papa and Vasya

Aelya folded up the last page of the letter and slid it into the pocket of her tunic, right next to *Aelita*. For once, the propaganda being spread on the home front matched the reality. Written in late January, by the time she received the letter, the German 6th Army had surrendered. Stalingrad had been liberated and the enemy was on the run. Comrade Stalin had ordered the Kremlin chimes to ring in the victory. For Aelya, it had been a foregone conclusion since the attack on the airfield.

Looking back at the destruction the Sturmoviks had wrought, she knew that the Luftwaffe would be giving up on the battle. It had just been a question of whether she would live to see it. But since that day, that question had been almost secondary.

She adjusted her greatcoat. She still felt numbness in her arm, but it hadn't stopped anything. She'd flown again the day after she was wounded. Donning an *ushanka* to go outside, she was greeted by Lucky from the back of an open truck.

"Are you ready, Comrade Commander?" She wanted to correct him. She was only his senior pilot, but correcting protocols could wait another day.

"Actually, I'd like to visit the revetments. Say goodbye to number 70."

"Too late," Tonya said, sitting with Lucky. What was left of the three squadrons could fit into a single truck. "Planes were packed off this morning."

So that was it. The front line had moved so far forward, this airfield was now considered a reserve base. The planes were being handed off to a training unit. Their regiment was being taken out of the line, its pilots soon to be boarding trains for who knew where. To train, to reequip and, most of all, to rest. The idea of rest made Aelya's hands shake as she was helped up into the truck.

"Not a cloud in the sky, finally," said Roza as they pulled away from the barracks.

"I think God is celebrating too," said Masha.

"Waited to see who was winning first, eh?" said Tonya with a snort.

"I think He's been cooperating the whole time," said Frost. "The weather may have been bad for us, but it was worse for Fritz on the ground."

The open space between the operations bunker and the runway was already crowded with people. As the truck pulled up nearby, two Yaks buzzed them low, startling Aelya. She recovered quickly. A few of the others hadn't even flinched. Even though only long-range enemy bombers could reach them, the 466th was flying cover today.

"Must be jealous," said Aelya.

Red was already on the field. Usy would be out of the hospital soon. Now minus a leg after suffering an infection, he would soon be out of the Air Force entirely. It was about the best outcome she could have wished for, Aelya thought caustically. Stitches had flown to Moscow to accept his gold star as a newly minted Hero of the Soviet Union. All the other pilots were disembarking from the truck. As they lined up in their places among the formation, Aelya realized just how many people were involved with the regiment. Pilots were just a tiny part of it.

Major General Platonov stood on the hood of a jeep. He started with the usual stirring tributes to the determination and courage of the Soviet fighting man and woman and a call to continue the glorious drive to victory, all the way to Berlin. Aelya knew better than to expect that to happen any time soon.

She shivered the whole time. They had left their heavy winter outerwear in the truck, all the better to be presentable for this ceremony. There were photographers on hand, after all.

Platonov got down from the jeep and began dishing out awards, followed by an aide holding on to the medals in an open case. They didn't mean much to Aelya, though it was nice for her friends to at least share in some applause. Red was recognized for his leadership in planning the airfield attack. Roza, Masha, and Wolf all received an Order of the Red Banner, in recognition for becoming aces. Tonya was given one of a lesser grade, and was no doubt calculating what sort of award she would have received if all those confirmations had gone in her favour. Eisenach was recognized for her contributions to keeping the planes flying. Really, all of the technicians should have gotten medals. Dmitriev, somehow, received more medals than anyone else.

Platonov stepped in front of Aelya, consulting a list in his hand.

"Senior Sergeant Aelita Petrovna Makarova. On November 17, 1942, you conducted a successful reconnaissance of enemy positions, despite heavy enemy fighter presence and ground fire. Your subsequent actions also resulted in the destruction of a Fascist fighter and the escort of a wounded comrade to safety."

November 17. Her gift to Lara: barely an extra month and a half to live. What had been the use? If she'd died that day, she wouldn't have become an outcast. A non-person. Aelya bit her tongue to stop from crying.

"You are hereby awarded the Order of the Red Star." As Platonov pinned the medal on her chest and a camera clicked, she felt as though she was watching this scene from afar, outside her own body. This wasn't Aelita Makarova standing here.

The ceremony ended. After they'd hastily retrieved their winter gear, no one was really sure of what to do. There were no planes to fly. No actions to review. No training to conduct. Aelya felt adrift in a vast ocean. Pilots milled around smoking, stamping their feet to keep warm. She'd barely gotten a word in with Zina when the technicians were called to continue packing up their gear. She sought out Roza, but "the Lily of Stalingrad" was surrounded by photographers and reporters and even a film unit.

Soon they would be singing the praises of a free hunter who had single-handedly strangled the lifeline of the enemy, ensuring this great victory. They would have no time for the wingmen who covered her or the mechanic who fixed her engine, let alone the truck driver who delivered her fuel. She should have felt happy for Roza, but she knew now how empty Roza was feeling. Aelya was angry. At Roza. At everything. At one time she'd been completely run through with fear, doubt, and worry. Now there was no need for that. Rage consumed her.

She stalked her way past more loiterers. Working her way around the other side of the operations bunker, she saw Tonya emerge from a copse just past a pair of anti-aircraft guns. Tonya was recognizable by her black sable hat. No unfashionable standard-issue *ushanka* for her. Aelya was about to greet her, but there was something undeniably odd and devious about her detour. Aelya hid by the side of the bunker until she passed.

It was easy to follow the footprints in the snow, back to the trees, to the base of a tall pine just inside the woods. The footprints stopped next to a rock by its roots. From the disturbance in the snow, it was clear the rock had been moved. Aelya knelt down and lifted it, revealing a folded piece of paper.

She looked around. If this was some sort of black market scheme of Tonya's, her contact might be coming soon. Her pulse quickened as she fell back into her combat senses. But there was nothing beyond the rustling of trees.

She unfolded the piece of paper. The face wasn't looking directly at her, but she could feel the warmth of its presence. It was a beautiful sketch of Lara. Aelya stayed for a while, stripping her glove so she could trace the lines of the drawing. Then she carefully folded the picture. Pulling *Aelita* from her pocket, she drew out Yura's last letter. Together with the drawing, she placed it beneath the rock.

Then she wept. She hadn't truly cried once since the war began. Not until now. She spent some time letting her tears run dry. When she was finished, she felt numb once more.

She composed herself and returned to the gathering.

Dmitriev sought her out quickly. "There you are. The last of my Sparrows."

He ushered her to the side of the other women pilots. Once lined up, they quickly tossed aside their winter coats, hats, gloves, and boot coverings. They all had new dress uniforms. Aelya tried to press out the creases in her khaki tunic and dark blue skirt. Dmitriev handed out blue berets to everyone and pointed out a scuff on Aelya's boot that she quickly rubbed away.

A photographer positioned Aelya between Tonya and Roza. She suddenly felt the urge to hold their hands. All six pilots soon linked arms.

"Don't you look pretty with your shiny medals?" the photographer said.

"I should hope so," said Dmitriev. "I spent ages writing their commendations."

The Red Star was a worthless trinket to Aelya. It took considerable effort not to shove it into Dmitriev's eye.

Her bare legs were freezing by the time the last photo was snapped. She doffed her beret and bundled up immediately afterward.

"Ah, I'm glad you're all here," said General Platonov, making an appearance. "I'd like to thank all of you for your contribution, which has gone far beyond what your country has demanded of you. You will be missed."

Aelya took a quick look around, but it was obvious no one had any idea what Platonov was talking about. He smiled wryly and made a gesture of resignation. "Military communications, eh? I suppose you might as well hear it from me. Now that the immediate danger to the motherland has passed, the chief of the Air Force has ordered a conclusion to this experiment. You'll all be rejoining your old unit."

Platonov paused, perhaps expecting some sort of fond farewell. The look of confusion and anger on their faces quickly disabused him of that notion. He mumbled more thanks, then beat a hasty retreat.

"Well, girls, you should be happy to get the attention of the chief of the Air Force," said Dmitriev. He was greeted with death stares and made himself scarce as well.

The pilots looked at each other.

"They can't do that to us," said Masha, "can they?"

"What now?" said Olga.

Roza put her hands on her hips. "Big deal. It's just another fight, isn't it?"

The Warbird will continue in
RAVEN'S SHADOW

HISTORICAL BACKGROUND

Putting yourself in Aelya's shoes might feel like you've stepped onto an entirely different planet. Besides taking place many decades ago, this novel is set in a totally different society than what we are used to in the West. A brief account of recent history leading up to the events of this novel may offer some helpful context.

The Russian Revolution
By the beginning of the 20th century, the Russian Empire was a powderkeg of discontent against the ruling czar. The economy strained to industrialize and catch up to the other European powers. Its vast population of peasants struggled to navigate these changes after generations of servitude under the nobles. Meanwhile, conservative factions tried to keep peasant freedoms in check. Any opposition to the ruling class was violently suppressed.

In 1914, Russia was drawn into the First World War, and it proved disastrous for the empire. By 1917, the war had ground to a bloody stalemate that had cost millions of lives. Suffering from food shortages at home, soldiers and civilians alike rose up in rebellion. They overthrew three hundred years of rule under the czars. After a struggle between revolutionary factions and a civil war against czarist forces, the Bolshevik faction of the Communist Party, under Vladimir Lenin, came to power.

The Bolsheviks united the remnants of the Russian Empire into an entirely new kind of country: the Soviet Union. The term "Soviet" referred to the local governing councils set up in the wake of the revolution. Being Communists, the Bolsheviks believed that property should be owned collectively, not privately; that the working class should direct the government; and that the State should tightly control the economy and many aspects of daily life. Opposed by Western governments fearing the spread of Communism, Bolsheviks instituted a police state to root out and destroy all enemies, real and imagined, within this new nation. As the Communist Party, they established single party rule with no meaningful elections.

The Rise of Stalin

With Lenin's death in 1924, his ruthless deputy, Josef Stalin, took the reins of power. He continued to transform the State, placing it under his complete personal domination, using secret police, networks of informers, and a pitiless bureaucracy to maintain his control.

Stalin instituted a rapid and brutal drive to industrialize the country. The nation felt constantly on the edge of war, surrounded by enemies that sought to roll back the revolution. The main threat came from Adolf Hitler's newly established Nazi Germany. Hitler viewed the Slavic people who made up most of the Soviet Union as inferiors, taking up valuable living space that would better serve his "master race."

Through most of the 1930s Stalin's cruel policies and purges of political opponents resulted in millions of deaths. Seizing property from farmers and forcing them off their lands and into state-run collective farms led to widespread famine in Ukraine and other agricultural regions. Millions were sent to forced labour camps to develop Siberia and the north. Thousands were simply executed. Even making the wrong type of joke could land someone in prison.

Despite these harsh conditions, many of the people were also optimistic about the future. By the start of World War II, a whole generation had grown up under the Soviet system. They earnestly believed in the ideals on which their new nation had been founded. Whatever they suffered and sacrificed now was in the service of a greater good, to bring about equality and collective well-being for all people.

The March to War

In the decade leading up to the war, many people believed that a massive clash was inevitable between the forces of Fascism, led by Nazi Germany, and Communism, led by the Soviet Union. Demonstrations and street battles took place between supporters of both ideologies all across the world. Despite the tragic lessons of the First World War, militaristic governments increasingly saw war as a viable option to get what they wanted. Threats of war allowed Nazi Germany to expand its borders in 1938 and 1939. Wars of aggression were launched by Italy (invading Ethiopia in 1936) and Japan (invading China in 1937.) It was only a matter of time before the rest of the world followed.

In August 1939, the narrative for the coming war was derailed by the Nazi-Soviet Pact. In a move that shocked the rest of the world, Hitler and Stalin callously agreed to each look the other way while they carved up control of Eastern Europe between them.

World War II from September 1939 to June 1941
Assured that the Soviet Union would not interfere and ignoring Britain and France's warnings, Hitler made the next move. In September, Germany invaded Poland, ostensibly to take back ethnic German lands lost in the First World War. Britain and France declared war in support of Poland and World War II in Europe began.

The Nazis swiftly conquered Poland using a new style of mobile warfare known as blitzkrieg. Emphasizing deep strikes with tanks and other vehicles and coordinating with air attacks, the Germans shattered expectations for the long, drawn out trench warfare of the First World War. Poland fell after a month and as agreed upon, the Soviets took over its eastern half. Within a year, nations in Scandinavia and Western Europe, including, most shockingly, France had all fallen under Nazi rule. Britain was saved from invasion by its fleet and its air force. Germany continued its war of conquest in the Balkans and North Africa.

Within occupied lands, the Nazis brutally oppressed conquered peoples. They continued their pre-war persecution of Jews, as well as Roma, gays and lesbians, political opponents, the mentally and physically impaired, and anyone else deemed unworthy of the Third Reich. All the while, the Nazis made preparations for mass murder on an industrial scale.

While staying out of the war so far, Stalin was preparing for a fight with Germany that still felt inevitable. The Soviets seized the Baltic nations, as well as land from Romania and after a bitter war that exposed many problems within the Red Army, parts of Finland.

By June 1941, Hitler's eyes were squarely focused on the Soviet Union. The economy and armed forces of the Communist nation were still rapidly modernizing. These efforts were hampered by the loss of many military and civilian experts after Stalin's purges. Those that remained were often fearful of taking any action that might make them stand out. As a result, Hitler believed that an invasion would succeed easily.

On June 22, the largest invasion force in history was ready: nearly 4 million soldiers, over 3,000 tanks, and almost as many aircraft. War between the two largest military powers in the world would unleash catastrophic death and destruction, not only in terms of its scale, but in its cruelty and hatred.

AUTHOR'S NOTE

This novel was written with the intent that everything in the story could reasonably have happened in real life. Many of the events are on the historical record or are drawn from the recollections of people who were there. Despite my best efforts to be accurate in detail, there will inevitably be errors in my work, either inadvertent or deliberate in the service of the story. I hope to honour the men and women who inspired it by telling it the best way that I can.

Kostyakovo, Orlovka, Urmanovsk, and Maloye Zakharovo are all made up places. Most other locations described in this book are real. The 466th and 497th Fighter Aviation Regiments are meant to be fictional units and no such regiments ever existed, as far as I know. The same goes for the 212th Fighter Division. The Red Banner Falcons also didn't exist, but a real all-female aerobatics team did provide several fighter pilots during the war. The films, filmmakers, authors, and works of literature mentioned by the characters all existed as well. Like Aelya, I preferred *Volga-Volga* to *Shining Path*.

An estimated 800,000 women joined the armed forces of the Soviet Union during the course of the war. Many took on dangerous frontline roles, such as snipers, medics, combat engineers, tank drivers, bomber crew, and fighter pilots. Marina Raskova was an actual person, famous for her pioneering flights before the war. Aviation Group 122 was the training unit that she formed with Stalin's approval. The three regiments arising from this, the 586th fighter regiment, 587th dive bomber regiment, and 588th night bomber regiment (the famous "Night Witches") all had distinguished records of service during the war.

The 586th did experience difficulties similar to what is portrayed in this novel, culminating in the transfer of eight pilots to the front at Stalingrad. I've attempted to stay true to the course of the Battle of Stalingrad, where the world's first female aces, Lydia Litvyak and Katya Budanova, established their reputations. The women pilots were spared little of the savage fighting and within a year, five of the eight would be dead.

FURTHER READING

I am indebted to far too many sources in my research to count. The list below is by no means complete and is intended to only offer a sampling of books that can help you learn more about the people, places, and events that appear in this novel.

On life in the Soviet Union: *Everyday Stalinism: Ordinary Life in Extraordinary Times: Soviet Russia in the 1930s* by Sheila Fitzpatrick

For a succinct summary of World War II: *The Second World War: A Short History* by R.A.C. Packer

On the war between Germany and the Soviet Union: *Hitler's War on Russia* by Charles D. Winchester

On the Battle of Stalingrad: *Stalingrad: The Fateful Siege 1942-43* by Antony Beevor

On the Soviet Air Force during the war: *Red Phoenix Rising: The Soviet Air Force in World War II* by Ilya Grinberg and Von Hardesty

On women in the Soviet Air Force during the war: *Wings, Women and War: Soviet Airwomen in World War II Combat* by Reina Pennington

For first-hand accounts from Soviet women combat pilots: *Women in Air War: The Eastern Front of World War II* by Kazimiera Jean Cottam

ACKNOWLEDGEMENTS

Writing a novel is an enormous undertaking, something that is impossible to do alone. There is no way that I can properly thank all the people I am indebted to, but I will give it a try.

First of all, there would be no story to tell without the men and women who experienced and sacrificed so much during the war. I recognize how privileged I am to be able to write about it and I do not take it lightly.

Friends and family have always been supportive of this endeavour and their enthusiasm and positive comments have kept me going through thick and thin. I am particularly grateful to Charles Hannah for encouraging me to turn my idea into a novel in the first place.

Every author needs a support team and mine has been fantastic. My beta readers, Charlotte Kieft and Pete Dulgar, were invaluable in fixing up my early drafts. My excellent editor, Caroline Kaiser, kept my writing on the straight and narrow, and my spelling Canadian. Kit Foster came up with the fantastic cover design and helped to get the book ready for publishing. Daria Tikhomolova provided the amazing artwork for the cover and book launch, bringing Aelita and her comrades into vivid, colourful life.

A vast amount of research went into this book. Hours and hours were spent poring over the minutiae of everything from Soviet box office hits to Klimov M-105 engine specifications. While help came from many places, I have to single out a few people for their particular assistance. Maria Garbuz helped me double check my Russian content. David Handyside answered key questions about piloting airplanes. Renald Fortier of the Canada Aviation and Space Museum assisted with avenues for research on flying and aviation history. I apologize for any inaccuracies or errors, they are entirely my own responsibility.

Finally, I have to thank Annabel, for always believing in me.

ABOUT THE AUTHOR

DL Jung is an enthusiastic student of history and enjoys blogging about it, in addition to writing historical fiction. He also writes fantasy and horror fiction as Darius Jung.

Jung is married, with two children, and lives in Toronto, Canada. They are lucky enough to spend part of the time in New Zealand. Outside of writing, he has tried stints as an industrial engineer, a film and TV script supervisor, and a professional game show contestant. Sparrow Squadron is his debut novel.

You can follow the author on Twitter at @DariusJung or visit the author website www.dariusjung.com.

Independent authors are greatly dependent upon online reviews to promote their books. If you enjoyed this book, please consider supporting the author by leaving a review online.